life is always
full of surprises...

also by
emmie mears

the ayala storme series

storm in a teacup — book 1
any port in a storm — book 2
taken by storm — book 3
eye of the storm — book 4

the stonebreaker series

hearthfire — book 1
tidewater — book 2

standalone novels

look to the sun

Some days the quiet
  called to her,
and she gathered words
  around her like a cloak.

a hall of keys and no doors

~ a novel by ~ EMMIE MEARS

bhc press

Livonia, Michigan

a hall
of keys
and no
doors

Copyright © 2016 Emmie Mears

All rights reserved. No part of this publication may be reproduced, distributed, or transmitted in any form or by any means, including photocopying, recording, or other electronic or mechanical methods, without the prior written permission of the publisher, except in the case of brief quotations embodied in critical reviews and certain other noncommercial uses permitted by copyright law. For permission requests, please write to the publisher.

This book is a work of fiction. The characters, incidents, and dialogue are drawn from the author's imagination and are not to be construed as real. Any resemblance to actual events or persons, living or dead, is entirely coincidental.

Published by BHC Press

Library of Congress Control Number: 2016952685

ISBN: 978-1-64397-080-6 (Hardcover)
ISBN: 978-1-946006-01-1 (Softcover)
ISBN: 978-1-948540-19-3 (Ebook)

For information, write:
BHC Press
885 Penniman #5505
Plymouth, MI 48170

Visit the publisher:
www.bhcpress.com

dedication

Once there was a boy with hair like red wine who knew how to make the milkweed pods fly. Later he knew how to make an outcast pubescent teen feel like a friend. He blasted loud music and told soft stories. He grew up, but never away. He got to see his baby born, he planned a wedding he never got to live, and he was taken from us far, far too soon.

This book is for Nate, because sometimes I still feel like if I close my eyes, I can smell the storm clouds on Pelee Island in 1999. I can hear his voice through a phone line as I navigated high school on the opposite side of the country. I see his face in his baby girl's smile.

There's a hole in our family where he once was, and there's no way my words can fill it. I hope he would have liked this tale.

For Nathan Stuart Layton (December 5, 1981 - December 16, 2011), who is always remembered and therefore never truly gone. I miss you, cousin.

table of contents

part one | I
death and houses

13...chapter one
21...chapter two
32...chapter three
47...chapter four
57...chapter five
64...chapter six
78...chapter seven
91...chapter eight
105...chapter nine

part two | II
markets and roses

113...chapter ten
122...chapter eleven
127...chapter twelve
136...chapter thirteen
146...chapter fourteen
153...chapter fifteen
163...chapter sixteen
176...chapter seventeen
186...chapter eighteen

part three 207
keys and families

209...chapter nineteen
219...chapter twenty
227...chapter twenty-one
235...chapter twenty-two
246...chapter twenty-three
255...chapter twenty-four
263...chapter twenty-five
282...chapter twenty-six
292...chapter twenty-seven

part four 305
doors and futures

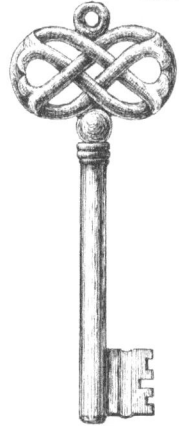

307...chapter twenty-eight
316...chapter twenty-nine
327...chapter thirty
334...chapter thirty-one
342...chapter thirty-two
350...chapter thirty-three
355...chapter thirty-four
362...chapter thirty-five
373...chapter thirty-six

377...epilogue

part one
death and houses

chapter
one

At 2:03 PM on Wednesday, December the seventh, Ella Keyes decided that everyone on the planet was picking their nose. The thought came to her as she fixated on a small brass elephant with eyes of lapis lazuli. It wasn't picking its nose or doing much of anything. But, Ella thought as she read an obsequious argument in favor of Thor as the Norse Jupiter, the writer of the term paper certainly was.

She would remember that imagery on occasional moments throughout the rest of her life, because precisely three seconds later, Easton Gellerman, her rather pimply graduate assistant and adjunct professor, knocked on her office door with a telegram between his fingers and a bemused expression on his face.

Ella took the telegram in her hand, holding it between two long fingers and a thumb with a nail in desperate need of clipping.

"Grandmother expelled. Stop. Come to house. Full stop."

Expelled what? Ella wondered about that for a moment before correctly deducing that the telegram ought to have read *expired*. Neither word, Ella decided, should ever be applied to the death of a human being.

There was only one person in Ella's life who might send a telegram in the twenty-first century. Grammy Helen's twin sister Eunice was ninety-three years old with a mind like Swiss cheese. The holes were where abilities like word choice and refraining from public flatulence had once made their homes.

"Better out than in," Auntie Eunice would say on such occasions.

Expelled, indeed.

Grammy Helen was dead.

Easton made his continued presence known with a small cough. "Everything okay?"

Grammy Helen wasn't, apparently.

Ella gathered the stack of term papers she'd been grading into a tidy pile and tucked it into a folder labeled, "Fall Semester NORMYTH203" and slid the folder into her hanging file next to "Fall Semester NATAMERMYTH301" and "Fall Semester EARNORFOLKLORE402SEM," which had a name altogether too long for the tab on the file. That bothered her.

She looked up from the file at Easton, who stood in the doorway awaiting an answer. "My grandmother passed away," she told him.

Easton frowned, opened his mouth, closed it, and opened it again in that way people do when they're not sure what to say about death. "I'm sorry?" His voice took an upturn at the end, which made his condoling sentence into an odd question.

"Thank you." Ella straightened the three pens by her keyboard, keeping them parallel to the edge of the plastic. Red, blue, black. "I'll be out for the rest of the day. Can you finish up grading the intro course's assignments?"

"Of course." Easton backed out of the office and shut the door.

Ella picked up her desk phone and held the weight in her hand for a moment. She looked down at the edge of her desk, her hair falling in her face. Grammy Helen. Ella hadn't known there was anything wrong with her, aside from the occasional battiness. Her free hand went to the single blue lock among the loose brown waves and gave it a tug. Ella had had tea with Grammy the week before. She'd seemed fine. Grammy had cooked cottage pie at her old farmhouse and served it to Ella with mint tea and a Jell-O parfait for dessert. The entire kitchen had smelled of beef and mint and artificial cherry, and in that space Ella and Grammy Helen both had known there was a presence missing. Ella felt hollow, the strange telegram's news ricocheting off insides that seemed polished and smooth like marble buttresses. Not releasing the blue lock, Ella punched the plastic buttons for Aunt Eunice's number with the middle finger of her phone-holding hand. After seven rings, a quavering voice answered.

"Ahoy." Auntie Eunice heard long ago that when the telephone was invented, Alexander Graham Bell had wanted the salutation to be *ahoy* instead of *hello*. Because it was his original intention, she refused to say anything else when answering.

"Aunt Eunice, it's Ella. I got your...telegram."

"Oh. That. Funeral's Sunday. Have you got anything nice to wear?"

"I'll find something."

"And bring something to the wake. Maybe a newt plate."

"Fruit plate?"

"That's what I said, dear."

Ella hung up the phone, swiveling in her chair. The window behind her desk wore a veil of frost that cast a muted glow over the office. She clicked on the antique lamp, flashing gold against the silvery winter light. After a moment, she turned it off again. Grammy Helen. Something nice to wear.

And then Ella would have to see about that newt plate and the prickle behind her eyes that seemed to echo.

ella tugged her cerulean blue scarf tighter around the lower half of her face and tucked the ends into the folds of her jacket. Snow buffeted her exposed bits, and she already wished she had stayed in her office with the little brass elephant for company, freshman term papers notwithstanding.

An icy blast chilled her wrists. She'd have to get a coat with longer sleeves one of these days. Ella's boots crunched the snow on the footpath. At least it wasn't getting dark yet.

Getting the tiny silver key into the bike lock in a Buffalo winter was a skill akin to magic. Ella did it twice a day. In went the key. Pop went the lock. The cable, so used to the carefully wound coil it lived in, almost circled itself up immediately. Ella's gloved hands packaged it into a tidy round and tucked it into the outside pocket of her briefcase along with the lock and pulled out a small towel.

She brushed snow off the bike's seat, drying it enough to sit on for the ride back to her loft.

One of the anthropology professors hurried past her, barely nodding in greeting. He didn't mention the bike. No one did anymore.

Ella mounted the bicycle and started pedaling down the salt-crusted path toward the road.

A person could get used to anything.

The snow had mostly stopped by the time Ella rounded the corner to her building. She pressed the button on her garage door opener — she shared with the neighbor — and chained her bike to an exposed girder next to her six-year-old green Subaru. The garage door rumbled closed behind her. Stomping her feet, Ella headed into the building.

Her loft was on the top floor of what was meant to be a duplex and wound up being a makeshift art studio. Ella rented the nicer of the two apartments; the more unfortunate one never got built past efficiency status, like a stunted growth or a half-finished Lego creation.

Poof the cat came running toward her when she opened the door with a loud *prrrrow?* He rubbed against her ankles, his cream-colored fur turning beige with the melted snow.

"You're going to be very unhappy in a minute if you keep that up, Poof. Just wait until it soaks through to your skin."

Sure enough, Poof rubbed once more as Ella took a step — almost sending her pitching face first into the wall — and bolted up into his cat tree to lick away the cold water.

"I told you so."

Ella moved her drying rack closer to the heating vent. Coat over one end, scarf on the top, gloves stuck on each of the bars on the ends. Boots over the floor vent in the foyer. Just like every day. Getting home had its own rituals. Heater up to seventy-three, teapot on.

Poof came back down from his perch when the sound of kibble hitting his bowl reached his ears. Ella scratched him once under the chin. His purr sounded like an old Corvette revving its engine. She could always hear him from the opposite side of the loft.

Prince, on the other hand, she almost never heard. He was very quiet for a frog. Ella tapped once on the glass of Prince's aquarium. Prince hopped out from inside his log and sat in the glow of his heat lamp, throat pulsing. Behind him, the soft purple LED glowed with the trickles of water that filled Prince's water fountain.

"Hungry? I'm still not going to kiss you."

Prince turned his back. Ella dropped in his three crickets.

"Don't take it so hard. You've given me no proof you deserve a kiss. If you ever want to eat anything besides crickets, you might want to work on that."

The teapot began to whistle with a shrill squeal. Ella snapped the lid on the aquarium back into place. She thought she might regret feeding them early today when five in the morning rolled around. She pulled the teapot from the burner and dropped a bag of chamomile into her favorite hand-thrown mug.

Something nice to wear for Grammy Helen.

Ella brought her tea up the stairs with her to her bedroom and set it on a coaster atop the nightstand. She opened the closet. Her clothes were all organized by color. Red through violet, just like a rainbow, followed by white, black, gray, and brown. Above the hanging clothes, all her shoes fit into cubby holes by color. Shouldn't be hard to find something. Except Grammy Helen hated when people wore black to funerals. She'd want Ella in something colorful. Something alive.

Ella decided on a bright green sweater and dark gray slacks. She had a pair of matching green pumps she could wear with it. She reached up to get the pumps, and something hard fell out of one of the shoes and hit her on the head.

Ella didn't think to say *ow*. She already knew what it was.

A rock.

This one was gray swirled with milky white. Pretty. They were always unique. She held it in her hand until it warmed to the temperature of her skin, ignoring the light throb at the top of her head where the rock had hit. Her heart did a slow turn inside her chest as if to say, "Ah, yes. Just making sure."

Ella backed out of the closet and placed the pair of green heels on the foot of her bed, stepping around the corner to the large plastic jug she kept just out of sight. She dropped the rock in with the others. It was almost two-thirds full now. Ella never thought it would get this full. Not now, when the person who had left them scattered around her home had been dead for three years.

A twang plucked in her chest, as it always did at the thought of her twin brother. The hole wasn't gone, just covered over in brush and vulnerable to rocks like the one that had just fallen on her head. Ella rubbed the part of her skull the small stone had struck, unable to allow herself to think about Stuart, unable to do anything else, as usual.

She laid the rest of the outfit out next to the shoes. She'd have to press it before Sunday.

Sunday Grammy Helen would be buried near her brother, and the wrongness of it made the tips of her fingers feel cold.

Grammy Helen's death made that hole feel stripped bare again, and bigger. Ella wanted to cry and found she couldn't. Instead she felt as though the rock had bounced round inside her where that hole made her hollow.

She ought to call her parents. Was it midnight in Johannesburg or was it noon? Ella should be able to remember the time difference by now. It'd been five years since her parents moved to South Africa. Midnight or noon, Grammy Helen was Dad's mother. He ought to know. Auntie Eunice might well have forgotten to send him a telegram, and even if she didn't, Dad was never very good at figuring out what words went where when it came to her.

The phone rang seven times before going to voice mail. Ella didn't think it was appropriate to let her father know about his mother's death in a recording, so she simply told him to call her back and hung up.

When was the last time they'd spoken? Ella couldn't recall. With the time difference, it was never easy to get a hold of her parents. She'd try again tomorrow.

Ella flopped down on her bed, thinking of Grammy Helen's worn, wrinkled face and the bright green eyes that never aged with the rest of her. Ella's hand sought out the tiny gold key at her throat that Grammy had given her ten years before. She didn't want to watch Grammy get put into the ground. A tiny part of her mind tried to pipe up and remind her that she didn't get any say in that, but she squashed it down, punching a deep well in her pillow in the process.

She never touched her tea.

chapter
two

Sunday came with a sharp brightness that turned the snow to glitter and sent jabs of cold into Ella's lungs with every inhale. After taking a long look at her bicycle and calculating the length of time it would take to bike the five miles to the funeral home, she put her silver key away and got out the keys for the Subaru instead, gritting her teeth as she fastened her seatbelt. She checked it once, twice, then a third time before taking four deep breaths, flexing the toes on each foot twice, and turning the key in the ignition.

She almost hoped the engine would shriek, whine, and refuse to turn over. Instead it started with a rumble and a hum, and Ella sat and waited for her heart to resume a normal tempo while the car grew warm. If she couldn't drive today, when could she?

Five miles always turned to fifty when she got behind the wheel these days.

The funeral home was gray on the outside and faux-warm on the inside. Everywhere Ella looked, something gleamed at her, polished and shining. Grammy was clashing crocheted afghans and mismatched knickknacks, not spit-shined caskets and spritely flower arrangements.

Ella trailed a finger down the wooden box that held her grandmother. So far Ella was alone, and she was glad for it. That was her whole reason for turning up early. A picture of Grammy Helen sat on top of the casket. One of those fancy glamour photos where they dress up your top half and poof out your hair like it's the 80s all over again. Grammy Helen and Auntie Eunice went together for their ninetieth birthday.

Grammy Helen wore a flaming red dress covered in sequins and lipstick that matched the dress. Her white hair — which she kept long all her life — was curled and teased into a silvery cloud like spun sugar. Eunice had worn the same dress, hadn't she?

In fact — Ella squinted at the photo, searching for the tiny mole on the left side of Grammy's neck that was the one visible difference between her and her twin Eunice — yes. There it was. Ella took a relieved breath. It would be just like Eunice to accidentally put her own picture on her dead twin's casket.

Ella winced at the thought and gave her blue lock of hair a tug.

"Ella?"

She turned to see Jace Wong, coat and a purple beanie slung over her arm, hovering in the doorway. Just Ella's height and slender where Ella curved — mostly in the bosom — Jace dumped her outerwear on a nearby chair. Her angled bob of black hair lifted off of her scalp from static.

"Your hair." Ella gestured, and smoothed both palms over it until it lay sleek and static-free on her friend's head. "You came early."

"Because I knew you would. Eunice here yet?"

"I haven't seen her."

Jace nodded and linked an arm through Ella's. "You doing okay?"

"I guess. She was ninety-three. It's not like…" Ella swallowed. "I mean."

"I know."

Not like Stuart. The words hung in the air. It wasn't like losing Stuart.

For a long moment, Ella watched their reflection in the casket.

"My parents send their condolences."

Ella turned her head to look at Jace. "What did they really say?"

Jace's lips twisted in a smile that looked more like a grimace. "They said to rejoice in Helen's return to the Lord."

"Was that all?"

"Nope. Something about grief being an affront to God when he plans to reunite his children in eternity. You know, the run-of-the-mill, most-offensive-sympathy-ever spiel."

"I'd be worried if they said anything but."

"You and me both."

They stared into the shiny wood of the casket again.

"They know we're not Christians, right?" Ella said.

"I think they repress that knowledge on my account."

"Still haven't told them?"

"Not coming out to them till I'm on my deathbed." Jace blew a kiss at Grammy Helen's picture. "Grammy Helen got it, didn't you, you old fart?"

"There's only one old fart in this funeral home, and she's still kicking."

Ella pulled her arm away from Jace and turned. "Auntie Eunice."

"Well, don't be shy, boys. Come give us a hug."

Jace and Ella exchanged a glance, and Ella put her arms around Eunice's bony shoulders. She felt her great-aunt's hand flapping around until Jace's arms enfolded them both, and Ella sighed into Eunice's long, white waves.

"I'm so sorry about Helen, Aunt Eunice," Jace said. Auntie Eunice started insisting Jace call her that the day Ella brought her home for Thanksgiving her freshman year of college.

"Oh, tosh. She'll never have to deal with one of these awful vintners again."

At Jace's confused look, Ella mouthed winters as soon as Eunice turned her head. Or perhaps she really did mean vintners. The two of them used to raise hell in the local wineries.

"Where is everyone?" Eunice bustled over to the casket and started straightening the already-uniform bouquets.

"It's still early, Auntie Eunice. The service isn't due to start for another half hour."

Ella didn't want to mention the real reason no one else had arrived — at ninety-three, Helen and Eunice were by far the oldest of their friends. Most of the others had died years before, and those who hadn't couldn't get around half as well. Eunice still drove, though whether that was in anyone's best interest was up for debate.

"I was forty-five minutes early for Jacob Barton's funeral two years ago. But that was mostly Helen's doing. She always had the hots for him."

Over the next twenty minutes, exactly four other people trickled through the doors into the memorial room, and one of them was the officiant, who shook Ella's hand with a pitying expression on his face, then promptly thumbed his nose with a handkerchief and stifled a sneeze.

Ella didn't remember much of the service, only that Jace kept eying her as if expecting her to shatter into tiny shards. Eunice's eulogy remained unintelligible to everyone — including Ella — except for the loud fart that escaped her halfway through.

Ella decided that the lack of reaction from everyone in the room said they were deaf (most likely the case of old Mrs. Morgenstern), arduously trained for such uncomfortable events (the officiant), or knew Eunice far too well to be surprised by any public bodily functions.

When the eulogy was over, Eunice pressed the play button on a decrepit boom box, spilling "Can't Buy Me Love" into the room. Grammy Helen always did favor McCartney's songs when it came to The Beatles. Ella felt the first smile of the day creep over her lips. Grammy'd been the one to introduce her to the band. Aunt Eunice shuffled back to her seat next to Ella and plunked down. Ella looked over at her, surprised to only now be seeing tears drip from her eyes.

She reached over and took Aunt Eunice's gnarled hand in hers. "Good choice of song, Aunt Eunice."

Aunt Eunice covered Ella's hand with her other one and patted it twice. "I know, dear. I know."

not much made for a sadder funeral than when there were more cemetery employees acting as pallbearers than there were mourners, Ella thought. And yet, there it was. The gravediggers had to help position the casket over the hole in the ground.

She guessed her parents hadn't gotten her messages. She'd left four more after the first, the last saying that it was urgent and they needed to call. Still nothing.

Ella couldn't hear much of the officiant's words over the wind. The rushing of air built pressure in her ears, and she thought she might blow away if Jace hadn't linked their arms again. Auntie Eunice snuffled into the officiant's handkerchief until the wind caught it, and it fluttered away to land on the corner of an unmarked headstone, the name swallowed by the wind and rain over the centuries.

Watching the burial was too much. Ella's fingers tightened around the stems of the three white roses she'd meant to place on Grammy's grave.

She pulled her arm from Jace's and stumbled away, tears dripping down her cheeks at last. She knew where her feet were taking her, but she didn't want to stop them. Not this time.

It wasn't far. Her family's graves took up a good chunk of the Twin Pines Cemetery. Grammy Helen had wanted to be buried next to her late husband, Glen Keyes.

They were surrounded by older family, dating back several hundred years.

Her feet halted in front of a newer stone, only three years old. Ella's fingers went to the blue lock in her hair, twisting it around her knuckle. She made herself read the tombstone.

Stuart Keyes. Beloved son, brother, grandson.

Auntie Eunice wasn't the only one in their family to have lost a twin.

Ella pulled one of the white roses from her left hand and set it in front of the headstone.

It had been cold that night, and Ella had been toasty warm inside her loft with Jace, giggling about Jace's new girlfriend and painting each other's nails stupid shades of pink. And then her life had ripped down the center.

Ella shook herself. After three years, she still couldn't bear the thought that they'd put Stuart in the ground. She couldn't bear the sense that she'd spent the last three years going about her life with frayed wires fizzing sparks where her brother was supposed to be.

She couldn't bear knowing she'd never hear his voice again.

His funeral had been so different from Grammy's. The service had overflowed with mourners. Stuart's friends, Ella's friends, their parents' friends. All of them on the verge of collapse. If Jace hadn't been there, Ella might still be a puddle on the floor of the funeral home.

A hand on her shoulder brought her back to herself.

"This must be so hard for you." Jace. Ella reached up and took Jace's hand.

There were a hundred things she could say, like "Isn't it supposed to get easier?" or "Why hasn't this hole gotten smaller?"

Ella knew how pointless those things were. Grief hits like a missile to the chest. Hollows you out. Makes you cold. Even after three years, you can still fall right in no matter how well you think you've learned to skirt the hole's edges.

"I should go back to Auntie Eunice," Ella said instead.

Her feet took her back to the graveside, near the array of flower arrangements already stiff and buffeted by the wind. Ella plucked the tag from the nearest arrangement and read it.

For Mother, who will be missed forever. Stephen and Susan Keyes.

Ella's parents.

They sent flowers but didn't come themselves? Then they did get her messages. Ella tucked the card into her coat pocket and pulled her arms around her body, wondering why her parents would send flowers but not pick up the phone.

grammy's house was just as Ella last saw it a week earlier. Same dormant flowerbeds lining the walkway up to the wraparound porch. Same bright green door with the brass troll knocker. Books piled on built-in shelves from wall to wall in the living room. Knickknacks sandwiched between them and stuck on top of them.

At least there were a few more people at the wake.

Grammy had been a member of a gardening club, and ten of her fellow gardeners — all in their mid-sixties — arrived in three carloads bearing lasagna and chili and various dessert "salads" that had never seen a vegetable and consisted of mostly Cool-Whip and Jell-O and marshmallows. It reminded Ella of her last visit with Grammy Helen. Ella's fruit plate looked out of place, like a pineapple trying to blend in with fujis.

After a few polite hellos and discussion about what would happen to Grammy's prize-winning irises, Ella and Jace escaped upstairs. The second floor was all bedrooms and bathrooms, and Ella kept going up another floor to the third. She'd come up here to read as a child when her parents got sick of having her and Stuart around all summer. Grammy let them drink as much cream soda as they wanted and never confessed when she sent them home and their parents fussed about how hyper they were.

"What is this?" Jace asked, stopping short at the top of the stairs.

"You've never been up here?"

Jace shook her head. Ella supposed it would look strange if you'd never seen it before.

At the top of the stairs was a corridor. And that was it. Just a long corridor that stretched across the house. No rooms. No doors at all. Just long walls. And hanging from every square foot of hallway were keys. Keys of all ages and sizes, from long knobbly skeleton keys to more modern varieties of flat metal with tiny ridges.

Ella felt a wave of vertigo and blinked away a sudden blur in her vision.

"What are they for?" Jace touched a key that looked as though it might open the door to the Holy Grail, then pulled her hand back as though it were hot against her fingertips.

Ella shrugged, the blur and wobble in her head subsiding. "A family joke. Keyes family, key collectors. Like this," she pulled out her necklace with the tiny gold key. The key was warm from touching her skin and flashed brightly in the overhead light. Ella dropped it back under her shirt where it always lay. "Grammy gave me this when I was about ten. I used to come up here to read."

As a child, Grammy Helen had always told Ella not to touch them. Once, Helen had caught her straining to reach a particularly shiny one, and it was the one time Ella had ever been punished during a visit. She'd been sent to her room without any books, and when she was allowed out again, somehow every key seemed to have slid upward on the walls to rest just out of her reach even were she to strain. Eventually, she'd given up, a sense of distaste filling her any time she thought of touching them. Now the keys were all easily within reach, but Ella felt no urge to touch one. Not today.

"It's quiet, I guess." Jace paced to the opposite end of the hall, then turned her head to look over her shoulder at Ella. "Did I ever tell you how weird your family is?"

"Hey. You're the one with the holy rollers for parents who'd pass out if you ever brought your girlfriend to a church potluck."

"You have a point there. But I think you mean have apoplexy. Passing out isn't giving them enough credit."

"Ella? Are you up there?"

Ella started. Auntie Eunice might be as old as this house, but she had a voice like a construction foreman. "We're up here!"

"My knees can't do scares, Ella. Helen's liar wants to talk to you."

"Oh, god," Ella muttered. "I hope Grammy's lawyer didn't hear her say that."

"Lawyer? Did Helen have a will?"

"She always said she was going to leave me a little something when she went whoop." Ella made a sound and twisted her thumb up toward the ceiling. "Direct quote."

"You probably shouldn't keep the liar waiting then." Jace turned back down the stairs.

Ella followed her down. At the bottom of the stairs, Auntie Eunice funneled her into the study and shut the pair of French doors behind her. A woman in a navy blue suit turned to greet her.

"Ella Keyes? Your grandmother told me all about you. She was very proud of you. She said you're a professor at the university?"

"Mythology and folklore, yes." Ella proffered her hand. "I'm sorry, what was your name?"

"Andrea Harper, Esquire. Helen made me the executor of her estate a few years back after her previous liar passed away." Andrea Harper's eyes glinted with a smile.

Ella gave her an apologetic wince. "Sorry about Auntie Eunice, Ms. Harper. She doesn't do too well with words anymore." It was worse when Eunice was upset about something, and today she had every reason.

"It's quite all right. And please, call me Andrea."

Ella nodded, sitting on a seldom-used blue velvet chair. She couldn't remember the last time she was in this room. Grammy never came in here. Andrea sat across from her on a matching love seat and pulled a folder from her briefcase.

"Helen's will is quite straightforward. She had a bit of monetary assets, which she left to her sister Eunice to ensure she had proper care for the remainder of her life —" Andrea paused, as if waiting for approval. Ella nodded at her to go on. "— but she did have one other asset that she wished to leave to you."

Nothing sprang to mind as being an asset. Grammy didn't have much use for traditional things of value. She had no jewelry or diamonds, always preferring travel and experience to material objects. She collected trinkets, small things unique to the areas she visited. A tiny porcelain bowl with a blue Star of David, the bowl's curves lace-like as if crocheted rather than sculpted — that was from the synagogue in Budapest. A set of Russian matryoshka dolls painted blue and gold from Nizhni Novgorod. And of course, the keys.

Ella lost herself so much in the myriad treasures Grammy had used to fill her home that she missed the very obvious direction in which Andrea was leading her.

"It was her wish that you would inherit her home, Ella," Andrea said.

The house? Ella's fingertips went cold in her lap. The house. "But I have a home," she said blankly. A home close to the university, where she could ride her bike or walk in the springtime when the campus bloomed to life. A small loft, yes, but a comfortable one. She had all space she needed and no more or less. Poof and Prince for company.

"Helen wanted you to have hers."

"But I don't need it."

"You're allowed to sell it if you like, after a year, but she wanted it to be yours."

Ella sat still on her ornate little chair, counting seconds. This wasn't what she expected. She'd expected nothing, really. Maybe a small admired tchotchke or two from childhood, like the mother-of-pearl handled antique letter opener from Scotland that always looked like a fancy dagger to a young Ella who wielded it as such when playing pretend with Stuart. Or the gold filigreed locket that held a pocket watch in lieu of photographs. Not…

Her gaze took a tour of the study. Its walls were emerald green, her Gramps' favorite color. This was more his room than anything else, but he'd passed away when Ella was very young, and the color was all she remembered of him. There was the oak roll-top desk with its perfectly arranged slots for papers and inkwells and sealing wax and blotting paper and all the little things no one used anymore for writing since computers made it all irrelevant.

Hers. Ella's.

chapter
three

Several hours later after the unwelcome announcement, Ella and Jace settled into Ella's living room — her real living room, at her real home — and Poof settled into his favorite perch on Ella's lap.

Even Prince the Frog seemed to understand that Ella had had a bit of an upset, because he came out of his log and crawled atop his one large rock to look out over the living room at Ella and Jace, beady black eyes darting back and forth. Ella even heard a venturing, "Grb-but?" from his direction.

"I don't understand why you're so upset. Even if you don't want to keep it in the end, she gave you something hugely valuable. And I don't mean its monetary worth."

To Jace's credit, she left off the implied, *you should be grateful* from the end of the sentence.

"I don't have any use for it, Jace. It's not like I can pick up and move out there." The thought made the little hairs on Ella's cheeks tingle. A little voice that sounded unnervingly like Stuart's pointed out that the house had been Ella's favorite place growing up, but Ella pretended not to hear it. Listening meant admitting the voice was right, and that she'd heard it at all.

"Look at it this way. It's a chance to get to you know your grandmother better. Think of all the things she left there. Things about your family. Things that came before all the tragedy of the last few years."

She meant before Stuart. Things that wouldn't be tainted by Stuart's death. Older things. History.

Maybe Jace was right. Ella had done her undergraduate work in history before moving onto postgraduate study in mythology and folklore. But she'd never explored her own family's history. She thought of her weekly visits with Grammy Helen that had punctuated the last three years. Grammy's knobby knuckles clasping a teacup of Earl Grey or Moroccan mint. Her green eyes with all their smile lines as she asked Ella about work and did everything in her power to distract her from thinking of Stuart. The way she told Ella she loved her every time she left the house. Ella had forced herself to drive out there once a week at first, but later the driving just became something that had to happen to see Grammy Helen. And now the house was hers. Maybe she could find out about the keys on the third floor and why they'd all been gathered in the first place.

No.

Ella found herself shaking her head at Jace. "You're doing it again. Making it sound all logical and normal. I have normal. I have a job I love. I have friends —" She added a plural that wasn't strictly correct, but plowed on, "— I have a home and a routine, and I don't need a new project or anything. I'm supposed to apply for the Fulbright professorship soon. I'm up for tenure."

Her fingers scratched at Poof's shoulders, and he reached out both front paws to her knees, kneading the air. Poof didn't need any upheaval either.

Jace's face went blank and unreadable.

"What?"

"Nothing."

Ella pushed her back farther into the couch cushions. "I don't need a house, Jace."

Jace raised her hands. "That's fine. That's fair. I'm just saying it could be good for you."

Ella shook her head, stroking Poof from head to tail. His fluffy cream-colored tail swished in the air and curled around her wrist. "I'm fine with things just as they are."

finals week.

Ella pulled off her hat, shaking her head to rid it of snowflakes. They scattered like dandruff onto the carpet. She had two tests to give this afternoon, but nothing until two o'clock. She could have stayed home.

Routine, Ella thought. Just get back to life as usual. Deal with the house later.

Ella stashed her boots by the space heater under her desk and changed into a pair of flats. The smell of coffee percolating reached her nose, and she stepped out of the office to find a pot brewing in the department's kitchenette.

"Morning, Easton," she said.

Easton looked up from his desk. "Dr. Keyes. I didn't expect you back today. Wasn't the funeral yesterday?"

Looking into the barren cupboard, Ella selected a plain white mug and waited for the coffee to finish dripping. "It was," she said. "But it's finals week. I should be here."

"I can moderate all the exams if you need me to. I don't have anything else going on this week." There was a desperate tone in Easton's voice that poked at the edges of his sentence like a child pressing his face against a flimsy tent flap.

Ella looked over at him. His fingers drummed on the desk, and his face seemed to have broken out more than usual over the weekend. "Are you okay?"

"I'm fine. I'd just like a distraction."

"From what?"

Easton's eyes darted back and forth in his eye sockets. "It's not a problem. It's stupid, really."

The coffee finished hissing and burbling into the pot, and Ella poured herself a cup. "Really, Easton. What is it?"

"It's-my-birthday," he muttered. "Really. Not a big deal."

"Do you have any plans for the day? You don't really need to be here, you know. All I have is finals, and today it's just the upper levels. None of the lectures are until later in the week."

There it was again, the bulging desperation. "I don't have any plans."

Suddenly, Ella got it. No plans. No parties. Just a lonely birthday. "Your family's in Alaska, right? Fairbanks?"

Easton nodded. "Well, that's where they live. They're actually way up in Barrow for Christmas. My older brother works on the oil pipeline up by Prudhoe Bay, and they didn't want him to be lonely. But the weather's been bad and phone service gets spotty."

"They haven't called, have they?"

"They still might." Easton's face flushed red. "It's five hours earlier there."

"Of course." Ella took a long sip of her coffee and jerked the cup back from her lips. The liquid scalded the top of her mouth, and she dabbed at the burned skin with her tongue.

For a long moment, the only sounds in the kitchenette were the coffee pot winding down and a printer from down the hall warming up.

This won't do at all, Ella thought.

"How about this — I have a quick errand to run. You get started on the next batch of term papers, and I'll be back in twenty minutes. Then we'll conquer Monday together. Sound good?" Ella hadn't seen Easton quite so forlorn ever. He was always a quiet sort, which suited her, because she liked quiet. But birthdays were miserable days to be lonely.

She should know. When you share a birthday your whole life with someone with whom you also shared a womb, birthdays are never anything but lonely once that someone is gone forever.

Ella changed back into her boots and tugged her still-damp hat over her head, shimmying into her coat.

She left her bicycle where it was this time and headed west across campus. The first intersection brought her to a small bakery that did custom cakes, but also sold confections a la carte.

A string of bells jangled as she entered, and a gust of sugar-scented warmth blew across her face.

"Welcome to Sweet Treats, can I help you?"

Ella smiled and pointed to an eight inch black forest cake. "Can you write a message on that?"

"Of course. What would you like it to say?"

"Simple. Just 'Happy Birthday, Easton.'"

While the cake went into the back to be lettered, Ella pulled out her cell phone and dialed her favorite Italian restaurant. She'd ordered for Easton before, and she asked them to send his favorite sausage ravioli to her office along with a family-size order of spinach lasagna and as many breadsticks as they could cram into the to-go bag. She asked them to bring it to the office at five.

Ella made her way back to campus with the cake and stashed it in the fridge while Easton hunched over a stack of sophomore term papers. He wouldn't look into a brown paper bag that wasn't his.

Back in her office, Ella sent out an email to the department asking them to gather at five to celebrate Easton's birthday. Once she hit send, she sat still for a moment and pondered. They should have hats.

There had been a few hats at Sweet Treats, but she hadn't thought to get them.

Ella pushed back from her desk and wandered back out toward Easton's desk. He looked up for a moment, and she gave him a smile. "Did you happen to see today's newspaper laying about anywhere?"

He blinked at her. "I think the dean took it."

"Thanks." Ella hurried down the hall to Dean Jonas' office. He was usually the first to get the newspaper. When he was done with it, he left it rolled up on the chair in front of his assistant's desk — yes. There it was. Ella nodded hello to Freddy and took the newspaper back to her office.

They'd forgive her. It wasn't like she was about to defile the Sunday paper.

Ella closed her door behind her and locked it, pulling the blinds. Then she booted up her computer, cranked up her favorite Rob Zombie album, and started folding.

It took three tries to get a proper pirate hat out of the front page, but after that, Ella sped through the remaining sections of newspaper until there were enough hats for everyone she'd invited. Plus two or three, in case someone else showed up. When she was finished, she stashed the creations in the bottom drawer of her desk and reopened her office, leaning around the door jamb to get Easton's attention.

"You know, I could use your help during those exams later after all."

ella felt quite pleased with herself by the time the last student finished the exam at four forty-seven that afternoon. She instructed Easton to gather up the finished finals and meet her back at the department, and she hurried back to the office.

A few faculty members milled around her office already.

Dean Jonas shook her hand. "Ella, Ella. Nice of you to think of Easton. He doesn't have many friends, does he?"

Ella rather resented that. She didn't have many friends either, but that didn't make her that sad. Did it? "His family's far away, and he might not get to talk to them. I thought it would be nice to do something for him. Besides, he's done great work for the last year and a half. He deserves some recognition."

The dean clasped her hand once more before releasing it. "Of course. He's a hard worker and has a great mind on him. I'm happy to be here."

"Remember you said that when I give you your party hat," Ella said.

She fished the hats out from her desk drawer and handed them out. Everyone she invited had turned up. Either the free cake or goodwill — she wouldn't judge. Just as long as Easton got a happy moment on his birthday.

Ella just hoped he didn't hate surprises.

She'd sort of assumed he'd be fine with it. At least she hadn't planned on singing.

The glass door banged, and Ella motioned everyone to silence. A moment later, Easton's wind-reddened face appeared around the corner, and after a second of him staring at all the faces peering at him from underneath meticulously folded newspaper hats, Ella waved her hand and they all remembered to yell, "Surprise!"

It went much more smoothly after that.

Somewhere about halfway through the cake, Easton sidled up to Ella with a slice. "You didn't have to do all this, you know."

Ella thought about the three birthdays since Stuart's death. Until Easton said it, she didn't realize how much she'd felt like she did have to do all this. But she didn't explain all of that. Instead, she just said, "I wanted to."

"Well, thank you. I won't forget it."

"Just eat more cake before I eat it all. And please, take some of that food home with you."

Besides, it wouldn't survive a trip home on her bike.

Slowly, the faculty members evaporated back to their offices to grade finals, and Ella packed up her briefcase, bundling herself into her daily cocoon of winter wear.

As she stooped to unlock the chain on her bike, the door behind her opened. Dean Jonas and Easton walked out of the building, deep in conversation.

Ella raised a hand to wave, but neither of them saw her.

Jace called just as Ella was draping her scarf over the drying rack.

"Come down to Fido's for coffee. Alexa's here, and she wants to see you."

"I just got home."

"It's two blocks away. Come on, Ella. No pooping the party."

Ella started to protest that she couldn't poop a party she only just heard about, and in fact she'd thrown a very nice birthday party for Easton just an hour before, but Jace hung up before any of that could leave Ella's mouth.

Poof jumped onto the back of the couch.

"I guess I'm going back out again, Poof."

At least she wouldn't be stuck putting on a damp scarf this time.

The coat closet was just as much of a rainbow as her bedroom closet. Scarves in all colors with their matching hats. Today felt like an orange day. Ella picked a fluffy crocheted set the shade of an autumn sugar maple and wrapped it around her neck.

Fido's was actually called Fado. It was an Irish pub no one could never seem to pronounce. But Jace did mean coffee. Irish coffee.

Ella trudged the two blocks in the snow and reached the pub to a blast of heat and malty beer smell and a cascade of fiddles that rummaged through her ears as soon as she opened the door.

Monday. Traditional music night. No wonder Jace was here.

Ella found Jace and Alexa two tables away from the band. A heady little bubble of relief burst prettily when Ella saw that it was just the two of them. She waved.

Alexa hopped up from her seat and scurried toward Ella, wrapping her arms around Ella's neck. She smelled like Guinness and the tiniest touch of malt vinegar. "Oh, honey," she said into Ella's scarf. "I'm sorry about Grammy Helen."

"It's okay." Ella tried to pull back, but Alexa's hands grasped at her shoulders.

"If you need anything. Anything at all. You know where to find us."

"I'm fine, Alexa. Thanks. It's good to see you."

Alexa's almost black eyes stood out in her brown skin. Her hair made black waves against her scalp, and the fire-engine red highlights licked at the black like tongues of flame. How long had she and Jace been together now? Over three years. It'd been Alexa who Jace and Ella had giggled about the night Stuart died. Before their third date, Jace had dragged Ella all over Buffalo looking for a model U-Haul to give to Alexa as a joke, but they still hadn't moved in together.

Alexa studied Ella for another moment before waving a heavily-ringed hand at the table. "Got you an Irish coffee."

Jace snorted. "You mean Bailey's with a splash of coffee." She took a drink of her own — perfectly traditional with only whiskey — Irish coffee.

Ella could smell the Jameson from where she stood. She hung her coat over the back of the free chair, then folded her scarf into a square and tucked it in the hat, which she placed in the hood.

The band started a lively folk song, and a young woman with a bit of plumpness on her bones and rosy cheeks from the heat started singing the "Maid Who Sold Her Barley."

Ella's coffee was still warm. She took a drink.

"There you are!"

The coffee hit Ella's trachea, and she coughed, looking up. A young white woman with spiky blonde hair in a pixie cut dragged another chair over to the table and pushed the one holding Ella's coat aside. Jace got up, hugging the newcomer.

"Lynn, this is Ella. Ella, Lynn. Ella's the mythology professor I told you about." Jace kissed Pixie Lynn on both cheeks and settled back into her seat.

Ella felt a murderous look taking shape on her face. Not again. Not again, not again, not again. She chugged the rest of her coffee.

Lynn stuck out a hand and grinned. "Hello, Ella. Love the hair."

"Likewise," Ella said faintly.

"What are you drinking? I'll go get you a refill."

Ella looked at her now-empty footed mug. "Scotch. Neat."

"I love a woman who knows what she wants." Lynn winked and flitted off to the bar.

The murderous look coalesced and aimed itself at Jace. "Not again, Jace. She knows I don't date, right?"

"Honey, you don't know you remember how to date. Loosen up." Jace put her arm around Ella and pressed her face against Ella's cheek to whisper in her ear. "Lynn's fun. She knows you just lost a family member. She's not pushy. Just get to know her. Let her distract you."

Just lost. Three years ago was still just to Ella, Grammy Helen notwithstanding, and Jace knew it. She felt a surge of love for her friend that quickly dissolved again into panic when she saw the bob of Lynn's head over the crowd at the bar. Ella looked at Alexa for help, who shrugged. "I had no idea Lynn was coming."

"You're no help."

Turning back to Jace, Ella leaned forward over the table. "This has to stop. Just because we happened to meet lips-first doesn't mean I need you to matchmake for me."

"We're all on the same team," Jace said with a magnanimous wave of her hand. Alexa looked away, at the woman on Fado's tiny stage area who was currently making a bawdy gesture.

"Oh, god." Ella sat back in her chair, defeated. Lynn was already paying, a Guinness and a rocks glass of amber liquid held deftly in one hand.

She'd even gotten Ella a double.

"I'm going to kill you," Ella said to no one in particular.

"No you're not." Jace reached across the table and patted her hand. "You like me too much."

"I'm quickly revising that sentiment."

"I would too," said Alexa. "But then Lynn's not my type."

At least there was scotch.

somehow ella ended up on the dance floor.

Lynn's hands clasped hers, and they spun circles between two lines of clapping people.

"Six counts, then we go!"

"Go where?"

"You'll see!"

The scotch made Ella's stomach warm and her head fuzzy. Five whirls later, Lynn released her hands. Ella almost veered off into a burly redhead, but Lynn's elbow caught hers, and she whisked in another circle. The burly redhead caught her free elbow in his and spun with her. Then back to Lynn.

Down the lines of people they went. Jace and Alexa whooped from the sidelines.

Sweat beaded on Ella's forehead, trickling down her temple as a stranger do-si-doed her and laughed, smelling of beer and heat. Then it was back to Lynn once more, and she deposited Ella across from her at the end of the line with a laugh that bubbled up like carbonation and spilled over her lips.

The next couple came spinning down the line, and Ella spun the guy with her. He and his partner took the place of the end of the line, pushing Ella and Lynn closer to the top again.

The fiddles shredded the air, dancing from note to note with a building frenzy. Ella and Lynn were halfway back to the top of the dance when the fiddles and guitar burst into a ragged finale of strings and cries of excitement.

Lines of dancers evaporated into the perspiration-humid air. Lynn slapped Ella on the back.

"Good job! That's the only ceilidh dance I know. It's called a strip the willow."

"Fun," Ella got out. She snatched a glass of water from Jace's hand and gulped down half of it. "I need to get into shape."

"Yeah, well, plenty of time for that resolution when the New Year rolls around," Jace said.

Alexa leaned on Jace's shoulder, eyes fluttering shut and a dreamy smile on her face.

Jace planted a kiss on Alexa's forehead. "We're out, Ella."

Ella darted a glance at Lynn, who was at the bar again.

Oh, no more scotch, Ella thought. But it was two sweating glasses of ice water Lynn returned with. Jace and Alexa layered on their coats and gloves.

Lots of hugging. Ella might have hugged Alexa twice. Then she and Jace were gone, and Ella was left sitting on a still-warm bench with Lynn, staring at an old iron plowshare that had been rigged to the ceiling above the bar.

Fingers touched the back of her hand, tentative and soft.

Here we go again, Ella thought. Why did Jace get her into this? And yet Ella knew. Jace had tried setting Ella up with men after she'd left her fiancé, and Ella had turned tail and run like they were piranhas instead of people. Ella had dated a few women in her life — one for over a year— and maybe it was that they felt safer and Jace could sense it.

"Look, Lynn," Ella turned and tried to focus on the woman's face. She was pretty, and she had cute hair, but Ella didn't feel anything about that. Since the last not-quite-relationship had ended just after the six month mark of leaving her ex, Ella hadn't felt like kissing any boys or girls or anyone. Jace had been just fine with that until Stuart died. Now she seemed to think Ella was sharing her closet, when in fact Ella's whole family knew she was bi.

Lynn's fingers jumped back onto the table. Ella blinked at them. Yes, they were still attached to Lynn's hand. Too much scotch.

Lynn smiled and gave a little sigh, like Wendy might sigh out the window thinking of Peter Pan escaping back to Neverland and leaving her in a nursery with two little boys.

"I know. She told me."

"Told you what?"

"That you may or may not be interested. But you were cute, and a good dancer, so I thought I'd give it a shot. I'm not looking for anything serious myself. Plus," Lynn reached out and gave Ella's blue lock of hair a tug. Ella jumped. "A mythology professor with blue hair? Hot."

Ella grinned at that. "Yeah, it's a...thing."

"What sort of thing?"

Maybe it was the booze or the heat in Fado — or the toucan with a Guinness staring at her from a poster across the bar — but

Ella opened her mouth. "My brother. Ever since he was fifteen, he had blue hair. We were twins."

"Were."

"He passed away. Three years ago."

"I'm sorry." Lynn's blue eyes filled, and this time her hand on Ella's was strong and firm and not asking for anything more. Her fingers were cool and hard. Muscled, like she worked with her hands for a living.

"Me too." Ella never knew what to say about Stuart in cases like this. And she knew no one ever knew what to say to her. Losing a twin, yeah, that must be terrible. It was. Beyond terrible. Ella didn't like to talk about how losing Stuart severed her connections, left her open and fritzing and glitchy. They'd shared so much more than DNA. It was hard to talk about to anyone who hadn't gone through the same thing.

"Jace said you lost your grandmother recently, too." Lynn pulled her hand back and folded it with the other in her lap. "This was probably silly of me, to come out here."

"No, I had fun." Ella looked up from the table. "Sorry I'm not..."

"A cute little professor dyke looking for a one night stand or three?" Lynn's smile lit up her face. "Of all the things to apologize for. Don't even worry about it for a moment. You going to get home okay?"

"I live close. You?"

"I'll call a cab."

Ella nodded. "Thanks for the dance."

"Any time, professor." Lynn winked.

Ella unfolded her scarf and pulled her hat over her head. Lynn twiddled her fingers in farewell, sipping from her water glass. The band was playing another reel, but no one was dancing now. Ella looked at her phone to check the time. Half past twelve and a message from Jace. "Tell me everything!"

Of course. Ella shook her head at her phone and stepped out of the bar into the icy cold. The temperature had dropped what felt like another thirty degrees since she walked in, and her feet made squeaky sounds on the thin layer of new snow. Tiny flakes still fell through the air, perfect creations of ice formed around miniscule impurities in the air. Amazing how beautiful dust could be under the right conditions.

Ella made her way home, taking her time. The warmth of the scotch dissipated into the cold night air. Looking up, a smattering of stars appeared through a break in the clouds.

This had gone better than the last time.

chapter
four

That Wednesday, Ella forced herself to drive to work and then left promptly after giving her last exam to go out to Grammy Helen's — now Ella's — house on the edge of Niagara. Blue and purple Christmas lights on the neighbor's house lit the snow with a colorful glow even in the waning afternoon light.

There weren't any lights at Grammy's house. Come to think of it, Grammy hadn't even put up a tree.

She pulled up to find a familiar white Volvo in the drive and parked beside it. Auntie Eunice.

Ella opened the door to the house. "Auntie Eunice, are you here?"

She wondered what Auntie Eunice could be doing here. The house was the same as it had been last week, apart from the inhabitant. The moment the thought finished flitting through her head, Ella scolded herself.

Auntie Eunice probably just missed her sister.

No one answered Ella's call, so she shut the door behind her. The heat was on, bringing the house up to a toasty warmth. Grammy had solar panels installed on the back roof of the house, and she used the power they generated to heat the water and the house itself. The problem was, doing so didn't leave much room for adjustment. In the winter it was either hot or frigid, and many a holiday season had been spent here with the windows wide open to let in the twenty degree drafts.

Ella liked it warm. She hung her coat and stepped into the living room. She wasn't sure what exactly had brought her out here, just that she wanted to come take a look at the place alone.

Although, she amended, she wasn't necessarily alone if Auntie Eunice's car in the driveway was any indication.

A thud and a crash sounded from the basement in tandem.

"Auntie Eunice?" Ella rushed toward the back stairs and tripped over a cardboard box at the top, catching herself four steps down with one hand on the rail and her hair on the rail joint screw. She sat down on the step, massaging her head and trying to coax the caught strands of hair out from between the metal and the wall.

"Ella, dear, is that you?"

Who else would it be? Ella asked herself. "It's me. What are you doing down here? I thought you couldn't do stairs."

Auntie Eunice's face peered around the wall at the bottom of the staircase. "It's getting up that's the problem. Down is fine."

"You do know that once you're down in the basement, up is the only way out, right?"

Auntie Eunice blinked once, then scrambled into the frame of the stairs. "There used to be a door down here."

"I think it got boarded up a long time ago."

"Oh. Fancy cat. You'll be a dear and help me back up then, won't you?"

"Of course. But what are you doing down there?"

"Helen had something she was supposed to give me." Auntie Eunice looked over her shoulder at the tumble of boxes behind her.

Ella followed her gaze. Tumble of boxes was putting it lightly. No less than five full boxes of trinkets were overturned. Ella felt her lips turn downward in dismay. "What exactly was this something?"

Auntie Eunice stared at a small ivory box. "What?"

"What is it she was supposed to give you?"

The old woman frowned, two fingers tugging at her wrinkled cheek. "I don't quite know."

Ella pulled the last strand of her hair away from the screw. "Why don't you let me help you upstairs? We can have some tea, and maybe you can remember."

"No, no. That's fine, Ella. I'll just go home for the day. Sorry about the mess."

"It's fine. I'll take care of it." Ella pushed the dangerously placed box away from the top of the stairs and made her way down to the bottom. Auntie Eunice looped an arm around Ella's shoulder. Slowly they made their way back up to the top.

"You're sure you don't want some tea?" Ella asked while Auntie Eunice piled on layers of scarves and a parka that looked plenty suitable for a North Pole expedition. She reminded Ella of Mrs. Who in A Wrinkle in Time, bundled like that.

"Oh, no tea dear. No tea. I'll go home and leave you to it." With a bang of the side door, she vanished into the sunset.

Ella wondered how Eunice could still manage to drive.

The house fell too silent in her great-aunt's absence. Ella went to the living room. Grammy had a nice stereo, but it was the turntable Ella set her sights on.

Grammy Helen had been in the parent generation when the Beatles took the world by storm, but that didn't stop her from falling head-over-heels for John Lennon — even though her song-writer of choice leaned toward Paul McCartney. She had every Beatles record ever released in duplicate.

Sometimes Grammy Helen just thought ahead on those things.

Ella slid The White Album from its sleeve, blew an almost nonexistent layer of dust from the turntable, and reverently placed the record onto the pin.

She smiled as she closed the lid on the record player. Ella could remember the first time she heard this album. She was fourteen, and Grammy was telling her about her first ever crush.

Ella made her way up the stairs to Grammy's room. The door was shut, and she twisted the knob and pulled up at the same time. Grammy never shut the door when she was alive, probably because it was such a pain to open. All the doors in her house were solid wood.

The bedroom remained as Ella had seen it last. Handmade wave quilt on the bed in different shades of blue and green. A framed quilt on the wall that, family legend said, had been a gift from a fugitive escaping to freedom on the Underground Railroad. The house had been a stop just before the Canadian border. Matching pillow shams and throw pillows. Dark gray velvet curtains separated to show a view of the side yard and the garage — Ella caught a glimpse of her Subaru from the corner of the window — and two green upholstered armchairs angled toward each other. Those curtains would wear cat hair like a lint brush. A coffee table sat between the armchairs, wearing nothing but a lace doily, probably of Auntie Eunice's making.

Ella knelt at the foot of the bed, looking at the low shelves of a glass hutch that mirrored the bed's position. There it was, the twin brass elephant to the one that sat on a shelf in Ella's office at the university. Its lapis lazuli eyes looked back at her. She'd brought that home from India four years ago — or was it five? Behind it, something caught Ella's eye.

She pushed the elephant aside and reached back to pull out a rock. Her fingers closed around it, and she sat back on her heels.

What was that doing here? This one was shiny and such a dark gray it was almost black. Ella tucked it into her jeans pocket, heart hopping.

Crouching always made her knees ache. Ella stood and moved to the side of the bed, sitting on the edge. She picked a throw pillow at random and set it on her lap, hugging it to her stomach and looking around. She hadn't been in here much in years. Ella glanced down at the night table, and her heart started hopping again. Her fingers reached for her blue lock and gave it a sharp tug before taking the picture from the table.

A picture in a frame.

It was her. Her and Stuart.

They must have been five years old. The two of them sat on a beach — there was a favorite sandbar on Lake Huron in Ontario where Grammy and Auntie Eunice loved to take them — smashing rocks. It was their game, Ella and Stuart. They were convinced they could find gold if they smashed enough of them. Ella would find two large base rocks. Stuart would find the smashers. Then they'd gather up pebbles and crush them to bits.

Ella turned the framed memory over in her hands.

The cardboard back on the photo frame popped out of place. Ella looked it over, trying to press it back down enough to swivel the tab back into position. It wouldn't go. Something was behind the cardboard.

She flipped the remaining tabs around and pulled off the back.

A folded piece of paper was pressed between the photo and the frame.

A letter.

With her name on it.

Dear Ella,

I hope you'll forgive me for triggering old memories. You shouldn't fear them anyway. It'll drive you mad.

Lots of things will drive you mad. But I've always been a mad old bat. You know that. Look, I rhymed. Eunice would be proud, the old goat.

Here I am talking of goats and bats and madness when you're probably seething at me for giving you a house you don't want. I'm here to tell you that's just too bad. I only hope your sentimental side allows you to find this letter before you convince someone to buy the place off your hands and out of your life. You won't get anybody to sell it in the near future anyway, so don't even try. You're stuck with it for a while. I want it to be yours for a time, even though I know it's far from the refuge you want but won't admit you do. These last few years have been hard, and as much as it's been a pleasure to see you each week, to get to know the wonderful woman you've become, to become your friend as well as your grandmother, you need to find your strength now.

If, after a while, you decide that selling the house is what you want, you can.

I won't judge you for doing that. Some days I wish I'd done the same.

But this place holds a lot of keys, to a lot of different doors. Some of those doors you don't need or want to open. I know you've got your shiny, new loft, but Ella, sugar, that's not all that's important. Shiny and new aren't always the best options, you know. Sometimes even less than you think.

Sometimes you need a little old and cluttered. Like Eunice. Watch out for her. I know it sounds nutty telling an almost thirty-year-old to look out for someone three times her age, but you've been through what she's going through now. You can help her. Please do that, for your mad old bat of a Grammy.

Love,
Grammy Helen

Ella read the letter again. Then once again. It was more scattered than she would have expected from Grammy Helen, and it meandered enough that Grammy'd cluck at herself if she could read it.

This place holds a lot of keys.

What a fine joke that was. Ella chuckled. Just like Grammy to state the obvious and try and get figurative at the same time.

She pressed the cardboard back onto the frame and straightened the tabs, then turned the photo back to its place on the table. The children in it didn't look up or notice, so busy they were with their rocks.

The black rock in Ella's pocket was a hard ball against her thigh.

She tucked the letter in the back pocket of her jeans and looked up at the ceiling.

Maybe she'd go have another look up there, but not today.

Suddenly she wanted to listen to Meshuggah more than the Beatles.

poof landed in ella's lap the moment she sat down on her bed back at the loft.

Her phone buzzed on the comforter next to her, and she reached for it.

Three missed calls.

Ella's throat went dry and sticky, and she fought back a rising lump in her chest.

Her eyes felt sandy for a moment before prickling with tears.

Get a grip, she told herself. It's just a phone. It's just a phone. It's probably just Jace.

Ella made herself unlock the screen and look at the missed calls. Sure enough, two were from Jace. She had three messages. Ella punched in her password. Calming breaths. That's what the counselor had taught her. Deep breath in for four seconds. Hold for a seven count. Deep breath out for eight. Woo-sah. Or something. Her heart thudded faster than she wanted it to; in moments like this, it felt like it were about to run away and leave her behind.

"Ella, it's me. Alexa and I are having drinks down at the Prancing Pony. Lots of fun with the fairies! Come join us!" The last sentence was drawn out in a sing-song. Christ, Jace was already drunk. Ella's breath whooshed out. One message down. Her heart slowed, almost imperceptibly, and she kept up her deep breaths.

"Me again. You should come down instead of moping around with Poof. Hi, Poof. Not that I don't love you. Let Ella come out to play."

Her cheeks grew warm at that, even though she was alone in her loft with only a cat and a frog. Poof tucked his head under and looked up at Ella from upside down as if to say, "Don't you dare get up." Ella had to agree with him. She sent Jace a text promising drinks in the near future.

"Ahoy Ella! It's Eunice! I found Helen's Snuggie, and I was wondering if I could have it!"

The final message made Ella hold the phone away from her ear, wincing. Auntie Eunice always seemed to think you couldn't hear someone in a voice mail unless you hollered at them. She got phone manner all right. Messages were something else.

Ella erased the messages and tossed her phone onto her pillow.

Her throat still hadn't eased, and she knew why. Three missed calls.

It sounded like a bad horror movie, but for Ella, the horror was just reality.

That girls' night with Jace. Sticking her tongue out to concentrate on the evil shade of salmon she was applying to Jace's toenails. Her phone had rung several times, and she ignored it.

When she looked at it, she'd had three missed calls.

Ella stood, dumping Poof from her lap. He let out a flustered mrrrow before hopping back up to the bed and stretching out against her pillows.

She left her cell phone where it was and went to her computer desk. Her fingernails tapped against the polished wood in time with the clicks and whirs of the hard drive booting up.

She shouldn't be doing this again. The counselor said it would only accentuate her feelings of guilt. The counselor said she had post traumatic stress from that night, and she should avoid triggers. But then, who else was going to feel it if she didn't?

The trigger happened with the first sight of three missed calls. Going onward might not help, but it wasn't going to hurt anything more than Ella'd already felt before.

On the desktop was an audio file titled simply, "Remember."

"Eeeelllaaa! It's your stupid twin brother, doing something stupid again. You should come save me." A rustling noise cut off the sound of Stuart's voice, followed by someone else's laughter. "Seriously, sis. You should save me from myself. I'm about to be up to my elbows in blonde. That came out wrong."

Beep.

"Ella-ella-bo-bella-banana-fana-fo-fella. You should be glad we both got two syllable names. So much more conveeeeen-yent." This time a snuffle. "Serrusly, Ella. Can you come get me? Please. The blonde left me all'lone."

Beep.

"You didn't come, but I foundariiiide. See you in the morning. You owe me brunsh. Muuuah."

Morning never came.

Not for Stuart.

Ella clicked the music player onto repeat.

Three years later, and Ella wasn't sure morning had come for her either.

"Eeeelllaaa!"

chapter
five

"I think you'd be a tremendous candidate for the Fulbright program, Dr. Keyes. Where were you thinking of applying to teach?"

Ella cupped her hands around the coffee mug. The dean's office was bright with the sun shining through the window and reflecting off the new carpet of snow outside. The tiny, perfect flakes sparkled across the quad.

Somewhere with winter, Ella thought to herself. "Eastern Europe," she said aloud. "I've spent a lot of time in Scandinavia, and I'm very familiar with Norse mythology. I'd like to venture farther east for my sabbatical. When I'm not teaching, I'd like to conduct some research on the Slavic pagan religions. See what I could dig up."

The dean nodded his approval. "That sounds like it would suit you very well. Your sabbatical is scheduled for when, next spring?"

"Yes."

"Let me know when you need your letter of recommendation, and I'll provide it."

A warm glow started in Ella's stomach. Maybe that's what she needed. Only a year, and she would be in Moldova or the Ukraine, unearthing ancient tales and statues and far away from the memories of Buffalo and the house that seemed to sit on her shoulders even from five miles away.

"Did you get your schedule for the spring?" Dean Jonas asked as Ella rose from her chair.

"It's in my office."

"Good. Make sure you're making good use of Gellerman. He's got a quick mind, even if he applies it with a bit more tentativeness than he should."

"Of course." Easton would be happy. Ella made her way back to her office, and Easton looked up from his desk as she passed.

"Good talk with the dean?"

"He's going to write my recommendation for the Fulbright professorship," she said. "If you stick around, you'll probably get to adjunct my classes for a semester if I get in."

"You'll get in. They'd be foolish not to take you. And you'll come back just in time to get your tenure."

Ella smiled. "We'll see about that." She stopped in the doorway to her office. "Do you have any plans for the holidays?"

"My roommate invited me to come home with him to Ithaca."

"That'll be nice."

"Better than spending it alone in our apartment, that's for sure. What are you doing for the break?"

"Probably going through my grandmother's things. I'm spending Christmas with my best friend's family, though." Ella cringed inwardly. Last time she spent Christmas with the Wongs, she spent three hours at their church bored out of her mind and deeply uncomfortable when a group of people had wanted to put their hands on her to pray. She made a mental note to time her arrival better this time. Maybe right before dinner.

"Fun."

There was a beat. "When are you taking off?" Ella looked at the wall clock. "By my calculations, break started two hours ago."

"Thought I'd finish grading these finals and then go."

"Don't worry about those. I'll take them home with me. I need something to keep me occupied." The stacks of exams might ward off the open hole that was the holidays. Even with plans for Christmas, Ella wasn't looking forward to spending time alone for the other three weeks. Being alone never really bothered her — only when the world wore colored lights and carols sounded round every corner did the hole grow to encompass the rest of her. The holidays were only the most wonderful time of the year until the person you were supposed to share them with no longer existed.

Easton nodded, and Ella ducked into her office.

For once, she didn't feel like grading anything. Instead, she stood in front of the shelves that lined her walls. The brass elephant was only one among an array of trinkets from years of travel.

Most of the travels had been done with her parents and Stuart. That little horn box came from Poland when they were fifteen. Ella pulled it from the shelf and opened it. Her fingers did a little jump on the rim, almost dropping the lid shut again. She hadn't opened it in ages. Now there was a rock in it.

Stuart had only come to her office maybe once before the accident. But still he'd managed to leave a rock here for her. Gray-blue with tiny flecks of mica, the rock was oval like an egg. Ella shook her head and tucked it in her pocket.

Maybe it was time to go home for break after all.

"merry christmas, ella!" Mrs. Wong folded Ella into a hug, her plump arms soft like a teddy bear.

"Thank you, Mrs. Wong." Ella hugged her back, meeting Jace's eyes over her mother's shoulder. "Thanks for inviting me to share the holiday with you."

All of her other friends' parents insisted on Ella using their first names by now. Not Jace's parents. Sometimes Ella thought their drivers' licenses had no first names, only mister and missus.

"Whatever you do for the least of these, you do for me," Mr. Wong quoted.

Ella recognized the quote as something from the Bible, but she wasn't sure how she felt about being called the least of anything. Jace winced.

"Come in, come in, take off your shoes and get warm." Mrs. Wong ushered Ella through the door and bolted it behind her.

"It's too bad you couldn't make it to the service with us," Mr. Wong said, taking Ella's coat and hanging it in a closet. "It was a beautiful, beautiful service. Mr. Cadberry's daughters all sang O Holy Night. Gave me chills."

"The spirit has touched those girls," Mrs. Wong shivered. Not, Ella assumed, from the cold air that had come in the door.

Ella stood in the entryway, not sure what she was supposed to say to that.

Saved by Jace.

"How about we dig into those cheese balls, Mom? Ella doesn't know anyone at our church."

"Cheese balls sound great," Ella said quickly.

The dining room was set with wooden plates and a candelabra of the same fashioning. Ella thought that looked unnecessarily dangerous. The living room was full of candles and no tree. Jace's parents thought having Christmas trees was too pagan.

"You know Ella, if you need a new church home, our church has a very nice singles group for people your age. I'm sure they'd love to have you, and you better find yourself a husband soon!"

Ella stopped midway through smearing cheese on a cracker. "Oh. I'm all right. But thanks. I'll keep it in mind." Church home?

"We've been trying to get Jace to go for ages. Isaac Hormel keeps inviting her, but she says no every time," Mrs. Wong went on. "It's not right for you women to be alone this long."

"Isaac Hormel is a great kid, but he's not the brightest," Mr. Wong said from the kitchen before adding a belated, "Bless his heart."

He walked into the dining room with a plate heaped with ham and turkey. Mrs. Wong uncovered a soup tureen of mashed potatoes. Food. There was food.

Jace's face was turning redder and redder by the second. "I don't need to meet anyone."

"Of course. The Lord will bring your husband to you when it's his time," said Mr. Wong encouragingly.

Ella formed a fervent wish for wine.

Fat chance. The Wongs didn't drink, though Jace looked more and more like she was about to try and turn the water pitcher at the center of the table to a font of wine with every comment her parents made.

"Do you have anyone new in your life, Ella?" Mr. Wong laid his finger against his nose. They all sat down around the table, and Ella had the sudden urge to pull her chair closer to Jace's. Safety in numbers.

"Dad, please."

"I'm just asking. You ever hear from that guy you dated at Harvard? What was his name?"

"Brett." Ella didn't want to think about Brett. Not marrying him was on her top five list of life accomplishments, right after getting her Ph. D. "His investment firm lost everything when the real estate market went down the toilet in '08. I think he works in construction now."

"What a shame," said Mrs. Wong. "He was a nice boy. That's what happens when we elect socialists to the White House."

Ella coughed and tried not to remind her that 2008 was still Bush.

"Can we leave the politics for another time?" Jace stabbed a piece of lettuce.

Mr. Wong and Mrs. Wong exchanged a glance as if their daughter were a stray cat.

Jace stuffed a bit of lettuce in her mouth.

"Jace, honey, we haven't said grace."

Maybe cheese balls didn't need to be blessed.

Ella closed her eyes and thought of all the food she was smelling and not eating.

"Oh, Lord. How gracious you are to us. We thank you for the birth of your son and for the time we have tonight to honor him as a family. We thank you for the food you have so bountifully provided for our sustenance, and for the fellowship you bring to us with Ella's presence at our table. We ask for traveling mercies on Pastor Wade as he goes to help the needy children and do your work. May tonight be a night to honor your glory. In Jesus' name. Amen." Mr. Wong let out a sigh and gave Ella a beatific smile.

"Jace says you've inherited your grandmother's house, Ella. Are you going to move out there?" Mrs. Wong took Ella's plate and gave it a dollop of mashed potatoes.

"I'm going to stay in town. Closer to work for me. I don't need to be driving in from Niagara every day."

Jace looked at Ella over her water glass.

"You could have Jace list the house if you decide to sell it," Mrs. Wong said brightly.

"I don't know what I'm going to do yet. I still need to go through all Grammy's stuff."

"Let me know if you need any help with that. The church ladies would love to help."

Mr. Wong nodded. "They have a great drive for ministry."

"Thank you, but I think I'll do it myself. It's kind of personal."

"Well, keep us in mind."

"So Alexa just got a promotion at work," Jace broke in.

For the next fifteen minutes, Ella concentrated on stuffing her face with food, listening and marveling at how Jace's parents had yet to discover that Alexa was more than just Jace's good friend.

People see what they want to see, she thought.

chapter
SIX

On Boxing Day, Ella rose early and went out to Grammy's house. She didn't have a plan in mind, only that she didn't want to be at home for once.

The house was warm — almost too warm — the moment she stepped inside. Ella opened two windows and sat cross-legged on the floor in front of Grammy's bookshelves.

Grammy kept almost every book she'd ever bought. "Ella," she'd say, "there's no friend you can have like a well-worn book. Even when they make you cry, you always know where to find them."

Ella smiled at the row of Nancy Drew mysteries and took down the first one. Her eyes wandered toward the ceiling. She always used to read up in the third floor corridor. Maybe today would be a good day for that.

Grabbing a cup of Earl Grey tea and the next couple of Nancy Drews, Ella made her way upstairs to the hall of keys.

Nothing had changed. Suddenly she was ten years old again, trying to get away from Stuart and his obsession with blowing things up with his chemistry set. She'd usually been game to help him, but some days the quiet called to her, and she gathered words around her like a cloak. Those days she'd tuck herself in the back corner of the corridor, far on the opposite end from the stairs, and read until Grammy or Stuart realized they hadn't seen her in half a day.

Halfway through The Hidden Staircase, Ella's tea sat forgotten and half-drunk by her side. She stretched her legs out against the floor, leaning back on the wall.

She didn't need old clocks or hidden staircases. These old keys were enough of a puzzle for her.

No matter what went on in the rest of the house, this corridor stayed quiet, almost reverently so.

Ella chastised herself for the thought. It was just because all the empty space around it sealed in the silence. But she'd always enjoyed it here.

Ella returned downstairs to warm up her tea and stood for a long moment by the kitchen sink. The linoleum on the floor could use a refresh. She had savings enough to do almost whatever she wanted. Even on a professor's salary, Ella lived modestly and managed to spend her summers in Stratford at the Shakespeare festival or in Banff, Alberta. Or traveling elsewhere. Maybe this summer she could patch up the house.

For what? A snide part of her mind intruded. You don't even want the place.

It was true. Ella didn't want the house, and she didn't particularly need it. Selling it would be the logical option for a house one neither wanted or needed.

Funny, she thought, how difficult it could be to think of getting rid of something she didn't want in the first place.

With a fresh cup of tea, Ella headed back up the stairs to Nancy Drew and her mysteries.

She spent the day up there, reading, replenishing her mug. She read her way through five books until her rear end went numb from sitting on the floor, and her back spawned an ache that crept out from her tailbone and up into her spine.

Ella gathered up the books around her, stacking them in the crook of her arm and dangling the empty mug on her pinky.

A good day. A relaxing day. She felt warm and sated, like she had as a kid. Maybe this place wasn't so bad. Maybe the house could be her retreat.

One of the keys caught her eye, and she stopped, the coffee cup swinging on her pinky joint. The key stuck out among the others, short and stubby and graceless. It was like the house in that. Full of clutter and memory with little order. With her free hand, Ella plucked the key from the wall.

Her fingers twitched at the touch. She'd expected it to be cool, metal-at-room-temperature. Instead it was warm. The metal looked beaten, crafted. Bits of tarnish lived in the creases. Ella wondered what the key opened, once upon a time. Where had Grammy found this one?

She put it back on the wall.

Making her way downstairs, Ella carefully replaced the Nancy Drew books on the shelf and washed the mug, tilting it in the drying rack. It felt strange, making herself at home here with Grammy's things. She ought to go through everything.

The basement would be a good place to start. Just as Ella turned toward the back stairs, a thump sounded from below.

her heart gave a hiccup.

She peered out the kitchen window toward the garage. Just her Subaru. No white Volvo, which meant no Auntie Eunice.

"Hello?"

No other sounds. Ella pulled her cell phone from her pocket and unlocked the screen, ready to call 911.

This is silly, she thought. It's probably just the house settling. That's what old houses do. They settle.

She flicked on the light and put one foot out onto the stairs. Ella paused, listening.

Nothing.

She stepped carefully down the flight of stairs. At the bottom, all the boxes her great-aunt had fumbled through littered the carpet. And one thing that she hadn't seen before.

It looked like a jewelry box. Carved wood. A thicket of roses covered every surface of the box, etched by hand into the wood. About the size of a shoe box, it sat upside down on the floor. Ella looked at a stack of boxes nearby. The top one had fallen into the box below it, tilting it precariously to one side.

Ella wanted to laugh at herself. The rose box must have fallen out when gravity shifted. Thump. Not a robber.

Just because it was silly didn't stop her from feeling relief.

Ella picked up the box, fingertips exploring the intricate carvings. Some of the edges were rough hewn, like it had never quite been finished.

She pulled on the seam of the box. The wood gave way with a squeak, and it opened, something glinting at Ella in the fluorescent light of the basement.

Jewelry?

Grammy didn't have much jewelry. She didn't put much stake in baubles of that sort. Aside from her wedding band — which was in itself a simple band of yellow gold — Ella couldn't remember that Grammy Helen wore any jewelry at all.

The box was filled with jewelry. All jumbled together. Necklaces with bracelets, rings dotting the mess. Earrings. Ella dumped the whole thing onto the floor and began to untangle it. After twenty painstaking minutes, she sat back on the floor to survey the contents of the box.

Her fingers throbbed from pulling apart knotted chains of delicate gold, and they smelled of metal.

Six necklaces, all different. One had a single star ruby hanging from it. Another was a chain of sapphires. One was made from beaten panels of gold that glowed warm in the cold artificial light. Nine rings. Emeralds surrounded by pinprick diamonds. Green gold with vines etched all around the band. Some of the jewels seemed to go together, like the chain of sapphires that matched a pair of earrings and a bracelet.

It had to be worth...Ella stopped herself. Her gaze raised to the tower of cardboard boxes, and she scrambled to her feet. What else was in that box? She pulled back the flaps and peered in.

A bird nest. A Faberge egg. An assortment of tea towels, and what looked like a christening gown from the 1800s.

Ella looked back and forth between the cardboard box and the pile of precious gems and metal.

Okay, Grammy, she thought. I don't understand your filing system.

She gathered up the jewelry and arranged it carefully in the box. There was a small, worn pad for rings, and the bottom of the box was partitioned into six small compartments and four larger ones, so she placed everything in the box by color.

Ella slid the rose-carved jewelry box back under the flap of cardboard and straightened the leaning tower so it wouldn't fall out again. She'd have to deal with it later. Grammy had obviously wanted to keep those things, though why she never wore them was beyond Ella's imagining. Ella resisted the urge to play dress-up, to rummage through boxes of Grammy's vintage clothes and cover herself in jewels until she dripped sapphires and rubies.

That would just be silly.

But maybe...

She opened the box one more time and pulled out the star ruby necklace. The star appeared as she turned it this way and that under the light, its center shifting and sending white rays that stretched to the edges of the small gemstone. About the size of a pea, it dangled from a tiny gold chain, hanging from a simple gold loop. Ella fastened it around her neck. It fit snugly, the ruby dangling in the hollow of her throat. The twin chains, one from the key that hung low past her breasts and the new one that held the ruby, were cool against her skin.

There.

Had Grammy ever worn it? She must have. Why else would she have it? Ella pictured Grammy Helen back in the sixties, when she was young and full of laughter and wit. She imagined her dressed in smoke gray or bright yellow with the star ruby around her neck and her green eyes twinkling.

There it was, the aching hole of loss. Three years of weekly visits, ever since Ella's parents had left the country and seldom returned or called. Ella and Helen had kept their family going, sharing time and words and tea. The necklace felt at home, some little secret of Grammy's own history to carry with her.

Ella touched the ruby at her throat and smiled.

her finals wouldn't grade themselves. Ella sat at her kitchen table, wishing the opposite were true. Poof occupied the other end of the table, his tail wrapped around his feet like a fluffy blanket, waiting for the papers to rustle again.

Ella looked down at the paper, wondering how it was that she'd come to read the same question four times when it was clear the student had marked the wrong answer. She made a slash with her red pen.

She pushed herself through three more exams before shoving them across the table. Poof pounced, both paws landing on question three.

The problem was that she was bored. It was winter break, and she had no plans to do anything but grade papers. Ella calculated the remaining amount of time she had to grade the one hundred forty seven exams that glared at her from inside manila folders, decided that ten days would suffice, and five minutes later was in her car, counting backward from twelve and double-checking her seatbelt.

What was it, Ella wondered, that made her so ready to drive for the first time in years?

It had to be a psychological thing. Ella had spent so many peaceful hours reading in the third floor corridor of Grammy Helen's home that she wanted to replicate it. What did that say about her life?

Ella snorted as she pulled her car out of the garage. Her life was as good as it could be. She had her own home, a great best friend (questionable blind date set-ups notwithstanding), a low-maintenance cat, and a frog that seemed to record everything he saw. Not to mention her job. And next year she'd go on sabbatical to Eastern Europe and learn all about pre-Christian Slavs.

Halfway to Grammy's, she realized that maybe she was trying to recreate the feeling of peace from childhood because it was a time when nothing was missing, when there wasn't a void where Stuart was supposed to be.

It could be that.

Or maybe she was just burnt out and needed to take a break now and then.

The streets were quiet in the lull between Christmas and New Year's Eve. No new snow, only clear pavement.

Grammy's house looked inviting, set back from the road.

Inside, Ella skipped Nancy Drew and picked out the first few Boxcar Children books. These Grammy had gotten for Ella and Stuart. Ella even remembered Grammy coming home with a huge crate of them one summer. She'd driven past a yard sale and someone had been selling the entire series. Grammy kept them all these years.

Again, Ella brewed a cup of tea and headed up to the top floor.

She looked around for the key that had caught her eye the day before, eyes searching out its short, stubbiness among the blanket of formed metal that covered the walls.

After looking around for five minutes, she still couldn't find it. There must have been hundreds of them, she decided. Ella plucked a key off its hook at random, a worn brass key with three prongs on the end. It felt warm, just as the one yesterday had.

Ella shrugged and put it back. She sat down in her corner of the corridor and stacked her books next to her. Just as she went to take a sip of her tea, a pounding from below made her jump.

Tea sloshed onto her jeans, and Ella brushed it away.

The pounding sounded again. Ella set the mug down and hurried downstairs to the front door.

She started again when the door shook with the knock. "I'm coming!"

Ella peeked out the small window in the door, which was just above her eye level. UPS?

She opened the door. "Can I help you?"

"Package for you."

Ella propped the door open on her hip, eyeing the large box on the porch. "My grandmother passed away a little over a week ago."

The guy shrugged. "You can still sign for it." After a moment, Ella's words seemed to sink in, and he blinked. "Sorry for your loss."

Ella gripped the plastic stylus and scribbled her name on the screen of his gadget. "Thanks."

"Happy New Year," he said. The man trotted down the steps of the porch and back to the brown truck in front of the house. It rumbled away in a cloud of exhaust.

The package was about the size of a laundry hamper. Ella hefted it over the threshold, looking for the address label.

Her heart gave a thud. It was addressed to Ella Keyes.

She pried back the edge of the packing tape with her fingernails, yanking the end away from the seam of the box.

It was full of packing peanuts, the strange biodegradable kind. Ella had eaten one once, just to see what they tasted like. They tasted faintly of puffed rice — or the rice paper used in Japan to wrap candies — and cardboard, neither of which was wholly a surprise.

The box held another box, buried underneath the packing peanuts. Ella pulled it out with a muffled whoomph and nudged the shipping box to the side with her foot.

This box wasn't taped, just tied with a bit of twine. Ella picked at the knots with her nails until they came undone and shrugged the twine over the corner of the box.

She couldn't figure out why there would be a box addressed to her. There had to be some sort of logical explanation for its appearance. Maybe Grammy had done something, ordered something for her.

But Grammy had died over a week ago, and Ella thought it would have arrived sooner. The UPS man didn't say anything at all about this being a second delivery attempt. Besides, she would have seen the little door hanger. She got them at home whenever she ordered books and spent too long at her office. "First delivery attempt. Another attempt will be made on — (day of the week checked)." Nothing like that had been here since she started coming out here.

Ella opened the box.

More packing peanuts. She was starting to notice a theme.

But instead of her hand encountering more cardboard, they found something cool and hard. Ella's fingers discovered the bottom of the object, and she pulled it from the box, brushing biodegradable dust from it.

The surface of the thing was black like ebony and shiny enough to throw Ella's reflection back at her, perplexed expression and all.

inlaid into the polished black surface were tendrils of pearly-silver. Like seashells. Mother-of-pearl. They formed whorls and undulating, wave-like designs across the expanse of the box.

Boxes, boxes, everywhere, Ella thought.

The star ruby felt warm against the soft skin of her throat.

Ella turned the box over. A small silver pin was set into the bottom. She turned it, listening to it click and the deep, muffled pings within. When it wouldn't go anymore, Ella righted the box in her lap. The lid rose easily under her fingers.

The first notes to reach her ears drained tension from her shoulders that she hadn't known was there. A smile flitted at the corner of her mouth. There were no words with the melody of the song, but Ella knew what went with it. "…A girl with kaleidoscope eyes."

One of her favorite Beatles songs. Grammy had introduced her to it.

"Lucy in the Sky with Diamonds." It had always seemed like a magical song for Ella, a world within her world, a world she glimpsed through the genius of four boys from Liverpool.

Even nowadays when she listened to almost nothing but Converge and Meshuggah, she'd sometimes turn on that song. She and Stuart used to dance around with hairbrushes and sing to it.

"Where did you come from?" Ella asked the box.

Its only answer was the continuation of the song in pings and plucked notes.

Ella brought it with her back up the stairs. The sight of the keys made her stop on the landing, looking down the corridor at her long-forgotten tea and stack of Boxcar Children books.

A thought pushed into her mind, and she brushed it off. A moment later, though, it came right back.

Yesterday she'd heard the thud in the basement just after touching one of the keys. Today the UPS man had shown up just as she put one back.

Ella traced her index finger across the wall between the metal keys, the music box cradled in her other arm.

It wasn't possible. It had to be some sort of coincidence. The jewelry box downstairs was explained by gravity, and someone obviously had to send this package, didn't they? Ella touching a key on a wall didn't make it poof into existence any more than she could change the laws of physics.

But still.

She remembered how Grammy had sent her to her room the one time she'd almost touched one as a child. She'd been a good girl, Ella had. She didn't like upsetting people. She'd never tried again after the keys had seemed to shift out of her reach, and the keys had become like the wooden paneling behind them. A fixture, not a curiosity.

Ella carefully set the music box on the floor next to the drying puddle of tea she'd sloshed when the UPS man had startled her.

She turned to the opposite wall this time, surveying the keys.

There. That small gold colored one. It was dull and beaten, and its shaft almost looked twisted as though something had heated it up and bent it. It was an unfortunate-looking little key. Ella pulled it off the wall.

A loud bang sounded from downstairs.

Skin tingling, Ella replaced the key and hurried down. A gust of frigid air blew through the house. The side door stood open. Ella pulled it closed and waited, shivering.

She took two steps back.

The whistle of the wind outside picked up.

The door flew open again, banging into the wall hard enough to vibrate the panes of glass set into the top half. A thin coat of dusty blowing snow covered Ella from head to foot.

Ella took a slow breath, her lungs seeming to crack in the freezing wind that gusted through the kitchen. She stuck her head out the door, and the wind subsided.

Grammy always kept a pair of clogs somewhere. Ella leaned over to look underneath the kitchen table. Sure enough, tucked between the wall and a table leg were the wooden clogs. Ella dragged them out and stuffed her feet into them. She stepped outside into the wintery December day.

She immediately wished she'd grabbed her coat. The wind bit at her bare neck and face like a school of tiny piranhas. Her Subaru sat, innocuous, in the driveway. There wasn't anything out here but Grammy's garden. Wrapping her arms around herself, Ella turned right and headed toward the back of the house where Grammy's tiny garden lived.

Grammy Helen didn't have much of a green thumb, but she kept a well-tended plot about the size of three sidewalk squares together. It backed up against the garage and a trellis, and since Ella was a child, the roses had climbed up almost to the gutter on the garage.

The bushes were dormant now, their vines brown and sleeping.

Except one.

One of the vines was a dark, vibrant green. From it sprang a curling tendril, and a bud just beginning to open.

Ella stepped closer to it, unable to take her eyes off what she was seeing. It was the end of December. Nothing should be growing now. Nothing at all.

But it was.

The bud was half-open, its white leaves the color of the pristine snow that coated the ground. The edges gave off a light shimmer, just as the snow did.

Ella was afraid to touch it.

Had she fallen asleep upstairs with her tea and the Boxcar Children?

No, the cold that pulled shivers from her body said she was very awake. Her teeth chattered in her mouth with a rat-a-tat-tat. Ella walked up to the edge of the garden. The rose was there, oblivious to the fact that it was supposed to be long-dormant, hibernating for the winter in order to bloom in the spring. It was blooming now. One single vine from one single bush. Ella traced the green down to the ground. Two others branched off the singular taproot, but they were as dead and silent as the rest of the garden.

The rose continued to exist.

Ella didn't want it to die out here. Whatever crazed glitch its DNA had given it, she didn't want to see the bush wither come spring. She shouldered aside her brain's reminder that thinking that way implied she intended to still have the house when spring rolled around.

The side door of the garage was unlocked, and Ella pushed it open. Gramps had kept a wood shop in here and built furniture when he was younger, but the place was tidy and as clean as a garage can be.

Ella stepped around the old Buick — Grammy hadn't driven in years — and pawed through tools on the low work bench until she found a pair of hedge clippers.

She rubbed her hands over her arms before picking them up, and a shiver squiggled through her back.

The rose was still there, still impossibly there, when she emerged from the garage with the clippers in hand.

She positioned the shears just below where the rose branched off and squeezed them. The rose fell into the snow.

Ella picked it up and blew on it once, sending a shower of sparkling snowflakes to the ground. She set the clippers back on the work bench and gingerly brought the rose inside. A vase. She needed a vase.

She found one under the sink, simple green-glazed porcelain, and Ella filled it with cool water. In went the rose.

Was this proof of whatever crazy inkling had taken over her? A rose blooming in winter. It was just strange enough. Ella went back to the third floor corridor to tidy up. The keys hung there, silent and unhelpful. Books in hand, she picked one more, a dark colored skeleton key that might have been silver long ago. She held it for a long moment and then replaced it on its hook, waiting.

Nothing happened.

Ella shrugged and went downstairs, a buzz of disappointment in her ears. She washed her mug and put back the unread books, just like yesterday. Just a series of strange coincidences, then, she decided.

The vase and music box came with her when Ella went home.

chapter
seven

"You need to get out. You've been alone all break except for spending Christmas with my 'everyone-but-us-goes-to-hell' parental units. Go out. Go have coffee. I have someone who wants to meet you."

"Seriously, Jace?" Ella scowled, but Jace of course couldn't see her from two miles away.

"Seriously. You'll like this one. Nice. Not crazy. Not too butch. About squeed at your picture."

"You decided I'm need this, not me."

Ella flopped her head back on a throw pillow, dumping Poof off her stomach. She did need to get out of the house. Ella groaned into the phone. "Fine." Agreeing to a blind date. Maybe it was just the best thing to do. Jace wouldn't quit until Ella agreed. "Where do I go, how do I find this nice, not crazy, not-too-butch person?"

"You'll go? Perfect. Three-thirty, coffee shop on the corner of Alder and Spruce. I can't remember what it's called. Green sweater."

"Alder and Spruce. I should be able to find a coffee shop on a corner." Ella threw her legs over the side of the couch and sat up. "You're going to have to stop trying to set me up one of these days."

"Just trying to get you out of your comfort zone."

"I know you are, and you don't have anything to prove. At least not that way."

"Suit yourself. Just be nice."

"I'm nice, I'm nice. Also not crazy." Maybe.

Jace made a kissy sound into the phone. "Have fun. Let loose. Get over-caffeinated."

"Mm-hmm. You still coming over tomorrow night?"

"Wouldn't miss it. Mr. Poof needs his kitty snuggles."

"Cat-spoiler."

"Someone's gotta do it."

Ella hung up the phone, watching the spoiled cat in question bathe his face with a tufty paw. "Your life is much simpler than mine," she said to Poof, then looked over at Prince, sunning himself on his log. "And yours even simpler than that."

Neither of them responded. Ella felt vaguely cheated.

What did one wear to a blind date during the holidays? Ella chose a black sweater with an asymmetrical neckline and buttons that went down the left side. She should stop humoring Jace. Maybe the only reason Jace kept doing this was because Ella let her get away with it. It wasn't fair to the people Jace picked out, whatever caveats she layered when she sent them Ella's way.

The white rose sat on her nightstand, the music box beside it. The rose had opened a bit more since yesterday, its petals cool and velvety. Ella gave it an eyedropper full of plant food and turned off the bedside lamp.

A light snow began to fall as Ella rode toward the corner of Alder and Spruce. She arrived at the corner at twenty after three and chained her bike to a rack with chipping orange paint. Straightening, she looked around the corner. There. Coffee shop, right on the corner. Ella took two steps toward it, then stopped on the curb of the street. Right across from it on the opposite side of the street was another coffee shop, one door down from the true corner.

"So which is it?" Ella said aloud, then looked around to make sure no one was looking at her.

They were both at the intersection of Alder and Spruce. Ella frowned. If Jace forgot the name, texting her was useless.

She started walking toward the coffee place directly on the corner. When in doubt, get literal. The Jumping Bean, it was called.

The roasty scent of coffee suffused the street before Ella opened the door. A tinkly bell rang as the door swung open, and Ella shut it behind her, looking around for a woman in a green sweater.

There. Ella walked in the direction of the flash of green she'd just seen, then stopped short fifteen feet away.

"Can I help you?" A barista came up to the counter. "We're still running our holiday drinks. Peppermint mocha? White chocolate raspberry latte?"

"The latte, please," Ella said absently, still looking at the back of the person in the green sweater.

The fizzing gurgle of the espresso machine invaded her thoughts.

Broad shoulders. Bright green sweater. Short, dark hair. It had to be who she was here to meet, but...Ella squinted, feeling like her eyes should be poking the sweater-wearer between the shoulder blades.

"That'll be four seventy-three. Did you want any muffins, lemon cake, sweet confections?"

Ella turned back to the barista. "Um, no. The drink is fine." She handed the barista a five dollar bill and tucked a single into the tip jar, picking up the coffee.

Jace had snapped. That was it. Or maybe she'd just gotten desperate after three years of failure. Ella ignored the snide little bit of her mind that asked why Ella always said yes to these silly blind dates with women when she never wanted to date at all. Maybe because they were automatically safer because they weren't Brett, her ex-fiance. Hard to get scared of relationships when you can't even entertain the idea of a third date with a person of any gender even when supposedly, you like all of them.

But the person in the green sweater wasn't safe and female. He was unmistakably male.

Ella's feet propelled her forward. She had to at least meet the guy. Maybe he was gay. Jace had a terrible sense for gay men. She could point out another lesbian on the 700 Club, but you could put a guy in tights and a tiara spewing stereotypes, and she'd shrug at you.

"Hi, I'm Ella." The words spilled over her lips before she could stop them. At least the guy was punctual. Three thirty, and he'd beaten her here.

Gray eyes met hers, looking up from a crossword puzzle that had left a crease between his eyebrows. He'd already scrubbed out his answer to thirty across a couple of times, and Ella pointed to it. "Mjolnir. Thor's hammer."

The clue read, "Most famous Norse tool."

He blinked, looking back down at the newspaper. "I think you're right."

Ella sat down across from him. "I should be. I wrote my dissertation on that hammer."

He smiled, sticking out his hand. "Callum Penrose."

"Ella Keyes. But I already told you half of that."

"It's nice to meet you, Ella Keyes."

Callum Penrose had gray eyes like the winter sky outside and dark hair he combed carefully to one side. He had a smooth face, unlined except for the crinkles at the corners of his eyes. When Ella shook his hand, his grip was firm and strong, and she couldn't help wondering where Jace had found such a person.

Ella turned her phone to silent and tucked it away inside her messenger bag. Callum chuckled and did the same, then turned the crossword sideways on the table.

"Want to help me finish it?"

"Carbon monoxide," Ella said by way of answer, pointing to the blank length of twenty-nine down.

When the crossword was finished, Callum went up to the counter and returned with two cranberry orange muffins. He placed one in front of Ella. "Spoils of war," he said.

"So what do you do aside from crosswords?" Ella asked him.

"I'm an actor."

"Really?"

"Really."

"Stage or..." Ella never knew quite what to follow up with when it came to the arts. Everything came out like, "Make it big yet?" Which was stupid, because if he had, she would have seen his face plastered on a poster and magnified ten times on the side of bus stops.

"Stage. I'm getting ready to go up to Stratford to get ready for the festival this summer."

Ella nibbed at the edge of her muffin. "I go up there every year. Do you know what productions you'll be in this year?" She'd never seen him, but then again, there were a whole heap of shows and many, many actors to populate them.

"This year I'll be in *A Midsummer Night's Dream*."

"Oh, proper Shakespeare for the Shakespeare festival. I hope you won't be stuck playing the wall."

"Nope. I auditioned for Oberon, but it's looking like they're going to cast me as Puck instead."

"Big role," Ella said, impressed.

"I'm excited. If you go up this year, you should come."

"I will." Ella was surprised that she meant it.

"So what do you do aside from taking over other people's crosswords?" Callum grinned. He had a nice smile. Medium lips that didn't disappear with the expression. White, even teeth. Almost too white. Ella guessed actors had to take pains for that.

"I'm a professor at Niagara University. I teach mythology and folklore."

"Mjolnir."

"Yup."

"How long have you been working there?"

"A few years. I'm hoping to get a tenure track position after I go on Fulbright next spring semester." A little thrill went through her at the thought of her sabbatical. Fulbright. She hoped she'd get it. They didn't just hand out Fulbright professorships willy-nilly.

"That's a nice way of saying six month vacation."

Ella laughed. "It's not quite that easy. I'll apply to be a guest professor at a university in Eastern Europe, like the Charles University in Prague or the Jagiellonian University in Cracow. I'd keep busy. Teaching during the day and doing my own research at night. You know. Lazy stuff."

Her phone buzzed inside her bag. Ella ignored it. Probably just Jace preening via text message.

"Are you from Buffalo?" Ella asked.

"Albany. But I live here now."

"Why?"

"It's as close as I can get to Canada without needing a visa."

"You like Canada?" Ella felt a warm flush in her cheeks, and this time not about her sabbatical.

"Love it. It's beautiful, open, and friendly." Callum polished off his muffin and brushed the crumbs from his fingers into his empty coffee mug. "What about you?"

"I'm from here. My family's been here for ages."

"Ah, a Buffalo blue blood."

"You could say that. My parents left, though. They live in South Africa now." That was dancing closer to a subject Ella didn't want to breach with someone she'd only known for thirty-seven minutes. She went back to the subject of their neighboring country to the north. "I love Canada myself. I usually spend my summers in Banff or in Stratford watching the plays."

"I've never been to Banff, but an artsy-fartsy chap like me might never leave. Places that beautiful are dangerous for creative types."

"I'll admit to being tempted myself," Ella said. "What are you doing between now and summer, then? Hanging out in coffee shops?"

"Well, rehearsals will start soon. I'll be relocating up to Stratford in a couple months to do that. Until then, I bartend downtown to save money and try to lure strange women by failing to complete crosswords."

Ella's phone buzzed again, breaking her smile off before it could begin. She frowned at her bag.

"Do you need to get that?"

"Maybe."

"I promise not to be offended."

Ella did smile then, and she dug her phone from the bag. Jace. "It's Jace."

"Who?"

Ella blinked at Callum, her finger hitting the messages screen. "Jace. She set us up?"

"What?"

Heat filled Ella's cheeks. Sure enough, there was a slew of texts from Jace.

Where are you? Angie's been waiting for twenty minutes.

Are you okay? You rode your bike into a snowbank again, didn't you?

Ella. Come on. Where are you?

And then two missed calls.

"Oh, dear." Ella met Callum's eyes. If the warmth in her face was any indication, her cheeks were redder than the stripes on a candy cane. "You don't know Jace."

"Nope."

"And your name's not Angie."

"Not even a little bit."

"Oh."

"Let me guess. You were supposed to meet someone called Angie?"

"Yes. No. I mean, Jace didn't give me a name. She didn't even give me a gender."

Callum laughed, the smile lines around his eyes bursting into being. "You thought we were on a blind date?"

Ella gestured at his bright green sweater. "It was the sweater. I was told to meet someone in a green sweater."

"Brave woman. You didn't know if you were supposed to meet a man or a woman?"

Ella slumped in her chair, letting out a gust of a sigh. A giggle trailed off the end of it. "Nope." Her eyes fell on the completed crossword. "You probably thought I was insane, barging in on your table."

"Not at all. I found the whimsy of it rather charming."

"I'm not usually that whimsical."

"Well, for what it's worth, I don't feel like I wasted the dollar eighty-nine I spent on your muffin. But if you usually like girls, I won't be offended if you want to leave. Well, a little offended if you don't even want to be my crossword-completing friend."

Gray eyes sobered in front of her, and Ella felt her lips tilt. If she normally liked girls. Her bottom lip quivered, and she stilled it. Oh, Jace. It must have been the other coffee shop. Across the street.

Ella burst out laughing. "I uh, like people who are my gender and also not my gender. That's the whole problem. My best friend. She always only sets me up with women, and I don't usually date at all, so I feel really bad about it and I'm just…resigned to it." The laughs came in gulping hiccups, and tears cooled at the corners of her eyes. "Oh, god. You must have been so confused."

A smile ghosted across Callum's face. "Like I said, rather charmed. I take it you don't want to leave, then?"

"No, not especially." Ella swallowed a giggle and coughed. What a mess, she thought. And he was looking at her like he was actually charmed by it instead of wanting to set his newspaper on fire and run screaming from the coffee shop. "But I hope you'll let me buy you dinner."

"I can live with that."

"Good." Ella looked at her phone and felt the titters rising in her stomach again. "I should probably explain to Jace why I stood up her friend."

"i still can't believe you went to the wrong coffee shop." Jace frowned, juggling a bottle of wine and two glasses in her left hand and kicking the door to the dishwasher shut with a foot. "Poor Angie."

"She'll live. And she'll probably be better off anyway." Ella took the bottle of wine and twisted her corkscrew into it.

"A guy though. You haven't dated a guy since…"

"I know who I haven't dated a guy since." Ella didn't want to think about it. Plus, she wasn't sure if she was dating Callum Penrose at all. She owed him dinner next week after he took a trip up to Stratford.

"Funny you happened to meet someone in a green sweater, though. What are the odds?"

"Right after Christmas, probably not that bad."

Jace shrugged, plopping down on the couch and setting the two wine glasses on the coffee table, pushing a stack of National Geographics askew in the process. Ella poured the wine, then plugged the bottle with a wine stopper. She leaned forward to straighten the magazines.

"You like him?"

"He's nice. And easy going."

"So, your opposite."

"I'm nice."

"But you're a control freak."

"Hey."

"Magazines," Jace said, pointing to the now-perfectly- even stack.

Ella frowned.

"You know I'd stop trying to set you up if you told me to, right?" Jace's hair fell in her face, and she pushed it back. "I just... I'm really happy with Alexa and I want you to be happy too."

"I know." Ella fought a little lump that tried to lodge in her throat. She reached out and squeezed Jace's hand.

"Is he cute?"

"Dark hair, gray eyes. Nice body."

"Ooh, la-la."

"Hush." Ella gave her wine glass an experimental sniff. She liked wine and tried to pretend she knew what she was looking for. Mostly she just smelled fermented grapes. "Do you want to come with me to Grammy Helen's this weekend? I want to try and get all the stuff in the basement organized."

"Sounds thrilling."

"I found a box of jewelry down there the other day. Real jewelry, not that costume stuff Auntie Eunice always gets as a gift with purchase from Dillards." Ella pointed to the star ruby that still hung around her neck.

Jace leaned forward, peering at the necklace. "Real jewelry, huh? Sure. I'll join you for the organizational treasure hunt. Do you know what you're going to do with the place yet?"

Ella tapped her fingers on the edge of the glass. "No. I'm not ready to sell it." Mentioning the jewelry made her think about the keys. Did she really think that could have had something to do with it? There was a rose blooming heartily on her nightstand and a dinner date in her appointment book that whispered she should.

Her friend had an expectant look on her face. Jace tucked a chunk of hair from her angled bob behind her ear. "And?"

"And that's it. I want to see what's there, organize what I can. The place is a cluttered mess, no thanks to Auntie Eunice."

"She still pawing around the place?"

"I haven't seen her in a while, but yeah. Looking for something, and she won't tell me what."

It certainly wasn't a bunch of old keys. Eunice wasn't forgetful enough to think those had vanished. Ella stared at the red liquid in her glass, wondering if she ought to tell Jace about the keys. Jace wasn't as skeptical as Ella. She might even believe her.

"You okay?"

If nothing else, they could have a laugh about it. Ella set her wine glass down on the coffee table and angled herself toward Jace, pulling her stockinged feet onto the couch cushion. "I have to tell you something. And it's weird, so just…bear with me."

"Sounds ominous. Did green sweater guy get you pregnant?"

"What? No. I didn't sleep with anyone." Ella shifted backward on the couch, ignoring the fact that she'd contented herself with mechanical toys for almost seven years and that she didn't think she'd mind letting Callum Penrose take over that job. Or at least share responsibilities. "It's nothing like that. It's the third floor corridor at Grammy's, the one with all the keys?"

"Oh, that hallway."

Ella squinted one eye at her friend, then shrugged her eyebrows and exhaled. "Something strange has been happening when I move any of the keys."

She told Jace about the timing of the thump, how it turned out to be the jewelry box. Then the UPS package. Then how she'd waited after the third key, but nothing had happened — until she landed in the wrong coffee shop and met the wrong person on a blind date.

Jace sat quietly at the end of Ella's story. "That's what Alexa would call 'woo-woo.'"

"And what do you think?"

"I think you've been through a lot of loss in the last few years," Jace began.

"Thanks for the patronizing. Helpful."

"That's not what I meant." Jace reached out and took Ella's hands in her smaller ones. "I mean, you don't believe in stuff like this. You study folklore and mythology and Thor and all the Native practices around here, but you don't really believe any of it."

"I respect it."

"That's not the same thing. And this isn't the same thing at all."

"So you think it's just coincidence?"

"I don't know. Do you? Really?"

Ella thought about that. "Stay here." She went upstairs and fetched the green-glazed vase and the rose from her night table. Back downstairs, she set the vase in front of Jace.

"That's a rose."

"Good call. Do you know where I got it?"

"Rose store?"

"Rose store. Really?" Ella snorted, and Jace shrugged, so she went on, "Grammy's trellis."

"It's December."

Ella raised her eyebrows.

"I know you know that. Are you messing with me?"

"No. I found it on the trellis out in back of Grammy Helen's house."

Jace picked up the vase and examined the rose. "It's really pretty. White, but not."

Even indoors, the rose had a slight shimmer when turned in the light, like silver dust.

She set the rose back on the coffee table. "That's weird."

"Yeah. It's weird." Ella picked up her wine again. "So to answer your question, I don't know if it's coincidence. All these things, they feel like gifts. They're like treasures."

Jace pointed to the ruby at Ella's throat. "Literally. And how does that make you feel?"

"Thanks, Dr. Phil."

"I'm serious. If this is true, which, let's face it, would be bonkers — how does that make you feel?"

"I don't know." And it was true. On one hand, each key was a little mystery, like hundreds of old clocks lined up in front of Nancy Drew. On the other hand, the more logical, Ella-like hand, the keys were just keys on a couple walls in a strangely-designed house. "I think they feel like gifts."

"Then let them be gifts. You could use some happiness."

Ella sipped her wine.

She really wanted to agree.

chapter
eight

dust.
Everywhere, dust.

Ella sneezed at a magic eye poster that was creased in three places. It looked like it had been sat on, sometime between the point where someone rolled it up and the point when it got shoved into a cardboard box.

"Bless you," Jace called from the other room.

The basement only had two rooms, and Ella was rather grateful for that. Her sinuses agreed.

They'd spent the better part of their Saturday organizing the contents of Grammy's mountain range of cardboard boxes into plastic storage containers. The clutter still prevailed, but Ella knew she'd get the better of it.

A squeal from Jace made her look up.

"Spider?"

"Mouse. It's gone now." Jace shuddered. "I don't mind mice when they're in cages, spinning on their little wheels. But when they run out of the box I'm going through, it makes me jumpy."

"Understandable."

"Mouse turds. Do we have a box for mouse turds?"

"You can make one, if it means that much to you."

Jace shot her a surly look through the doorway. Ella shrugged.

"I can't believe you talked me into spending my New Year's Eve like this."

"You said Alexa is on call and has to stay home."

"I know."

"You said you don't want to go out on the town this year, because it's always a waste of money and hopefulness."

"I get poetic when I'm feeling melodramatic."

"I'm just saying."

"I know what I said." Jace kicked at the box at her feet. "I'm probably covered in turd dust. Over a layer of regular dust, which is pretty much just the turds of smaller organisms."

"Don't remind me."

"You declared tonight for orange chicken and bubble tea." Jace plucked at her clothes, her face wearing nothing but distaste.

Ella took the sole remaining item from the box she was emptying. A wooden carving shaped like a duck. That went in the animals bin — there was an animals bin — and she brought her foot down on the cardboard box. "We can wrap this up if you want."

"I want, I want. I surrender to the mess."

"I don't, but we can retreat for the night if you want."

"Thank you. Just point me toward hot water and towels."

"Second floor, third door on the left. There should be towels in the linen closet in the bathroom."

Ella considered showering in the other bathroom, but then decided not to risk upsetting the plumbing of Grammy's very old house. Instead, she washed her hands — and arms, up to the elbows — in the kitchen sink and called in their food order.

As soon as she heard the gurgle-groan of the pipes that said Jace was out of the shower, Ella turned on the water in the downstairs bathroom. She was just toweling off when the doorbell rang. She couldn't help a smile. She'd forgotten the doorbell played Monty Python's "Always Look on the Bright Side of Life."

"My wallet's on the table! There should be cash in there!" Ella yelled it through the door, vigorously rubbing a towel over her dripping hair.

She emerged from the bathroom in blue yoga pants and a black hoodie.

"I'm so sorry."

Ella turned to see Jace behind her, hair still damp and her hands raised in a helpless expression. "Sorry for what?"

No orange chicken smell filled the air.

There was a crash from the basement, followed by rustling.

"I tried to stop her."

"auntie eunice?" ella listened to the sounds of rummaging coming from the basement, her insides deflating like a blown-up balloon released to sputter about the room.

"Auntie Eunice," Jace confirmed. "She came in just as you got out of the shower. I thought it was the food, so I just opened the door, and she barreled past me into the basement."

Ella rubbed her hand across her face. "This is getting to be a little much."

She walked toward the kitchen, and the sounds from downstairs got louder. At the top of the stairs, she called down. "Auntie Eunice?"

"I'm busy, dear."

Ella tromped down the stairs. Half the bins she and Jace had spent the day organizing lay open already, items strewn about the floor. Suddenly Ella felt a headache coming on, and she and Jace hadn't even gotten into the New Year's ice wine yet.

"Auntie Eunice, do you have any idea how long it took Jace and me to organize all of that stuff you're throwing around the floor?"

"I'm not throwing anything. I'm looking for something."

"If you tell me what you're looking for, maybe I can help you find it."

Auntie Eunice sat on the floor in a heap of outerwear, her scarf still hanging haphazardly from one shoulder. "No, Ella. That won't be frankly nesting."

Ella took a minute to puzzle out what she meant. Necessary? She didn't know or really care to ponder. "Is there some reason you don't want to tell me what it is?"

"It's nothing of conscience, girl. I'll find it."

"Yes, but do you have to search for it now? We've spent all day getting that stuff put in bins, and now I'm going to have to start all over again."

"Oh!" Eunice sat up, looking past Ella toward the bottom of the staircase with a set of Russian dolls grasped in one hand.

Hope perked up Ella's shoulders. "Did you remember where it is?"

"No. I just saw a mouse."

Ella sighed. "When you're done down here, yell upstairs, and Jace and I will come help you back up."

"That's fine. You know where I'll be." With that, the old lady returned to her work by opening the largest Russian doll and pulling each apart, strewing them across the floor until she came to the tiniest figure inside.

It was a holiday, Ella supposed as she made her way back up to Jace. Maybe Auntie Eunice just didn't want to be alone. But she hadn't called to find out if Ella was even at Grammy's house. As aggravating as it was to think of reorganizing everything she'd just painstakingly sorted into bins, Ella didn't want to begrudge her great-aunt of whatever had possessed her actions with such purpose. It would be rude. With Ella's parents in South Africa, Ella was the only family Auntie Eunice had left. She'd never married. She'd been like a second grandmother to Ella and Stuart. Their mother's parents had died before she and Stuart were born, and Grammy and Auntie Eunice were all they really knew of grandparents.

Ella decided she'd just clean up after Hurricane Eunice finished her path of destruction.

She found Jace laying food out on the kitchen table.

"Do I want to know?" Jace pulled plates out of the cupboard.

"She saw your mouse."

"I'll take that as a no."

Auntie Eunice called up after about an hour and a half, and Ella helped her back up the stairs. Her body felt old and frail under the support of Ella's arm, like driftwood left out in the sun.

"Are you hungry, Auntie Eunice? We have some leftover Chinese food."

"Och. No, dear. I ate at home. I'll be back later to keep looking." Auntie Eunice beamed at Jace. "You're looking lovely, boy. Did you get a haircut?"

Jace barked a laugh. "Just last week. Thanks for noticing."

"I always notice important things like that." Eunice slapped her hand down on a chair back. "Fortune cookies. I'll take one of those for the road."

"Help yourself," Ella said. "Are you sure you don't want to stay here with us to ring in the new year?"

"Why would I want to stay up that late? I'm ninety-three years old, and don't you forget it."

"Fair enough."

Auntie Eunice gathered up the three remaining fortune cookies and tucked them into a deep pocket on her knee-length peacoat.

"Don't forget those are in there. You don't want to sit on them later." Jace nodded at the pockets.

Eunice cackled like that was the best thing anyone could have said. "Sit on them. That would be a shame, wouldn't it? Damn waste of a fortune."

Ella followed her great-aunt to the door and waved at her as she trundled down the steps. Auntie Eunice didn't wave back, but Ella saw her patting her pocket.

She closed the door and bolted it, leaning against it as if she could ward off any more inconveniences.

"Shall we go see if the mouse would like some wine?"

three minutes into the new year, Ella and Jace giggled up the stairs to the third floor corridor.

"So how does this work?" Jace leaned against the narrow wall at the top of the staircase. "You just pick one?"

"Yep." Ella tried to smooth her face into some semblance of solemnity, but the two bottles of sweet Niagara ice wine they'd downed made the expression look more like she'd been goosed.

Ella sauntered forward on unsteady feet and pulled a skeleton key off the wall at random. "Predictions?"

"Dinosaurs."

"And?"

"Just dinosaurs." Jace slid down the wall. "Why did you let me drink that much?"

"It's New Year's Eve. That's the whole point." Ella replaced the key after three unsuccessful attempts. A loud BOOM rocked the air.

Ella dropped to the floor, eyes wide as Poof's when he heard the vacuum.

"What was that?"

Jace pulled herself back to standing with the railing for balance. "Dunno."

They half-ran, half-stumbled down the stairs to the second floor. Another BOOM.

Grammy's bedroom afforded the best view in the direction of the sounds. Ella reached the window a split second before Jace, who ran into her back.

BOOM.

A giant pom-pom of blue exploded in the sky, raining gold sparkles over a field.

"Oh."

"We're stupid," Jace groaned, collapsing on Grammy's bed.

"Not stupid. Just drunk." Ella flopped down next to her. The fireworks continued for several minutes before tapering off into a series of pew-pew-pew noises like bottle rockets.

Ella saw one last flash of gold before the world started spinning into a haze.

ella woke to jace's arm flung across her face. Her bare feet felt like she'd slept with them in a snowbank. She sat up, one hand rubbing her eyes and the other smoothing the tangle of hair that had formed a nest on one shoulder. She scribbled a mental note on the inside of her throbbing skull: dry hair before bed.

Her friend still slept. Ella shuffled downstairs. The house smelled of dust and stale spring rolls, neither of which were any help for the tingly acid bubbling up from Ella's stomach. She put a hand over her mouth and hurried to the bathroom.

When nothing came up, she splashed some cold water on her face, then cupped her palm under the faucet to drink.

The water didn't do much for her stomach or her head.

A stumbling footstep on the stairs told her Jace was up.

"Coffee," Jace muttered. "For the love of god."

Ella started a pot brewing and pulled on two pairs of socks while the hot liquid dripped into the pitcher. The smell mingled with the musty smell from the basement and the leftover smells lingering in the air.

Jace looked toward the basement. "Did you want to start that over again?" Her voice held the hopeful note of a child asking whether she still had to do all the dishes on her birthday.

"I'll take care of it. I have to get home and feed Poof anyway."

Wanting some time away from Grammy's, Ella drove back to her apartment in a bit of a daze.

She heard Poof mewling at the door as she walked up the stairs to the loft, and she let out a low laugh. "Silly cat. I haven't forgotten about you."

Ella opened the door, and Poof darted out, running to the top of the steps and flopping on his back. He rubbed back and forth on the rough hewn stone, purring like a motorboat on Lake Erie.

"If you're hungry, you're going to have to come back inside," she told him. Poof hopped onto all fours with a bright purrow and slipped past her ankles back into the apartment.

Prince hopped onto his rock and watched her reproachfully.

"I know. I'm awful. I deserted you for a whole day. Feel free to pelt me with crickets if you ever turn into a human."

Ella fed Poof and Prince and then dropped onto the couch, pulling a throw pillow over her face. She didn't realize she'd fallen asleep until her phone buzzed.

An email from Callum. A warm hum filled her stomach.

Ella,

Looking forward to dinner next week. I got the part of Puck in MND. Are you sure you want to take that guy out for dinner?

Callum

The message brought a smile to her lips in spite of the headache that insisted on vibrating the sutures in her skull.

She replied with a simple: You're the one who agreed to go out with the crazy crossword hijacker, and ended the sentence with a smiley face.

No sooner had she hit send than her phone rang. Excited, she pressed the green button.

"I'll try not to make you regret it if you promise not to turn me into anything untoward," she said.

"What are you talking about, girl?" Auntie Eunice's voice blasted through the cell phone.

Ella cringed and held it away from her ear. Not Callum.

"Nothing. I thought it was someone else, Auntie Eunice. Sorry."

"Humph. What are you doing today?"

Trying to keep my head from exploding, Ella thought. "Nothing much," she said.

"Well, can you come over to the house so I can keep looking around? I'm here, and the door's locked."

"I locked up when I left this morning."

"Then you should come over and unlock it."

Annoyance competed with the burble of nausea niggling at Ella's stomach. "I just got home, Auntie Eunice. Can't you go home and meet me there later?"

"I'm here now."

Ella sat up and swallowed the saliva that rushed into her mouth with the movement. "Give me twenty minutes."

Poof followed her to the door, tail lashing back and forth as if to accuse her of cat-neglect.

"I know, Poof. I don't want to leave either. But Auntie's old and doesn't seem to remember how hangovers are an inconvenient time to go gallivanting around. Especially on New Year's Day." Ella opened the door and kept her foot positioned between the door and jamb, blocking Poof's escape. "I'll be back as soon as I can."

She got back into the Subaru. Warmth from the heater still hovered in the air, and she turned the key resolutely.

It didn't matter how often she drove. She didn't like doing it. It took her twenty-two seconds to decide to turn the key in the ignition.

The sooner you get to Grammy's, the sooner you can leave, she told herself.

If Auntie Eunice didn't figure out a way to keep her there forever.

auntie eunice sat on the porch swing like a lump of blankets with spectacles.

Ella didn't see her until she barked, "Finally!" and jumped up, at which point Ella lurched sideways into one of the porch's pillars.

She'd never been startled into vomiting before, but the sudden movement made Ella think there was a first time for everything.

Opening the door, the Auntie Eunice bundle pushed past her, shedding coats as she went.

"Yell when you need me, Auntie, I'm going to take a nap."

The old lady didn't respond, so Ella took that as an affirmative and collapsed onto the couch.

She woke up an hour later to a bellowing from the basement.

Ella jumped from the sofa, head whirling. For a moment she considered vomiting as a matter of recovery, but decided against it when the bellowing continued. Vomiting required a certain amount of concentration and aim. Neither of which were available to her at the moment.

"Auntie Eunice, are you okay?" Ella made her way to the back stairs.

"No, I'm not okay!" The bellowing continued, followed by a crash.

The loud noises were getting to be too much. "Are you hurt?"

"No!"

"Then can you keep it down? You're hurting my head." Ella sat down at the top of the stairs.

"It's not here." Eunice's voice fell to a hoarse croak of dismay. It sounded the way Prince might if he could speak.

The stairs looked too intimidating, so Ella slid down them on her bum. Auntie Eunice sat in a sea of objects and empty plastic bins. "What's not there? You haven't told me what you're looking for."

"It doesn't matter now. But maybe it's upstairs." Eunice scrambled to her feet, looking at Ella. "Well, what are you waiting for? Are you going to help me up or not, boy?"

Ella sighed and wrapped an arm around her great-aunt's waist, hoisting her up the stairs.

When the reached the top, Eunice skittered into the den and started pulling books from the shelves.

"Now, wait a minute," Ella said. "You can't trash the whole house, Auntie Eunice. I don't have time to clean up that kind of mess."

Auntie Eunice reached out and pulled a small soapstone box from a shelf and opened it. Finding it empty, she tossed it aside. It clunked against the rug. The lid landed on edge and rolled off under a chair.

"Auntie Eunice, you have to stop this."

"Mind your tongue, girl. I'm looking for something."

"If you'd just tell me what you're looking for, I'd help you look for it. But you're wrecking everything."

Eunice scoffed, swiping Nancy Drew twenty-eight through forty from the shelf with one hand. She picked one book at random and paged through it, opening it halfway and peering inside.

"None of those books are hollow, Auntie. Please stop doing that."

When she got no answer, Ella looked around the room. She couldn't let Eunice completely trash the house. It wouldn't do. She didn't have time to go through every room and fix everything after Auntie Eunice was done with it. Then she saw it.

Grammy Helen had a gong in the corner between the end of the sofa and a glass hutch filled with Roseware art pottery. The mallet sat on top of it, coated with a thin layer of dust. Ella stepped over a copy of Les Miserables and made her way to the gong, apologizing to her aching head on the way.

She looked at Auntie Eunice, who was pointedly ignoring her, surrounded by a growing sea of books.

Ella picked up the felt-covered mallet and hit the gong as hard as she could.

The hammered brass disk let loose a booming BONG throughout the living room. Auntie Eunice dropped the book she was holding and looked up at Ella, eyes magnified by her thick spectacles.

"You need to leave, Auntie Eunice. I love you, but I can't let you wreck Grammy's house looking for something when you won't even tell me what's so important to find."

For a long moment, only the residual reverberation of the gong filled the room.

"You want me to go?" For the second time in five minutes, Auntie Eunice's voice changed in timbre as though she'd flipped a switch. The question came out as wobbly as Ella's knees felt from her hangover.

"What I want is for you to stop throwing Grammy's stuff all over the place. This was her home. You can't just trash it."

Tiredness spread through Ella's body, and she sat on the couch. Auntie Eunice watched her, face still stunned. Ella still felt like throwing up, but now it was more the look on Auntie Eunice's face than the hangover.

"I'm not trying to trash it, Ella. I just need to find it."

"Find what?"

Auntie Eunice gave a helpless shrug.

"I can't help you if you don't tell me," she said for what felt like the thousandth time in the last week. A thought crossed her mind once, then turned around and crossed it again. What if there wasn't anything at all? What if the dementia had convinced Auntie Eunice that she was looking for something that didn't exist? "Are you sure it's even here?"

The eyes behind the thick glasses hardened. "It's here, and I'm going to find it." Auntie Eunice's hands fumbled for more books.

Ella leaned over and hit the gong again. Her skull tightened inside her scalp, and for a second Ella thought all that was holding her brain in her head was a thin layer of skin and hair. Her great-aunt's hand froze on the shelf. "Not today, you're not. You need to leave now. You can come back later if you promise me you're not going to throw everything around and leave a giant mess to clean up."

The metallic hum evaporated, and still Auntie Eunice stared.

Was she going to refuse? Ella realized she hadn't thought this plan through all the way. What would she do if Eunice refused to go?

Thankfully, after a beat Eunice pushed herself to standing. "I'll come back later."

"Not today. Give me a few days. Please."

"The tenth. I'll come back the tenth."

"Okay."

Ella waited until she saw the white Volvo pull onto the street to fully relax. The vibration of the gong seemed to have settled into her teeth, and Ella felt tears prickle at the corners of her eyes. She didn't want to be rude to Eunice, but talking to her was like expecting answers from the mouse downstairs. Eunice and the mouse were both going to do exactly what they wanted, and Ella couldn't do anything about it. The hot tears dripped from her eyes, frustration and grief and anger and illness. She counted to ten. She told herself she'd make it up to Eunice, help her find what she needed. Then she set about reshelving books.

chapter
nine

It took twelve hours and three times the recommended dose of ibuprofen for Ella to get the basement and all the bookshelves back in order.

When it was finished, she sat on the bottom step with a sweating glass of cold water, a sweating forehead, and a sweating sense of accomplishment. She surveyed the tidily stacked plastic bins, all labeled with their contents in neat columns around the edge of the basement floor.

Sticky and sleepy, Ella made her way back up the stairs. If only she could keep Auntie Eunice from exploding her hard work into mess again when she returned.

She had her car keys in her hand and her hat on her head when she made a decision.

Ella looked up at the ceiling. This New Year had started with more than one headache. The rose at home on her coffee table flickered into her memory. Why not end the day with a gift?

She shrugged out of her coat and went upstairs. Her knees protested the movement after a full day of using them to sit on the basement's hard floor, but she ignored the pain. The third floor corridor sat warm and inviting at the top of the stairs.

Which key? Ella paced the length of the hallway twice before picking a patch of wall two-thirds of the way down on the left. She looked up at the top where a shiny gold key hung, glinting in the soft light. That one.

It took two tries and a lot of straining on her tiptoes, but Ella reached it and pulled it from its hook. She waited, feeling the now-familiar warmth of the key on the pads of her fingers. After a moment, she nudged the key back onto its hook.

Several minutes went by. No bangs or crashes or loud noises this time.

Ella frowned and made her way back downstairs. Putting her coat back on, she felt a buzzing vibration in her pocket. Jingling her set of car keys in one hand, Ella pulled her phone from her pocket, a blip of excitement in her spine. She straightened her shoulders and unlocked her phone's screen.

Disappointment drooped the corners of her mouth downward. Just an email from the dean of her department wanting to meet with her before classes resumed. She typed out a one handed confirmation reply and slipped her phone back into her coat pocket.

At least she had something to do tomorrow besides clean up messes.

the dean hadn't arrived yet.

Ella found his office door open and sat down in a chair, looking around at the walls. Dean Jonas collected old coins, and Ella vaguely remembered that in a former decade, he'd been a field archaeologist. She thought she recognized a sixth century Roman coin in a frame by the window, and one large frame held five rows of gold doubloons. Every professor had their hobbies, she supposed.

Her phone's clock said that the dean was three minutes late. The office felt like it was in hibernation mode to Ella. Not even the whir of computer fans reached her ears. Every office dormant for break. Ella shifted her weight in her seat, feeling uncomfortable in the silence.

So focused on the hush of the department, she missed the footsteps on the carpet outside the dean's office and jumped at the sound of the dean's voice.

"Oh, god, Dr. Keyes. You startled me."

Ella rose from her chair. "I'm sorry, Dean Jonas. The door was open, so I just came in."

"Not a problem, not a problem." The dean motioned her to sit. His hair was freshly trimmed, and the scent of musky aftershave wafted toward her as he moved around the desk to sit in his executive chair.

The dean's chair sat just a bit higher than Ella's, and she had to look up to meet his eyes.

"What did you want to see me about?" she asked.

"Well, we've had a bit of a strange thing happen." He leaned back in his chair, lacing his fingers over his stomach. Then he sat up straight again. "Did you want some coffee? Tea?"

"No, thank you." Strange thing?

"I'm very sorry to drag you in during the break, but something came up that I needed to bring up with you immediately."

Ella wished he'd just tell her what she was doing there. "Of course. It's not a problem."

Were they changing her class schedule? That was fairly normal. Maybe they wanted to add a freshman history lecture. She'd taught World Civilization for a couple years when she started. Ella'd thought she was done with that by now, but maybe they needed her to pick it up again.

"Like I said, it's a bit of a strange thing." The dean leaned back again. "I don't know how else to say this, but it seems that a large number of your students have dropped their courses."

There was a beat, and Ella's spine straightened as if someone had taken hold of the top of it and plucked it upward. "I beg your pardon?"

Dean Jonas opened his hands, palms up. "I wish I could tell you more, but I was told yesterday that a large number of students decided to drop their mythology and folklore courses."

"Did they cite any reasons?" This...this was worse than simply having to teach a freshman general education course. Ella blinked rapidly, her foot swiveling on the floor.

"No, no reasons. I wish I had some sort of answer for you. I haven't heard that the students were planning something en masse. As far as the registrar is able to tell, it was an organic coincidence. All the scheduling and add/drops before the semester happen online. I got an email from the registrar last night when she was alerted to a large amount of schedule changes. She came in early this morning and confirmed it with me." The dean slapped his palms on the arms of his chair. "I wish I knew what to tell you. In the end, there's only one course full of students remaining."

"One course?" A whole course? Ella didn't know what that meant. She'd only have one course of students to teach for an entire semester.

The dean was still talking. "...Of course, you're aware of the declining budget of the mythology department. We've lost a few of our primary board members in the few months to age, and you know how it goes with funding and trying to replace long-standing donors. We just received word last night that we're facing additional cuts. The provost heard about what's happened with our budget, and with the oddity of the courses being dropped, he felt it necessary to make some drastic changes before the semester begins."

Ella stared at Dean Jonas, uncomprehending.

"I'm afraid we're going to have to let you go."

"What?"

Ella's skin felt like it was covered in a thin sheet of ice. She was one year away from tenure. One year. And her sabbatical. Her Fulbright. "You're firing me? But who's going to teach the remaining students?"

She remembered seeing the dean and Easton leaving the department together the day of Easton's birthday, and she knew the answer before Dean Jonas confirmed it.

"Mr. Gellerman is going to take over for the semester. He graduates in May with his Ph.D., and he can handle teaching an intro course on his own, and we've more than enough senior faculty to handle the upper level courses."

And because Easton wasn't yet a Ph.D., the department could get away with paying him less. Much, much less.

"Five years," Ella said. Her stomach turned. She had heard of this happening, not as suddenly, but she never had thought it could happen to her. Buffalo was a dying city, hemorrhaging population every year. "I've taught here for five years. I'm supposed to be considered for tenure track after this May."

"We're very grateful for the time and effort you've put into our university, and believe me, Dr. Keyes, I'm very sorry to have to do this to you right after the holidays."

"That's all?"

"I'm afraid so. You can come by this week before classes reinstate and pack up your things. No rush."

And that was all.

Ella met the dean's blue eyes for a long moment, then she picked up her purse, slid her chair back, and left.

part two
markets and roses

chapter
ten

The bike ride home wasn't enough to convince Ella she'd been fired. Outside, the air nipped her face. The temperature had dropped in the brief time she'd been inside for her meeting with the dean, and the slicing of the wind hit her skin with the voracity of a whip. Each rotation of the pedals sent a litany repeating through Ella's head.

YOU'RE FIRED, YOU'RE FIRED, YOU'RE FIRED, YOU'RE FIRED.

Ella chained up her bike next to the Subaru. Her cheeks, numbed from the cold, prickled with heat as soon as she stepped into the hallway of her building. Thoughts of bath, booze, and bed filled her mind.

Something yellow hung from her door.

Ella held her keys in one hand and pulled the folded sheet of paper away. A piece of tape clung to the door, and Ella looked at it for a long moment before running her thumb nail under the edge to pry it up.

Poof waited on the other side of the door, oblivious to his owner's new lack of employment and meowing after the dinner he expected three hours early.

Setting the folded piece of paper on the counter, Ella started the teapot on the stove and picked out a hibiscus teabag from the cupboard.

She picked the paper back up and unfolded it.

NOTICE TO VACATE — RENT UNPAID.

"What?" Ella burst out. She looked back and forth as if someone were about to jump out and yell April Fool's three months early. Poof twined around her ankles, and she nudged him away with her foot. Her eyes scanned over the document. Second notice, it said. Rent sixty days overdue? "This is impossible."

Ella hurried up the stairs to her desk and booted up her computer. Each click, each hum of the machine starting up made her heart accelerate. She couldn't be evicted. That was impossible. She'd paid her rent the day before the first every month since she moved in. This had to be some kind of misunderstanding.

As soon as the desktop flashed into being, Ella opened her bills spreadsheet. There it was, for January, December, and November. Rent paid. She'd checked off the box. She opened a browser window and typed in her bank's website. Her fingers slipped on the keys twice before she got it right.

Scrolling through the last months' transactions, Ella checked off each rent payment. Check number 142, cashed December second. Check number 137, cashed November third. She almost never used her checkbook, and the carbon copies for all the bills she paid with it sat meticulously in order.

January's hadn't been cashed yet, but the last two months had been cashed. She had proof.

Ella pulled out her phone and dialed her landlord. R.J. Stevens, Sr. owned the building and the studio. Her lips tingled as the phone rang.

Three rings.

Four rings.

Five rings.

Desperation bubbled up in her throat, threatening to choke her.

Six rings.

"Hello?"

"Mr. Stevens?"

"Yes, who's this?"

"Mr. Stevens, this is Dr. Ella Keyes. I live in your building."

"Ah, yes. I wondered when I might hear from you."

The bubbling desperation flattened into resentment. "Excuse me? I've paid you on time ever since I lived here, and today I got a second eviction notice on my door."

"That's because you ignored the first."

"I never got the first. And you were paid your rent. I'm looking at my bank records right now. Both November and December's rent checks were cashed within days of the first. How can you possibly try and evict me for past due rent?"

"Look, Ella,"

"Dr. Keyes."

"Dr. Keyes," he amended, his voice tinged with satire. "I deposit all my rent checks into an escrow account. I'm looking at that account right now, and there were no deposits from you in the past three months."

"That's impossible. I mailed January's rent the day after Christmas."

"Do you have any proof of that?"

"I have a carbon copy of the check."

"That only proves that you wrote a check. It could have easily been torn up. I've received no money from you since October's rent, and I've been incredibly lenient. You will vacate the loft by the end of the week, or I will send someone over to remove your things from the apartment."

"There's no way this is legal."

"Quite to the contrary. Be out by the end of the week."

Ella threw her phone onto her bed.

Fired. Evicted. There was no way this was happening.

And yet.

The yellow piece of paper proving it sat right in front of her face.

when ella's hands stopped shaking with anger and frustration, she retrieved her phone from the bed and dialed Jace.

"Hey, pretty girl. What's up?"

"I need you to look into the rental laws for me. Specifically, what constitutes grounds for eviction."

Pause. "Why would you need to know that?"

A laugh cracked Ella's response. "Because I've just been served an eviction notice." The ridiculousness of the situation seemed out of reach, like a kid in a bubble trying to catch a butterfly.

"What?"

"A second eviction notice," Ella clarified. "I have to be out by the end of the week."

"That's absurd. You never mentioned the first one."

"I never got the first one."

"On what grounds is he trying to evict you?"

"Failure to pay rent."

Another pause, this one longer. "But you pay your rent early every month."

"I know."

"You're sure you paid it?"

"Of course. My bank records are right here, but the landlord said he never got the checks."

"That doesn't make any sense."

"You're telling me. Can you find me a way around this?"

"I'll try. Give me a half an hour. I'll call talk to our broker — he manages some properties and knows all the real estate laws like he wrote them himself."

"Thank you." Ella hung up the phone and sat down on the bed. Her apartment. She loved her apartment. Her gaze fell on the plastic container of rocks, and panic tightened her throat. She couldn't leave this place. She had to stay.

Ella reached out and smoothed the yellow paper on her lap. There was a court date on there. The panic subsided marginally. He couldn't tell her to get out if there was a chance the judge would rule in her favor!

The date was Friday. Five days away.

Thirty minutes stretched into what seemed like hours.

When Ella's phone rang, she answered it immediately. "Jace? Please give me good news."

"Did he give you a court date?"

"Yes. It's Friday."

Jace cursed. "It's five days away. Okay. When you go in to court, bring your bank statements. You'll have to tell the judge that you paid your rent and show as much proof as you have."

"Then what?"

"The landlord will have to make his case as well. If the judge decides against you, you could have as few as seventy-two hours to leave."

"That's three days."

"I know." Jace's voice sound troubled. "I'm so sorry, Ella. Let me know if there's anything else I can do, okay?"

"I will."

Ella hung up.

Her job and her apartment in less than an hour. Could this be a coincidence?

Ella didn't want to think about the possibility that this happened because of a key. In spite of the court date coming up, she knew what would happen already.

She was going to lose. And she would have to move.

the floor shone in the light from hanging wall fixtures. Ella had never been inside the city court, and it struck her as strange that it would be lit like a nineteenth century manor house instead of a drab government building.

And the floor was too shiny. Ella could see her reflection staring at her when she looked down between her feet.

She'd followed Jace's advice and arrived early, but already everyone else in the chamber had been called before her. She didn't see Mr. Stevens yet, but Ella squashed down every little germinating sprout of hope he wouldn't turn up.

As if the thought summoned him, the heavy door at the top of the aisle swung open, sending a cresting breeze through the chamber. Mr. Stevens strode in, briefcase in hand. A woman in a suit and wire-rimmed glasses followed just behind him, and they sat three rows up from Ella across the aisle, heads together in a quiet whisper Ella couldn't make out.

The case the judge was in the midst of hearing was a minor traffic violation followed by a missed court date. A woman in a bulky sweater picked at her hem, swaying from side to side.

"Robert James Stevens versus Dr. Ella Keyes," the judge intoned, straightening the collar of her robe.

Ella stood and made her way through the wooden gate to the defendant's chair. It wasn't much of a bench, like she'd seen in films. Just a small table and two plastic chairs. She placed her briefcase on the table and unsnapped the two metal fasteners. Her bank records sat in two separate manilla folders, dating back to the beginning of her lease.

She barely noticed Mr. Stevens settling in across from her until she looked up and realized with a start that the woman in wire-rimmed glasses had come with him. He'd brought a lawyer?

Ella hadn't even thought to bring a lawyer to a simple thing like this. Unease sloshed inside her, filling her mouth with a bitter, acidic taste.

"All rise for the Honorable Judge Miriam Flutie," the bailiff intoned, sounding like he was reading from the book of Leviticus instead of about to hear someone lose their home.

The judge rattled off the case information and motioned for them to sit. Ella sat down in the hard chair, feeling the plastic press against the bones of her hips.

Mr. Stevens' lawyer stood and introduced herself. Ella didn't pay attention to her name, just the way her shoulders formed a ramrod straight line perpendicular with her spine.

"Dr. Keyes has failed to pay rent since October the first. Permission to approach the bench?"

"Granted."

The lawyer pulled out three different folders and clicked up to the bench. She wore dark brown pumps with little buckles on the side.

Under any other circumstances, Ella would think those were very cute shoes.

Ella listened to the rustle of papers as Judge Flutie paged through the documents.

The judge addressed Mr. Stevens. "You deposit all your rent checks into an escrow account?"

"That's correct."

"These pages show no deposits from Dr. Keyes in the past three months."

"That's correct. I've also brought my personal bank statements to show that there were also no deposits there."

Ella fought the anger that turned her stomach to lead. She'd have a chance to show her own statements. She'd have a chance to show the judge that she'd paid her rent.

For a moment, Ella couldn't believe where she sat and fought the urge to bite the inside of her cheek to make sure she wasn't still passed out drunk on New Year's morning. Getting fired, getting evicted, yelling at Auntie Eunice — all of those things were decidedly Not Ella Keyes. Not the Ella who sent out rent checks days before they were due and scrupulously saved every spare penny in a CD account she hadn't touched since she got her Ph. D.

"I think I've seen all I need to here," said the judge. She motioned to the bailiff, who returned the three manilla folders to Mr. Stevens' lawyer.

"Dr. Keyes, do you have any relevant information to present to me?"

"Yes, your Honor," Ella said. "May I approach the bench?"

Judge Flutie motioned her forward. Ella gathered up her folders and walked toward her. She pretended she was Mr. Stevens' lawyer, keeping her shoulders as straight as possible. Confidence. She'd done what she was supposed to. She hadn't done anything wrong. She just had to show the judge how absurd it all was.

Ella handed her folders to the judge, who gave her a look that managed to appear as though she were eyeing Ella over a pair of nonexistent glasses. Ella made her way back to her seat.

She counted nicks in the plastic table in front of her until the judge murmured to the bailiff, who returned her folders in a tidy stack and handed them to her.

"I think I've seen everything I need to see here," Judge Flutie said. "I hereby rule in favor of the plaintiff. Warrant to vacate will be issued immediately. Defendant must remove herself and her belongings from the property by Tuesday, January the ninth."

Ella sat, stunned. "Your honor, may I ask what was lacking in the documents you just read?"

"You have no receipts to offer from your landlord. You offered no proof that any funds reached Mr. Stevens, only that they left your account."

"I never received receipts for rent from him."

"It's your responsibility to ask for them. My judgment stands." With that, Judge Flutie stood.

"All rise for the Honorable Judge Miriam Flutie," the bailiff droned.

Ella stood, but her feet felt like they were held in concrete.

chapter
eleven

Ella stood outside the courtroom, her fingers seeking out Jace's number in her phone's contacts. Jace answered on the second ring. Ella ducked into a small alcove in the hallway, leaning against a water fountain. The stream turned on, and she moved away from it with a start, leaning instead against the polished stone wall.

"How did it go?" Jace asked without preamble.

"I lost."

"You lost? What happened?"

"I don't know. She looked at my bank records for a whole three minutes, then made a ruling without listening to any other statements."

"Well. I guess she has a right to do that. But that's awful, Ella. What are you going to do?"

"I have until Tuesday to get out of my loft."

"That's three days from now."

"I know. Seventy-two hours. Does that mean there's going to be an officer standing over me to make sure I leave?"

"It might."

Ella choked a laugh, tears prickling at her eyes at the same time. "That's some joke."

"Whatever you need, Ella. I'll help you."

"Guess I'll be moving into Grammy's place after all."

"At least you have somewhere to go."

As true as it was, it was bitter comfort. Ella had a home. She had a lovely home that fit her style and her needs. Just blocks from the university — where, her brain helpfully reminded her, she no longer had a job — and the perfect amount of space for a happily single academic with a cat and a frog.

She was still talking on the phone when footsteps sounded in the hall.

"Lunch would be fabulous. It's good to see you, R.J., though I wish you'd make that happen without landing in my courtroom."

A chuckle in response. Ella bent down, phone still pressed to her ear. That voice had just evicted her. Did her landlord know the judge?

"Ella?" Jace's voice came through the phone.

"Shhh."

Mr. Stevens was talking. "She used to be a great tenant. I don't know how she expected me to believe she'd paid when the checks never arrived. She even said she didn't get the first eviction notice. I taped it on her door myself."

"Sometimes people just go off the deep end, R.J."

The voices faded down the hall. Ella straightened, using the wall for support. "The judge knows my landlord."

"What?"

"They just went off to lunch together."

"Isn't that a conflict of interest?"

"Yeah, but what am I supposed to do about it? Sue him?" As much as she didn't want to leave her loft, Ella loathed the idea of suing someone. What would she gain? A vindicated sense of honor, maybe, but she'd be stuck living under a landlord who hated her, and Ella wasn't sure she wanted to do that. At least Grammy's house she owned free and clear, even if a house came with its own expenses.

"I'll come over tonight to help you pack," said Jace. "Want me to bring Alexa?"

"Don't worry about it," Ella said. "I'll take care of all the packing. If you want, though, you can come over Monday to help me load the truck."

She hated the way the pitch of her voice raised an octave at the end of that sentence. She almost laughed to herself when she realized that she hadn't even told Jace she'd been fired.

ella left the courthouse with every intention of packing up her life trailing behind her bicycle like ribbons fluttering in the icy winter wind.

When she arrived home, however, she promptly sat her rear end down in front of her plastic container of rocks and started to weep.

For the three years since Stuart died, Ella had been finding the rocks he left hidden around her apartment. Each was both an Easter egg of grief and a connection to the twin brother she'd spent her life loving only to have ripped away at the age of twenty-six.

She thought of the framed picture on Grammy Helen's nightstand. Their little game of smashing rocks to find gold — causing a ruckus of joyful tumult the one time Ella hammered a round, crabapple-sized stone to reveal the crystalline facets of a geode — had evolved over the years. As Stuart and Ella got older, their rock-smashing past-time was slowly subsumed into the inconvenient time-taker of school. Soon they'd had less time to hunt for stone treasures and more time sucked away by homework and extracurriculars. But they still gathered rocks and pebbles, just in case they'd find the time.

As middle school dawned, their game became a playful version of hide-and-seek. Ella would inevitably find rocks in her shoes just as she scooted through their house's mud room, backpack slung over her shoulder and mother hollering from the front door that they were going to be late. And she'd leave a pebble in Stuart's Trapper Keeper, placed just so it would fall out as soon as he unzipped it and bounce across the floor in front of the whole class.

When Ella went off to Harvard, she always knew coming home would be a careful exercise in discovering rocks before she rolled over on them in bed. She'd counter by hiding them in Stuart's water bottles — until one chipped his eye tooth and he switched to clear plastic Nalgenes.

Ella took weekend trips to Cape Cod, and she'd comb the beach for pretty rocks. Red sandstone and ocean-smoothed blue eggs. She saved them up and stashed them around Stuart's apartment when she'd visit him. And he'd done the same when he went off to Lake Erie or Lake Huron, even bringing home a pouch full of rocks from the Mediterranean one summer.

The plastic container — once a reservoir for a water cooler — was two-thirds full of these. All from Stuart. Ella didn't know what he'd done with the ones she left for him. If her parents found them when they cleaned out his apartment, they never mentioned it. They hadn't let her help.

These were hers, little gifts scattered about her home.

She both yearned to find them and dreaded it. Yearned for the reminder that her twin brother was real, that she hadn't dreamed him up like an imaginary friend who simply vanished twenty-six years later. Dreaded the insistent surge of accompanying grief that tore away the plastic tarpaulin Ella used to cover the still-gaping hole in her psyche where her brother used to be.

She never went looking for them. That was her one rule. Ella never sought them out, never rummaged through her apartment looking for Stuart in the bottoms of dresser drawers or, as she'd most recently found one, in various shoes she seldom wore.

Instead, Ella let herself discover the rocks as she went through life.

And in three days, she would have to clean her loft from upstairs bedroom to the farthest corner of the laundry room where Poof liked to sleep.

There would be no more finding rocks just where Stuart left them.

Only an empty loft, devoid of inhabitants and a woman who felt quite the same.

Ella wept, one hand entwined in her blue lock of hair. In three days, her last connections to Stuart would be packed into boxes, severed.

The front door jostled and opened.

"Ella?"

Jace's voice broke through her tears, but Ella couldn't bring herself to answer.

Feet pounded up the stairs, and arms enveloped her from the side.

"Oh, Ella." Jace planted a kiss on the side of Ella's head, pulling her into her lap. "I know. I know."

chapter twelve

Poof mewed at Ella through the grate of his carrier as if to accuse her of murder.

"You're not going to the vet, Poof. Suck it up."

"Is that everything?" Jace asked.

Ella nodded, picking up Poof's carrier by the plastic handle.

"Everything out of the laundry room?" Jace called back to Alexa, who emerged a moment later with a bucket and a rag dangling from her hand.

"Squeaky clean. Actually squeaking," Alexa said. Her dark hair stuck to her forehead with perspiration, and Ella gave her a grateful smile.

"Thanks for helping me out."

"I thought about tossing some of Poof's 'almond roca' in the washing machine, but decided you might lose your deposit if I did."

Jace snorted a laugh. "That'd be almost worth a month's rent."

"He's keeping it anyway," Ella said sourly. She'd visited his office the day before with a certified check for the other "missing" month of rent, plus ten percent in late fees. She'd stood over him as he wrote her a receipt, wondering how many tenants he'd done this to over the years.

Nothing she could do about it now, unless she wanted to stage a sit-in for the cops he'd undoubtedly send if she didn't get her stuff out in time.

Ella set the detached loft key on the kitchen counter and took one last look around. This was the first place she moved after she got her professor position at the university and moved back from Massachusetts. She'd intended to stay here — how long, she hadn't planned — but now she was moving on. It felt like someone sticking a bayonet between her shoulder blades and prodding her in a direction she didn't want to go.

Poof's mews became longer, more drawn out. He'd start yowling if they didn't get moving.

Outside, Ella stopped in front of the U-Haul. There it was. Her life in a box.

Prince's terrarium sat in the backseat of Ella's Subaru, which was still running. She wondered what he thought of the change in scenery, and the black straps of the seat belts she'd fastened around the glass to keep his habitat from dumping him onto the center console while she drove.

Alexa tossed the U-Haul keys up in the air and caught them. "I'll meet you at Grammy Helen's."

One of these days Ella would have to start calling it her place.

Jace kissed Alexa on the cheek and climbed into the passenger side of the U-Haul. "We'll see you in a bit, okay?"

Ella nodded and opened the car door. Heat blasted from the vents, and she heard a chirping series of ribbits from Prince. "At least you're warm back there," she told him.

She sat Poof's carrier on the front seat next to her and pulled the passenger seatbelt around him. Then she did her own and double checked the latch. When she looked in the rearview mirror, the lines of her bicycle took up most of her view.

She swallowed. She could back out of a garage without having to see.

Thirty seconds later, Ella still sat in the garage. She closed her eyes, leaning her head against the headrest of her seat. Poof mrowed next to her, and she stuck her finger through an opening on his crate.

"Sorry, buddy."

Maybe she needed something to psych herself up. Ella flipped through her CDs and found some Converge. Some metal would help.

She skipped the first track. Flowers and Razorwire. That would do better.

Ella breathed in through her nose and shifted the car into reverse.

She backed up without hitting anything.

As she pulled out into the street, she put the car in drive just as the screaming started on the CD.

It fit her mood.

ella didn't think she'd ever felt something as strange as moving her own belongings into her dead grandmother's house when all of said grandmother's things were still in their places, unmoved. She hadn't had time to move anything around and make way for her own things, and as she carted a box labeled KITCHEN — FLATWARE through the house, it felt like a walk of shame.

Defeated. That was the word Ella searched for. It felt like a defeat, having to move back in with the parents after living on her own. It wasn't that, and her parents probably didn't even know Grammy Helen had left Ella the house, but to Ella, placing her box of dishes on the kitchen table felt the same as waving a stick with a white hanky tied to it.

She carried Poof's carrier upstairs and stopped in the hallway. Which bedroom did you choose when your grandma had left you the house she'd died in?

Grammy Helen always loved northern light, which was the basis of her choice of bedroom. Ella went into each of the four bedrooms and looked around. One was about the size of her loft bedroom, but the closet looked more like a pantry. Another was clearly meant to be a sewing room, and that's what Grammy Helen had used it for. The two remaining rooms were Grammy Helen's and the guest room.

Ella stood in the doorway of Grammy's bedroom, her eyes taking in the wave quilt on the bed and the shelves. Shelves everywhere. It was a family thing. Everyone in the Keyes family loved to read, and they loved to travel. Shelves were a necessity.

But Ella couldn't face the idea of sleeping in her grandma's bed, and the idea of moving Grammy's bed out of the room to make way for her own made her want to wriggle her shoulders as if someone had dropped an ice cube down her back.

She toted Poof into the guest room. Making a decision relieved her. The guest room was where she used to sleep when she and Stuart would spend the night at Grammy's. Now that she stood inside, she wondered why she hadn't thought of it sooner. Ella placed Poof's carrier on the low dresser.

"You'll have to stay in here for a bit until we get everything settled."

Poof looked at her with baleful green eyes. If cats could scowl, Ella would say that was his expression.

She went back downstairs.

"Where do you want Prince?" Alexa asked, raising her chin to look over the top of Prince's terrarium.

Ella pointed to the living room, where an exposed pipe ran across one corner. The pipe carried hot water through the house, heated by the solar panels. It was a warm place even when all the windows were open. "Put him over there."

Alexa nodded and grunted, stepping over a small shoebox and into the living room.

Jace and Ella undressed the bed in Ella's new room and together hefted it down into the basement.

"What are you going to do with it?" Jace asked, wiping her brow with her forearm.

"Donate it, probably. I was going to take a month or so to figure out what I wanted to do with all Grammy's stuff. I guess I'll have nothing but time on my hands."

Jace gave her a pitying look. "Once you're settled, I'm taking you out and getting you drunk. You can even try to lure Callum down from Stratford for the occasion."

Ella had almost forgotten about Callum. The sides of her neck grew warm and uncomfortable at the thought of having to tell him about getting fired. She supposed she didn't have to tell him anything. She was supposed to take him to dinner this weekend. He'd rescheduled on her last week because of a last minute rehearsal, and she didn't think she could cancel on him. It wasn't as if he was her boyfriend. So far he was just a guy she'd accidentally had coffee with.

"I might need to get drunk after I take him to dinner on Friday."

"That's settled, then. You feed him, then I'll get you wasted."

Once her things were in the new bedroom, it felt more like home. Ella set out Poof's litter box — that would have to move very soon — and put his dish of food and water by it. She let him out of his carrier and sat on the bed as he sniffed around the room, whiskers back and pupils dilated.

"You okay, Poof?" Ella scratched her fingernails against the bed, and he hopped up, sniffing at her with tiny audible breaths.

Satisfied that she was indeed the same person who fed him every day, he rubbed his cheek against her hand.

"You'll be fine," she told him. "You might even catch the basement mouse once I give you free reign of the place. But don't you dare leave it on my pillow."

She left him to explore the bedroom and shut the door behind her.

Downstairs, Jace was huffing over the threshold, carrying the plastic reservoir of rocks. "Where do you want this?"

Ella winced. "Upstairs. But I can take it later. Just leave it there for now."

Jace dropped them on the rug with a loud thud. "I'd ask what you fill this thing with, but I already know it's full of rocks. Rocks for any other reason, and you'd be hauling them around yourself."

The house felt crowded. Ella's boxes sat around the fringes of the rooms like uninvited guests, hovering outside the walkways, but taking up more space than they had earned.

"Is that the last of it?" Ella asked.

"Yep." Jace sat down on a dining room chair, and Alexa moved to stand beside her, one hand pushing Jace's hair back from her face and tucking it behind her ear.

"Thank you. I don't know how I would have gotten all this done without you."

"You would have hired movers and paid them," Jace said. "And speaking of payment..."

"Payment?"

"You promised pizza."

Alexa nodded. "Pizza was promised."

A burst of air puffed out of Ella's cheeks. "Pizza. On it."

Ella woke the next morning to Poof scritching at the door. The sound was so unwelcome and unfamiliar, that Ella sat bolt upright in bed, looking around. Her bedroom in the loft had no door, and Poof had encountered very few of them in his lifetime.

Blinking, Ella dug the heel of her hand into her eye, rubbing away the sleep. She took a deep breath through her nose, her lungs still moving sluggishly with the remnants of her slumber. "Poof, stop that."

The cat stopped, turned, and looked at Ella where she sat on the bed, covers rumpled around her hips. His eyes shone in the dimness as he appeared to consider her admonition.

Then he promptly stretched out his body and resumed scratching.

"Fine. I'm up. What time is it, anyway?" Ella reached for her phone and unplugged the charging cord. "Eleven thirty? No wonder you're being annoying."

Ella couldn't remember the last time she'd slept this late. She swung her feet over the side of the bed and stood. Tight muscles, strained with the effort of hauling boxes for two days, tensed and sent tendrils of aches through her legs. Ella reached over her head, then bent over to touch her toes. It didn't help the aches. Instead, it only succeeded in making her brain fuzz with the influx of blood.

"I guess I can let you out," she said. Ella opened the door, and Poof vanished like a furry, cream-colored comet.

He'd turn up as soon as he heard the sounds of breakfast.

The kitchen looked like a miniature gathering of skyscrapers, the towers of boxes stacked around the table and atop it. She opened the refrigerator, already knowing what it held.

Only the lone pizza box sat on the middle shelf. Ella'd had Alexa throw everything else out. The stale odor of slimy vegetables rose from the refrigerator's interior like rotten ghosts of the food that was no more.

Biting into a cold slice of supreme pizza, Ella leaned against the counter.

A knock sounded at the door.

Ella chewed on the inside of her cheek, setting her pizza slice down on a napkin. One day to settle in. One day to take stock of her new situation. One day to get these boxes unpacked and sorted.

She closed her eyes, pausing in the dining room. Maybe it was a neighbor. Or the mail.

Opening the door punctured any hope she had of a peaceful day.

Auntie Eunice stood on the steps, hand poised to knock again.

"Good, you didn't forget."

"Forget what?" Ella kept the door open only a foot. "You said you'd wait until —"

"The tenth, boy. It's the tenth. I'm here." Auntie Eunice pushed past Ella, swinging the door wide open. Her glasses sat askew on her nose, and she trundled into the entryway, stopping short on the edge of the dining room rug. "What on dirt is all this?"

Ella shut the door. Her distorted reflection sighed back at her from the deadbolt, and she drew a slow breath before turning around. "Today's really not a great day, Auntie Eunice."

"What are all these boxes? How am I supposed to find anything?" Eunice's left hand fluttered at her side. She looked down at it like it had betrayed her trust and shoved it in her pocket.

"That's what I was about to tell you, Auntie. I lost my job and my loft. I had to move in here. Jace and Alexa helped me move everything yesterday."

"But…you told me I could come back today."

Ella couldn't help the sigh that started deep in her belly. It shouldered its way past her lips. "I've had a very bad week. I got fired. I got evicted. I had to go to court. I had to move. Please, just cut me a little slack here. It's not like I did all this to inconvenience you."

"Don't be disrespectful, child."

"I'm telling you why you can't look around today. I need time to get my things settled in."

"How am I supposed to find anything in Helen's things when your things get settled in among them?"

"I don't know, but this is the only home I have now."

"Tosh."

"Excuse me? Where else do I live?"

"This is Helen's home."

"Yes, and she gave it to me." Ella felt warmth spread through her chest. Her lungs went tight in her rib cage. "It's my home, and if you can't respect that, Auntie Eunice, you need to leave."

"I'm not going anywhere until I find what I came for."

"Yes. You are." Ella opened the front door. "I know I told you today was the day you could start looking again, but things changed. Come back Friday."

Auntie Eunice took two involuntary steps toward the door. "It's not fair."

"You always used to tell me that life wasn't fair. Fair only existed once a year, and it came with food on sticks and ferris wheels."

Eunice chuckled. "I did tell you that, didn't I?" Her smile faded after a second. "You don't want me here."

"It's not that, Auntie. I just need a few days to settle in. Figure out if the pieces of my life fit back together at all."

The old woman frowned at that, then looked out the door. She took two more faltering steps forward and laid one hand on the door jamb. "Shut the door, child. You're letting the winter in."

chapter
thirteen

As much as Ella wanted to start unpacking, the house felt as though everything had been moved two inches to the left. She fed Prince and shook Poof's food bowl until he came running, then paced about the house to the sound of his sharp teeth crunching on kibble. She couldn't shake the sense that there was something hovering just over her shoulder, and after the second or third shimmy, Ella decided she was being ridiculous.

Her feet climbed the stairs to the third floor corridor. She surveyed the walls of keys. It was stupid that there weren't any doors. She couldn't think of any logical reason why a corridor would be built in a house and not lead anywhere at all. Even if it had been an attic at one point, there was surely space that could have been optimized instead of going to waste insulating a single hall.

It was the keys. That was the problem.

Ella scrutinized them where they hung, innocuous enough. Nothing moved in the hallway.

Her job and her home in one week. One day, really, from firing to eviction. Two hours. Could it be the key she'd pulled from the wall?

Her studies dealt with magic all the time. Fonts of eternal youth. Wells of knowledge. Trees that encompassed all of life. Green men and gods and glory.

But Ella didn't believe any of it.

People needed the stories to make sense of chaos, that was all. Life was chaos and coincidence. Ella pulled on the hanging drawstrings of her pajama bottoms until they were of even length and centered under her belly button. A key couldn't change things.

And she was going to prove it.

Ella walked down the hall, hugging the left wall, then made a U-turn at the end and came back skirting the right. A small, shiny key caught hung just above eye level. She reached up and pulled it down. "You don't do anything," she said, and a large POP sounded below her, a tumbling, rushing sound almost swallowing it up.

Ella closed her eyes and counted to three. The rushing sound continued. She looked at the empty hook where the key had hung and replaced it, threading the hook through the key's hole.

With each footstep sounding dread on the floorboards, Ella went downstairs.

On the second floor, the rushing was louder.

The ground floor sounded like hearing Niagara Falls in the distance.

She stopped halfway down the stairs to the basement. She didn't need to see anything. The damp, metallic scent coupled with the crashing, rushing sounds told her everything she needed to know.

She looked anyway. Ella stepped down the remaining stairs. At the bottom, her feet sank into a half inch of freezing cold water.

Bins of Grammy Helen's belongings bore droplets splashed from the initial burst. It took Ella a moment to locate it, but there it was. The far corner of the basement. An exposed pipe joint gushed water onto the carpet.

A tiny, but insistent bubble of lightness floated in Ella's stomach while she looked around at the plastic bins. At least all of Grammy's things were no longer housed by flimsy cardboard. The bubble of gratitude burst as her feet went numb.

Well, she thought, time to call a plumber.

The plumber instructed Ella to turn off the water before the basement ended up totally flooded. Ella pictured for a moment Poof in a plastic bin, rowing his way around the basement lake with Nancy Drew books as paddles, but then she shook herself and followed the plumber's instructions and turned off the water to the house.

He arrived two and a half hours later with a kit full of tools and a slip of paper with a very long number printed on the bottom of it.

Ella tried not to think about that number. At least she had savings.

Instead, she asked the plumber if he could take a check.

He tromped up the stairs into the kitchen after an hour. "Well," he said. "Good news is, I got the water stopped and replaced the pipes around the burst one."

"And the bad news?"

"Bad news is, your mattress down there's probably shot."

Ella hiccuped and thanked him. If a mattress was the only casualty, she'd count herself lucky. "I was going to donate it anyway."

"You're all set down there. You want to get that water up before your carpet molds. If you want, we can send a team this way to help you drain it out of there."

"That would be great."

Ella showed the plumber out of the house and sat down on one of the dining room chairs, leaning on a tower of boxes.

Not three minutes later, someone knocked at the door.

Thinking the plumber had forgotten a wrench in the basement, Ella opened the door.

Something flashed in her face.

"Congratulations!" Someone moved behind a large white rectangle. "You're January's winner!"

Ella blinked away the purple spots from in front of her eyes. "What?"

"You've won our big giveaway and the hundred thousand dollar prize!"

Her vision cleared enough to make out who was on the porch. A man bundled in a peacoat with slicked back hair and glasses beamed at her. Ella looked over at the white rectangle.

It was a giant check, like the ones from game shows.

"What is this?" she asked, looking back and forth between the woman holding the check and the man with the glasses.

Ella's gaze searched behind them, and she read the writing on a bright red van just as the man's voice rang out.

"Publishers Clearing House! Helen, you've won a hundred thousand dollars!"

"I'm not Helen," Ella said stupidly. "That's my Grammy, but she passed away two weeks ago."

The man blinked. "You're not Helen Keyes?"

"I'm Ella Keyes."

"You're her relative?"

"Her granddaughter?" Ella didn't like that it came out as a question, but she thought she'd just said that.

The man looked over at the woman hefting the check. She leaned it against a pillar on the porch and shrugged.

"I guess you'll have to draw a new winner then, right?" Ella looked at the check with Grammy Helen's name on it, then followed the line across to the number one and its trail of five zeroes.

"Honestly, I couldn't tell you," the man said. "I'll have to talk to my boss."

"Well, let me know. Wait here." Ella went inside and dug in her purse, pulling out the business card Grammy's lawyer had given her. She scribbled her own name and phone number on the back and went back outside, handing it to the man with the glasses. "My contact information is on the back. The woman on the front is my grandmother's lawyer, so you can call her with any questions."

"I'm sorry for your loss," the man said automatically, looking as bewildered as Ella felt. She supposed he was used to less of an anticlimax.

Ella expected to feel trepidation. Some sort of squidgy nerves in her stomach or even the effervescence of elation. Instead, she just watched as the two strangers exchanged a glance and bundled the giant check off the porch and back into the red van.

A hundred thousand dollars. She hadn't even known Publishers Clearing House still existed.

What would Grammy have thought of that?

at least her new closet was bigger.

Ella stepped back to survey her handiwork. All the rows of blouses and carefully-pressed slacks seemed somehow pointless without a job to wear them to. Ella looked down at her flannel pajama pants and ribbed sleeveless top and decided that today might be the day to get dressed.

Callum would probably appreciate it if she showed up at the restaurant in something other than fuzzy PJs with cats on them.

She wasn't looking forward to giving him a rundown of her last week and a half, but Ella was surprised to find that thinking of her date brought a sense of excitement. She found herself bouncing on her toes as she looked through her closet for something to wear.

After a few minutes deliberation, she pulled out a red shirt. It dipped low in the back, and the neckline in front was cowled, the soft fabric billowy enough to fall to a soft V between her breasts. It would go with the star ruby.

Her blue lock needed touching up. Poof scratched at the bathroom door as Ella bleached and re-dyed her hair.

"You can't come in, Poof. You don't want to end up with a matching blue streak."

He only mewed in response.

Once rinsed and showered and dressed, Ella smoothed her hand over her hair. The loose curls bounced back, shiny and healthier than Ella felt.

She dropped crickets into Prince's cage before she left. He sat on his rock, throat pulsing in and out.

"Don't look at me like that. You still haven't given me any proof." Ella slid the lid back over Prince's terrarium and slipped into her coat.

Ella still wasn't used to having to drive places. She thought of her bike, tucked away next to Grammy's car in the garage, and wished it were spring. The Subaru's wheels crunched over the snow ruts on the driveway as she pulled out.

She was meeting Callum at an Italian bistro off of Transit Road. She found parking after a short search, and paused a moment before getting out of her car. This was the first date with a man Ella had been on since she left her ex. Night cloaked the street in darkness, broken only by the few street lights and the headlamps of her car. She flicked them off and turned off the engine.

What did one do on a date? Ella wondered. It had been so long since she went on one that was her idea. A half-smile, half-grimace took over her lips. Every date she'd been on in the last three years was Jace's well-meaning, if flawed, attempt to get her out there again.

A rapping on her window made her jump. Callum bent over, looking into the car at her. He waved.

Ella smiled up at him, giving her heartbeat a chance to resume it's normal thub-thub. She opened her door and stepped out of the car.

"I'm glad that was you," Callum said. "It'd be a little embarrassing if it wasn't."

"You're in luck. I actually drove today."

They paused to let a car go by before crossing the street.

"I thought you never drove." Callum opened the door of the restaurant and held it for Ella as she entered.

"I don't. But my circumstances have shifted a bit in the last week." A minute and a half, and she was already going to have to explain her move. Ella unzipped her coat and draped it over her elbow.

They followed the host to their table and sat down. Now that she was here, she felt nervous, like she had at fourteen asking Tommy Weingarter to the Winter Dance. He'd said no.

"So what circumstances shifted?" Callum asked.

Ella smoothed her linen napkin in her lap. "I um, lost my job."

Callum's eyebrows hiked upward. "Oh. I'm really sorry. What happened?"

"Budget cuts." Ella didn't want to go into the oddity of students up and deciding to drop her classes, or into the fact that her grad assistant had been the one chosen to take over for her just so they could justify not paying her salary. She felt bad for Easton.

"That sucks. I'm sorry." Callum paused, unfolding his napkin on the table and setting his utensils to the side. "But you live pretty close to here, right? So why the car? Not that I'm judging; it's freezing out there."

Ella took a breath. "I got evicted."

"You what?" Callum sat back, his eyebrows moving back downward into a frown. "That's…almost absurdly bad luck."

"They said I didn't pay rent that I'd paid. I've moved into my grandmother's house for now. She left it to me when she passed a couple weeks ago."

"It sounds like you've had a pretty awful month." Callum grinned suddenly. "Good thing you get to buy me dinner."

"I don't know what I'd do without this opportunity," Ella said, pretending to dab at her eyes. Light-hearted. That's what she needed.

After ordering their food, Ella sipped her Italian soda. Callum watched her, a small smile hovering about his face.

"What?"

"I think I expected you to get wine or a mixed drink of some kind."

"Oh, I didn't tell you? My friend Jace is supposed to get me drunk later. I think she expected you to come, but —"

"Jace. Is this the person who was always setting you up?"

"The very one."

"I don't think I can possibly refuse the chance to get drunk with someone like that." Callum lifted his water glass and toasted. Ella clinked her Italian soda against the water goblet.

Through the meal, Callum told Ella about his family, being the only child, and how his mother reacted when he started learning about Shakespeare and how in all the old plays, men played all the roles.

"She found me dressed as Juliet once when I was eleven. At the time, I just thought her eyes were going to pop out of her head and roll around on the floor like marbles. Looking back though, I know she was trying extremely hard to be tolerant and understanding."

"What did she say?"

"I don't even remember. All I remember is her face, which looked like something was about to erupt out of it."

"Ever play a female role?"

"I actually did play the nurse in Romeo and Juliet in high school."

"Brave."

"I was the star point-guard on the basketball team. I think everyone was too confused to do anything but laugh at me. They got over it in a week. Most of my other acting friends had it a lot worse." A cloud passed over his face, but it vanished after a moment. Callum tapped his fork against the table. "What about you, Dr. Keyes? What were your high school days like?"

"Alternately very quiet and very loud. I spent a lot of time in the library reading anything about mythology I could get my hands on, and when I wasn't there I was breaking my eardrums listening to metal with my brother."

"You have a brother?"

Ella fought the urge to curse under her breath. There were moments when she forgot Stuart was gone, moments he was just across town or up in Toronto. Moments where she thought of him as she had three years ago: an ever-present fixture in her world, like the ground itself or the sun in the sky. Her fingers reached for her lock of blue hair, and she twirled it around her knuckle.

"Ella?"

She looked across the table at Callum and pushed her lips into a smile. "I'm sorry. Yes, I have a brother. Had. I had a brother. My twin brother Stuart. He passed away three years ago."

It was a strange sort of thing, mentioning dead people in front of new acquaintances. There was a moment, a short moment, where you could catch pity on their faces. Ella thought if she'd had a net, she would have an entire box full at home. And then came the confusion, followed by discomfort. That was when the walls went up, because no one liked to think about death. No one wanted to hear, not really, that someone had vanished decades before anyone could pat your shoulder and tell you it was just their time. No one ever really knew what to say at all, and Ella never knew what the right thing to say really was. Or if she'd even recognize the right thing if it came out of someone's mouth. She looked at Callum, nerves grating in her core.

The pity was there and then gone, but his face remained calm, open. "It must be awful to have to tell people that after first meeting them."

Ella's hand gave a little jump, and she waited for Callum to continue.

"On one hand, you want to remember your brother. You want to be able to talk about him the way other people talk about their siblings, but it always just reminds you that he's gone, doesn't it?"

Ella nodded, disentangling her finger from her hair and placing both hands in her lap. "If I don't mention it, someone inevitably asks what my brother does now, or where he lives, or if he still messes with me."

"It's a lose-lose for you. I'm sorry." Callum's gray eyes watched her from across the table. "I'd love to hear about him if you want to tell me."

Who was this guy? Ella fiddled with the hem on her linen napkin on her lap. Why not? She thought.

"Well," she began, "from the time he was fifteen, he always had blue hair."

chapter
fourteen

Ella couldn't remember the last time she'd talked about Stuart so much. Even with Jace, she avoided the subject. Jace had known Stuart for several years. She knew all about him. And grief was a fickle thing; after the first few months of losing a loved one, no one wanted to hear about it anymore. They wanted you to hush, to move on, to live your life like they lived theirs and not remind them that lives could end at any moment.

She told Callum about Stuart's hair and how they accidentally dyed their ancient cat when they were seventeen. The cat had a smurf-blue spot the size of a walnut that faded to green but remained for the rest of her life. She told him about introducing Stuart to heavy metal and how neither of them ever listened to anything but that and The Beatles. How Stuart used to sing "Come Together" at the top of his voice when he was drunk. She talked so much that her seafood linguini grew cold on her plate, half-eaten, and the ice in her Italian soda diluted the cream to a watery, tasteless substance.

And through it all, Callum listened. He asked the right questions, laughed at the right moments, and when Ella finally had to pause to wet her parched throat with now-iceless water, she leaned forward with her elbows on the table and met Callum's gaze.

"Thank you," she said.

"He sounds like the best brother anyone could have. I wish I'd gotten to meet him."

A lump pushed at Ella's throat. She wasn't going to cry on a first date. She wasn't. She took another drink of water that refused to wash away the lump. In spite of her best efforts, her voice still cracked when she said, "I do too. He would have liked you."

Every so often, Ella felt that if she just turned quickly enough, she'd catch Stuart sitting there with a smirk on his face, shaking his head at her, ready to reach out and cuff her on the shoulder. She looked to the right, but all she saw was a portly diner sawing into his lamb chop and whispers of unseen ghosts.

When their server brought the check, Callum's long fingers snatched it off the table before Ella dug her wallet from her purse.

"Wait," she said. "I'm supposed to be treating you."

"Oh, that was just a ruse to make sure you came."

Ella reached for it, but Callum snatched it back out of her grasp.

"No, no, no. If you want, you can get the next one. This one's all me. You just lost your job and your place. Fair's fair. Or you can buy me a shot when your friend starts grilling me."

"She might not grill you." Who was Ella kidding? Of course Jace would grill him. "Never mind. She'll grill you."

"Then buy me a shot to loosen my tongue."

Ella frowned, but tucked her wallet away again. "I get the next dinner."

"That's fine."

They met Jace and Alexa at Fado, and Alexa immediately bustled Callum off to the bar to fetch drinks with her.

Ella hugged Jace. "Go easy on him," she said into Jace's ear.

"Not a chance."

Pulling back from the hug, Ella straightened her shoulders. "Seriously. He's nice. Don't...scare him off."

The words sounded ridiculous the moment the air hit them. If going on about her dead brother for forty minutes hadn't scared him off, Ella hardly thought a mischievous lesbian would succeed where Ella had failed. Jace looked at Ella, her eyes dark and accentuated by gold liner that made her look like she belonged on the cover of Vogue. Her short, asymmetrical bob gleamed in the dim lighting of the pub, and Jace pushed it back from her face, expression curious.

Callum and Alexa returned, both with drinks in each hand. Callum turned to Jace.

"I hear I owe you a thank you."

"Ooh, for what?" Jace took her beer from Alexa, making twinkle-fingers with her free hand.

"For giving Ella bad directions to the coffee shop where she was supposed to meet your friend."

"I gave perfectly good directions," Jace said, but a smile teased her mouth. "I just might have forgotten the name of the place."

"Either way. Best interrupted crossword puzzle of my life."

Ella went to take a drink from her beer, but Jace snatched it from her hand.

"Nope, nope. You'll be sick if you drink that first."

"First?"

"I promised Alexa drunk Ella. And you know what that means." Jace mimicked lighting a fuse and dropped her fist on Ella's shoulder, making a sound like wheeeeeeeeee-PSSSSHHH.

"What was that?" Callum asked.

Ella sat down. "She's off to get Jäger bombs."

at some point in the evening, between shot rounds four and six, Ella's phone rang.

She pulled it out of her pocket and held it at arm's length, squinting at the unfamiliar number.

"Hello." The word didn't come out right, and Ella giggled. Jace was trying to teach Callum the Electric Slide while the guitar player in the Irish rock band tuned his instrument and looked on.

"Ella? This is Andrea Harper. I'm sorry to call after normal business hours, but I thought you might want to know. I spoke to the folks at Publisher's Clearing House, and they agreed that you are legally entitled to your grandmother's winnings since she was drawn for the contest and notified before her death."

Ella blinked, trying to clear the liquor-fog from her head. "I get it? What about Auntie Eunice?" It came out more like whabout Aunteeyoonis? Ella thought she should remember to feel embarrassed about that in the morning.

"Is this a good time to talk?" Andrea Harper's voice sounded half-amused, half-exasperated.

"No, not really." Ella leaned sideways in her chair. Her head landed on Alexa's shoulder. "My friend keeps buying me shots."

"How about I call you back tomorrow?"

"Mm-hmm. 'Morrow."

Ella hung up the phone and jammed her nose against Alexa's sleeve.

"Who was that?" Alexa asked, pushing Ella upright again.

"Grammy's lawyer." Ella frowned, picked up a half-full shot glass and downed it, then snorted into the empty. "Think I just won a hundred thousand dollars."

"Oh."

Some time later, Ella helped shove Jace and Alexa into a taxi. She waved at them, then promptly turned around and ran into Callum's chest.

"Easy there."

Ella pried her nose off the zipper of his jacket and backed up a step. "Jace always does this to me. I shouldn't let her get me drunk. Gonna feel like hell in the morning."

"That makes two of us." Callum waved.

Confused, Ella waved back, then felt rather silly when a second taxi pulled up to the curb.

"You can take this one." Callum opened the car door. "I had a lot of fun tonight, Ella. I'll call you tomorrow."

"Me too," Ella said, not sure of which sentence she was agreeing with. The world tilted when she looked at it. Callum was at a sixty-degree angle to the ground. Seventy. Eighty-five. Back to ninety, like he ought to be.

She felt his arms around her and pressed her face into his shoulder. She hadn't realized he was quite that tall. Hugging him made the world tilt just a bit less, and she wanted to stay there. Ella looked up at him. This was a bit embarrassing for a first date. She shouldn't have let Jace get her this sloppy.

Instead of looking annoyed, Callum met her gaze. "You're a cute drunk."

Ella didn't know what to say to that. Now that she was gazing upward, his lips were awfully close to hers.

As soon as she noticed it, they got farther away. Seventy-degree angle again. Ella winced and pulled back. "I had a good time too," she said before realizing they'd already gone over that.

Callum shut the door of the taxi and waved through the window. When had she gotten in the car? She gave the driver her address and sat back against the seat. Wait. She'd given him the loft address.

"Wrong address," she said. "I just moved."

The taxi driver grunted his acknowledgment.

Ella looked back once, but Callum was already gone.

Ella woke the next morning to her phone ringing against her head and Poof's paw batting at it.

Neither sensation helped the throbbing going on inside her skull.

"Hello?" Ella pressed the cool plastic against her cheek. If the room would stop spinning, it would help her situation immensely.

"Ella, this is Andrea Harper again. Is this a better time to talk?"

Her cheeks warmed as the memory of her drunken phone call the night before surfaced, bringing with it a surge of bile from her stomach. "Yes, this is fine," Ella said, willing it to be true and telling her stomach to simmer down. "Sorry about last night. Hard couple weeks."

"It's quite all right. After speaking with those in charge at Publishers Clearing House, we've decided that you are to be the recipient of the prize. They apparently contacted your grandmother before her death, so the money was legally hers. Because she passed away before it could be disbursed, it goes to her next of kin."

Ella closed her eyes, which helped slow the sensation of movement. "Shouldn't that be Auntie Eunice?"

"I believe Eunice's exact words were, 'What's an old fart like me going to do with that kind of money?'"

Old fart indeed.

Guilt filled Ella's stomach at the thought of Eunice saying that, knowing it would be Ella who got the cash. She really needed to be nicer to Auntie Eunice. Maybe they could come to some sort of arrangement.

The room still spun in spite of Ella's refusal to look at it, and she cracked her eyes open again. "So it's mine."

"So it's yours."

"A hundred thousand dollars."

"Minus taxes."

"Of course."

"The final sum will be —" a rustle of papers sounded through the phone, "—about seventy-one thousand dollars."

That didn't settle Ella's stomach.

She hung up the phone. Her stomach felt like it was turning somersaults in her gut, but her head felt clear for the first time in a week. Seventy-one thousand dollars.

Ignoring the fact that she had a similar amount of funds tucked away in savings and investment accounts, Ella thought for the first time about what it would mean to have the money.

She stared up at a still-unfamiliar ceiling, allowing Poof to bat at her earlobe.

Maybe this was just what she needed. It wasn't the prestige of a Fulbright professorship, but she also wouldn't have to wait through months of uncertainty. She could just go.

Ella knew what she wanted to do.

She got out of bed and went downstairs, digging around for her laptop.

Booting it up, she opened a browser window.

The cursor blinked in the search field. Ella thought for a moment, the towers of boxes lurking in her peripheral vision. Did she really want to do this?

She opened up a travel site in a new tab and clicked back to the search bar.

Buffalo pet sitters, she typed in.

chapter
fifteen

two months later

everything was bigger.

Ella stood at the baggage carousel, waiting for her bag to appear on the slide. After two months in Eastern Europe, she wasn't prepared for a return to the supersized America she'd left. She hadn't thought that would be her first impression upon returning. She'd thought it would be the smell of the air or the sound of her native language instead of Moldovan, Russian, Polish, or Ukrainian. Maybe even an overabundance of junk food.

Ella had never felt chubby in her life, but exploring mythology in Eastern Europe had made her wonder about her weight for the first time. All the walking had made her pants fit looser and her bra fasten on the tightest hooks.

She'd shrunk and everything around her seemed bigger. The airports were so much larger. The cars. The luggage.

She turned on her phone as the bags clunked onto the conveyor belt. Five new text messages.

From Jace: **Welcome back!**

And then: **Poof thinks you deserted him forever. Prince didn't seem to notice.**

Then: **We're at the cell phone waiting area. Let us know when you get your bags!**

Ella shook her head.

Her heart did a flop in her chest when she saw the next message.

From Callum: **Welcome home, cute drunk. Call me when you're in?**

She didn't expect him to understand why she'd up and planned a long trip right after their first date. That would be too much to hope for. But he seemed to be okay with it.

The time she'd passed in hectic planning had left little chance for them to see each other, what with him up in Stratford for rehearsals, even though they'd kept in touch.

Ella hadn't had the guts to kiss him when they met for coffee the day her plane left for Odessa. Instead she'd given him an awkward handshake and a hug that left the scent of his aftershave clinging to her blouse for the entire journey.

She'd emailed him the occasional picture of onion-topped palaces from Moscow and tiled mosaics in Lviv, but there hadn't been any indication that he was still romantically attached, even though the email thread between them had reached something like seventy messages since she left. Nothing heavy, just her observations and his responses. Friendly banter.

Oh, well, Ella thought. At least he was a new friend.

She brought herself back to the moment just as her bag disappeared around the bend in the conveyor belt. Sending a quick text to Jace, she hurried over to chase it.

Jace met her seven minutes later with an attack hug that almost sent her flying into an elderly woman's baggage cart.

"Sorry," Ella gasped at the woman, who ignored the apology and trundled off, muttering about young people and airport parking fees.

"I am so glad you're back. You look good. Too skinny, though. I thought the food over there was supposed to be hearty. Doesn't eating sausage for six months make you gain weight?"

"I walked a lot." That was an understatement. According to the pedometer she'd bought before leaving, she'd averaged around twenty thousand steps per day.

"Girl, you walked your ass off, apparently." Alexa circled around to hug her. "No, seriously. Your ass is gone."

Jace raised an eyebrow, and Alexa shrugged.

"Don't tell me you didn't notice," Alexa said.

"I wasn't going to say anything about it." Jace gave Ella a wicked grin and tossed the first suitcase into the trunk of the car. "So, what'd you bring me?"

Ella feigned confusion, blinking wide eyes. "You wanted presents?"

Jace fell against the car, the back of her hand over her eyes. "You've destroyed all my hope."

"Over actor," Alexa muttered. She winked at Ella and got in the car.

"You're going out with us this weekend, right?" Jace climbed into the back seat and leaned forward over the console.

"Sure. As long as you don't shove my lips on anyone else's this time."

"Bring Callum, and I'll shove your lips wherever you want."

Ella chose to ignore that. "I think he probably has shows this weekend."

Did she want Callum to come? It had been six months since she saw him. Ella wasn't sure what she wanted. The landscape outside the car was the same as it had been all the other times Ella had returned from far-flung countries around the world. The landmarks were the same. Why did Ella feel different? The car felt strange, more foreign than had Cracow or Moscow or Kiev. Ella tucked her hand through the handle in the armrest and watched Buffalo appear through the window.

Home.

for a terrifying instant before Ella opened the door to Grammy's — her! — house, Ella had the horrible feeling she'd discover Poof, curled up and emaciated on the rug.

Something about her footsteps on the porch must have rung familiar for her little cream-colored kitty, because he raised a cacophony of mewling cries as soon as her feet hit the wooden steps.

"Poof, I'm back!"

"I checked in on him a couple times a week while you were gone."

Ella hefted her suitcase and jiggled her key in the lock, turning sideways to look at Jace. "You didn't have to do that."

"I have kitty envy. We played laser pointer and went fishing, and Prince was very jealous. I didn't want them to get lonely."

The still-unpacked piles of boxes dropped lead into Ella's stomach as she opened the front door to her house. Poof wound himself around her ankles, purring like a lawnmower. Ella dropped her suitcase and scooped him up, nestling her face into his soft fur.

"You little mongrel. I missed you." She picked up a note from the pet sitter from the coffee table and skimmed it. There was a Polaroid of the blonde girl with Poof, her hair in waves and her hipster glasses the size of baseballs. Poof's eyes were bright and his whisker in the picture was caught under the sitter's finger, making him sneer like Elvis, if Elvis were a dopey, fluffy cat.

A rumbling in the driveway made Ella peek out the window. Jace's car — with Alexa behind the wheel — turned out onto the road and vanished.

"What's going on? Where's Alexa going?"

"Alexa is going home. I'm staying here with you tonight. I missed you, Ella. You have to tell me all about your trip, and I have to concoct a way to get Poof away from you."

"Not likely," Ella said. "The Poof thing, I mean. I'm glad you're here."

Ella surveyed her friend, who looked around at the piles of boxes. Jace's hair had gotten longer, reaching down to her collarbones now, though it still angled up sharply and went pixie in the back. There was a line between Jace's eyebrows that Ella didn't remember being there before, and her face had a pinched-look that Ella knew was new.

"You look unhappy," said Ella.

"We don't need to talk about that."

"Are you and Alexa okay?"

"Yes. I mean, no. But she and I are fine. It's...other stuff."

Poof scrambled from Ella's arms and jumped up on top of a box. Ella didn't quite know what to do with herself. She could go shower or change — both of which sounded appealing — but she couldn't muster the motivation. Instead, she stepped over her suitcase and sat on the couch, patting the cushion beside her.

"What's wrong?" she asked Jace.

"You just got back. It's nothing that can't wait till tomorrow."

"Look around, Jace," said Ella. "My life's still a pile of boxes. I have no job and I was enough of a jerk to leave my cat and frog in a stranger's care for almost two months because I was such a mess."

"Are you less of a mess now?"

Ella blinked, chewing on the inside of her cheek. "Well, no," she said finally. "I'm still a mess. But that doesn't mean I can't be a good friend and listen to whatever's making you look so down."

"Alexa wants me to move in with her."

The yearning in Jace's voice was clear enough, and Ella felt a burst of warmth. "But that's wonderful news."

"I mean, she really, really wants me to move in with her. She's been asking me every six months for the last two and a half years."

Ella pressed her tongue against the inside of her teeth. She hadn't known that. She'd thought they were happily independent. Maybe she'd been wrong. "And you don't want to?"

Jace's brown eyes filled, and she looked away. "I want to move in with her more than I've ever wanted anything in the world."

"Then why don't you?" Ella already knew the answer, but she had to ask.

"It's my parents. I've kept this from them for so long. I won't be able to give them a reason they'll believe for moving in with Alexa. We both have stable jobs and savings. We don't need the financial help of a roommate."

"You're still convinced you'd have to justify it to them?"

Jace put her hand in the air, then let it fall to her lap. "They talked a member of their congregation into sending his daughter to one of those gay deprogramming camps. They gave an annual donation to Exodus International until it shut down, that ex-gay ministry. They thought the ministry had fallen to Satan when it closed and apologized to the queer folk it had hurt. What do you think?"

Ella thought it was horrid for any child to fear losing their parents' love. Even though hers were on the opposite side of the planet, Ella never doubted their love for her when she'd come out to them, or their acceptance — at least she hadn't when they used to return her calls. Ella squashed that thought. That was just a side effect of them living on the opposite side of the planet. She couldn't empathize with Jace, but she could understand.

"I think you need to do whatever makes you feel safe. If that means staying in your own apartment and postponing moving in with Alexa until you feel safe doing it, then do what you have to do. I've got your back whichever you choose."

The smile that twisted Jace's lips wavered almost before it began. She pressed her lips together as though she'd tasted something bitter.

"I love her, Ella," Jace said after a beat. "Shouldn't that be enough to pull me out of the closet? We have the right to marry now, nationwide. Isn't love supposed to be enough?"

That was one question Ella couldn't answer.

bills. grocery store ads. The mail never contained anything useful anymore.

Ella paused in the doorway, one foot propping open the front door of the house as she flipped through the stack of junk. Something brushed up against her pant leg.

"Poof!" She dropped the mail inside the door and ran after him. "Damn it, cat! Where do you think you're going?"

Poof wasn't an outdoor kitty. He wasn't even a brave indoor kitty. Ella thought she'd seen the basement mouse chasing Poof across the floor as she searched for the jewelry box downstairs the night before with Jace. Poof darted under the Subaru.

"Come on, Poof," Ella said, bending down to one knee in the gravel of the driveway. "Come on out. Kitty-kitty-kitty, come on, Poof."

She continued calling him for several minutes, but he didn't come out. Ella bent over farther to look under the car. No Poof.

The gravel was damp under her knee, soaking through the denim of her jeans. Ella looked around the Subaru. How was she supposed to find a cream-colored cat in that? The house was surrounded by fields of waist-high grass still dormant with late winter. She glanced over her shoulder three times as she made her way back to the house. Maybe he'd come back for dinner.

Ella forced herself not to look at the road or think of the neighbor's teenagers who drove on it twenty miles an hour over the speed limit.

"What took you so long?" Jace asked when Ella came back inside.

"Poof ran out."

"He did?" Jace stood, peering out the window. "You couldn't find him?"

Ella shook her head.

"I'm sure he'll be fine."

It wasn't much reassurance.

It had been a chilly March so far, and the temperature outside was colder than Poof was used to. Barely rising to thirty degrees during the day, today was a dreary 28. Ella tried to repress the worry that rose in her stomach. "I'll try to call him again in a little bit."

Jace nodded. "I'll help when you go back out." She looked upward. "Have you been up in the hall at all since you came back?"

"I've been with you the whole time."

"After everything that happened right before you left, I can't help wondering if you thought it was because of the keys. Your job, your apartment, the pipes in the basement, the prize money."

Ella shrugged, then shifted her shoulders. She didn't want to think about that any more than she wanted to think about the neighbors turning up at her door with a lump of cream-colored fur in their hands and sorrow on their faces.

"Come on," Jace said, tugging at Ella's hand. "Up."

Ella let Jace drag her up to the third floor corridor. "What is it you want me to do?"

"I want to know if you really think there's something more to this hallway than just a bunch of shaped metal and walls."

That was the question, wasn't it? Ella curled her toes inside her slippers. "I don't know."

"Why don't you know?"

"Correlation, causation, all that stuff. It could just be a bunch of coincidences."

Jace pointed to a small skeleton key. "Let's see, shall we? Take it."

"Why don't you?"

"Because it's your house and your magical whatchamahoosit of a hallway."

"We don't know that."

"Then prove me wrong."

Ella frowned at the key Jace pointed to. What if she touched it and fell through the floor? But that was ridiculous. The keys hadn't caused the burst pipes any more than they'd caused her eviction. Both of those things had precedents set in motion months before she touched any keys. That meant it couldn't be real. Right?

She reached out and pulled the key from the wall. Ella held it in front of Jace's face for a three count, then replaced it, waiting.

The silence that greeted her ears was a relief.

Jace looked only disappointed.

Ella made her way back down the stairs, listening to the trudge of Jace's footsteps behind her. But when she reached the ground level, a different sound met her ears.

Scritch - scritch - scritch. Scritch - scritch - scritch - scritch - scritch.

The sound grew more insistent. The front door. Ella opened the door, and Poof breezed past her, tail high in the air.

He had something white in his mouth.

"Oh, my god." Jace fell to her knees. "He's got —"

"A kitten." Ella bent down to the floor. Sure enough, Poof had a white ball of fluff in his jaw. He placed the kitten on the rug and began licking it.

The kitten couldn't have been more than a few weeks old. Its eyes were open and clear, but its tiny body trembled, trembled, trembled.

"It must be freezing." Ella hated calling the kitten an it. She scooped it up from the floor and cuddled it to her chest. "Where's your mama cat, kitty?"

The kitten, of course, did not answer.

"I'll go warm up some milk. Maybe we can get it to drink something."

Ella nodded, distracted by the fluttering of the small paws against her hand. She walked into the living room and draped a chenile throw over the warm, exposed pipe by Prince's terrarium. Prince himself paid her no mind. After a minute, she pulled the now-toasty blanket from the pipe and sat down on the couch, laying it in her lap. She placed the kitten in the middle and formed the blanket around it.

The burbly purr that started then made her jump. It was a tiny sound from a tiny kitten. Ella tucked one edge of the blanket over the kitten's body and rubbed her hand over the top. Poof's weight dented the couch cushion as he jumped up next to her, his motor overshadowing the small bumble of the baby in the blanket.

Poof nudged at Ella's elbow as if to ask, "Did I do good?"

"You did good, Poof. You did good," Ella murmured, scratching behind Poof's ears with her free hand.

chapter
sixteen

Ella decided to call the new kitten Puff, in spite of Jace's eye-rolling. Puff was exactly what the kitten was: a tiny, white puff of fur. The kitten's eyes were still the sapphire blue of a newborn, and when Ella and Jace took it to the vet, the nurses all cooed and told them the kitten was probably only four weeks old.

And Puff was a female. Ella made sure she got all her shots, and Puff slept sandwiched between Ella and Poof every night thereafter. Ella liked to watch her try and climb the stairs. Her still-stubby tail stuck straight out as she scrambled up, and little needles of claws scrabbled on the grains of the wood. Poof acted like Puff's wet nurse, curling up around her to keep her warm and retrieving her in his mouth when she got too far away. Ella fed her wet food and within a couple days, Puff's emaciated ribs vanished under a healthy layer of kitten fat. She purred and pounced easily, going after Poof's tail enough that Ella wondered if Poof would eventually regret rescuing the little ball of white fluff.

Two months after Puff was dropped on the rug and into Ella's life, Jace came over for her weekly playdate with the growing kitten and sat with a little smirk dancing across her lips.

"You know this was the key, right?"

Ella paused, a feather dangling from a string in front of Puff's eyes, which never wavered from the quivering toy. "We don't know that."

Neither of them had brought up the keys since that day. Ella had settled into an easy friendship with Callum, and spring had given way to June's budding warmth.

Jace raised an eyebrow and quirked her lip as if to say, *I don't believe you.* "So for Pride this weekend. Are you going to crash at my place?"

It was all Jace had talked about all week — aside from assessing the continued cuteness of Puff — and Ella couldn't help but wonder if Jace threw herself into Pride so much because she felt ashamed about hiding her sexuality from her parents.

"I'll probably come home. I don't want to leave the kitties alone too much." Puff jumped paws-first at the feather, landing clumsily and tumbling off to the side, feather eluding her tiny claws. Ella grinned.

"Taxis aren't going to be cheap, you know."

"I know how not cheap they are," Ella said, tugging the feather along the floor. Puff scurried after it, wriggling along the rug with her belly almost to the floor.

"I wouldn't be able to stay away from her either. Poof jealous yet?"

"Not that I can see." Poof sat on top of a cardboard box, keeping a watchful eye on the little white ball of fluff rolling around the floor. Ella thought back to the week she'd arrived home and Jace's own problems. "Have you and Alexa talked any more about you moving in with her?"

"I told her I'd have to think about it more."

"How'd she take it?"

"Not well."

Ella waited, but Jace didn't elaborate. After a few moments, Ella handed Jace the toy. "I'm going to keep unpacking stuff."

She was slowly chipping away at the piles of boxes. Ella couldn't bring herself to throw away Grammy's things, so the rooms she finished unpacking began to meld the two sets of possessions together. Other than her many books and trinkets, Grammy Helen hadn't kept much clutter. Some things, like old electric bills dating back to the 1970s, Ella cleaned out and threw away. Other things she kept, like all the tchotchkes from Grammy's travels. To those she added her own, giving each shelf a bit of Ella to go with Helen.

This box was all old photos. Ella looked around the living room, shaking her head at kitten pounces. There was a section of bookshelf that would do well for the albums. Ella picked one out at random and opened it.

It was from their family trip to Greece when she and Stuart had been fourteen. His hair wasn't blue yet. And there they were, standing in front of turquoise water, an ancient crumbling temple behind them.

Sandwiched between the pictures, under the center rings, a rock sat nestled in the crevasse that divided the tagboard pages. Ella pulled it out. Red sandstone. Deep red, the kind that left rusty dust behind when you smashed it and turned the color of blood when it got wet. Ella remembered that, remembered always hunting this kind of rock with Stuart. Once they were done smashing them, they always mixed water into the dust and painted each other's sun-browned faces with red whorls across their cheekbones. Ella clasped the rock against her palm and shut the album.

Puff caught the feather.

there hadn't been any sign of Auntie Eunice since Ella returned from Eastern Europe, so when the doorbell rang the next day, Ella assumed it had to be the old lady, back to pout about her extended absence and to wreck the house Ella had painstakingly gotten in meticulous order. Perspiration beaded on her forehead. After the cold snap the previous month, spring had returned with a gust of blooming flowers and soaring temperatures.

She opened the door and took a step back as much from the hot air that poured into the house as from who was on the other side.

It wasn't Auntie Eunice.

Easton Gellerman stood on the doorstep.

Ella cleared her throat and shifted her weight, drumming her fingers against the open door. "Easton. What are you doing here?"

His acne had mostly cleared up. He looked smart in brown trousers and a linen button down shirt, and Ella stepped aside.

"Come in, if you want. Watch out for the kitten."

Puff sat by the door, looking out but making no move to bolt through it. Poof licked his paw a few feet away, one eye always on his tiny charge.

Easton nodded. "I'm sorry to barge in on you." He stepped through the door, looking down at the little ball of white that was Puff. "New kitten?"

"Poof found her outside and brought her in. I decided she'd be better off staying in."

"She's cute."

"She is that." Ella motioned to the living room. "Have a seat. Do you want anything to drink? I think I have water. And water."

"Water sounds good."

In the kitchen, Ella paused with one hand on the filter pitcher. What was Easton doing there? She poured the glass of water. Condensation gathered on the outside immediately — she'd have to start turning on the air conditioning soon if this kept up.

Ella handed Easton the glass of water and sat down across from him on an ottoman. "So what brings you to my living room?"

"I needed to apologize to you."

Shifting her weight on the ottoman, Ella crossed her right leg over her left. She folded her hands on top of her knee, then looked up to meet Easton's gaze. "What happened wasn't your fault."

"I feel awful about it. When I heard you'd left the country, I wanted to email you. There were about five thousand times this semester when I wanted to call you to ask you a question, and I just couldn't bring myself to pick up the phone. I had about three email drafts saved for four months." Easton scrubbed at his hair with his hand and took a big gulp of his water. The pale skin of his neck bore red splotches in a U shape around his collarbone.

"It's not your fault, Easton," Ella repeated, her voice as gentle as she could make it. "You didn't fire me. The dean did."

"But I took your job."

"You didn't. You filled in after they got rid of me."

Easton appeared to consider that for a few moments. "I still feel very guilty. As soon as I heard you were back, I wanted to come see you and tell you that personally."

"I appreciate the gesture, but I'm very sorry you've been feeling like this was your fault. You didn't do it."

"I'd tell you to apply to get your job back for the fall semester, but with all the budget cuts, they've let go two more professors in the past month."

"Two more? All in our department?" Funny how she still thought of it as her department. Ella's thumbnail made a miniature washboard sound on the knee of her jeans.

"Rankle and Elan both. There've been a lot of budget cuts. A lot. The university's struggling, and our department in particular lost three trustees last year."

Ella frowned. She remembered the dean mentioning that when he let her go. "Are you going to continue to work there?"

"Yeah. I've got about three classes to teach this fall." Easton brightened for a moment. "They approved my Ph.D. last week."

"That's wonderful. Congratulations." Ella gestured to the half-empty water glass. "Sorry I don't have something stronger to toast your success with. Still getting settled in."

"No, no. That's not necessary at all." Easton set the glass down on the coffee table. "I won't take up any more of your time. I just wanted to make sure you knew that I didn't mean for this to happen. Do you have another job lined up?"

"No." At his panicked look, Ella held up a hand and shushed him. "It's not a problem. Really. The house is paid for. All the property taxes are paid for the year, and all I really have to pay for is the utilities and lawn care. I have enough in savings to carry me over for quite some time."

"You always did seem to live quite simply." Easton stood. "Thank you."

"For the water?"

"For being so kind. You were always a joy to work for."

"That sounds like something you'd put on a kindergartner's report card," Ella said, smiling to show him it was a joke.

"Maybe, but it's still true." He walked toward the door. "If there's ever anything you need, please don't hesitate to let me know."

"I won't."

Ella walked Easton Gellerman to the door. When he got to the bottom of the steps, something flipped in her chest. "Easton," she said.

He turned and looked back up at her. "Yes?"

"I'd like to make a donation to the university."

"Excuse me?"

She had about sixty thousand dollars left in the bank after her trip, not including her savings and investment accounts. "I'd like to donate fifty thousand dollars to a scholarship fund in my brother's name."

"Fifty...what?"

"Call it the Stuart Keyes Scholarship. A merit-based scholarship for low income students who are past their freshman years." Stuart would appreciate that. He'd given a friend of his $500 his junior year when the friend was about to be kicked out of school for failing to pay tuition. This would mean something to him. It would.

"Dr. Keyes —"

"For god's sake, Easton. It's Ella. Just find out what I have to do, and I'll do it."

He nodded hastily, his eyes wide.

For Stuart. She could do that.

"you. me. separated by several feet and surrounded by strangers."

"What on earth are you talking about?" Ella pressed the phone to her cheek, chuckling inwardly at Callum. The past two months had been a flurry of settling in, with every attempt to reconnect with Callum turning to disaster. But still he texted her every day or so, sometimes pictures from rehearsal or Stratford, sometimes just asking about her day.

"Dress rehearsals are in full swing. I finagled a front row seat ticket for you if you want to come up to Stratford and see me covered in oil and flouncing about on stage."

"Do you really?"

"What, flounce?"

"Yes."

"Absolutely. So, will you come?"

"I'd love to. When is this spectacle?"

Ella imagined Callum on the other end, twirling a non-existent phone cord and smiling.

"Tomorrow night. It'll be a blast. Hopefully I'll do something miraculously embarrassing, like slip on a prop and get a concussion."

"Your job sounds dangerous."

"Remember you said that."

"Why?"

"Because when I'm wearing a loincloth and glitter, you might think you came on a date with someone less badass."

"Never think that loincloths and glitter negate badassery," Ella said seriously.

"I'll hold you to that statement." Callum paused. "But really, I'm glad you want to come."

"It'll be fun." Ella'd been to enough shows alone not to feel self-conscious about going by herself. Mostly. Front row, he'd said?

"I have to get back to rehearsal. I'll see you tomorrow, then."

"Until tomorrow."

"And Ella," Callum said. "I think I miss you."

friday dawned hot and muggy, almost as if summer had seen the date and come running through the sun's rays, shirt-tails still untucked and sandals dangling from one hand. Ella dabbed at the moisture on her forehead that gathered in spite of the air-conditioning and tried to summon the powers of a fashionista. This hot already, and it was only the tail end of May.

She didn't know what to wear.

It was an unusual problem for her to have. She wished she were Alexa, who picked her clothes in the morning by closing her eyes and reaching blindly into her closet. Ella hadn't felt this way in some time. Since college, maybe. High school, definitely.

She wanted to look good, and she wanted Callum to notice that she looked good.

That meant she had to find something nice to wear. Something a grade above the rank of business casual that had invaded her closet during her years as a professor. At least she hadn't gone the route of some of the archaeology profs and taught her lectures in dungarees and pocketed button downs.

Ella had very few of those.

She drew the line at going shopping. Ella hated malls. Sweaty, crowded places full of bright lights and loudness — noises and smells alike. Whenever she had to venture into one, she sought out her specific items with the singlemindedness of a squirrel with an acorn.

The hangers slid across the closet bar with a *snick-snick-snick* as Ella paged through her clothes. She went all the way through the rainbow and shoved the entire bulk of the hangers to the left with a disgusted sigh as she reached the end of her black section. Nothing there she wanted to wear. How was it possible to have so many choices and hate them all?

Part of her felt amused by the sensation. She liked Callum. He was funny and nice and definitely good-looking. He'd probably think she looked fine if she showed up in jeans and the Vitamin Water t-shirt she'd been handed on campus during an event one day.

Ella reached for a garment bag and unzipped it. Dresses. She was looking at dresses.

She shook her head at herself. Red polka dots. Cute and punk-y, but no. Three Little Black Dresses, none of which that suited her purposes. A red gown with a very low — very low — cowl in the front. Also no. Too formal.

Three dresses from the back of the bag, she saw it.

Dark blue satin. The dress was knee-length and strapless and had the delicious smoothness of fine fabric. Ella pulled the hanger out and held it up in front of herself. That would be perfect.

Dress decided, she laid it out on the bed with a pair of strappy silver sandals. She'd wear the sapphire necklace and earrings from Grammy's jewelry box. Her overnight bag gaped open like a wide frog mouth on the bed. She added a pair of pajamas and a rayon sundress to the bag, double checking that her confirmation email for the B&B still occupied the outer pocket.

Ella had thought that figuring out her attire would calm the nerves that fluttered around in her stomach like the leaves on the sycamore in the back yard when ruffled by a breeze. It hadn't. She wiped her upper lip with her hand. She'd have to turn up the air.

Or maybe it wasn't the heat making her perspire.

Ella paced around the room. After staring hard at the dress on her bed, she made her way up to the hall of keys.

It was even hotter up here, and the perspiration she'd wiped away returned in seconds. Ella didn't know what she was doing in the hallway until her fingers grasped the shaft of a shiny key and pulled it from the wall. Her heart gave a hiccup, and her hair stuck to the back of her neck. She put the key back and hurried downstairs, feeling jangled.

Her phone bleeped.

Not the tone for a text message or the three notes for an email. It sounded like a smurf squawking. Ella plucked it off her night stand and unlocked the screen.

SEVERE THUNDERSTORM WATCH.

Ella sat on the bed with a whoomph of mattress coils. The radar showed a massive thunderstorm aiming toward Buffalo and covering most of northern New York and southern Ontario. It was supposed to hit in four hours. She'd have to leave earlier if she wanted to beat the storm to Stratford.

She was in the middle of throwing lipsticks into her toiletries pouch when her phone bleeped again.

SEVERE THUNDERSTORM WARNING.

Unnerved, she looked at the radar again. The storm was now set to hit in two hours. Hurricane force winds, it said. Niagara region warned of 2-6 inches of rainfall in the next hour.

As if to prove a point, something clicked against the window of Ella's bedroom. She looked outside and immediately took a step back in alarm. Dust devils swirled in the field across from her house. The clicking came from a twig — bearing three maple leaves — pressed up against the glass by the wind. The light outside had dimmed from the bright gold of summer sun to a dingy yellow, contrasting with the eggplant purple of the bloated clouds that gathered to the west.

A zig-zag of incandescent lightning cracked the sky.

Ella counted to eight and jumped at the clap of thunder that burst through the silence like an exploding drum head.

Moments later, the sky opened, and water drenched the land.

ella poked at her phone's screen. Refresh. She scowled and poked it again. Refresh.

The torrential rain outside had yet to slake. The cats, made sleepy by the pounding of the deluge against the roof, curled up between the two pillows on Ella's bed and dozed in fluffy little balls.

No matter how many times she refreshed the weather page, the thunderstorm warning wouldn't go away. The play was now only three hours away, and she was going to have to start driving if she wanted to reach Stratford in time.

Drive over two hours in weather like this.

Water ran in thick rivulets down the driveway. The ditches on either side of the main road swelled, the surface of the water only a few inches from breaching the banks.

Ella gathered her overnight bag and garment bag. "Okay, kitties. You've got Jace coming by to feed you tonight, and I'll be home in the morning."

The cats didn't look up from their cuddles.

Ella had one hand on the doorknob when her phone bleeped again.

FLASH FLOOD WARNING.

And, right below that:

TROPICAL STORM WARNING.

As if to accentuate the point, the house lit with the buzzing flash of lightning, followed after a split second by a rumbling BOOM that lasted for a three count and clenched the inside of Ella's chest.

Her phone rang.

Dismayed, Ella looked at the screen. Callum.

"Hi, Callum," she said.

"Have you left Buffalo already?" he said without preamble.

"Just about to."

"Don't. The shows tonight have all been canceled. There are already trees down across a couple streets in Stratford, and the director canceled the dress rehearsal."

With a sigh, Ella set her bags down on the dining room table. "They canceled it?"

"Yeah, the news is cautioning people to stay indoors. I guess some of the roads are washing out."

Flash flood warning, indeed. "I can still come up to Stratford if you want."

Now, what made her say that? Ella wondered. Willingly drive in this weather?

"No, no. Don't worry about it. I'll get you a seat for another show when the weather is being more cooperative. We should be having bi-weekly dress rehearsals from here on out."

There was a moment of silence, and Ella listened to the crashing of rain against the roof. "Just let me know," she said finally.

"I will. I'm sorry it didn't work out; I was really looking forward to seeing you."

"Me too. Maybe next time." The damn key. This had to be it. Had to be. The storm had come on too quickly, minutes after the weather app on her phone had given an additional four hours before it was to start.

If Callum had waited this long, Ella supposed she could wait another week.

"Have a good night, Ella."

"You too."

Ella hung up the phone, feeling like someone had stolen her shoes before a long hike.

No more keys. No more.

chapter
seventeen

In spite of her mental declaration, Ella stomped up the stairs to the third floor corridor.

There was no such thing as magic. The dark-paneled walls contrasted with the brightness of the shiny keys and blended with those tarnished with age. Each wall was a mass of bumpy texture, little lumps of wrought metal all meant to open doors that just didn't exist. Maybe they had once, maybe each of these keys had opened something before, but now they hung from their hooks and mocked Ella where she stood. A hallway that went nowhere, just like she was going. Nowhere.

They weren't magic; they were metal. The rose, the jewelry box, the pipes bursting, everything that had happened since Grammy passed couldn't be blamed on what was certainly a family joke, just as Ella had always thought. There was no story behind them that Ella had ever heard, nothing. The place that had given her so much comfort and warmth as a reading room for her whole life suddenly felt hostile and cold. She missed Stuart. She missed her job. She missed her parents, far away in South Africa. Even after Grammy's death, they still hadn't returned her calls.

Nothing was as it should be. Nothing at all. Jace couldn't move in with her lover because of her parents. Five years they'd been together. Five loving, happy, joyous, raucous, crazy years. If Jace was Ella's best friend, Alexa was almost a sister-in-law. And their lives, their happiness — all of it was put on hold because of prejudice and intolerance. The thought made Ella's hands quake with anger.

She grabbed as many keys in each hand as she could hold and threw them to the floor. There was no way these bits of old metal had power over her life. She controlled her path. Her choices. Not the whimsy of inanimate objects.

The keys clattered to the floor and slid across the wood. The heat misted her forehead and upper lip with sweat, and her skin hummed and tingled with the electricity from the storm.

Ella sat down hard, landing on a key and not bothering to remove it from under her rear.

Her breathing came fast, and she tried to slow it. This — all of it — was too absurd.

She couldn't be there anymore. Not in a house that wasn't really hers. Not in a life she hadn't chosen. Everything she'd worked so hard for had been jerked from her grasp. Her job, her home.

Her brother.

She couldn't force the dean to return her job, and there was no way she'd convince Mr. Stevens to give her the loft back. Both of those things were gone for good.

There was one thing she could change.

Downstairs, Ella rummaged around her grandpa's study and pulled a thick Yellow Pages directory from the bottom drawer of his desk.

She flipped to the Rs.

Real Estate.

She made a list of every company in the area. Then she got out her phone and dialed the first number.

Before she could hit the green call button, her phone buzzed in her hand. An email from her accountant.

"No," Ella said out loud. The little push notification didn't vanish. She opened the email.

> *Dear Dr. Keyes,*
>
> *I'm writing to alert you to the fact that certain stocks in which you have invested have declined rapidly in value over the past few days. Until further notice, all funds in your portfolio will be frozen until the market stabilizes. I apologize for the inconvenience and will keep you abreast of any further developments.*

Ella's stomach twisted. Her right hand rested on the open Yellow Pages, and her fingers clenched together, rumpling the thin paper.

This couldn't be happening. Ella went to her laptop and opened her bank account page. She had the remaining money from her winnings, but she'd already pledged a fifty thousand dollar donation to the university. She couldn't back out of it now. That left — Ella did some quick calculations — just over six thousand dollars.

There was a flash, accompanied by a cracking sound. A moment later, a crash.

Ella rushed to the kitchen window, but couldn't see anything. She flung open the side door and pushed it open against the wind. Sheets of rain pummeled her face, and her eyes searched through the falling water for the source of the sound.

She found it. Half of the sycamore had fallen, crunching through the back corner of the garage. One branch swayed in the wind, only a couple of feet from a power line.

Ella stood in the rain, water dripping down her face.

even though the house was four times the size of her former loft, Ella felt like the walls grew closer together with every passing second.

Ella pushed her list of real estate agents aside and dialed the electric company. After eighteen minutes on hold, she spoke to a frazzled operator about the fallen half of the tree and explained that it was near the power line to the house.

Another boom of thunder rocked the house, and the room plunged into darkness.

"And my power just went out," she said lamely to the operator.

"We'll work to restore everything as soon as possible. Keep an eye on our website for updates. You can also find a number for tree removal on the website."

Ella'd rented ever since moving out of her parents' house. "Is that something the electric company takes care of or —"

"No, ma'am. Tree removal is at the expense of the property owner."

"My power's out. I don't have the internet. Do you have the number handy?"

"I'm sorry, but no."

Ella hung up the phone.

Her chest constricted, and her hand went to the blue lock in her hair. She braided it, then unbraided it. She did it twice more before sitting back and opening the browser on her phone. The loading bar never budged past twenty-five percent.

Tree removal would have to wait, it seemed.

Still drenched from the rain outside and now sweating in the heat with the air conditioning off, Ella stripped off her soaking t-shirt and jeans and traded them for a pair of cotton shorts and a tank. She curled up on her bed next to the cats, who were as oblivious to her impending financial doom as they were to Ella's shattered date plans.

When her phone rang, it startled both cats into making a *prrow?* in unison.

"Hello?" Ella answered without looking at the number.

"Ella. It's Aunt Eunice."

Not now. Ella couldn't deal with Aunt Eunice right now. Part of her mind piped up in an acerbic tone that she'd ignored her great aunt for six months when she left the country, and broken her word that the old lady could continue to look through her deceased sister's things. Ella ignored it.

"If you're wanting to come over, the power's out over here, and it's too dark to see anything properly."

"Child, have you looked outside? It's snowing like crazy."

Confused, Ella's gaze darted to the window. Still just late spring rain, and lots of it. Eunice and her word choice again. "Yes, Auntie. I know."

"Well, then you should know I'm not going anywhere till this lets up. But I wanted to find out if I could come over this week."

Ella felt very tired. No "welcome back," no "how was your trip?" Just more demands to ransack the house she lived in. "Sure. Whatever."

"Don't be sullen, boy. It's unbecoming."

Ella didn't much care what was becoming at the moment. "Come whenever you want. I'm not going anywhere."

"Fine. I'll be there in a couple days. Make sure you're ready for me."

"Whatever you want to find, you better find it quickly," Ella said. "I'm putting the house on the market as soon as I get the garage fixed."

"What? You can't do that. What happened to the garage?"

"A tree fell on it an hour ago."

"You can't sell Helen's house."

The tone in the old lady's voice lost it's edge. If Ella had expected the statement to sound angry and sharp, she instead got a flabby statement of disbelief.

"I can't live like this, Auntie Eunice. I don't belong here."

"No one belongs anywhere. You make do with what you have. Don't you dare put that house on the market." The edge was back, honed and bright. "I'll be there in two days."

A click told Ella that her great aunt had hung up.

if ella hadn't known about the half a tree pushing into the garage when she woke the next morning, she would have thought she dreamed the entire previous day.

Pride Day opened its eyes as if it had a head to pop off its pillow. Bright golden sunlight flooded the house, and sometime during the night, the electricity had come back. Ella's skin felt like it had been stretched tight with drying sweat, and her sheets were still damp, cooled by the chilled air from the vents.

She dressed quickly in a green shirt and blue shorts and dug a pair of leather sandals from the depths of her closet. If she was going to be surrounded by people and on her feet all day, she had to be comfortable.

The air outside was blessedly cooler than it had been before the storm. The fresh scent of wet earth suffused the warm breeze with life. Today the grass seemed just a little brighter.

Ella didn't want the world to be brighter. Part of her mind balled up like a dark sore born from frustration and hurt, and she tried to keep it boxed away in a corner. She supposed if she was in a grumpy mood and opposed to brightness, going to a Pride Parade full of rainbow flags and glitter wasn't really the best option. Or maybe it was just what she needed. To support Jace and Alexa and herself, to be around people who got it.

She met Alexa and Jace at a diner outside of the downtown rush and parked her car in a long term garage.

"I ordered you waffles," Jace said. "I want to get down to the parade in a half hour."

Sure enough, they already had their food. Ella's waffles were piled high with strawberries and whipped cream, and she dug into them as soon as she sat down. As they left the diner twenty minutes later, Jace opened her purse to show Ella a glint of metal.

"Flask?" Ella asked.

"Yep. None of us are going to Pride sober." With that, Jace pulled out the small metal container and took a swig of something that smelled spicy and warm.

"Well, I'm driving," said Alexa. "I'll have to wait to get drunk till we get there."

Ella watched them both, looking for any signs of tension that would betray the hurt about their living situation. She found only a playful smile. How did they do it? How did they continue to go about their lives when they had to fear the consequences of their love? Ella's parents had shrugged and Stuart had just hugged her when Ella told them she was bisexual. She couldn't imagine if they'd reacted poorly. Or she could — she saw the effects of that on Jace every day.

Downtown, the streets already bustled. Ella came to Pride with Jace every year, and every year it buoyed her. Jace was silent as they walked up the street together. She didn't have to say anything for Ella to know why. Going to Pride was something Jace did, had to do, even though in much of her life, she remained hidden away from any chance of outing herself. Ella wasn't even sure if anyone at Jace's job knew about Alexa. Yet each year she came, got drunk, waved rainbow flags, and danced until her knees went floppy.

Ella slung one arm around each woman's shoulder, taking her spot in the middle. "Let's go," she said.

The throng swallowed them after only a block. They found the start of the parade and tucked themselves into the crowd next to a two-dad family with three kids, beaming proudly, their faces shining with excitement. Ella smiled at them.

Families like that gave her hope for Jace and Alexa. She thought it did the same for them, because when she looked down, Jace's brown hand was entwined with Alexa's darker one, and as she watched, both hands squeezed a little tighter.

Someone's whistle blasted a shrill, ecstatic series of tweets. A chant started up ahead of them a ways, but Ella couldn't make it out. So many smiling faces surrounded her. The parade began to move at a slow shuffle, inching forward until it picked up pace. Ella watched the people around her, feeling as though she were bathed in color and joy. Rainbows danced at the ends of sticks and waved on banners and undulated throughout the crowd in hundreds and hundreds of colorful shirts and painted bodies.

They rode that river of joy to the end of the parade route, where a fair and stalls had been set up to peddle handmade crafts and causes alike. Ella walked a little behind Jace and Alexa, occasionally taking a swig from Jace's flask until her skin buzzed and the sun magnified the warmth in her stomach.

Jace crowed with laughter at a sign and pulled Alexa over to her. "Dip me in honey and throw me to the lesbians," it read.

Taking Alexa's hand, Jace spun her out and dipped her backward, meeting her lips in a long kiss. The crowd burst out in cheers and laughter, and Alexa came up blushing and giggling.

Ella loved to see them like this. Happy. Proud. In love.

It made her think of Callum, and she felt her own cheeks color.

The strobe light flashed, making Ella stumble on the dance floor into a burly man who vogued at her before sashaying away. She turned her face away from the rapidly blinking lights, trying to locate Alexa and Jace in the crowd.

Sweaty bodies pulsed around her to the beat of a Madonna remix. Ella pushed past a gyrating couple, aiming for the bar. Her skin brushed against a bare shoulder, slick and smooth. A foot came down on her foot, and a man clapped a hand down on her shoulder, mouthing an apology. She smiled a tight smile and slid between a group of people bouncing to the refrain.

The throng at the bar was four deep, and Ella still didn't see her friends.

"Hey, there!" A man's voice, just behind her. Ella turned to see one of Alexa's friends. Tall and muscular, he waved at her and pulled her in for a damp hug. Jared was his name. Or was it Jarek?

"Hi!" Ella yelled over the music. "Have you seen Alexa anywhere?"

"She went outside with Jace!"

"Thank you!"

Ella slipped through the crowd, her skin thirsty for the cool night air. The rum had long since worn off, leaving her body tired and her feet protesting.

Outside the thump of the bass was still clearly audible over the chatter of passers-by. Halfway down the block, Ella spotted Alexa and Jace. She hurried up to them, but skidded to a stop fifteen feet away.

Alexa had her arms wrapped around Jace's shoulders, and Jace sat in a crumpled ball. The shake of her shoulders wasn't from laughter or happiness.

Ella took two steps toward them and stopped. Maybe this wasn't her job. How could she comfort a friend who wasn't free to be herself around the people she loved the most, the people who'd raised her, supported her through college. Pinpricks of tears formed in the corners of Ella's eyes. She turned to go, but the scuff of her foot on the pavement brought Alexa's eyes up to meet hers.

She didn't say anything. Ella didn't know what to say or do. Instead, she swallowed, pushing her lips together. They tasted of salt and heat. Ella started to walk toward them, one hand stretching toward Jace involuntarily, but something sharp rose in Alexa's gaze that made her stop where she was.

"This is my job," Alexa mouthed. Something heavy dropped into the pit of Ella's stomach.

She put one hand over her heart and walked away.

Around the corner, she raised her hand to flag a taxi.

She couldn't get the image of Jace's wet face out of her head.

chapter
eighteen

"Can you give me some sort of reason for not taking the listing? The house is in perfect condition on a good-sized lot. It's incredibly energy efficient, with the solar panels and the water-based heating system. I don't understand why you wouldn't want to sell this kind of property." What Ella didn't say was that this was the fifth real estate agent to turn down the listing.

"I'm sorry. Not that property."

The line went dead, and Ella's fist smacked the desk. Five no's. The first agent had been enthusiastic at first. Then she'd heard the address and looked it up on the Multiple Listings Service. After that, her voice went chilly and she apologized, saying she couldn't take the listing.

Ella didn't understand. She wanted to pull her hair out. The anxiety of the fruitless phone calls made her feel warm and itchy, and she scratched absently at her arm. There was already a red spot there. She remembered the note Grammy had left, but she hadn't really thought Grammy could do anything that would keep people from taking the listing. Grammy Helen had a lot of friends, and their family had been in Buffalo forever, but to keep people from wanting to sell a house and make money? How had she managed that? How long was this supposed to last?

She dialed the next number.

Two hours later, Ella had worked her way through half the agents on her list and was no closer to finding someone to help her sell the house. Poof and Puff pounced a jingle ball on the floor, making a rolling tinkly sound on the wood.

A clunk came from upstairs, and Ella's teeth ground together. Aunt Eunice had been up in the spare room for the past three hours.

Ella was afraid to go up and check the state of the bedroom after the old woman's rummaging. Instead, she went into the kitchen and slapped together a couple of ham and cheese sandwiches.

"Auntie Eunice!" she called up the stairs. "Do you want some lunch?"

"I'll be right down!"

Ella sat down at the kitchen table, wishing she had something besides water in the house. She'd been afraid to go grocery shopping much after the email from her accountant. The white bread — the cheapest she'd been able to find at the store — gummed up in her mouth and stuck in the crevasses of her teeth.

Auntie Eunice popped into the kitchen a moment later. "Sandwiches?"

"If you want something else, feel free to make it." Ella gestured to the chair next to her. "Have a seat. There're some potato chips in the bag."

"Thank you, dear."

The thank you made Ella raise her eyebrows, and she took another bite of her sandwich. "Have you heard from my parents lately?"

"Not since Helen passed," Auntie Eunice said around a mouthful of sandwich.

The simple sentence made a blip in Ella's heartbeat. Her parents had called Auntie Eunice but hadn't called her? "You heard from them? I must have called them fifteen times."

"Yes, well. They were in the middle of a trip or a meeting when they called and wanted to let me know they'd heard."

Ella forced her esophagus to push the bite of sandwich down her throat. She gulped down half a glass of water, but the sticky feeling remained, halfway to her stomach.

They'd heard and they hadn't come. Grammy Helen hadn't spoken much about them in the past three years, but could they have been estranged? Enough that Ella's father, Helen's son, wouldn't have come home for his mother's funeral?

"Any luck finding what you're looking for?" Ella was careful to keep her voice level, though her tongue stuck to the roof of her mouth. She drank more water. She didn't really expect Auntie Eunice to tell her, but it was better than sitting in silence and wondering why her parents hadn't gotten back to her.

Eunice blew out her lips like a horse.

"I'm going to take that as a no," said Ella.

"Yes, it's a no. I can't find any trace of the damn thing. I'm starting to think she swallowed it before she croaked."

"Auntie Eunice!"

"I can say croaked if I damn well please. She was my sister."

Ella gave up on the bread and rolled up the remainder of the ham and cheddar from the inside of her sandwich. She'd have to go grocery shopping soon. "Are you going to keep looking today?"

"I thought I might come back tomorrow."

"Did you put everything back in the spare room?"

"Ella, child, don't talk to me like I'm a child. I'll put everything back when I'm done. I closed the door."

"I'm sorry, Auntie Eunice," Ella said. "I just don't want to have to clean up a big mess again."

Auntie Eunice stood up and pushed her chair back under the table. It smacked into Ella's knee and smarted, but Ella kept her mouth shut.

"It's all cleaning up messes. Big messes, little messes, all the medium messes in between, that's life," Eunice muttered on her way to the door.

Ella rather thought she was right this time.

Ella gave up on calling real estate agents and went straight to the Realex office the next day. The receptionist looked pleased to have a walk-in seller and signaled to Ella to wait while she called an agent.

The tile floor was clean and free of dirt, and everything in the waiting area had a sheen to it. A bouquet of fake flowers sat on the glass coffee table in front of her, surrounded by carefully arranged back issues of Better Homes and Gardens.

"Dr. Keyes?" A man of medium height walked toward her, his hand proffered. Ella shook it firmly and followed him back to a small conference room.

"I'm Greg Winters," he said as she settled into a chair. He had round glasses and blue eyes. His hair had a liberal sprinkling of grays, and his teeth were as white and straight as a runway model's. "You're looking to sell your home?"

"Yes," Ella said, relieved. Maybe all it took was to talk with someone face to face.

"Well, it's still a difficult housing market, especially here in Buffalo. But I think I can help you. Do you know what the house appraised for?"

"About a hundred and ten thousand, according to my grandmother's will."

"You inherited the property, then? Is it in your name?"

"Yes, I did, and it is."

"Shouldn't be a problem."

Ella glowed with the promise of success. She'd sell the house. Buy a flat downtown. A loft or a condo. She could do this thing. She'd spend her summers in Stratford or Banff as she had before, watching plays and hiking through mountains that birthed aquamarine lakes. She'd write a book on Norse mythology and one on Eastern Europe's early pagans. She'd create a new life for herself. Maybe she could even arrange tours of Scandinavia, tours of the fjords and the ancient standing stones.

"What's the address?"

Ella snapped herself back to the present and rattled off the address of Grammy's house. Hope bubbled inside of her. She didn't have to be a professor to teach. She could do something else, meld her love of academia with her love of travel.

So lost was she in her contemplations of the future that Ella didn't notice the stretching silence in the conference room.

Greg Winters had his eyes on his computer screen, scrutinizing something.

"Is there a problem?"

"I'm afraid I can't take this listing."

Ella's daydreams vanished into a wisp of smoke. "What? Why?"

Not again. This couldn't be happening again. She'd already tried the other big companies. Every agent at every office had turned down the listing with no explanation. This was beyond the possibility of coincidence. There had to be an explanation for why no real estate agents in Buffalo would approach her Grammy's house.

Winters shrugged, pushing his knees together and straightening his spine. "I can't take this listing."

"Please give me some sort of explanation. I have a house I legally own and want to sell. There's no reason for this."

"I'm sorry. I just can't take this listing."

a hall of keys and no doors — 191

Ella waited, but no further explanation arrived. "This is ridiculous," she said. "I'll sell the damn house myself."

She strode out of the conference room with heavy footsteps. On the way back to the house, she stopped at Home Depot and bought a sign. For Sale by Owner.

The metal wires stuck into the dirt of the front yard. The sun reflected off the white background of the sign, and Ella gave it a tight-lipped smile. If no one would help her, she'd sell it herself. With a thick Sharpie, she penned her phone number on the bottom of the sign in large print. She was good with computers. She'd make fliers and brochures.

Ella spent the rest of the day taking pictures of the house and editing them until they showcased the best aspects of it.

She didn't photograph the third floor corridor.

A trip to the store yielded glossy paper for fliers and brochures, and when Ella printed the proofs, she couldn't help but admire her handiwork.

Updated late eighteenth century farmhouse on three acres in Niagara, it read. **Four bedrooms, two baths. Perfect for families. Energy efficient, with solar panels. Finished, repiped basement ideal for rec room or storage, den and study a dream for working at home.**

When she was finished, she had a stack of gleaming fliers and brochures sat on her desk. She'd do it. She could do it. Ella pulled Poof into her lap and scratched the big cat's head. "We'll get our lives back, Poof," she promised him.

He jumped off her lap to chase Puff and a jingle ball.

jace was already drunk.

Two steps into Fado, Ella sighed and almost turned around to walk back out. Jace sat on a bar stool, leaning forward onto her hand and giggling at something the bartender had said. Ella contemplated the consequences of just leaving, but Alexa wasn't here, and it was just her and Jace tonight. She'd have to play catch-up. Jace was great to be drunk with, but drunk Jace with sober company got old pretty quickly.

She sat down on the bar stool next to Jace. "Hey, tipsy girl. What are you drinking?"

Jace squinted into the remaining ice in her glass, then looked up at the bartender with a frown creasing her forehead. "What was that?"

"Lemon drop on the rocks." The bartender turned slightly toward Ella and made a slight cutting gesture with his hand, then pointed to Jace. No more.

"I'll take one of those and a big plate of cheesy fries for her. And a screwdriver, minus the screws." Ella hoped the bartender would know she meant orange juice, and when he nodded, she relaxed a bit.

"So," Ella said to Jace. "You started early." It was barely four in the afternoon.

"Mmhmm."

"Something you want to talk about?"

"Noooope." Jace drew out the word with a puff of air at the end. "Tonight we're going to have fun. Lots of fun."

"We'll have to leech some of that booze out of you before that happens."

Jace wasn't listening. Instead, she raised her left hand and waved frantically. A curly-haired woman in a dark green blouse looked over and smiled, heading their direction. Jace motioned at Ella when the woman got closer.

"Angie, that's Ella. Ella, Angie. You look good together."

Angie's hand was soft, and her nails gleamed in the dim light, perfectly manicured and painted a dark red with golden glimmers. Her fingers lingered, gripped around Ella's hand, and Ella met Angie's eyes to see a crinkle of a smile at their corners.

"So you're who stood me up."

Ella shot a look at Jace. She hadn't. Not again. "It was sort of an accident."

"I heard." Angie sat down next to Ella. "I'll forgive you if you buy me a drink."

What had Jace gotten her into now? Ella nodded absently. "Whatever you want."

She half-heard Angie ordering a complicated martini, most of her attention on Jace, who sat with her face in her palms, still staring into her empty glass. The bartender set a glass of orange juice down in front of Jace. She brightened and slurped part of it down, eyeing Ella's lemon drop. Ella nudged it out of reach.

"Tell me about yourself, Ella," Angie said. Did she not notice how far gone Jace was?

The bartender shook the martini shaker with a rattle-rattle-rattle. Ella didn't think she had much patience for this. "What did Jace tell you?"

"She said she wanted me to come meet you and that you needed a little pick-me-up. Cheers," said Angie, holding out her martini glass.

Ella clinked it with her lemon drop. "Look. I don't want to be rude or unfair, but Jace probably should have told you that I'm sort of seeing someone."

Sort of indeed. And "seeing" was putting it optimistically. Ella hadn't laid eyes on Callum in months, but he was clearly still interested, and so was she.

Angie blinked. "She said you were single."

Jace giggled into her orange juice. A steaming plate of greasy fries and cheese arrived.

"Eat that," Ella told her friend. Maybe it would soak up some of the drunk. She turned back to Angie. "I'm really sorry. I guess I'm technically single, but there's someone I'm interested in, and he likes me too."

"Is this perhaps the someone you met the day you were supposed to come meet me?"

"Yes. This is kind of awkward. I'm sorry she gave you wrong information."

"You just don't know I'm right," said Jace.

"She did say you balked when your boyfriend proposed." Angie sipped her martini, looking genuinely curious.

"That had nothing to do with not liking men. It had to do with not liking him." The thing Ella hated about being bi was people deciding she just hadn't made up her mind. Boobs were great. So were penises. But the people wearing them were what mattered to her.

"Fair enough."

"You're not upset?" Ella thought she'd be upset in Angie's place. It made everything more awkward, more uncomfortable. How many times had she had this conversation now? She usually tried to get it out of the way when she first met the women Jace sent her to meet. Jace hadn't stopped setting her up, and Ella never told her to stop, but she didn't like the idea of any more collateral damage than necessary. Now was probably past time to tell Jace no more.

"She means well, doesn't she?"

Ella nodded. "She does."

"Still here," Jace said, her mouth full of fries.

"Then I'm not upset. But I'll let you deal with drunk Jace. Last time I did that, I ended up with her puke in my hair." Angie drained her martini and winked at Ella. "Thanks for the drink."

"Sorry for the inconvenience. And your vomit experience."

Angie put her hand on Jace's back. "Once you sober up, try and remember that your friend's taken." She kissed Jace's cheek and swished out the door.

"Why couldn't you just talk to her?" Jace asked. "This screwdriver's weak."

"It's virgin. You got cut off." Ella didn't want to try and address the other question. Instead, she swiped a couple of Jace's fries. "What's with the day drunk, hon?"

"Nothing."

"Well, that doesn't sound true at all."

"Just wanted to hang out with my bestie."

Ella rolled her eyes. Jace hated the word bestie. "Well, here I am."

"You're not drunk enough."

"Now that is true." She finished her lemon drop and asked for another. "You're a lot more of a fun drunk when I'm not sober."

"I'm a fun drunk no matter what."

"You've got cheese on your cheek."

five hours later, ella and Jace sat in Tim Horton's, slurping coffee from travel mugs. Three half-eaten doughnuts graced the table, a trail of crumbs leading in a circle around the plate.

Ella didn't quite remember getting there. The warmth of the alcohol was beginning to fade, but Ella knew if she stood up, she'd walk about as well as a fourteen-month-old baby.

"Why do you want to sell your house?" Jace asked. Her words were still slurred, and her eyes shone with the alcohol.

"I can't be there anymore." The hours of being drunk weighed down on Ella. She never drank this much or this often. She blinked owlishly into her coffee. "The house is ruining my life. I went to every real estate agent in town, and they all said no."

"Not every one," Jace giggled.

Of course. Hope rose in Ella's stomach. Or maybe that was a doughnut. Either way, she swallowed it back. "You're a real estate agent."

"Was wondering how long it'd take for you to remember that."

Ella grinned. "No one'll sell my house. But you will, right? You're my best friend. And a real estate agent. You can sell it."

"'Cept I won't." Jace's giggles turned into titters as she nibbled on a corner of a doughnut.

"You won't sell it? You have to. You're the only one left."

"Nope."

She had to be joking. Ella struggled to focus on her friend. Just Jace being drunk Jace. The slowly-sobering part of Ella reminded her that maybe she hadn't chosen the best time or venue for the conversation, but the rest of her ignored the thought.

"Jace. You have to sell my house." Now the welling feeling was tears, not hope or bile. Ella felt one spill over and dabbed at it. "I can't live there. Can't."

"You can."

"Why won't you do this?"

Jace stuffed the rest of her doughnut in her mouth. "You can't control it, Ella."

"What?"

"Life. You can't control everything. You can't make it what you want it to be."

Her words were less slurred now, and the tightness in Ella's chest contracted. Her heart stuck on a beat, then re-started at twice its normal pace. "I know."

"No, you don't. You try to fix everything the way you want it. You're a control freak, Ella, and you can't change life to the way you want it. I won't take the listing."

"Why are you doing this? Why won't you help me?" Ella didn't really think she could sell her house by herself. Jace was her only remaining hope of having a professional to guide her through it, and she was refusing? For almost ten years of friendship, Ella couldn't recall Jace ever refusing to help her. When she needed tutoring in

Spanish? Jace helped her. When her courage slaked leading up to dumping her girlfriend? Jace encouraged her. When she got the call about Stuart's accident? Jace consoled her.

Loneliness crept up around her, entwining its fingers around her neck, threatening to choke her.

"Why won't you help?" Ella hated the tinny note in her voice, the slight slur that muted the consonants, blurred the lines of speech.

"Because you can't bring Stuart back!"

The words hung in the air, silencing two chattering workers behind the counter. A woman with a mop froze two tables away.

"I know that," Ella said, her voice sticky and thick.

"No, you don't. You try and mold everything in your life into perfect little boxes because you have to prove to yourself that you can keep stuff like that from happening. You want to move out of Grammy Helen's house because it's easier for you when you don't have the constant reminder that he's gone. And the keys."

"This has nothing to do with the keys!" It was a lie the moment it left Ella's lips, and from the glint in Jace's eyes, she knew it.

"This has everything to do with the keys. You can't stand not having control over your life. This is me saying no. Deal with it like the rest of us, Ella. Grow up."

Jace picked up the tray, strewn with crumbs and walked on still-stumbly feet to the trash can.

Ella sat, stunned.

Her head buzzed and spun with the alcohol. She lurched for the door, feet tumbling pell-mell after one another, but when she got outside, Jace was already gone. Had she walked? Taken a cab? Ella blinked away the film on her eyes and leaned against the corner of the building.

The night air was moist and warm against her skin, the humidity holding the heat of the day to ward off the coolness of the brisk northern air. Ella dialed a cab and sat on the curb. The hard concrete dug into the backs of her bare legs. She tucked her head between her knees, waiting for the nausea to come. Waiting for her body to purge itself of poison.

Sitting there staring into the gutter, Ella wasn't sure if she meant the alcohol or the anger at her friend.

Minutes slid by, licking at the dangling lock of blue hair in front of her face. Ella didn't hear the taxi until the driver rolled down the window and hollered at her.

"You Ella? If you need a lift, hurry up. Got people in the queue."

She pushed herself to her feet, feeling the knobbly indents in her legs from the concrete.

The taxi left her at her car.

Ella's stomach roiled and twisted, but not from the booze. She got into her Subaru and sat behind the wheel. The key turned, sparking the engine to life. She ignored the clumsy tug of her foot on the accelerator and shifted the car into drive.

The front passenger wheel clipped the curb, sending a series of jitters through her spine, but she kept going. The road tilted in front of her, illuminated only by streetlights.

Home. Bed. Far away from judgment and any reminders of how far her life had crumbled into dust. Far away from the anxiety and fear of what would happen when the money ran out and she was stuck with a hemorrhaging house and two cats and a frog to feed.

Night cloaked her vision as she drove. The wheel slid beneath her hands, and a loud honk tightened her grip. An oncoming car flashed its lights once, twice, three times. When the next did it, Ella's head swiveled. She took her eyes off the road to look at the dash. No lights.

Her hand fumbled for the headlights. She switched them on, and yellow-white light pooled in front of the car. The streets were quiet except for a low murmur of traffic and the brightness of their headlights flicking toward her. Or maybe that was the streetlights. Flick, flick, flick.

Streetlights. Car lights weren't as regular.

Her vision blurred around the edges.

The world was the colors of Christmas. Fuzzy bulbs of green and red and gold and white. The brakes squeaked as she stopped at a red light, peering over the wheel to watch the cars on the boulevard. Did she even know where she was? Ella tried to make out the street signs, but the world swirled, leaning to the side before she could make sense of the letters.

The light flicked green, and Ella felt it push her forward, felt her foot stumble on the petals, pressing both accelerator and brake until the engine revved and her foot slipped onto the gas. The car jumped forward through the intersection.

Forward.

She kept going forward.

The lights blurred together as she drove, unsure of the direction, unsure if she were even heading toward Grammy's house.

The wheels of the car turned of their own accord, and Ella twisted the wheel back in the other direction. Yellow lines moved under the car, first to the right, then to the left.

Still. Hold it still. Ella chanted to herself. Still. Hold it still. She wasn't sure if she was talking to the wheels or the steering column.

Streetlights and buildings streaked by. Faster. Faster. Green and gold. Green and gold. Green and gold.

Red.

Screeching tore through the air, and a loud honk.

Green minivan. Right in front.

She was going to hit it. She was going to plow the front of her Subaru into the driver's side door.

A face in the window, tight with terror.

For a fraction of a second, the face was Stuart's, his blue hair green in the gold street lights.

A whir. A squeal. The face and the minivan flew to the left.

Ella's Subaru streaked through the intersection.

No crash.

It took two blocks to pry her foot from the gas pedal and apply it to the brakes. Ella pulled the car over to the side of the road, her breath scraping through her lungs in gasps.

She'd almost killed someone's Stuart.

What was she doing? The world outside looked like the view from a carousel horse. Moving, spinning, up and down. Tearless sobs convulsed Ella's body. She fumbled with her seatbelt, hands futile on the release. She pushed her head back into the seat of the car, willing the movement to stop.

It couldn't be real. She wouldn't do this. She wouldn't.

Why had she gotten in her car?

It seemed to take forever for her to pass out.

fwap.

Ella's eyes stuck shut. She forced them open.

A yellow piece of paper hovered in front of them, attached to nothing. Suspended in the air, it pulled her gaze. She groaned and squinted. The letters were wrong. Backward.

She made out two words in block letters.

PARKING VIOLATION.

Ella's face scrunched up as she twisted in her seat. Someone tapped on her window.

For one second, she almost expected it to be Callum, but the having-none-of-it face of the parking enforcement officer was far too squishy to be Callum's. Besides. Callum was in Canada.

She turned the key in the ignition and rolled down the window.

"You're lucky I don't call the cops. You can't sleep here. Next time call a cab. Move your car before I change my mind. I'm coming around again in twenty minutes. If you haven't slept it off yet, I'll call a tow truck and a taxi and let you pay for all that on top of your ticket."

Ella's closed her eyes to slits and nodded, swallowing.

"Lucky you didn't kill no one," the ticketer said.

She waited until the parking officer drove away, then opened her door and was violently sick into the gutter. Vomit splashed on the running board of the car, and the sight of the half-digested doughnut chunks from HoJo's made her heave again.

A water bottle from two days ago sat in the center console. Ella swished her mouth with the stale liquid and spit. The next mouthful, she forced herself to swallow.

Twenty minutes, the officer said.

Ella closed the door to her car and sat back against the seat.

The yellow paper still hovered there.

Part of her wanted to laugh. She'd almost killed someone less than eight hours ago, and she had a parking ticket to show for it instead of a DUI and a suspended license. Or a corpse. What had she been thinking?

The rest of her felt sick, and the feeling had nothing to do with the hangovers.

A drunk driver was why Stuart was dead. Granted, Stuart had gotten in the car with the guy, but only because Ella hadn't gone to get him. She'd been too busy painting her nails a color she'd refused to wear for years.

How had she gotten here?

Fragments of the conversation — argument — with Jace hit her like broken glass to the face.

Grow up, Jace had said.

Ella looked at the yellow parking ticket, glowing softly with the rising sun, and thought it looked like a large step backward.

The early morning was quiet, full of the chirps of insects still deciding whether to be nocturnal and a cool breeze that sent air tickling against Ella's cheek through the open car window. She opened the door again, leaning around the steering wheel to tug the ticket off the glass and collapsed back into the seat. Rebuckling her safety belt, she pulled the car away from the curb.

This wasn't how it was supposed to be. This wasn't how any of it was supposed to be.

"That's the rub, isn't it Stuart?" She said aloud. "You're supposed to be here to keep me from fucking everything up. You were supposed to be here!"

But he wasn't.

Ella pulled into a Starbucks drive-thru. She didn't recognize the area or the street she was on. After ordering a frappucino with an extra shot of espresso, she parked and pulled up the GPS on her phone.

She'd driven across half the city in the wrong direction.

Ella punched in the address for home, yearning for her bed and her cats, who were probably unhappy about her absence.

It wasn't until she got back on the road that she realized she'd thought of Grammy Helen's house as home.

She didn't have much of a choice, it seemed.

Home. She thought the word, then said it aloud. "Home."

Home was family and warmth.

That day, Ella felt like she lacked both.

A WHITE VOLVO SAT in the drive when Ella pulled up.

Her stomach gave an unhelpful twist, and her shoulders slumped forward against the seatbelt. Auntie Eunice.

Ella got out of the car, tucking the parking ticket into her purse. Her great-aunt wasn't sitting in the car, and Ella didn't see her on the porch. Frowning, she started toward the house.

Halfway there, her stomach acids burbled up again, and Ella fell to her knees by a juniper bush, retching into the mulch.

She wiped her mouth on the back of her hand and stood, brushing the dirt and juniper needles from her knees. Ella stuck her key in the doorknob. When it didn't click, she pushed the door open. Had she left it unlocked?

A rustling noise from upstairs confirmed it. Ella closed her eyes, shutting the door behind her. "Auntie Eunice?"

Raising her voice hurt her head. She turned off the lights downstairs. Those she knew she hadn't left on.

"Auntie Eunice!" Still no answer but rustling.

Ella mounted the stairs with feet that felt as though she were wading through mud. There was no sign of the kitties, just a rustle-clunk-thud coming from…

Not her bedroom. Ella flung open the door to her room. Auntie Eunice sat in a pile of Ella's clothes, every drawer on her bureau pulled out.

"What. Are. You. Doing." Her molars tightened against each other, and Ella forced herself to swallow the hint of bile.

Auntie Eunice's head jerked up from examining the back corner of Ella's middle drawer, her fingers tense on the hem of a t-shirt Jace had bought Ella three years before. She dropped the t-shirt in her lap and scrambled to her feet.

"I have to find it," was all she said.

It was too much. Ella had put up with Eunice digging through boxes in the basement and the study. Going through old drawers of her sister's things, hoping to find whatever mystery object she sought tucked among ivory carvings or handmade colored baskets from Africa. Ella had put up with her turning up on the doorstep without explanation and demanding time to ransack her house.

Her house. If Ella couldn't sell it, it was hers in earnest. She was stuck with it, and she had to make it her home.

And someone who was supposed to be her family, someone who was supposed to come with some tiny inkling of intrinsic respect for her space, had thrown her things about like they were so much trash.

Ella felt bubbles of anger forming in her feet, slowly merging, popping, rising until her very body boiled. Her voice came out quiet and even and terrifying. "Get out of my home."

"I have to find it," Auntie Eunice repeated, but her eyes were wide as the decorative plates she collected at home. She looked around at the mess she'd created of Ella's belongings, and her wrinkled skin flushed with shame.

"I said get out. Get out!"

The old woman's mouth slackened, lips trembling like she couldn't keep them still. "Ella," she began.

"No! You've violated my home and my trust one too many times, Eunice!" Ella had never omitted the familial address when speaking to her great-aunt. Her family felt broken, shattered by Stuart's and Grammy's deaths and her parents' long silence in South Africa. "You can't just do this. I don't know how you don't understand that. These are my things. There are personal and private things in my room that you don't have a right to go through. I lost everything, and this is the only place I have in the world! How could you do this, Eunice? How could you?"

"I didn't mean to —"

"What, invade my space like that? This isn't your house. Your sister left it to me. I'm sorry if that angers you—"

"It doesn't! You should have it. I don't have any use for it."

Ella looked around her room, which looked like a Goodwill donation truck had blown up in the center of it. She couldn't ask why or what Eunice was looking for again. She wouldn't get an answer. Instead, she moved aside and pointed to the door. "You need to leave. Now. Before I call the police."

She knew she wouldn't go through with the threat, and from Auntie Eunice's injured expression, she did too. But she straightened her linen blouse, swallowed, and walked past Ella without meeting her gaze.

For the second time that day, Ella waited for someone to leave before she collapsed.

She pulled a pillow to her chest, curling herself around it. She wanted Jace to be here, to tell her she wasn't a horrible person for the way she'd threatened a ninety-three-year-old lady. Ella felt guilt creep into her core, turning round three times before settling in to rot her emotions. Shame settled over her, hot and heavy and cloying. A weight jumped to the bed, followed by a smaller dip in the mattress. Poof and Puff. The cats didn't come up as far as Ella's face.

Instead they balled up at her feet, not touching her even when she scritched her fingernails against the sheets to entice them toward her.

Her fingers went limp on the bed.

Alone, Ella closed her eyes and wished for sleep. She wished slumber would take her to a dreamless dark. Instead, the thub-thub, thub-thub of an anxious heart pulled her back from the edge of relaxation each time she neared it, reminding me of each facet of her broken life, shattered like a giant crystal into jagged, shining bits.

Alone.

part three

keys and families

chapter
nineteen

lla sat on the park bench, fingers seeking out cracks in the wood, which was in dire need of a paint job. A squirrel sat at the base of a maple tree about twenty yards away. He — even from twenty yards, his sex was evident — rested on his haunches and looked at Ella. She'd been staring him down for the past six minutes.

It was what she got for being early. Callum was supposed to meet her here. After calling to tell her he'd be back in Buffalo for a few days, he'd asked if he could show her a park he liked. So far Ella wasn't entirely sure what was so special about it, aside from the squirrels having a staring problem. She almost wished she'd brought a bag of peanuts. From the way the squirrel's eyes bored into her face, she figured he was willing her to have food and failing. She hadn't seen Callum in — how long was it? Ella felt excitement grapple with nervousness in her belly. The squirrel hopped closer, still staring intently.

"It doesn't work that way, buddy," Ella murmured.

"What doesn't work that way?"

Whoops. Ella hadn't meant to speak aloud, and she greeted Callum with a rueful smile. "That squirrel seems to be hoping I'll feed him."

"Ah. That would explain something. Maybe. Did you expect him to answer?"

"Not really, though after this week it wouldn't surprise me much."

Callum sat down next to her on the bench. A soft breeze swirled the air around them and ruffled the branches of the squirrel's maple. Clouds obscured most of the blue sky, but the day was hot and humid. The grass tickled Ella's feet in her flip-flops.

"So this is your favorite park?" Ella asked.

"Well, it's the park in which we had our third date." Callum turned to look at her, a smile playing at the corners of his mouth. "So it's my favorite now."

"You don't have any other favorite parks, do you?"

"Oh, you mean have I just run through all of the parks in Buffalo with various women? Yes. How'd you know?"

Ella laughed. "This one isn't bad."

Electronic music filtered through the trees to the tune of Pop Goes the Weasel. Callum looked in the direction of the sound and grabbed Ella's hand. "Come on!"

"Where are we going?"

"To teach you about ice cream trucks, apparently." Callum towed her off the bench and took off at a jog toward the repeating nursery rhyme.

Trotting alongside him, Ella's hand felt warm, a tingle spreading from where their palms touched and fingers intertwined. It almost made her want to pull her hand back; it had been so long since she'd felt anything for anyone. Instead she grabbed his hand harder.

She hadn't run since high school, and the last six months without riding her bicycle everywhere had taken their toll on her stamina. By the time they reached the ice cream truck, perspiration beaded on her chest and face, and she panted.

"I need to get back into shape, and you want to feed me ice cream?"

"Ice cream fixes everything."

"I'm not sure it fixes my inability to run."

"It makes it not matter as much."

"True."

They stood in line behind a gaggle of kids with crumpled bills in hand.

"So what do you like? Rocket pops, Klondike bar, ice cream sandwich?" Callum gestured widely as if to call the ice cream truck their oyster to crack.

"Drumsticks. Those were always my favorite when I was a kid."

"Then I'll have what you're having. Good choice. Chocolate in the cone? Can't lose."

Callum paid for their Drumsticks and handed one to Ella. She pulled the paper from the edges of the cone and resisted the urge to lick off a chunk of chocolate and peanuts.

She threw the wrapper in the trash and took a nibble from her cone. Callum's hand took hers again, fingers interlacing with hers, and he nodded toward the path.

They didn't speak for several minutes as they ate their ice cream cones. The coldness of the ice cream teased Ella's lips, and it made her think of the contrasting warmth of Callum's hand.

"I tried to forget about you, you know," Callum said suddenly.

"You seem to have failed." His words made Ella's heart squish. She tried to keep her voice light, embarrassed when it cracked on the word failed.

"Yeah, well. I went out on a couple dates while you were gone, up in Stratford. None of them had anything on your crossword abilities."

Ella smiled down at her feet, listening to the flap-flap-flap of her flip-flops on the path. "If it makes you feel any better, I haven't wanted to date anyone in years."

"That only makes me feel better if you qualify it with 'until you.'"

"Until you," said Ella.

"That's much better." Callum stopped and reached out toward Ella's face. His fingers cupped her cheek, and his thumb brushed something hard away from her lips. "Peanut."

Ella hoped that was what he'd wiped away and not her new pet name. She popped the remaining end of chocolate-filled cone into her mouth, looking over at a swing set not far down the path. Swings. When was the last time she'd been on one of those?

She turned back to Callum to tell him they should go play on the swing set and found herself staring at his Adam's apple. Ella looked up, struggling with the breaths that wanted to race faster and faster. Gray eyes met hers.

His lips touched hers, still cold from the ice cream and soft, soft. The kiss was almost a brush of skin, and Ella closed her eyes to the tingles that flooded her. Callum's mouth moved against hers, still soft but more pressing now. He tasted of vanilla ice cream and hints of chocolate, and their lips warmed from the kiss.

A loud whoop startled her, and Ella jumped back.

A pair of pre-pubescent kids flew by on bikes, laughing wildly.

"I think this is my favorite park now too," Ella said.

ella set down her keys on the dining room table. Her lips still felt tingly from her kisses with Callum. She'd kissed someone. More than that, she'd wanted to kiss someone. Ella didn't want to think about how long it had been since the last time that happened. Her mind fought with the sensations coursing through her body.

"Poof, Puff, I'm home!"

Everyone said cats didn't care when you got home, but the pitter-patter of kitty paws fumbling down the stairs proclaimed otherwise. A moment later, Poof trotted toward her, Puff still following kittenishly clumsy to the rear.

"There're my babies," Ella said. She knelt down and filled her hands with soft fur. Poof's purr rumbled into a loud idle immediately, accented by the more delicate motor of Puff.

Puff's tail was starting to fluff out more, looking more like an adult cat and less like a stumbling kitten. Ella scooped her up and put her on her shoulder. She was still small enough — and had weak enough claws — that she could stay up there without falling or causing permanent damage. If the keys did change things, she'd gotten a couple good things out of the bargain. She reached up and scratched Puff's cheek, then set the kitten on the floor again next to Poof.

Upstairs, Ella flopped down on her bed. She'd moved the photo of her and Stuart smashing rocks onto her nightstand and replaced Grammy's letter in the frame. Now she pulled it out and studied the letters again. One vague paragraph stood out to her.

> *But this place holds a lot of keys, to a lot of different doors. Some of those doors you don't need or want to open. I know you've got your shiny, new loft, but Ella, sugar, that's not all that's important. Shiny and new aren't always the best options, you know. Sometimes even less than you think.*

Shiny and new aren't always the best options.

Ella thought about the keys upstairs, trying to remember what had happened when she'd picked the shiny keys. The one she remembered was the shiny gold key she'd had to strain to reach.

Twenty-four hours later she'd been fired and evicted.

Ella sat up on the bed, dumping Poof and Puff from her stomach onto the coverlet. They flailed around for a moment before curling up in the warm spot her back had left. They could stay there. Ella had something to look for.

She headed up to the third floor and looked around the hallway, Grammy's letter clasped in her fist. Some of the keys in the hall glinted at her, shiny and almost untouched. It didn't make sense why they would look brand new and others were tarnished by the oils of generations of hands.

At that thought, something clicked.

What if the shiny ones were the ones to avoid? What if those were untouched for a reason?

Some of the keys she'd taken down were old and lumpy. Ella paged through her memories, trying to place which ones she'd pulled down before what happened, but the memories of the keys were nothing but a fog. She hadn't believed they were connected then, hadn't expected any sort of need to remember which keys triggered what events.

On impulse, Ella reached out and took a key of medium wear from the wall to her left. She held it, feeling it's strange, above-room-temperature warmth against her skin.

Her phone's ring broke the silence as she replaced the key on its hook.

Not her normal ring — Stevie Wonder's "Superstition" blasted from downstairs. Jace's favorite song, and the ringtone Ella'd always assigned to her.

She ran down the stairs and caught her phone on the last bar before it went to voicemail.

"Hello?" Out of breath. Ella blamed Callum and his ice cream. She took a deep breath through her nose and exhaled. "Jace?"

There was a snuffle on the other end. "Ella?" Jace's voice sounded like she had a bad cold, or like…

"Are you crying? What's wrong?"

"Can you come over?" The question barely made it out of her mouth before dying to a choked whisper at the end.

"I'm on my way."

Jace's front door was open when Ella arrived at her apartment. She pushed the door open and threw her purse on the floor.

"Jace?"

"Over here." Her voice sounded even more stuffy and broken in person.

Ella hurried into the living room, where she found Jace clutching a copy of the newspaper, the edges crumpled and floppy with wear. Jace's skin was puffy and splotchy, and a pile of tissues made a small mountain in the center of the coffee table.

"What happened?"

Wordlessly, Jace passed her the newspaper.

Ella took hold of the paper, noticing that the edges were damp from sweat or tears. It was the living section, and emblazoned across the entire top of the page in full color was a picture of Jace dipping Alexa low, kissing her near the sign that read, "Dip me in honey and throw me to the lesbians!"

"Oh," Ella said.

"Now the stupid dyke who still hung out in the closet is out to the world," Jace said. She pulled her laptop from where it sat on the table and opened it.

Ella saw why a moment later. Jace brought up her email account and aimed the screen toward Ella.

The words on the screen dropped Ella's stomach.

Jace,

How could you lie to us for so long? You have deceived your family and your church home, hiding your sin and abominable lifestyle in the filth of secrets. You are no longer welcome in our home.

Second Timothy 3:1 says, "But mark this: there will be terrible times in the last days. People will be lovers of themselves, lovers of money, boastful, proud, abusive, disobedient to their parents, ungrateful, unholy, without love, unforgiving, slanderous, without self-control, brutal, not lovers of the good, treacherous, rash, conceited, lovers of pleasure rather than lovers of God — having a form of godliness but denying its power. Have nothing to do with them."

You have fallen away from the Lord and been stolen into the filth of Satan.

We will pray for you.
In Christ do we live.

"Your parents wrote this?" Ella couldn't help the cloying sense of panic that coated her throat. An email. They'd sent an email disowning their child. "Your parents?"

"That's not all. I called them." Jace's voice quavered as she spoke, and her hands shook as she closed her laptop again. "I called them as soon as I got this. When they answered, they asked who was calling, and I said it was their daughter. And my father said..."

Jace swallowed and closed her eyes. Tears stood in her lashes, and one dripped onto the outside of her computer.

"My father said—" her voice cracked, and tears streamed down her face. "—He said he had no daughter."

Ella pushed the computer aside and took Jace into her arms, pulling her shaking body against her chest. "Oh, my god," was all she could think to say.

Her best friend's shoulders quaked against Ella's arms.

Ella knew that grief. Ella knew what that felt like, when pain gutted you from the inside out, and the shock of it sent your body into spasms of sobs that wouldn't quiet or slake. She held Jace close to her, stroking her hair.

"They won't answer when I call them," Jace sobbed. "They won't even pick up the phone. I went over to their house, and they wouldn't come to the door. I saw them close the blinds. I saw them! How can they just stop loving me?"

There was no answer, no solace Ella could offer. She couldn't say that they hadn't stopped loving Jace. Ella didn't know what was going through the Wongs' heads, other than that she knew they believed they were doing the right thing, that this — Ella's face pressed against Jace's hair, her own tears falling in rivulets — that this was what God wanted.

Something incomprehensible came out of Jace's mouth, muted and blurred by tears and sobs.

"I didn't hear you, love," Ella said.

"This is my fault. I had this coming."

Ella froze, one hand mid-stroke of Jace's hair. "What are you talking about? How could this possibly be your fault? You didn't do anything wrong."

Jace pulled back. "It's me. I'm a hypocrite. I've gone to Pride all these years, and it was all a lie. I never told my parents because I was scared, and now they've found out a different way, and..."

"Shhh," Ella said. "You were trying to preserve your family. You didn't do anything wrong. They don't have any right to know about your sexuality if you don't want to tell them. Or if you're not safe."

The revulsion she'd felt at seeing the email, at seeing her crumpled friend kindled into something hotter, something sharper. Anger. Tongues of it licked at the inside of Ella's ribcage until she felt herself quivering.

"What they did is the abomination. You should be first, Jace. You should be the first thing they defend, the first thing they trust and accept. You're their child. What they have done is cowardly and cruel, and don't you dare take it on. Don't you dare take it on." Ella took Jace's hands and pulled them into her lap. She reached up and tilted Jace's chin up. "This is not you. This is them. You live a beautiful life. You have a loving, wonderful, brave, caring girlfriend who worships the ground you walk on. She loves you. I love you. If your parents can't see that what makes you happy is beautiful, if they can't see that your love is real love, then they can go to hell."

Jace's face looked like she wanted to believe Ella.

Ella knew that look. And she understood why Jace couldn't.

chapter twenty

emotions drained, Ella returned home as soon as Alexa burst through Jace's door, the memory of the other woman's almost accusatory look that night at Pride still fresh in Ella's mind. She thought she got it now, especially now that she was dating a man. She could date Callum, have a loving, fulfilling relationship. And they could kiss in a park and get only good-natured laughs from teens. No one would mutter that they were dirty, not really. Even though Ella had dated women, been with one, Leah, for over a year in college before meeting Brett, she could find someone she loved and society wouldn't ever shun her for it. But Jace and Alexa, to be together faced this no matter what. Ella remembered the whispers with Leah, the way people averted their eyes — or worse, the men who stared lasciviously and hooted that Leah and Ella could come back to their rooms as if love between two women was only meant to titillate nearby men. Ella knew what it was like to be told she just couldn't make up her mind or was somehow greedy. But she hadn't had to go through this, not with her family.

Poof greeted her at the door again, and Ella looked around for Puff. "Where's your buddy, Poof?"

Poof, of course, didn't deign to answer. Instead, he twined himself around Ella's ankles, purring. Ella wandered through the ground floor of the house, calling Puff's name. Poof followed her, meowing as if to say he was right there, and why was she looking so hard for him?

Perhaps it hadn't been the best idea to name the new cat something so close to Poof's name.

The house was quiet except for the sound of the air-conditioning and a few staccato chirps from Prince's terrarium.

"You didn't eat the kitten, did you?" Ella asked Prince. Like Poof, Prince didn't answer.

Ella searched the basement. The house felt hotter than it should, and the long chain around her neck stuck to her skin. Ella pulled out the small gold key that rested under her shirt and flapped the chain around to dry it. No kitten in the basement.

She started to feel the beginnings of worry. Ella frowned as she went upstairs. No Puff in her room.

"Where's Puff, Poof?" Ella asked. Puff was still a small kitten. Ella berated herself for not closing the doors. The kitten shouldn't have free reign of a house this large. Not until she was older.

Grammy's room held no sign of Puff. Ella checked the sewing room next, peering under the sewing table and behind a stack of boxes.

The last room was a guest room. Ella went inside. "Puff? Here, kitty, kitty, kitty."

A small mew came from under the bed. Ella lifted the dusty bedskirt to see the tiny white kitten stretching, little paws out in front kneading the floor.

"There you are," Ella said, relieved. "This isn't the best place for kittens."

She reached under the bed and pulled out the kitten, who nestled into Ella's chest and yawned in her face. Her breath smelled of salmon from the wet food Ella had given her for breakfast. Ella was about to drop the bedskirt back into place when a book caught her eye. She pulled it out from under the bed. A smile tugged at the corners of her lips when she sat the paw prints in the dust that covered the book's outside.

Sitting down on the bed, Ella held Puff in one hand and the book in the other. It didn't look like a novel; there was no writing on the spine or the cover. Poof jumped up on the bed next to her, and Puff scrambled out of her arms to pounce his swishing tail.

Ella opened the book.

Writing covered the pages, not printed words. Grammy Helen's writing. Was this her journal? Why was it under the bed in the guest room?

The word "key" made Ella stop.

Grammy had written about the keys.

Ella forgot about Jace and the dusty smudges on the front of her shirt along with long white hairs. The lettering on the pages was in a slanted but smooth scrawl of cursive. Ella knew that writing, and if she hadn't, the letter in the picture frame on her nightstand would have been her first clue.

January 17, 1987

> *I'm starting to have suspicions about the keys upstairs. With Robert gone, I haven't anything to do in this big house but sit around and hope my son brings the grandbabies over for me to play with. Yesterday I pulled one off the wall, and an hour later the mail came with a check from the life insurance company we dropped twenty years ago. I'm going to use the money to put a new roof on the house.*

Ella scanned through a few more entries, finding nothing more about the keys. Grammy seemed not to write often, maybe one post every month or two. One mentioned Ella and Stuart dunking all their stuffed animals in her toilet, which brought a rueful smile to Ella's face, but there was nothing else about keys until June.

June 21, 1987

My hands are still shaking.

After touching a new key, my glass hutch collapsed downstairs. It broke the porcelain one of Robert's friends managed to send us from Poland. I know it wasn't my fault, and that Robert wouldn't judge me, but I can't help feeling as though I've betrayed him. That pottery was his. Now all that's left are blue and white shards in a heap in the dustpan.

It's sitting on the counter. I can't bring myself to throw it away.

June 29, 1987

I can't figure out where the keys came from. I should have asked Papa before he died — he always used to come up here and sit for hours on end with his books. His grandparents built this house. Maybe he knew something. I found one on the walls (without taking it down) that had a Russian word engraved into the shaft. I copied it down as faithfully as I could, but I'm afraid to ask around when things are so tense with Russia right now. Maybe I remember McCarthy too well.

July 3, 1987

The kids are here for two weeks, and I took them to the library this morning for a reading. They remind me of when Eunice and I were little. We couldn't sit anywhere without holding hands. Watching them together brought tears to my eyes. I haven't seen Eunice in a while. I think I'll call her this weekend.

While I was at the library, I dug out an English-Russian dictionary and found the word. It only means "good," and as far as I can tell isn't the name of any prominent key manufacturers. I've come no closer to finding out where my family got all these keys. I wish there was someone around here I could ask.

Ella flipped through the journal, watching the years slip by under her fingertips, like the sound of the turning pages.

April 8, 1998

I finally found something. Papa wasn't much of a writer, but I was going through some things in the basement, and I found a journal he wrote. At least I think he wrote it. He only wrote in the first quarter of it before putting it away about ten years before he died. He mentions a box that will reverse the effects of the keys. I don't know how serious he was. The dementia that runs in our family had already taken big bites out of his mind by that point. It's worth looking into, though. It is that.

Reverse the effects? The words sent a shiver down her back as if she'd turned around to find someone watching her. Grammy didn't write more about the box. Ella ruffled the pages, scanning the cramped handwriting for any clues. Could she do that? Really?

Admitting there was a way to reverse the effects of the keys meant admitting the keys had an effect in the first place.

The idea of getting her job back, her loft back — Ella closed her eyes and held tight to the journal in her lap.

Her gaze fell on Puff, curled up next to her with Poof's tail between her paws. What would resetting everything mean for Puff?

Ella returned to the journal, opening it where she'd wedged her finger between the pages.

February 3, 2011

The date felt like a punch between the eyes. Three years ago. The day before Stuart's death.

Ella forced herself to read.

> *I climbed up on a step-ladder today to pull a key from the top of the wall. It was bright silver and looked as though it had never been touched. I know I shouldn't touch the shiny ones. I've learned that over the years. With Ella grown now and thriving at her new job, maybe I'm just hoping for an end. I'm ninety years old and have seen a new millennium arrive. I'm done. I'm finished. Eunice will have to understand.*
>
> *So I took the key down and held it a good long while. I held it thinking that I'd trip and fall off the stepladder and break my neck.*
>
> *But nothing happened.*
>
> *I put it back, and for a moment the stepladder wobbled so that I thought I'd done it. I felt fear, then. And not a little bit of hatred for myself for wanting this long life over when my heart just keeps beating and beating and beating on and on. I miss Robert.*
>
> *I didn't fall. I stepped down from that ladder and nothing happened.*

Even sitting down, Ella's legs felt as wobbly as the stepladder Grammy mentioned.

Someone pounded on the front door.

Ella jumped as though she'd just taken a shiny key from the wall.

a hall of keys and no doors — 225

journal in hand, she ran down the stairs. Maybe it was Jace. The knocking sounded frantic, like someone who had lost everything.

Ella flung open the front door to see Auntie Eunice with her hand poised in a fist to pound again.

Remorse filled her at the sight of the old woman. She'd been so rude.

"I know you don't want me here, boy, but I had to come and try to make things right. I'm an old lady, and I know what the doctors tell me about my brain falling apart at the scenes."

Ella beckoned at Auntie Eunice to come in. "Please. I was out of line. I shouldn't have spoken to you that way."

"Tosh." Eunice held up her hands. "I'm not coming in. I had a long think about what you said. I've been treating this house like it was Easter Sunday and there were eggs hidden all over. I didn't think much about you living in it. I should know better. Been on this earth almost a century."

Shifting her feet, Ella moved the journal to her other hand. "It's okay," she began.

"Where did you get that?" Eunice pointed to the journal. "Where did you get that?"

Ella blinked at the journal. "I found it under the bed in the guest room. Or rather, Puff found it."

Eunice's hand flicked out and snatched the book from under Ella's arm. "You found it. It has to be in here. It has to be." She opened the pages and flipped through them, feeling along the book with gnarled fingers. When she came to the end, she let out a cry and dangled the book by the spine, shaking the thing as if she expected something to come out.

"Auntie Eunice," Ella said, alarmed. "What are you doing?"

"It's not in here," Eunice said, ignoring Ella's question. Her fingers felt along the binding of the book. A wail escaped her throat. "It's not in here!"

"What isn't in there?" Auntie Eunice couldn't be talking about the box Grammy had mentioned. There was no way a box could fit in the pages of a book. Or maybe she was talking about the box, and her mind had her confused.

Eunice grasped the book in shaking hands, her head moving back and forth. "It's gone."

Ella gave up on finding out what was gone. "Would you like some tea, Auntie Eunice?"

"What?"

"Would you like some tea?"

"That would be lovely." All traces of agitation vanished from her voice.

Ella slumped toward the kitchen. Auntie Eunice was losing her mind. That had to be the explanation. She put the teakettle on the stove and lit the burner with a match. A new stove. That's what this kitchen needed. The thought surfaced before Ella realized she didn't have any money. She'd have to start looking for a job soon. Very, very soon.

She turned to ask Eunice what kind of tea she'd like.

Eunice was gone.

She'd taken the journal.

chapter
twenty-one

Callum was meant to come over that night, and Ella wasn't sure what to tell him when he asked about her day. Kooky great-aunt stealing journals? Hall of keys with no doors or explanation? In the end, she decided to keep things vague.

He showed up with a bottle of pinot noir and a rotisserie chicken and homemade macaroni and cheese.

"He cooks," Ella said, impressed.

"You don't grow up with as a latchkey kid with a single dad without learning some tricks." Callum followed Ella into the kitchen. "Nice place."

"It's not bad." Aside from the crazy relative and the keys that may or may not make pipes explode, Ella thought.

Poof and Puff, enticed by the scent of chicken wafting through the air, appeared in the kitchen. Both cats hopped up onto chairs, whiskers forward and pupils dilated.

"Nice peanut gallery," Callum said. "What are their names?"

"Poof's the big guy, and Puff's the kitten."

"Poof and Puff?"

"I thought it was fitting."

Both cats ignored the discussion of their names, eyes on the chicken Callum pulled out onto the counter.

"I also have a frog named Prince," Ella confessed. "And no, I've never kissed him. He's mostly gotten over it."

Callum's laugh boomed through the kitchen. "Maybe I'll kiss him later. To mourn my departure."

Ella started to tell him that she'd rather he stick to kissing her, but Poof chose that moment to leap onto the counter and take a swipe at the chicken.

"Cat!" Ella nudged him off the counter, and he ran under the table, licking the one paw that had managed to touch chicken. She looked at the chicken, which was missing a few tiny spots of skin. "I hope you don't mind cat paw."

"We'll live."

Ella dished up their plates, feeling awkward under the combined stares of the cats, Poof from under the table and Puff from the chair. Callum put his hand on the small of her back to reach around her for glasses, and she felt a wave of panic to accompany the warmth of his palm. Her dating hiatus had stretched from when she finished her bachelor's degree, and that meant more years than she wanted to admit. The many blind dates with Jace's friends didn't count. Or did they? Either way, she hadn't had a romantic prospect this close to her bedroom since she had to throw an engagement ring at her ex-boyfriend when he didn't get the point that she'd said it was over.

She wasn't even sure she knew what to do anymore. What if he wanted to take things upstairs? Worse, what if he wanted to move things forward down here? Ella felt her chest flush as she sliced through the joint of a drumstick and dropped it on her plate. It wasn't like she hated sex — unless seven years of near-celibacy made that true. She was quite fond of sex. She liked Callum. She liked that he was filling water glasses and opening the wine, not asking where anything was. He made himself at home.

It was more, Ella thought a bit ruefully, than she'd managed to do in this house by herself.

She brought the plates into the dining room and set them down. "I better guard these from kitty invasion," she called. "Can you bring in forks?"

"Got it," Callum said from the kitchen.

Ella sat down at the table, palms down on the polished wood. She remembered Thanksgiving at this house as a child, an adolescent, even as an adult. Years of memory. How many times had Grammy had the table refinished? Ella'd spilled blue nail polish on it once, trying to paint her nails black with electric blue lightning bolts.

The house still didn't feel like hers, as much as she'd been present in it throughout the years.

When Callum entered the dining room with two water glasses balanced in one hand and forks in the other, Ella couldn't shake the feeling her grandmother was watching her.

"You look a little spooked. Everything okay?" Callum set everything down on the table, sliding her water toward her.

"I told you how I got the house, right?"

"Inherited it."

"Yeah. There's a lot of memories here, but it still doesn't feel like mine."

"That makes sense. Most of the furniture isn't yours, is it?"

Ella nodded. "It's all Grammy Helen's. My stuff's either piled in the garage or scattered around her stuff."

"Any thought of redecorating?"

The question was a bit alarming. Redecorate Grammy's house? The thought was another reminder that Ella didn't think of it as her home, and she gave Callum a tight smile. "That would be the smart thing to do. But it feels weird, thinking of moving her stuff out and mine in."

"I meant a bit farther than that. Paint the walls, hang your own pictures, make it yours."

That was even more alarming. "I really hadn't thought of doing that."

"You probably won't feel at home here until you do something like it."

Ella hated to admit it, but he was probably right. Instead of conceding aloud, she took a bite of macaroni and cheese. Still hot and gooey, the sauce had a little kick to it. "Well done, Chef Penrose," she said.

"You like it? The secret is pepper-jack."

"That's not much of a secret if you tell me."

"Touché."

Ella ate a few more bites in silence. Callum looked good in blue, she thought. He wore a solid blue t-shirt and dark jeans that accentuated his nicely-muscular build. She suddenly wanted to see him shirtless on stage as Puck more than she wanted to finish her dinner.

"I should probably tell you that you're the first person I've dated in…a while," she blurted out.

"How long's a while?"

Ella winced.

"That looked ominous."

She poked at a bit of macaroni. "I had a great girlfriend in college who dumped me, then a crappy boyfriend in college who proposed, and after I turned him down and broke up with him, I just didn't want to meet anyone for a few years. Then Stuart —" she couldn't make herself say died, "— and I really didn't want to think of anything romantic. After that, Jace started setting me up, and I just focused on my job."

Callum appeared to consider that. "I don't think any less of you for taking yourself off the market."

"Neither do I, but I thought I'd tell you anyway."

"I'll be back from Stratford in a month," said Callum.

"I'll probably be right here."

"Probably?"

"Well, assuming I don't get evicted again."

Callum grinned. "At least you own this place. Getting evicted from here would be an impressive feat."

The chicken was getting cold on her plate. Ella cut off a bite from her drumstick and ate it, thinking of how drumsticks were the best regardless of whether they were poultry or ice cream. Callum had been about to say something, and she'd sidetracked him.

"What were you going to say about when you get back from Stratford?" she asked.

"I know we've only been on a couple dates, but I'd like to go on a couple more. Maybe get touristy and visit the falls. Get on a boat and get drenched."

"I'd like that," Ella said.

"I like you."

This was the part that made her nervous. Ella felt as though she had a flock of migrating monarchs in her stomach, all flapping at once. It had been far too long, and she couldn't remember if that part was normal or if she was about to panic and do something stupid.

"I like you, too," she said. For a moment she couldn't tell if that was something stupid.

It seemed to be the right thing to say.

This was lucky, she told herself. Most people didn't find mutual like with someone they pestered at a coffee shop, and even if they did, usually that like wouldn't last through months of distance and play rehearsals and traipsing across Eastern Europe. But with the words hanging in the air, the house was suddenly too quiet and the words too heavy for the silence.

"Do you like the Beatles?" Ella pushed back from her chair. "I think we need music."

For the next two hours, Ella forgot about the fluttering in her stomach and Auntie Eunice's antics. She and Callum sat in the living room, a cat on each lap, and they talked about everything from Peter Pan to nuclear disarmament.

This was what it was supposed to be like. Easy.

When Callum got up to use the restroom, Ella cuddled Puff to her chest, and Poof made his way over from the vacated cushion he'd been left on. She thought again of Grammy's journal and her grandmother's words. She could reverse the effects. What would that mean for her and Callum? What would that mean at all?

The tiny kitten nuzzling into her neck brought tears to her eyes. If Poof hadn't escaped out the door that day, Ella wouldn't have Puff in her lap. The kitten was the cuddliest cat she'd ever met. It was almost as if she knew every day that she'd been rescued and was grateful for it. Her soft purr vibrated Ella's collarbone, and Ella kissed the top of Puff's head.

When she heard the bathroom door open and close, she looked up and met Callum's eyes as he came back into the room. He sat back down on the couch, right next to her this time. His leg touched hers, and he scratched Poof behind the ears.

"I'm happy to take things slow, you know," he said.

The fluttering returned in her stomach, and Ella sat Puff down next to Poof on her lap. She didn't know what to say, and Callum seemed to sense it.

"You don't have to say anything. I just wanted to put that out there."

"Thank you," Ella said.

"There is no need to thank me. I didn't do anything."

She considered telling him she was thanking him just for being himself, but that sounded trite and silly even in her head. She settled for handing him the kitten and leaning back so that her shoulder touched his. Callum took Puff from her with a smile.

"You know, I never thought of myself as a cat person."

"Dog fan?"

"Never really thought about either," he said. Puff swatted at his earlobe, and he winced. "We never really had pets growing up. My roommate got a puppy when I was just out of college, but that didn't work out so well. We weren't allowed to have them in the apartment complex, and my roommate forgot that puppies tend to pee everywhere."

"Precisely why cats are better. Show them where to go, and they know the drill." Ella turned her head to the side to look at Puff scrambling to stay on Callum's shoulder. "What happened to the puppy?"

"He took him back to the breeder after the landlord threatened to evict us."

"Ah, so you have experience with the dreaded eviction notice."

"It worked out better for us than it did for you," Callum said. "Though not really for the puppy."

"Poor puppy."

"I'm sure he got a nice forever home. He was a purebred golden retriever."

The sound of Yellow Submarine played softly in the background. Callum pulled his phone out of his pocket with his spare hand.

"I ought to be getting out of here. I have to drive back to Stratford in the morning, and I have to be at the theater at ten." He handed Puff back to Ella, but paused before getting up. "If you want, I can try to get you a ticket before the end of the run."

"That would be great," Ella said. "I'd love to come see it."

"As long as you coming doesn't doom us to another storm," he said.

"I promise to try not to anger the gods of thunder."

"Thank you."

She walked him to the door and out onto the porch. "I'll see you soon then," she said.

He smiled and pulled her into his arms. He was warm and solid. Did she want this? Ella questioned herself. Almost eight years of ignoring romance of all kinds for myriad reasons. She tried to reason through it even as her cheek pressed against his neck.

Ella did know one thing. She didn't want him to let go. She turned her face upward and met his lips. Warmth spread through her from that spot, encompassing her body in a haze. His lips traveled from hers, along the curve of her cheek and down the side of her neck. She wrapped her arms around Callum's back, feeling his shoulder blades move as his arms tightened around her.

His kisses trailed around her collarbone, just above the star ruby that sat in the hollow of her neck, and back up to her cheek.

When he returned to her lips, she pulled him closer, pressing her body against hers.

The kiss ended a few seconds later, and Callum pulled back. His eyes looked like Ella's felt, soft and not quite focused. He smiled down at her.

"One month." With that, he was gone.

Ella stood on the porch, her arms wrapped around her own body as if she could replace his touch, wishing to herself that she'd asked him to stay.

chapter
twenty-two

With Callum gone for another month and Jace's parting words ("I just need some time to figure out what next"), Ella needed a distraction.

She found it in the basement. She'd organized most of Grammy's trinkets, but she hadn't given herself the time to really look at them beyond "animal, figurine" or "box, carved stone."

Now she went back down into the basement — which thankfully did not smell of mildew or anything beyond normal basement smell thanks to the plumber's cleanup team — and started going through the plastic bins of things her grandmother had left. Some things, like a mountain of small porcelain figures that looked like they came out of the Red Rose Tea boxes Grammy always bought when Ella was growing up, Ella kept where they were. Others, she set aside to take upstairs. The jewelry box of gemstones was one of those things.

Ella thought she would have loved to go through all of the boxes as a child. Each plastic storage bin was like opening a treasure chest. If she ever had children, Ella wanted to make a treasure chest for them with what Grammy had left to her. There was the brass lamp that looked like it could have belonged to Aladdin himself, tucked beside an incense burner and and a tarnished brass service. There were a bunch of locks with the likenesses of Hindu gods. Giant, clunky padlocks that looked like they belonged somewhere to guard treasures. Ganesh with his elephant face stared out at her from one of them. Ella didn't know what she wanted to do with it, but she liked it. She put it aside.

Ganesh was a god of new beginnings, rewarded for losing his head and getting stuck with an elephant head for eternity by being the one Hindus called on whenever they began an important endeavor. Ella liked that, and she loved elephants in general. She put the Ganesh lock with the jewelry box.

Under two full storage containers of wicker baskets — those Ella thought she could find another use for — Ella found the box of animal figurines. Her grandmother had an affinity for elephants too, it seemed. Between a few rustic carvings of grizzlies and a stylized menagerie from Kenya, Ella found elephants. Soapstone elephants, jade elephants, wooden elephants, even an elephant formed from small reeds bundled together. There was one carved from a large hunk of ivory that made Ella sad to hold, as if whoever took the elephant's life to make the carving had imprisoned him in it.

The elephants she gathered up, thirteen in all. She loved elephants. Their intelligence, their nobility, how they mourned their dead and cared for their living.

She carried everything upstairs in two trips and went to sit on the living room floor. Maybe Callum was right. Maybe she needed to make this house her own. She had a good start in her hands. Along the wall below the windows, Gramps had made built-in bookshelves. They lined the entire wall and filled in the space between the windows as well, reaching up to the ceiling. They didn't just hold books. Ella pulled the one elephant that already lived there from its place on the shelf and sat it with the others. That was the one she'd brought to Grammy, the one that matched hers. Brass with eyes of lapis lazuli.

Ella cleared off a shelf between the windows at eye level. Behind a copy of The Slave Dancer and a biography of Harriet Tubman was a small, egg-shaped rock.

She pulled it out, holding it between two fingers as if it could bite her.

The rocks were her game with Stuart. Grammy wasn't a part of it. Ella looked at the book she'd just pulled out. They'd had to read it in fifth grade — or was it sixth? Ella couldn't remember. When had Stuart put the rock there? It had to be after they'd graduated from high school. By then, they only stayed with Grammy when their parents were off traveling. There were only two college breaks she could remember when she and Stuart had stayed at Grammy Helen's: the summer between their junior and senior years because their parents had rented out the house and gone to help a start-up business in Spain, and spring break senior year. They'd both been broke and didn't feel like going anywhere, so they'd spent the week with Grammy, helping her...

The books. They'd helped Grammy organize all her books. Before, Grammy Helen had just shelved them wherever. But that spring break, Ella and Stuart had taken every one of these books off the shelves and arranged them by category, then genre, then finally author.

Stuart must have thought she'd move The Slave Dancer and find it that week.

She hadn't, and now here it was, six years later.

Some distraction she'd created for herself.

Ella carefully put the rock aside and started arranging the elephants on the shelf. When she was done, she had a whole herd. Some, like the jade and soapstone elephants, were small like babies. Others, like the wooden and ivory ones, were large and imposing. She sat the Ganesh lock front and center. She'd leave it there until she could figure out what to do with it.

She looked at the clock. All of her puttering had only taken two and a half hours. She picked up the rock and held it in her hand as she always did, waiting for the rock to warm to her touch.

Suddenly the house was full of memories Ella didn't want. She went upstairs and dropped the rock in the plastic container with all the others. She needed to get out of there. Outside, it was a nice day. Puffy white clouds drifted across the sky, which showed a duller blue in the day's haze. Ella thought of the elephants she'd just arranged. That was it. She could go to the zoo. See a real elephant.

She showered the dust from her body and dressed in a pair of black shorts and a blue t-shirt. She was about to go downstairs, but instead she looked up at the next flight. Her feet took her to the third floor corridor.

She hadn't been up there since reading Grammy's journal. Ella had been avoiding the corridor. But now Grammy's words stuck out in her mind like the shiny keys among the dull, worn ones. She wouldn't choose a shiny one this time.

Ella selected a small, knobbly key that looked like it had gotten just a bit too hot and melted a little. Then she put it back and waited.

Nothing happened.

With a shrug, she went back downstairs. The zoo. She'd go to the zoo.

ella didn't want her first stop to be the elephants, so instead she visited the big cats.

She'd always liked them, the way the snow leopard sat on top of his perch with bright green eyes watching passers-by. The tiger paced back and forth in front of a log, a chuffing sound coming from her throat each time she passed the end. Her whiskers were long, so long Ella thought they'd stretch from her fingertips to her wrist if she laid one out on her hand. They were pushed forward, just like Poof did when he was checking something out. What was this tiger waiting for?

The lions were all sunbathing in a golden patch of light as if to say, "No, we don't mind being here. Leave our food just there, will you? Good chap."

She made her way around, through the ape habitats and past the zebras. Ella wished Jace were there with her. They'd come here together before, but it had been years. Ella made an annual donation to the zoo.

At first the commotion blended with the giggles and screams of children. It was summer, and all the kids were still out of school. As Ella neared the elephant enclosure, though, the hubbub around her took on a different note.

Two zoo employees hurried past her. "How did she get out?"

"I don't know!"

"Where is she?"

"They lost her."

"How the hell did that happen?"

Alarmed, Ella followed behind them, not sure if she ought to turn back or stick close to people who knew what was going on.

She veered off on a path to the right and turned a corner.

And came face to face with something very, very large.

Dark eyes looked out at her from a sea of gray wrinkles. A bristly patch of hair grew from the elephant's head, and her trunk was curled in on itself.

Ella could hear the barking of sea lions not far away. The elephant looked at her and took a step forward.

Ella froze on the path. The heat from the day made her shirt stick to her midriff, and somewhere behind her a cry rose in the air. She couldn't make it out. The world narrowed to one hulking mass of animal in front of her.

She knew that this elephant was used to seeing people, day in, day out. Smaller than the African elephants, she'd met Asian elephants in Thailand with her family in high school. People rode them.

That didn't change the fact that they were still massive. And if it decided to sit on her, Ella knew who'd come out second best.

The elephant took another step toward her. What was she supposed to do? How fast were elephants? Ella thought of running hand in hand with Callum to get ice cream and decided she probably couldn't outrun even a very slow elephant. That left standing still and hoping, hoping the creature watching her didn't decide to hurt her.

Her mouth tasted like metal, like sucking on a nickel. Ella's hands curled in on themselves like the elephant's trunk. Behind her, people's voices raised, but she couldn't understand them.

The elephant stood less than ten feet away. Two more steps forward.

Ella held very still.

Every wrinkle in the elephant's trunk stood out to her. She smelled the warm, dusty scent of its — her? — skin. And Ella smelled herself, in spite of the deodorant she slicked on each morning after her shower. A tangy, apprehensive odor.

Her mouth felt as dry and dusty as the elephant's back. Ella looked to her right. The elephant could get by there if she wanted to. Enough space opened between Ella and the small fenced-off area of foliage. But the elephant didn't seem to want to get by.

She walked directly at Ella instead. Three more steps brought her within two feet of Ella's face, and that curled trunk was right at eye level. Ella looked up, into the eyes of the creature before her.

Her heart should be pounding. Instead it boomed in her chest only slightly faster than normal.

The elephant's trunk uncurled and slowly moved toward Ella's face. She saw the end of it flare and quiver. Was she sniffing Ella?

Ella felt the puffs of breath on her neck and ears. It smelled like sun-warmed hay.

With no other idea of what to do in the situation, Ella held eye contact with the elephant, blinking slowly twice.

"Hello," she said softly.

The elephant didn't move, trunk still raised.

Ella thought that she could be about to die, but for the moment, she didn't care. She'd never been this close to an elephant. Not face to face. Not looking into its eyes. There was intelligence there. Curiosity. Of course, a curious elephant could hurt a human quite by accident, but Ella didn't think the elephant looked at her as a toy.

She raised her hand, moving as slowly as possible. She didn't want to look like a threat. Ella held her right hand at shoulder level, palm up. "You just wanted to take a stroll, didn't you?" she murmured.

A long moment of silence brought the sound of raised voices back to Ella's ears. She turned her head to see a crowd of people twenty yards away. Children pointed, and not a few adult's faces held pinched anxiety and fear. It would only be a moment before the zoo's personnel arrived. What they'd do when they got here, Ella didn't know.

Something rough touched her palm.

Ella's head turned back. The elephant's trunk curled now around Ella's hand. Not firmly. Gently, as one might hold the stem of a flower.

The tears that formed in her eyes surprised her. Ella blinked again now, this time to clear her vision. The elephant's trunk was warm, wrapped around her hand and wrist. Ella raised her free hand and laid it on the trunk, feeling the coarse hairs and creases beneath her palm.

Tears fell from her eyes as the elephant's grip tightened ever-so-slightly and released.

Like a friend's reassuring grip.

"Don't move."

The words intruded into Ella's world, and for a moment she stood confused, the fact that the creature holding her hand had escaped from her paddock.

A middle-aged man stood behind her. "Don't move," he repeated.

"I'm fine, sir. It's fine. She's not hurting me."

Ella didn't know what to do, but she didn't want to pull her hand from the elephant's trunk. She didn't want the moment to end or for anything to sever the connection. She looked up at the elephant. The elephant's head nudged as if she wanted to turn, and Ella went with it. She walked carefully to the elephant's left side, her right hand still held in the elephant's trunk.

"I'm thinking I'm going to do what she wants," Ella said.

She craned her head back to look at the zookeeper, whose wide eyes said he didn't have a better plan.

"I'll follow behind," he said finally.

Hand in trunk, Ella let the elephant lead her back around the path. When they reached the elephant paddock, Ella saw that a large portion of the wall had crumbled away. The elephant stopped at the wall and turned to Ella.

She squeezed Ella's hand once more, then her trunk dropped away, and she shuffled past the debris and back into the enclosure.

Ella sat down on a rock and cried.

the zookeepers made her sign a waiver saying that she hadn't been harmed and that she'd approached the elephant of her own accord, indemnifying the Buffalo Zoo of any ill-effects her encounter might have had. Ella assured them she hadn't approached the elephant; she'd simply turned a corner and found her there. The whole thing seemed to leave them flustered.

She left the zoo's offices with a copy of what she'd signed. Rolling it up, she stuffed it in her purse.

"Excuse me."

Ella turned to see a woman with a digital SLR camera around her neck giving her a small wave.

"Can I help you?" Ella didn't much feel like talking to anyone. She wanted to go sit somewhere quiet and think. What she really wanted to do was return to the elephant paddock and sit and watch the elephant to see what she'd do, but the zoo had closed it off to the public until they could figure out how the wall had crumbled spontaneously and left an elephant-sized exit hole on the far side. All the zoo's elephants would be kept in their indoor habitat until it was repaired.

None of the others had tried to leave, which was strange enough in itself.

The woman pulled her camera strap from around her neck and motioned at Ella to come closer. "I saw what happened with the elephant. I thought you might want to see the pictures."

Ella blinked. "You took pictures?"

"I'm kind of an amateur photographer, but some of them are wonderful." The woman opened the camera bag that dangled on her shoulder. "I just got this new lens and wanted to try it out today. I was hoping to get a picture of the tiger yawning, but this was much more exciting."

At Ella's blank look, the woman barreled on.

"I mean, I'm really glad you didn't get hurt. That would have been bad. But I think you'll like these."

Moving closer to look over the woman's shoulder, she watched as the screen clicked on.

The first image was just of Ella's back, looking at the elephant. Slightly blurry.

"I was still trying to focus," the woman muttered. "Here."

The next was…magic.

It was still Ella's back, but the photograph was portrait-style and perfectly symmetrical. Just Ella with the elephant in front of her. It was only then Ella saw how small she must have looked coming up to a creature whose shoulder was at least eight feet tall. The elephant's eyes in the photo were clearly trained on the person in front of her, observing.

"Wow," Ella said.

"They get better."

Some of the pictures were blurry or a little sloppy. But there she was, the elephant's trunk sniffing her face. Ella with her hand out.

The elephant's trunk taking her hand.

Ella reaching out to touch the animal's trunk. Contact.

As the woman flipped through the pictures, Ella felt it all over again. "Stop there for a second," she said.

At the time, Ella hadn't noticed the sunlight on her face. The picture showed the elephant's trunk and her hand on it, a tear running down her cheek in perfect crystalline clarity.

The final photo was of the two of them walking away. The woman had even managed to cut out the zookeeper from the picture.

"I want you to have these," the woman said.

"You call yourself an amateur?" Ella cleared her throat when the words came out crackly.

"Yeah, well."

"These are amazing. Thank you."

They exchanged phone numbers and emails.

The woman's name was Sara Krakowski, and she handed Ella a business card for a floral shop. "My aunt owns the place," she explained. "I'll call you as soon as I have the photos edited a bit, and you can swing by to pick them up. I'll put them on a CD for you. The cloud's great and all, but it might be nice to have a hard copy."

"That would be lovely. Thank you again."

Ella tucked the business card into her purse with the rolled up copy of the waiver. A distraction. She'd found one.

As Ella drove home, all she could think of were the keys on the wall.

chapter
twenty-three

her phone rang almost before she got the front door closed. Jace. "Jace? How are you doing?" Ella juggled her purse and her phone and dropped her keys to the floor with a clack.

"How am I? How are you, more like! You're on the news."

"I'm what?"

"The news. They're talking about an elephant escaping at the zoo, and there're a bunch of pictures people sent in from their phones of you standing right in front of it. What the hell happened? Are you okay?"

"I'm fine," Ella said, her lips curling into a smile. "I'm more than fine."

She related the story and told Jace about the photographer.

"I'll show you the pictures as soon as she gets them to me. I think I might get them framed. They're amazing." Ella flopped down on the couch. "I've never experienced anything like that."

"Who has?" Jace's voice was full of wonder, devoid of pain for the first time since her parents had cut her out of their lives. "I can't believe it."

Neither could Ella. But it had happened. Her gaze rose to the ceiling, thinking of the keys upstairs. This she couldn't deny. Could she?

Her phone buzzed against her cheek, and she put Jace on speakerphone. "I just got an email from the woman who took the pictures."

"And?"

"And she attached a couple unedited." Ella forwarded the email to Jace. "Keep those to yourself for now, will you?"

There was a pause, then a sharp intake of breath. "These are incredible."

"I know."

She hung up the phone after a few minutes of chit-chat and sat back on the couch, staring at the shelf of elephant figurines she'd so carefully arranged before she left.

Ella needed to get Grammy's journal back. She had to find out what was going on the day before Stuart died, and she had to learn more about what Grammy Helen meant by reversing the keys' effects.

Too bad Auntie Eunice had the journal now.

She dialed her great-aunt's number and listened to it ring.

Six, seven, eight rings.

When the answering machine picked up, Ella sighed. "Auntie Eunice, if you get this, please give me a call. I need to see Grammy's journal. I was reading it before you ran off with it, and there was something in there right before the day Stuart died. I want to find out what it is. You should understand that. Please call me as soon as you have a minute."

She considered calling again, but decided against it. If Auntie Eunice were going to give her the journal back at all, leaving multiple messages wouldn't change her decision.

Ella didn't feel hopeful about getting the journal back.

Her thoughts turned back to Jace. She'd sounded happier, brighter. Less despairing. Ella didn't doubt that Jace's parents continued their stonewall silence against their daughter, but something had shifted. She couldn't understand how parents could do that to a child. Hers might be on another continent, but Ella knew they'd never disown her for loving someone.

If an elephant could treat a human with gentleness, how come people couldn't do the same for each other?

She'd never been good at sketching.

Ella crumpled the paper into a ball and tossed it at the end of the corridor.

The hall of keys was flooded with light; Ella'd brought up three floor lamps and placed them at intervals through the corridor to illuminate the keys. She couldn't get it right. The blank page mocked her, white and incandescent in the brightness of the hall. The tattered spiral edge of the recently-destroyed attempt made a jagged line across the top part of the notebook, and Ella tugged the remnants away.

This wasn't working.

The only thing she'd ever succeeded at drawing was in junior high when the teacher had made them copy another picture from the original to a new sheet.

And how had she done that?

Ella tossed the notebook aside and ran down the stairs. The teacher had made them overlay the original drawing with a grid, then she had copied it square by square. She could do that. The lines in the corridor's paneling would work.

She rummaged through her office supplies until she found it. A large notebook she'd bought in Eastern Europe. It wasn't lined like American paper; every sheet was a grid of centimeter-sized squares.

Ella brought the notebook back upstairs and pumped a bit more lead out of her mechanical pencil. She could do this.

It took three hours and several more crumpled balls of paper — which Poof and Puff chased and kicked through the corridor — but Ella succeeded.

When she was finished, she had two carefully transferred diagrams of the keys in the hallway. Each key location was marked with a circle and numbered.

Ella couldn't remember all the keys she'd taken down, but there were two she did. She found the small, half-melty-looking knobbly key she'd taken just before going to the zoo. On the back of the page, she'd written all the numbers of the keys down the margin. Next to A23, she wrote "elephant encounter." After that, she jotted down what she'd felt. "Wonder. Fear. Apprehension. Joy."

The shiny key at the far end of the hallway she'd had to strain to reach, that was A148, and she labeled it, "lost job and apartment." Following that, she wrote, "Anger. Resentment. Frustration. Nervousness."

The page was startlingly blank. Ella didn't know enough, didn't have the gall to try each and every key. But it was a start. She took the notebook back downstairs. The pages weren't perforated, and Ella found a pair of scissors, opening them to slide a single blade down the middle of the book, slicing the pages from the notebook. She placed them in a folder and slid it onto her bookshelf next to the bound copy of her doctoral dissertation.

It was a start.

Ella felt as though a warm sunbeam had pierced the fog of her life, burning it away.

Some people, Ella supposed, wouldn't try to figure it out. They'd take things as they came without needing a pattern. Jace was one of those people. Ella wasn't. This way she'd know, and future generations would know. Maybe not the how of it, but at least the what. Whatever existed in the hall of keys, Ella didn't know, but where as a child she had felt a strange aversion to snooping, suddenly that aversion had dissipated like the fog, leaving a fiery curiosity and determination. She would figure it out.

At least she hoped. For all Ella knew, the keys changed each time. She doubted people would run into an elephant every time they took that particular key, but it gave an idea. Her fingers ached and cramped from holding a pencil for hours, and Ella flexed her hands, massaging her right hand with her left. A sense of pride filled her. She'd figured out a way to make sense of the keys, even a tiny bit of sense.

Sometimes a tiny bit of sense was enough.

For a start.

She met Callum at a vineyard just over the Canadian border a week later.

"We didn't think this through all the way," was the first thing he said after greeting her with a kiss.

"What do you mean?"

"We came to a wine tasting in two cars."

He was right. Ella's heart gave a thump at the thought of driving the night she'd left Howard Johnson's drunk and stupid. She'd almost killed someone that night. Killed someone else's Stuart. Ella would never let herself do that again. She didn't know what had made her do it then, only that it was behind her forever, a terrible mistake. Her head was shaking before she could get words out of her mouth. "Then we'll just walk around the vineyard until we're sober again."

"That sounds like a fine plan."

Ella didn't pay attention to most of the tour. Her attention focused on her thumb grazing the back of Callum's hand. He had strong hands, calluses on his palms. They reminded her of the calluses she'd always had as a kid from playing on the jungle gyms and monkey bars on the playground. She decided it had to be from lifting weights. No one got that fit downing beer and potato chips and binge watching *Lost* on Netflix.

She wasn't the only one not paying attention. Callum's hand snaked around her waist, and he leaned over to kiss her on the temple. Ella slipped her own arm around his waist, feeling the hard muscles of his back.

Wine clocked in last on her priorities for the moment.

The sun lit the vineyard with gold that touched down on the curving vines of grapes, spotlighting tendrils that grew in curlicues from the central vines and the plump green grapes that hung down. All Ella knew was that these grapes were used to make ice wine, the sweet, light dessert wine the region was famous for.

A buzz of insects filled her ears, the backdrop for the tour guide's words. Ella tuned the words out, hearing only the symphony of the world around her and her own breathing matched with the rise and fall of Callum's chest. They fell farther and farther behind the group until the tour guide led the other six couples around a corner, leaving them alone in an grassy aisle of future wine.

"Only three more weeks now," Callum said, his fingers caressing her hip bone.

Three more weeks until he came back, and then what? They hadn't said the boyfriend-girlfriend words about each other yet. They hadn't even had the talk about being exclusive, though both of them had hinted at it. Not for the first time, Ella wondered if she were ready for a relationship. Ready seemed like such a strange word to apply. She decided that it had nothing to do with time; it had been eight years since she escaped marrying a jerk and anyone looking from the outside would shake their heads and say that ought to be enough time to get over just about anything. Sometimes three weeks was enough. Other times three decades probably wasn't.

No, being ready was about the person, and this person standing next to her with his arm around her waist and his hand on her hip — he was about as nice of an example of a person as she'd seen in her almost-thirty years.

Ella leaned into his shoulder. "This is nice."

"I agree." He paused and plucked a grape from the vine, popping it into his mouth. He bit down and squinted one eye. "Tart."

"I don't think they're ripe yet."

"Shows how much we've listened."

Ella smiled at that. Three weeks. She figured she could decide how she felt in that much time. Being around Callum was intoxicating. He was sweet like the wine these grapes would become. Funny. Definitely good-looking. What made the smile fade was wondering if the intoxication she felt around him was just her body waking up after a long period of celibacy or if it were just him.

She nudged him forward, and they walked at a leisurely pace toward where the rest of their group had disappeared. The group had stopped just around the corner, and the tour guide gave them a knowing glance before motioning them onward.

When they returned to the main building, Callum brought her a sample of ice wine in a small clear plastic goblet. Their two cups clicked instead of clinked, and Ella sipped the cool, sugary wine. It tasted of apricots, leaving a tingle on her tongue and a fruity scent in her nose.

"I wanted to ask you something."

Ella's heart flubbed at that, and she faced Callum, shifting warily to put her weight on her right foot. "What's that?"

"I found a ticket for you, if you want to come to the closing night show. It's two and a half weeks from now. It's sold out, but there was one seat left in the third row. It's not front row this time, but if you want to come, you're more than welcome."

She let out a breath, not sure why his initial statement had caused a spike of panic. Maybe it was the way he'd phrased it. "I'd love to come," she said.

He smiled at her then, and this time the fluttering in her chest had nothing to do with panic. "If you want to stay the next day, I can take you to brunch at my favorite spot. They've got the best pancakes in Stratford."

"Superlative pancakes," Ella said. "Count me in."

They browsed the small store, holding hands again. Ella picked out three bottles of ice wine and two pinot grigios that looked interesting. Maybe she'd convert part of the basement into a wine cellar. Looking at the basket in Callum's hand with the five bottles, she thought it would be a very lonely wine cellar. She'd have to get a job soon. Her bank account dwindled with each passing day.

Ella'd never had to worry about money before. She'd always saved scrupulously, invested wisely, and never had to fuss with a budget. She saved for what she wanted to do and always got what she needed first. Now it was running out. She considered putting the wine back for a moment, then decided against it.

She'd have to call her accountant soon, find out what her stocks had done since he'd told her they'd tanked.

But Ella didn't want to think about money. When Callum let go of her hand to rummage through a shelf of dark chocolate infused with dried berries, all she wanted to think about was the warmth it left in hers.

He'd be back in Buffalo soon, and Ella could figure out what she wanted in that time. She closed her now-free hand into a ball, watching Callum read the labels on various chocolates. He pulled one with boysenberries from the shelf and stuck it in the basket.

Ella would take the time to figure it out for sure, but for now, she thought she wanted him.

chapter
twenty-four

We have news, Jace had said.

Ella tapped her salad fork against the linen tablecloth and looked at the time on her phone again. Twenty minutes since she'd gotten to the table. Eighteen since Jace said she and Alexa were almost there. The sweating water goblet looked like Ella felt. She traced an E in the condensation and watched slip away as the drips fell down the side of the glass.

"Would you like me to start an appetizer for your table while you wait?"

The voice made Ella's tapping fork leap from her fingers onto the table. Her server stood with her hands folded on the hem of her apron. She had a sheen on her forehead much like the water goblet, and her eyes rested on the now-still fork with barely-veiled relief.

Ella thought the question sounded an awful lot like, "We are very busy and on a wait, and your reservation was for twenty minutes ago. Please for the love of god, order something."

"I'll take a white wine sangria and an order of mussels," Ella said. "They said they were on their way."

"I'll get that started for you."

The server scurried away, scooping up an empty plate from the table next to Ella and tucking a check presenter under one arm from the next. Ella flapped the napkin on her lap for the eleventh time, looking at her plate to avoid the accusatory looks of the people crowded in the entryway of the restaurant. Had she been here before?

The frescoed walls reminded her of Tuscany, even though the restaurant peddled a sort of contemporary French fusion. Vintage chandeliers dangled and swayed in the breeze from the ceiling fans, and Ella sipped her water, listening to the bustling drone of the diners around her punctuated by the clink of silverware on plates.

"Ella!"

Alexa and Jace squeezed through the throng at the entry and waved. Jace half-plunked down in her chair, leaning over the table to kiss Ella's cheek.

"Sorry we're so late. Traffic was awful."

"I ordered some mussels," Ella said. She smiled at Alexa, who sat down next to Jace. "So what's this news you wanted to tell me?"

Jace and Alexa exchanged a look and a should-we-tell-her smile, but at that moment the server returned with Ella's sangria and the mussels.

Even as they ate, Alexa and Jace kept their hands entwined atop the table, and every so often, Alexa turned to Jace with a small smile glowing at the corners of her mouth.

"You're not pregnant, are you?" Ella blurted. The rattle of mussel shells in the bowl stopped in surprise, and Ella held her breath for a long moment, carefully watching the faces of her friend.

"Oh, god, no," Jace said after a beat. "Not even close to pregnant."

"There's a 'close to pregnant' option?"

"We're lesbians, Ella. You can't get much farther away from pregnant, by default." Alexa grinned.

Ella had to concede that one. "So what's the news then?"

Jace drew a deep breath and licked a bit of butter from the corner of her mouth. "When my parents saw that picture, I thought my life was kind of over. I expected them to take it hard when they found out, but I didn't expect them to ostracize me. I've never felt that way before, like someone cut some sort of umbilical cord to my family."

That feeling Ella knew.

Alexa squeezed Jace's hand.

"What I wasn't expecting," Jace continued, "was the complete outpouring of support at work. The next day I went in, three different people came up to me and said they were so happy for me. They had no idea what my parents had done, but everyone seemed to think something amazing had happened to me. They asked about Alexa and giggled about how in love we looked, and it made me realize something. My parents might never approve, but what happened allowed me to live my life more freely than I've ever been able to. They might have cut a cord, but they also broke some chains I didn't know were there."

Ella reached across the table and put her hand on top of Jace's. "That's wonderful."

"So I made a decision. Alexa and I are moving in together as soon as my lease runs out." Jace ducked her head and smiled at Alexa, then met Ella's eyes.

Ella felt warmth pool in her stomach, and not from the sangria. For five years they'd lived apart, Jace always in fear of her parents finding out. For the first time, Ella saw Jace's face glowing with the knowledge that the happiness she thought out of her grasp was actually hers to keep. Ella thought her heart would burst in her chest, and tears welled up in her eyes.

"I couldn't be more happy for you," she said. "You two deserve this. You do."

Alexa beamed and patted Ella's hand.

"And you know I'll help you move." Ella raised her sangria.

The rest of the meal passed in a happy daze. As Jace and Alexa discussed what movie they were all going to see, Ella got up to go to the restroom. A smile still danced at her lips for her friends. She waded through the crowd, excusing herself when she bumped into someone's kid when he darted out in front of her. Just outside the door, a face caught her eyes.

Straight nose. Thin upper lip, full lower. Long brown waves. Ella froze in the midst of the waiting people, standing on her tiptoes to catch another glimpse of the woman.

"Excuse me," she said, pushing through the crowd for the door. It couldn't be. She got to the door after three tries and pulled it open. The sticky humidity hit her like walking into a bathroom where the shower's as hot as it can get. Outside there was no woman.

Ella scanned the parking lot, her heart beating a subdued patter.

Just one look, and she couldn't be sure. Her mother was supposed to be in South Africa. She was in South Africa.

Wasn't she?

ella forgot the movie almost before she left the theater. She'd laughed at the right places, told Alexa and Jace that she enjoyed it, but nothing about the film had managed to wiggle its way past her fuzzy conviction that she'd seen her mother outside the restaurant.

Back at home, Ella picked up her phone. She stared at her mother's number for seven minutes, watching each of them click by on the phone's clock. Just as the phone was about to tick by another, she pressed the send button and waited.

One ring. Two rings. Three. Four. Five. Six. Seven.

When her mother's voice appeared on the line, it was only the voicemail message.

"I had the weirdest thing happen tonight, Mom. I thought I saw you in Buffalo. It's been a while since we've talked." That was an understatement. It'd been what, a year? Ella couldn't remember. Her parents were so often out in the jungle with no reception that she almost never heard from them. "We missed you at Grammy's funeral last winter. I'd like to catch up with you. I met someone, sort of."

Ella stopped at that. She didn't spill personal details in voicemails.

"Anyway, call me back. I love you."

She hung up.

Puff pounced her knee, tiny paws batting at it as though it were a struggling mouse. Ella pulled the kitten into her lap, scratching both her cheeks until her velvety purr began.

"Your mom's probably far away too, eh Puff? At least we have each other."

Ella wandered through the house, not sure what she wanted to do with herself. After a while, she headed into the study, where Grammy Helen had kept all her photo albums.

Grammy had a whole heap of photo albums. Some dated as far back as the 1800s, their pages filled with immaculately covered black and white photos of flat-faced family members. Ella had loved looking at those as a child, seeing her great-great-great grandparents in front of the very house her Grammy lived in, back when the whitewash still gleamed and she could almost smell the freshly cut timbers and siding. Two of them showed a windowless room Ella thought must have vanished in one of the houses's remodels, a strange reminder of the house's place on the Underground Railroad, here at the gateway to Canada and freedom. But those weren't the photographs Ella wanted to see today.

Instead, she pulled out an album from the mid-nineties. It was one of the few summers they hadn't traveled, choosing instead to go to summer camp in Vermont and then spending the rest camping and never really ridding their fingers of marshmallow goo and tree sap.

Ella and Stuart fishing, both of their faces screwed up in intense concentration as they waited for their bobbers to move.

Ella and Stuart blowing frantically on flaming marshmallows.

Always Ella and Stuart, Ella and Stuart, Ella and Stuart.

And their parents. Her dad with the bushy mustache he used to grow until Mom made him shave it off. Mom brandishing a hunting knife over the fire telling ghost stories on a camping trip with the Cohen family who had moved away when Ella and Stuart were twelve.

The glimpse of the woman at the restaurant haunted her. Was that the same nose she'd seen? Or was the woman's at the restaurant too hooked, too wide at the nostrils? Was that the same hair color? Colors could be changed, but Mom never dyed anything.

No matter how long she stared at the pictures, Ella couldn't tell if the woman she'd seen was her mother.

Had it been that long since she'd seen her mother that she couldn't tell the difference between her and a stranger? The thought disconcerted her, left Ella's mind feeling troubled and sharp around the edges.

She turned her focus back to pictures of Stuart, watching the two of them age like watching a story unfold in a flip book. The blue appeared in his hair that summer, as soon as they got back. She still remembered her dad's face when Stuart came into the kitchen from the bathroom he and Ella shared, smelling like bleach and chemicals. He had a dribbly stain of green down one temple, but his hair was the color of a Smurf and his smile twice as wide.

The blue had stayed forever.

The more she looked at the photos in the albums, the more Ella wanted to see. There was proof, there in those pages, that her family had once been more than just puzzle pieces with no way to interlock. More than a bit of scenery here, an animal's eye there.

They'd been a unit. Mom, Dad, Stuart, Ella. They'd been happy.

There was high school. Stuart's first art show. He'd fallen in love with surrealism, idolizing Dali and Magritte. Her favorite painting of his was obscured in the photograph by his grinning face, but she could fill in the blanks. A tiger in the jungle, leaping through the air with its front paws, while the back two spread out into a rug on someone's floor. Not for the first time, Ella wondered where that painting was.

That was also the year Ella and her friend Daisy's science fair project got second place in the county. She and Daisy tagged along with a university dig and archaeologists from Seneca Nation and helped excavate the remains of an old Iroquois village. Daisy's family were Seneca, and together Ella and Daisy helped the archaeologists find the timbers of the longhouse, arrowheads, glass beads and shells — all of it fascinating and at once ghostly, like a window into the past opened with shovels and brushes. Daisy had become a historian, and after earning their doctorates, they'd collaborated on a few other projects before Daisy moved to Albany.

Stuart had been so proud of Ella's and Daisy's work, and Ella had been proud of him. Both families had taken the kids out to fondue to celebrate. Stuart had given Daisy one of his paintings,

Ella had given her a jade box from Grammy's travels, and Daisy had given Stuart a Green Day CD.

Ella paged through albums late into the night.

chapter
twenty-five

Stratford spread out in front of her like a picture from a storybook. The river wound through the town, and the occasional honk from a goose echoed from its banks. Ella had always thought the town looked like something enchanted. Quaint shops, Victorian houses, brick buildings, and a warm breeze that filtered through the narrow streets.

Ella knew that most of the people strolling down the sidewalks were just as touristy as herself, but that didn't matter. She passed a coffee shop advertising a white chocolate raspberry mocha and almost stepped inside to get it. She paused in the doorway, one hand on the door handle. It was almost ninety degrees outside, and drinking something hot would only make her sweat through her midnight blue dress. Ella had pulled it from her closet again as if to shake her fist at the thunderstorm that had dropped a tree on both her garage and her plans to visit sooner.

The play was to start at seven, and Ella found herself in front of the theater an hour early after picking up her ticket from will call. A small gift shop sat to the left of the theater, and she made her way inside, enjoying the cool bite of the air conditioning on her humidity-touched skin.

Jace would like that orange necklace made of glass beads, Ella thought. The beads were cold against her fingers as she picked it off the turntable, all different shapes and sizes. Swirls of red danced through the centers of the beads, and Ella picked out a pair of matching earrings. She looked at her phone clock again after paying. Only seven after six. Her shopping hadn't killed any time.

She stood in the theater lobby, folding the small paper bag's opening over and over until it pressed up against the necklace at the bottom. Ella didn't know what to expect from the night. She loved *A Midsummer Night's Dream*. She liked Callum. A lot. But afterward, she wasn't sure what would happen. They'd only kissed so far. Her stomach reminded her of that fact by fluttering its lining in tune with the piped in elevator music. When the doors opened, Ella made her way to her seat and tucked the paper bag into her purse where she couldn't do it any more damage.

Minutes stretched themselves out full-length, then touched their fingers to the next one's toes until the bell finally rang and the lights dimmed.

Ella tapped her fingers on the armrest of her chair, then stopped when the portly man next to her shot her a dirty look.

The curtain went up.

It had been a while since Ella saw a play. She used to spend almost every summer here, or at least part of it. Last year she'd spent the time traveling in Alberta and British Columbia and hadn't been in Stratford for the festival. Maybe it was the long absence that made her breath hitch in her throat as the play began, or maybe it was the familiarity of the characters that slumbered on stage, but Ella watched Shakespeare's world unfold in front of her and felt her anxiety slip away. There was no more worry about seeing Callum after or about what would happen when she did.

Instead there were just four lovers bound by a society that didn't value their choices for marriage.

When Callum appeared on stage in act two, Ella almost didn't recognize him.

She knew he was muscular, but seeing the proof clad in flesh-toned tights and leaves with nothing above the waist but a pair of horns sticking up from his tousled hair brought the fluttering back to her stomach again. His chest glistened in the lights from the stage. His lean build looked nothing but from where she sat. Ella swallowed as the light caught the etched line down the center of his belly. Did he really look like that?

He must. Ella started to wonder if she was bespelled like Lysander and Hermia.

Callum's voice rang out through the character of Puck, mischievous and wry. A half-smile flitted over his face as he delivered his lines, and Ella felt blood rush to her cheeks.

The story faded into the background as she watched him. When he looked out over the audience, she couldn't help but think he was searching for her among the hundreds of people crowding the theater. She laughed in the right places, fell silent in the right places, and her eyes strained for every glimpse of Callum on the stage.

The energy in the room felt like the fairies had sprinkled magic dust over the audience, catching the lot of them in a spell for the two hours of the play. Ella tried to relax in her chair, but saw only the remainder of a play that seemed to reach out its tendrils over the armrests, over the seat backs, and into the minds of everyone around her.

Except for her there was only Callum Penrose.

As he spoke his last lines of the show, his eyes scanned the audience. "If we shadows have offended, think but this and all be mended." On the last word, his eyes locked with Ella's. Her heart leaped in in her chest.

She stood with the rest of the audience as they rose for a standing ovation. Callum's eyes were only on hers as he bowed to the cheers around her. The swell of the applause brought rows of gooseflesh rising across her arms, and Ella felt a low tingle in the core of her belly. The actors vanished behind the drawn curtain, and Ella pulled her purse to her chest. What now? The high of the play's ending thrilled through her, turning her muscles to icy-hot humming.

She pulled her phone from her purse as she waited for the throng to allow her into the aisle.

"**Meet me out front in twenty.**" A text from Callum.

It had been sent ten minutes before. Ella made her way at an achingly slow pace through the aisle and out into the lobby. The crowd slid away from her mind in the polished marble surroundings of the foyer, slowly dissipating into the still-warm night. Ella bought an Italian soda from the theater vender and sipped it, the sweet creaminess coating her tongue.

Other cast members appeared around her. Their names in the programs were long forgotten to Ella, and she thought of them only as their characters. Lysander and Hermia signed programs for a family with three adolescent children. Demetrius and Helena posed for a picture with an elderly couple with American flags for shirts. There was Wall having an earnest discussion with a young woman, and Oberon looking irritated as someone stopped him on the way into the restroom.

"Looking for me?"

That would be Puck. Ella turned to see Callum behind her, his face scrubbed of makeup. His hands touched her cheeks, sending zig-zags of sweet shocks down the sides of her neck. He bent and kissed her, and for a moment Ella lost herself in the warmth of his lips on her chilled mouth.

"You taste like raspberries," he murmured.

Ella looked up at him. Her breath came shallow and choppy, like a fast river over rocks. "You were fabulous as Puck."

"I'm just glad you got to come."

The gleam in his eyes as he took her hand and turned away made her think that all his mischief on stage may not have been an act.

It was the first time Ella had seen Callum's home.

She followed him into the small apartment, looking up at the high ceilings that echoed with their footsteps.

"It's a bit sparse. I got a furnished place because it was just temporary, but the furnishings are limited to...furniture." He motioned to the couch and coffee table in the living area. "Have a seat. Would you like some wine?"

Ella nodded and sat. The sofa was firm underneath her. It reminded her of the one in her apartment in college, which she and Jace had lovingly dubbed the chastity couches. She shifted her weight and crossed her right leg over her left, looking around for a throw pillow to put into her lap and finding none.

The pop of the cork resonated through the empty apartment, and Ella jumped.

Callum's head appeared around the corner from the kitchen. "Sorry," he said. "The problem with temporary apartments is that there's nothing on the walls to keep it from sounding like a cave. My place in Buffalo is much more homey. It's even clean."

Ella smiled at him and tried to settle herself in the corner of the sofa. Her heart had picked up to a faster-than-normal tempo, and after three futile calming breaths, she resigned herself to the hurried beating in her chest. She didn't remember getting this fluttery with her ex. Granted that was almost eight years ago, and the only dates she'd been on since were with women. Women were safe, and though it got awkward sometimes when Ella had to inevitably flee, she never had to worry about this. It was of course possible to spend the night with someone without having sex. But Ella wasn't sure that was what she wanted, and suddenly the sparsely decorated apartment seemed to occupy another dimension, separate from the the rest of Earth.

Her heart and breath conspired against her, like she'd felt at her first middle school dance when she'd danced with Jason Kansas to No Doubt's Don't Speak. She felt the headiness of warm arms around her for the first time, reliving that moment even as she sat alone on the couch.

And then Callum was there, handing her a chilled glass of chardonnay, and the brush of his hand on hers turned her into a nervous twelve-year-old all over again.

"To new beginnings," he said, raising his glass.

Ella clinked her wine glass on his. "To new beginnings." Her voice came out with a breathy huskiness she wasn't used to, and from the way Callum swallowed before the wine even touched his lips, he noticed it too.

She sipped the wine, oaky and dry with hints of bright white plums. Setting her glass on the coffee table, she looked at Callum. Ella wanted to say something, anything to break the thick silence. "So what next?"

She'd meant for his life, for his plans in Buffalo and the rest of the year. Instead, he sat his glass next to hers and took her hand between both of his. "I was thinking maybe you could stay. If you want."

Her head nodded before her mind had a chance to process his statement, and after the briefest of pauses, his arms enfolded her, and his lips pressed against hers. Always before their kisses had been soft, like the wings of a hummingbird against your cheek. This time they moved against hers with a hunger she'd never felt from him.

"You still taste like raspberries," he murmured against her cheek.

Callum's lips trailed down the side of her neck, his hands on the smooth satin of her dress where the tight bodice gave way to only skin and no straps. In his touch there was a whisper of more against the line between fabric and skin, a desire to eschew that boundary and leave only one behind.

Warmth spread through her, but Ella shivered in his arms. She let her own hands seek out his chest, the sides of his ribs, his back, feeling the muscles she'd seen displayed so cleanly on stage less than an hour before. Ella let Callum lean her backward on the too-firm sofa, his kisses leaving trails of pulsing embers in the crook of her neck. His weight pressed down on her, his knees on the expanse of midnight satin skirt between her legs.

That skirt was all that stood between her and what?

Ella lost herself in Callum's kisses. When his hands ran over her breasts, she shivered again, exhaling a shuddering breath as his lips met hers again. His weight bore down into her, solidly there and firmer than the couch beneath her. Her satin dress kept her from moving, but it did nothing to conceal the growing warmth and hardness that pressed up against her. Ella swallowed, raising her hand to Callum's hair.

Soft and still tousled, she thought she could almost imagine Puck's horns still there. Ella ran her fingers through the dark strands, seeing them stand out against the milky paleness of her skin. Callum's arm broke into gooseflesh, and his lips sought out her jawline, tracing a path to her ear. He took her earlobe between his lips, teasing it lightly with his tongue. Ella reached her arms around him and pulled him closer into her, every inch of her body aflame with his touch.

When he pulled back, his voice seemed to have dropped an octave when he spoke. "I'm still sort of covered in oil from the stage." His fingers drew little swirling lines on her shoulder, and already Ella's body missed the weight of him.

She looked into his gray eyes. His pupils were dilated, his lips full and plump from their kisses. "Okay," she said.

"How about you go into the bedroom, and I'll take a quick rinse off and join you in a few minutes? Only if you want."

"Okay," she said again.

"Okay?"

"Okay." Ella felt a smile pulling at her lips.

Callum's weight lifted from the sofa, and he vanished down the hall into the bathroom. Ella stood, straightening the folds of her now-wrinkled satin dress. She passed the kitchen and the bathroom to the right, hearing the creak of the shower turning on. The end of the hall was the bedroom, and Ella's breath hitched as she crossed the threshold.

One queen bed and not much else. A pair of jeans folded on a chair. An alarm clock next to a lamp on the bedside table. She sat at the foot of the bed, her heart still pounding. Looking down, her chest was flushed mottled red, and her fingers trembled lightly when she held them in front of her face.

The bed was softer than the couch, and her weight sank into it. The mattress gave beneath her, and Ella laid back, feeling as though the down duvet and the mattress were about to swallow her whole. Eight years, it had been.

Eight years since her jackass of an ex and the ring he thought would erase all their problems. Eight years of just Ella alone in her body. Suddenly the softness of the bed seemed to reach around her, and she sat up, skin crawling with the memory of Brett. She couldn't do this. Could she?

This was Callum. Nice, gentle, funny, witty Callum. And her body sang in a low contralto when she thought of what had caused the flush on her chest, the warmth low in her belly. The raised downy hairs on her arms. She wanted this. She was an adult.

Ella scooted back on the bed, the muted rushing of the shower pervading her thoughts.

She could do this. She could stay the night.

If she said no to sex, she was certain he would simply smile and let her snuggle him as anyone ought to in such a situation.

The bare walls around her mocked her as if to say that they weren't afraid of being naked. Ella swallowed again, and this time not from desire. Eight years was a long time.

The buzz of her skin became electric like a bug zapper. Ella rubbed her hands across the skin on her arms, her breath coming faster. The sound of the water running in the bathroom crowded in on her, like a timer counting down.

Too much, too soon. Ella stood, looking around the sparsely furnished room. Too much.

She hurried from the bedroom and into the kitchen. A grocery receipt sat on the counter next to a pen. She scrawled the words with a shaking hand, listening for the continuing sound of the shower.

I'm so sorry. I can't.

She left the note at the foot of the bed and gathered her purse from the arm of the hard sofa.

The two glasses of wine remained on the coffee table, undrunk.

ella woke the next morning to her phone's ping. She opened one eye to look at the notification.

ACCOUNT ALERT: LOW BALANCE.

There were also three text messages, but Ella ignored them.

She sat straight up in bed, blinking the sleep from her eyes. Logging into her account, her heart tap-danced on her ribs. She couldn't have a balance that low, could she?

The screen showed that she had just over $2600. Ella stared at it for a long moment, wondering in what stratosphere that qualified as low until she realized that she had a $2500 minimum balance on her account. She'd get assessed a large fee if she didn't keep her balance above that, and then subsequent fees until she cleared the minimum again.

Her body felt achy and empty as she pulled the covers over her head, shutting out her phone and its bad news. A tiny weight landed on her chest, flattening the comforter against her breast. Puff, pouncing the blankets. She smiled and reached out, scooping the kitten under the covers with her. Puff scrambled over her shoulder, wriggling a kitty-style army crawl over her ribcage. Poof gave an indignant "Mow?" from the doorway.

"I know you want fed, cat. Give me a second."

She'd driven across the border at two that morning. The border guards shined flashlights into her car and asked her why she was returning so late, and for an instant, Ella had been tempted to just blurt out the truth. She wondered what they would have said if she'd confessed she was too messed up to be able to sleep with the guy she really liked.

Because she did really like Callum. Puff wiggled up to her throat, her tiny mouth snuffling at the skin on Ella's neck, little paws kneading her shoulder. "You're not going to find anything to eat there, kitten," she said.

Ella made herself get up and feed the cats and Prince to work up the courage to look at the text messages.

As she'd expected, they were all from Callum.

"God, Ella. I'm sorry if things moved too quickly. Please call me."

"I hope you're all right. Text me when you get home?"

"Please, Ella. I want to know you got home safe. Please call." That message was from — Ella looked at the time — four hours ago. He'd stayed up until four in the morning because of her.

Ella rubbed her hand over her eyes and sat down on a kitchen chair, listening to the crunch-crunch-snuffle-shuffle-crunch of the cats eating their kibble. Puff always purred when she ate, and that little whispery rumble overlaid the crunching.

She dialed Callum's number, thumb hovering over the send button.

Her thumb came down.

He answered on the second ring. "Ella?"

Guilt racked her. Was he still awake? Had he slept at all? She berated herself. She'd handled that so badly, so immaturely. Ella thought through all the ways she could have done it differently. Just waited for him to get out of the shower and then told him she couldn't. Talked to him. Anything but dip out and leave a note, leaving him to worry. It wasn't like he would have been upset with her or blamed her. He'd said they could move slowly, and Ella knew he meant it.

"I'm so sorry," was all she managed to get out.

The long pause sent her stomach churning.

"You're okay?" He sounded tired, but his voice wore concern draped over the exhaustion.

"Yeah. I'm okay." She should have texted him last night. Anything different. She wanted to start a litany of "I'm sorry," repeat it over and over until she felt some absolution. Just one more came out, though, and Ella bit it off before it could multiply. "I'm sorry."

"No, I'm the one who's sorry," Callum said. "We were going to move slowly, and things weren't going slow last night. When I asked you to stay, I meant stay in whatever way made you comfortable. I didn't mean to scare you off."

Ella barked a laugh. "It wasn't you," she said, hating the cliché the moment it left her tongue. "It's just…it's been a really long time. I freaked."

She'd freaked out like a fourteen-year-old who just found out she'd tucked the back of her skirt into her underwear.

"I wish you'd stayed and talked to me about it."

Ella was glad he said it. He was right. That would have been the adult thing to do. "I'm really sorry I worried you," she said. "I should have waited until you got out of the shower."

"How about this? I'm moving back in a week. When I get back, I'd like to take you to the symphony. We can go together. I'll pick you up, and afterward we'll do whatever you want, whether it's smack me and run away or go to HoJo's and drink coffee."

The symphony. "You're being awfully cool about this," she said.

It was Callum's turn to let out a bark of a laugh. "In case you haven't realized it yet, you sort of picked me up and wrapped me around your finger when you first sat down at my table and butted in on my crossword. Besides, any other reaction than letting you decide your own readiness is just asshole level."

Ella paused, her body going very still. She couldn't make herself speak.

"I'm crazy about you," Callum said. "Just...next time I make you want to run away, at least tell me why in person."

"Okay," Ella said. Her mind flitted from thought to thought, not managing to make sense of any of them. This was such a different reaction than Brett would have had. He would have stomped and moaned and plied heavy on the guilt trips. Asshole level, indeed. Instead Callum wanted to take her to the symphony. "I'd love to go to the symphony when you get back."

"Good. Because I want to take you. You brought it last night with the fancy dress; now it's my turn to show you that I clean up nice and don't just look good in spandex and leaves and fake horns."

Ella smiled, the heaviness in her chest lifting. "Sounds good. I'll...call you tomorrow, okay?"

"Perfect. I'll talk to you then."

She hung up the phone and set it down on the table. Ella thought about Callum staying up all night, waiting for a message from her and getting nothing. Brett would have rubbed that in her face. Instead Callum only met her with kindness.

Whatever hangups surfaced after eight years of ignoring people who showed romantic interest, Ella straightened her shoulders and determined that she wouldn't let the past ruin her relationship with this one.

ella peered into the refrigerator, dismay pooling at its bare shelves. She dug around in the bottom drawers until she found a green pepper and some spinach that hadn't yet turned to slime, and she threw together an omelet for breakfast. She couldn't go grocery shopping, or the check she'd written to the electric company would send her balance below the threshold. More than enough money had languished in savings for years, but with her investments tanked, her broker had all of it tied up to cover the loss.

She chewed her omelet, making a face. The eggs were soft and fluffy, but the vegetables tasted like fridge. She scraped them away from the eggs and shunted the vegetables off to the side of her plate. She needed to look for a job, and she needed to do that immediately.

As she dumped the egg-caked vegetables into the trash, she froze, fork on plate, her gaze rising to the ceiling. Maybe the keys would help. It was worth a shot, at least. Ella rinsed her plate and went upstairs, stopping only to pick up the painstakingly-drawn diagram of the corridor.

The shiny keys she avoided, hunting out the knobbly, tarnished ones. She settled on a long brass skeleton key that looked like finger bones. It hung near the floor on the right side of the hall, about a foot from the molding. Ella looked at her drawing. B17. She picked it off the wall and turned it over in her hands, feeling its warmth. The corridor was already hot from the day's sun and no air conditioning vents, and she replaced the key after a long moment. She left her diagram sitting beneath it on the floor and went back downstairs.

Just as she reached the ground floor, a polite tapping sounded at the door.

Heart taking a jump against her sternum, Ella peeked out of the window. A group of teens and two adults stood on the porch, big smiles stretched across their faces. She opened the door and poked her head out. "Can I help you?"

"That was more the question we were going to ask you," one of the teens said with a grin. The girl was tall and looked like a basketball player. It was only then that Ella noticed the gardening gloves tucked into the waistband of her shorts. "We're from the Unitarian Universalist Church of Buffalo, and we're going around to houses this summer to see if we can help with yard work. We saw that your grass is getting a bit long, and we were wondering if you'd be okay with us sprucing up your yard for you!"

A bit long. That was one way of saying it. Ella gave the girl a rueful grin. "That would be lovely," she said. "If you need a mower, I think my grandmother still has one in the garage."

"We brought everything we need," a man said from the back of the group. "We'll get the lawn mowed and edged for you."

All the teens except one scattered at the direction of the first girl who had spoken, but the man stayed on the porch, a young guy next to him. "This is Rob Stevens. I've got to run into town to pick up one of our other kids, but if you need anything, ask Rob or Iza over there."

"Sounds good," said Ella.

"You can call me Junior," the boy said. He had a slight build and longish hair. "I'll be in the back yard and Iza will be up front."

Ella nodded as he walked away, but the man lingered.

"Are you Helen Keyes' granddaughter?" he asked.

"Yes. I'm Ella." She reached out and shook his hand.

"I'm George Hemming." George Hemming looked around. He had a long face that contrasted with a short, rather stout body, but his eyes were full of warmth and concern. "If you're living here now, I guess that means Helen is no longer with us."

Ella pressed her lips together and nodded slowly. "She passed away in December."

"That long ago?"

"Did you know her well?"

"We came twice every summer to take care of her landscaping. She handled her flowers, but she let us help out with the rest. Some of these kids didn't know her that well, but I came for the last four years. She'd always make everyone mint iced tea and usually handed out little trinkets from her travels to some of the kids she'd pick by drawing their names from a hat."

Grammy would do something like that. Ella smiled, feeling the edges of that empty hole where lost loved ones left their chasm. "She was always a kind person."

"She was at that. I'm going to go get the kids moving. We'll let you know when we finish up."

"Thank you," Ella said. "I'm not that great at yard work."

George gave her a smile and stepped off the porch. Ella followed him down, feet stepping gingerly on the rough path to the mail box. Across the yard, Junior tugged a weedeater from the bed of their truck. Something niggled at Ella's memory, but she couldn't place it. She pried the mailbox open, frowning when it stuck. After a moment, she saw why. She stared at the stuffed box for a long second. How long had it been since she checked the mail? She pulled out a stack of envelopes and the shopper guide that curved around them, piling all the mail into the crook of her arm. Four days? Five?

Ella shook her head and nudged the now-empty box shut, making her way back to the house. She stooped to scoop up the two newspapers on the porch as well. She'd go through the classifieds to see what jobs were offered before moving the search online.

Suddenly she stopped short in the middle of the entryway. Robert Stevens Junior. Her former landlord was Robert J. Stevens; Ella had seen his full name when she signed her lease.

The checks.

Ella's mouth fell open.

She dumped the pile of mail on the dining room table just as the coughing roar of a mower began outside. Glancing toward it, she thought their appearance on her front porch was pretty fortuitous. Now she wouldn't have to wrestle the grumbly dinosaur of a mower Grammy always used in the summers — if it even still existed and worked.

She spread out the classifieds on the table, fetching a red felt tip pen from the study. The job market in Buffalo wasn't exactly booming, and Ella eyed the pen warily, hoping she wouldn't end up circling ads for fry cooks and administrative assistants. She didn't even know if she could get that sort of job without pretending not to have a Ph.D.

She set the pen down in the center crease of the newspaper and paged through the stack of envelopes, tossing single-page tagboard advertisements into a pile with the shopper guides.

A thank you letter from the university was the first thing she opened, and her chest constricted at the sight of Stuart's name. The letter was signed by Easton Gellerman, Ph.D.

In spite of the fact that Easton seemed to have completely taken over her old job, Ella smiled to see the letters following his name. Even better was the announcement in the letter that the Stuart Keyes Scholarship had five finalists chosen for the upcoming year already, and that Easton was looking into all their backgrounds as well as their personal essays and applications to see who would benefit from the money the most. With a little luck, the scholarship would last several years.

The rest of the envelopes were all pre-approved credit cards and bills until Ella got to the bottom of the stack. The final envelope was postmarked six days before and came from her stockbroker's address.

She opened it quickly, slicing through the crease of her thumb's knuckle with the envelope's flap. The cut stung, and blood welled up immediately. Ella popped her finger in her mouth, taking hold of the letter and shaking it out of the envelope with her free hand.

She scanned the page, eyes widening more with each line.

Dear Dr. Keyes,

When I did not hear a response from my last email,

Ella frowned at that. What email? She read it over again.

When I did not hear a response from my last email, I decided to send you a letter to document the actions undertaken on your behalf this week. Because of the nature of our last interaction, it will come as a surprise to know that the stocks that previously took a sharp downturn have not only returned to their previous levels of stability, but have exceeded their value by large margin.

Exceeded. Ella's gaze drifted over the figures at the bottom of the page without really understanding them.

While this was unexpected, it has greatly improved the viability of your portfolio, and you should find that your funds are free for you to use. Additionally, because of the volatility of these particular stocks, I have opted to remove your funds from these arenas and moved

> them to a low-risk account in accordance to our written agreement that you signed upon investing with our firm. We promised you a risk-averse strategy at that time and apologize for the inconvenience of having your savings tied up due to an unexpected shift in the stability of these bonds. We've sold those stocks and will reinvest the funds, pending your agreement. In spite of these rather extreme fluctuations, I think you will be very happy with the outcome.

Ella read the letter three more times before she could process the information at the bottom of the page. She'd invested a large amount of her savings five years ago, which had grown steadily into six figures — until a few weeks back when it had plummeted.

She read the figures again, trying to make sense of it. She'd bought the initial stocks in three different companies for five dollars per share. For five years, they had grown quietly to just over eleven dollars, then dipped down to about a dollar. If what her broker had written here was true, they'd all soared above twenty-five when he'd sold them.

She now had just over a quarter million dollars when five years ago she'd invested fifty thousand.

That just didn't happen.

Ella hurried to her computer and opened her email, paging through her inbox. Since losing her job, she didn't get much email aside from the junk that cluttered her inbox. No email from her broker.

She clicked the spam folder. Among emails that began, "Dearest Beloved Friend" and offers for Viagra, there it was. She opened the email from her broker.

It confirmed what the letter said.

Ella walked back out to the dining room where the red pen sat in the center of a sea of job ads.

Looked like she wouldn't be needing that after all.

She walked up to the third floor corridor, each step in rhythm with the pulse of the lawn mower and weedeater. Next to key B17, she wrote, "Financial windfall and free lawn manicure."

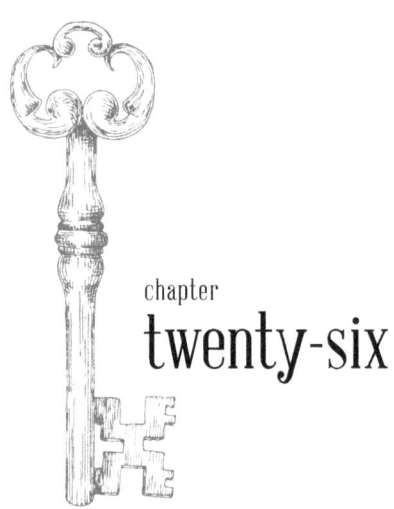

chapter
twenty-six

Ella met with her broker and her accountant that Monday and agreed to reinvest half the money in a low-risk, long term savings program for her retirement.

Retirement. It wasn't as though she could retire on two hundred and fifty thousand dollars, but she knew what she wanted to do with the rest.

What was she good at? She'd spent five years as a college professor, and she still enjoyed the thought of teaching. She liked traveling.

The thought had surfaced before, and as Ella left her broker's office and stepped into the hot sun, it returned, flirting with her mind. She could combine those two things. Organize tours of Scandinavia and the British Isles, Eastern Europe. Bring mythology and history to life.

The more she thought of the idea, the more she liked it. Buffalo wasn't far from New York City. Not so far that she couldn't easily arrange the tours to leave from there. Ella got in her car, a new dream germinating and taking root in her mind. She might not make much money, but without a car payment and a mortgage, all she'd need to do would be pay a pet sitter for when she was gone.

a hall of keys and no doors

Her phone rang before she even started the car's engine. Jace. The steering wheel was hot against her hand as she brushed it, and she turned on the ignition, cranking the air up to max.

"Hey, girlie," Ella said, answering just before the phone went to voice mail. "How are the moving plans shaping up?"

"They're good!" Jace's voice sounded ready to burst with chipper, and Ella smiled.

"Do you have a date for the move yet?"

"My lease runs out on the fourteenth of August, so I think we're just going to plan for the move to be the weekend before that."

"Just let me know when you need me, and I'll be there."

"Thanks. I'll keep you posted. Oh!" Jace paused. "How was your trip up to Stratford?"

Ella winced, fiddling with the knobs on the dash as though it would turn the warm blasting air cold faster than just waiting. "It was...rough." She quickly related what had happened.

Jace made a sound like *ow-owww* when Ella got to the couch and the fooling around bit, but went silent and sighed as soon as Ella mentioned that she'd fled. "You just left?"

"I started thinking about Brett and just panicked, I guess."

"Next time panic the other way, girl. You're probably dry as the Sahara down there."

Ella ignored that. "He was really sweet about it. Really, really sweet. He's taking me to the symphony next week when he comes back."

"Ooh, la la. When do we get to see him again?"

"I don't know."

"Well, figure it out. I like Callum. For a dude you're dating."

Ella wasn't sure what that meant. "Look, I've got a couple errands to run, but can we get together later? I want to trot some ideas past you."

"Of course. I'll come over after I'm done showing these new buyers some houses this afternoon. Probably around six."

Hanging up the phone, Ella took a deep breath of the artificial cold that had started spewing from the vents. The steering wheel still felt too hot to touch, but she put the car in reverse and backed out of her parking spot, gingerly touching the rubber. She'd come up with a business plan, sketch out some ideas for her tours, and then see what Jace thought about it. The idea tantalized her. Ella had never thought about being a business owner before, but the longer the idea spent taking root in her mind, the more its roots entwined with the rest of her.

She took the For Sale By Owner sign down when she got home. It bore sticky grass clippings round the edges from the gardeners' efforts. Ella threw it in the trash.

No one had even called.

Jace dumped a basket of muffins onto the kitchen counter. "I brought those for you. Left over from an open house this morning."

The basket contained a variety, and Ella pulled a blueberry muffin out and peeled back the wrapper. "Thanks."

"So what's this idea you had?"

Ella motioned to the table, and they sat down. Jace's face bore drying beads of perspiration, and she pressed her water glass against her cheek.

The thought of becoming an entrepreneur had never really occurred to Ella until she lost her job, but she loved the idea of being her own boss. She couldn't — or most likely wouldn't — fire herself, at the very least.

She took a deep breath. "I think I want to start a company that would organize and lead tours to famous sites of mythology. Temples, standing stones, cairns, places where legends are said to have come to life. I'd do a few tours a year for maybe ten to twenty people at a time. I'd organize the flights, the hotels, the transportation and everything, and all they'd have to do is show up with their suitcases and cameras at JFK."

Jace sat still, her glass still held to her face. After a pause, she set the glass on the table and wiped away the trickle of condensation from her cheek. "That sounds like an amazing idea."

"You really think so?"

"I really do. You've always been so organized." Jace turned her head, her gaze on the carefully alphabetized teas in their caddy on the counter. "For something like that, you'd need plans A through D ready to roll in case something went wrong, and you're just enough of a control freak to make it happen."

Ella couldn't help the glow that started in her chest. "I think I'll spend the fall and winter planning it all out —"

Before she could go on, someone knocked at the door.

"Hold that thought," Jace said.

Ella moved through the house to the front door and opened it.

Auntie Eunice stood on the porch, a wide-brimmed straw hat perched on top of her head and enormous, bug-like sunglasses taking up most of her face.

"Auntie Eunice," Ella said. "What are you doing?"

"I came to see you, boy." The old woman squeezed past her into the house. "You've got company? Good. Anything to eat?"

Aunt Eunice bustled into the kitchen and waved at Jace, eyes trained on the basket of muffins. She selected a poppyseed one and took a large bite from the very center of its top. Crumbs dribbled from the corners of her mouth as she chewed. Ella leaned against the counter, watching her and feeling exasperated. She wasn't in the mood to watch the woman dig through boxes again.

"Did you come to look for the thing again?" Ella felt stupid calling it *the thing*, but she wouldn't have known it if it landed on her face. It could be a chair for all she knew, but then if it were something as large as a chair, she supposed Auntie Eunice wouldn't have been looking for it in boxes.

Then again, Ella thought, looking at Auntie Eunice in her hat and massive shades, maybe she would at that.

"I haven't come to look for anything, Ella. I came to see you, just as I said." Eunice took another large bite of muffin. "Hello, Jace, dear. Lovely picture of you in the paper. Alexa's a lucky woman."

Jace's cheeks turned bright red, but she managed a smile. "Thanks, Aunt Eunice."

"Don't let her get away. Love's a tough nut to chase."

Jace blinked at that, but nodded when Auntie Eunice continued to stare at her, expectant.

"Have you heard from your parents lately?"

"No," Ella and Jace said in unison.

The dual answer made both Ella and Jace jump, and Jace turned even redder when she realized that the question wasn't directed at her at all. Auntie Eunice shot her a shrewd glance that showed she hadn't missed the answer from Jace, but turned her attention back to Ella immediately.

"Well, that's a damned shame. You haven't forgotten to call them every once in a while, have you? Kids. Always thinking everyone else ought to do all the work."

"I called my mom not long ago and left a message, but I haven't heard back."

"She always was a flighty one," the old woman muttered. "How your father managed to tie her down this long is beyond me."

Ella shifted her weight to her left foot and scratched at the edge of the counter with her thumbnail, unsure of what Auntie

Eunice was trying to say. "I'll let you know if I hear anything from her."

"You do that." Eunice frowned, looking back to Jace, whose cheeks were slowly beginning to return to their normal color. "And you. If you don't hear from your parents soon, I'll go give them a piece of my mind. No one who calls themself a good Christian should turn their damn daughter away just because she fancies girls over boys."

The color flared back up in Jace's skin immediately. "Oh, that's not necessary, Aunt Eunice. It's fine. Really."

Aunt Eunice smacked her hand down on the counter, making the basket of muffins shake. "It's about as fine as mouse-gnawed silk, boy. Don't you do that."

With that, the old lady plucked another muffin from the basket and waved it in the air. "Well, I'm off."

"You just got here." Ella blinked. Strangest social call she'd had this week. Which, she admitted, wasn't saying much lately.

"I've got things to do," Auntie Eunice said. "I'll see you soon."

She swept out of the kitchen, and after a moment, the front door slammed and Ella heard the sound of her white Volvo pulling out of the drive.

"European tours, you say?" Jace asked.

"That was the plan," Ella said, still looking toward the front of the house.

"I might need the opportunity to get far away from this town myself."

Ella couldn't say she'd blame her.

the door looked like it led to a prison. Or not really, but to Ella that didn't matter. She stood in front of it, gritting her teeth. She could do this. She could. She waited for Jace, who hurried over from the car, dropping her keys in her leather messenger bag.

Jace stopped a couple feet in front of Ella. "What are you waiting for?"

Ella looked at the door, trying to make out the shapes of people behind it. Finally she sighed. "Nothing, I guess."

She hated malls.

The air inside smelled like freon and pretzels, and Ella's nose wrinkled two steps into the long corridor.

"Hey, you're the one who needs a dress. I'm just here for moral support." Amusement lit Jace's face. "You've got your 'what stinks?' look on again."

"The mall stinks."

"Of course it does. This many teenagers who haven't learned to put on deodorant plus really bad Chinese food? What did you expect?"

"I keep hoping that someday I'll come here and it won't smell like feet."

"Dream on, sister."

Ella followed Jace from department store to department store. Most of the dresses they found Ella thought would look better on a prom queen than a grown woman going out for a night on the town. She supposed she could have gone downtown to a boutique and found something really nice, but Ella couldn't justify dropping several hundred dollars on a couture piece of frill she'd probably only wear once.

After two hours, she started to lose hope. The symphony was in two days. Callum would be back in town tomorrow, and even though they'd talked on the phone every day, Ella still wasn't sure she believed him when he said he was excited to see her again.

"How about this one?" Jace held up a red dress that looked like a toddler had filled a straw with glitter and blown it all over the fabric.

"Ew. Are you serious?"

"Fine, fine." Jace put the dress back on the rack. "You've got to help me a bit here, Els. Give me a blue or a black. Green. Puce. Anything."

"Black."

"See, now you're helping." Jace flipped through the rack, then circled to the other side, looking around.

"Thanks for coming with me."

"Oh, you know me. Helping the helpless is what I do."

The opposite side of the rack held only silver and gold dresses, and they moved onto the next.

"Ella?" A male voice cut through the elevator music and the clicking of hangers. "Ella Keyes?"

Ella knew that voice. She felt air on her eyeballs as her eyes widened, then blinked rapidly, turning around, hoping she was wrong.

She wasn't. Brett Matheson, her ex-almost-fiance stood in front of her, holding a six-pack of boxer briefs. His left hand sported a plain gold wedding band that seemed a little too loose. He was taller than she remembered; he probably had an inch on Callum, and his shoulders were broader. He'd played football for the first two years of college, and Stuart had always razzed her for dating a football player.

"It is you. My god."

"Brett," she said.

"You look great." He motioned to her hair with a vague sort of gesture. "I like the blue."

After dating the guy for three years, she knew how to spot his insincerities. She ignored it. "What are you doing here?"

Ella didn't like the idea that Brett was in Buffalo and shopping for something domestic. No way he'd moved here. Had he? She knew his real estate investment company had gone under in '08 when the industry took a nose dive, and the last thing she'd heard he was eking out a living as a contractor in Maine.

"I'm just in town for a meeting with a client. I was coming off a long night when I packed and forgot a few necessities." He waggled the boxer briefs and seemed to notice Jace for the first time. "And Jace! You two are still friends?"

"No, I just follow her around," Jace said.

Brett blinked, frowning. "Look, I'm sorry to bother you. I just… it's been a long time, Ella. How's your family? How's Stu?"

Stuart hated being called Stu, which was probably one of the reasons he'd hated Brett, who could never seem to remember. Jace went tight-lipped and silent, looking to Ella.

"Stuart died three years ago," Ella said.

Brett's mouth fell open, and he took a small step backward. "He what? How?"

"Accident." Ella didn't want to give him any more information than necessary.

Her ex swallowed, then moved forward again, one hand rising as if he wanted to give Ella a hug, but it dropped again after a second. Ella had never known him to be indecisive. Driven and ambitious, yes. Uncaring, yes. But not hesitant and nervous. Maybe the struggles of his job had changed him.

"I'm truly sorry. I always liked him a lot. He was a good guy." This time Brett's voice held no insincerity, only genuine grief.

Ella hesitated. "Thank you."

"Look, I have to get to a meeting. But it was good seeing you." Brett dug in his pocket and pulled out a slightly-wrinkled business card. "My email's on there. If you ever want to catch up, let me know."

He turned and started to walk away, then stopped and looked over his shoulder. "I'm really sorry about your brother."

Ella watched him go, wondering what the years had done to the man she'd fled marrying.

She put the business card in her wallet, though, wondering if she'd ever be curious enough to find out.

"This is why I never come to malls."

Jace clapped her hand on Ella's shoulder. "Let's just find your dress."

It was Jace who found it, a slinky, lightweight black gown that scooped low in the back and dipped almost as low in the front, the fabric falling in loose folds to the cleft of her rib cage. Ella normally wouldn't go for something that left her that exposed, but when she put it on, the soft material clung to her like a sheath. Jace squealed as soon as Ella stepped out of the dressing room, dragging her down to the three-way mirror.

"This is it! This is it, isn't it?" Jace turned her around, and Ella grinned at her, the pressure of running into Brett evaporating.

"I think we found it."

"You're going to knock Callum dead."

"Let's hope not." Ella smoothed her hands over her hips, and her mind whispered that it could be Callum's touch there that weekend.

Ella looked in the mirror, seeing Jace's beaming face over her shoulder reflected in the glass. She wouldn't run away this time.

chapter
twenty-seven

She needed a distraction. That's what it came down to. Ella stood in the living room, looking around at the walls. Paint. Maybe she could paint them. Not for the first time, she wished she had some of Stuart's artwork to hang on the walls. The tiger painting was her favorite, but he'd painted others, others that would fit well in this room. There was one of a tree growing out of the center of a library floor with titles scratched between the lines of its bark. Another of a man rising alone out of a sea of black.

As she imagined the walls filled with her brother's art, she turned at footsteps on the porch and reached the door almost before the knock. It was Auntie Eunice again, in the same hat and sunglasses, but this time clutching a large photo album. She looked up in surprise when Ella answered the door.

"That was quick."

"I heard your footsteps. What's up, Auntie Eunice?"

Auntie Eunice wet her lips and gave Ella a wide smile. "I found this album in my house and thought you might want to see it." She tromped past Ella into the house and set it down on the dining room table.

Ella followed with a shrug. She'd said she needed a distraction.

Auntie Eunice sat down at the head of the table and opened the album to a random page, smoothing it flat. All the photos were black and white, and Ella moved to stand behind her, looking over her shoulder. "Is that..."

"My grandmother? Yes." Eunice pointed to a photograph of a woman in a high-necked dress with poofy sleeves. "I think she was pregnant with my mother here, but barely. This was taken right at the turn of the century, 1902 or 1903. When I show you a picture of my mother from the twenties, you'll see a real difference." She chuckled as if she'd made a good joke.

The old woman's fingers traced the border of the photograph, and Ella caught the hint of a fond smile on her great-aunt's face. She looked closer at the picture, trying to make out any hints of family resemblance in the upright stoicism of the woman's face. She stood on the front porch of the very house they sat in, and as Ella looked into the photograph, she almost had the urge to open the door and check to see if her great-great-grandmother were indeed standing next to a pillar.

And looking closer, there it was. The straight nose, almost a bit too long. That same nose was on Ella's face and had been on Stuart's as well. And Grammy Helen had had it, as well as her identical twin who just then had gathering tears swimming in her eyes. Ella pulled a chair over to where Auntie Eunice sat and put her hand on the woman's gnarled knuckles, taking her hand and giving it a light squeeze. It reminded her of the elephant at the zoo, that reassuring moment of pressure, and it gave Ella an idea. Sara Krakowski, the florist-turned-photographer, had called a few days before to let Ella know she had a whole disc of edited photos for her to pick up.

"Auntie Eunice, would you like to come on a small errand with me?"

"What sort of an errand?" Auntie Eunice looked up from the photograph, her fingers still touching its edges as though maintaining a conduit to the past.

"I had a funny thing happen the other day, and I thought you might like to see the evidence."

That seemed to intrigue the old lady. Auntie Eunice folded her hands in her lap and nodded. "A mystery. How mysterious."

"I think you'll like it."

Fifteen minutes later, they pulled up to the florist where Sara had directed Ella.

"I hope you didn't bring me to get flowers for my own funeral, Ella Keyes," Auntie Eunice said.

"Not at all, Auntie. We just have to pick something up, and it's not flowers."

"Hmm."

Auntie Eunice followed her into the store and harrumphed at a large arrangement of orange flowers.

"Can I help you?" Sara Krakowski herself emerged from the back room, wiping her hands on her smock. "Oh! Ella!"

"Hi, Sara," said Ella. She gestured at Auntie Eunice. "This is my great-aunt Eunice. We stopped by to pick up the disc, if that's okay."

"I have it right here," said Sara. She reached under the counter and pulled out a jewel case with a pink sticky note attached to it. "There are about sixty images on here. I picked the best ones and edited them up for you."

"Images of what, boys?" Auntie Eunice shuffled over and peered at the disc. "It better not be porn."

Sara coughed to disguise a guffaw, which Eunice seemed to take as a confirmation, and she scowled.

"Why on earth would I bring you to look at porn in a flower shop, Auntie?" Ella asked, shaking her head.

"I don't know what you kids do these days."

"It's not porn. I promise."

Sara smiled and came out from behind the counter. A small pot of violets sat on a shelf, and she went to it, pulling a violet from the stem with a tiny snap. "Ms. Eunice, would you like a violet? I think it would look lovely in your long hair."

"Of course it would," Auntie Eunice huffed, but her eyes lit up. "Purple and silver go perfectly together."

Ella rolled her eyes at Sara over Auntie Eunice's head, and Sara tucked the violet into Eunice's French twist.

"Beautiful," she said.

Auntie Eunice beamed, reaching up her hand to finger the petals of the flower. "Is this the surprise?"

"No, but it's nice anyway," Ella said, mouthing her thanks for the disc at Sara. "I'll show you the rest at home."

Auntie Eunice smiled to herself the whole way back to the house, and Ella tried to remember the last time she and her great-aunt had had a day out together. She wasn't sure if it had ever happened without Grammy Helen present. Grammy and Auntie Eunice spent almost every day together after Gramps died. Ella looked over at the old lady's smile and felt tears prickle her eyes at the sight. Who did Auntie Eunice spend her days with now?

Only Ella, it seemed.

She pulled into the driveway and put the car in park. "Are you ready to see the surprise?"

"Honey, you weren't alive ninety-three years ago to know I was born ready."

Ella laughed and got out of the car. Inside, she got her laptop and set it next to the photo album on the dining room table. Inserting the disc, she looked over at Auntie Eunice. "This happened when I went to the zoo a little bit ago, Auntie."

"Oh, my gracious," said Auntie Eunice when the first photo popped up. "That's an elephant."

"It got out somehow. I just came around a corner and there it was."

"Are there more?" Auntie Eunice gestured at the screen. "I want to see more."

Ella paged through the pictures, flipping through one by one. Some of them elicited a gasp from Eunice, and the first of the elephant with Ella's hand in its trunk made her clap her hand over Ella's and squeal. Ella smiled to herself and kept flipping through the photos. Seeing them again brought back all of the wonder she had felt, and from the tightness of Auntie Eunice's hand on hers, she thought her great-aunt felt that wonder as well. When she turned her head to look at Auntie Eunice, Ella was surprised to see more tears in the old woman's eyes.

"Is something wrong?" she asked.

Auntie Eunice patted the back of Ella's hand. "Not at all. Do you know how much your Grammy loved elephants?"

"She kept a lot of figurines of them."

Eunice nodded, and Ella looked back at the picture. The computer now showed Ella's back as she walked away with the elephant, hand in trunk.

"Helen thought elephants could see your soul. She met one once when we went to Thailand and never stopped talking about it to me. Maybe she was right. Sure looks like that elephant saw yours."

Ella realized that Auntie Eunice had been almost entirely lucid throughout the day, but now as she looked over at her, her wrinkled face trembled from the inside, and she smacked her lips together.

"I should go, dear," she said. "Can I come back tomorrow?"

"Of course, Auntie," said Ella.

"Do you have plans for the weekend?"

"The man I'm dating is taking me to the symphony tomorrow night." There. She'd said dating.

"Then you'll have to show me your dress." Auntie Eunice rose and kissed Ella on the cheek. "I'll see you tomorrow."

She left Ella alone with an elephant-sized pile of thoughts.

When Ella woke the next morning, she hopped out of bed without languishing under the covers for the first time in weeks.

The day felt crisper, like a fresh notebook of paper with no writing in it yet. Ella made her bed, smoothing the covers as Puff chased wrinkles and Poof licked his paws and watched from on top of Ella's pillow.

Ella couldn't put her finger on what felt different about the day. Maybe it was the business plan she'd put together for her new undertaking. Maybe it was knowing she got to see Callum, or the renewed sense of fondness that had chased away some of the exasperation with Auntie Eunice.

No one liked to be lonely, and Auntie Eunice was alone for the first time in almost a century. When Ella thought of it that way, she cringed at how frustrated she'd gotten with the woman. She hadn't even been alone in the womb. Ella had been through the loss of a twin. She knew what it was like. And even though Grammy Helen had died at the end of a very long life, that probably didn't make it any easier. No wonder Auntie Eunice wanted to come over so much.

Ella made a trip to the grocery store before eleven and returned with a refrigerator full of food.

When Eunice arrived at half past twelve, Ella had a full spread of lunch foods on the kitchen table. Ham and cheese sandwiches with spicy mustard — Auntie Eunice's favorite — sliced honeydew melon, kettle chips, and cream soda. Eunice's face burst into a grin at the sight of the food, and she fell upon her sandwich with the vigor of a fifteen-year-old instead of a woman approaching her centennial.

After lunch, Auntie Eunice would hear nothing of Ella cleaning up, so Ella sat back with a bowl of honeydew and savored it piece by piece as Eunice put away all the food and washed all the dishes by hand in spite of her protests that the dishwasher worked perfectly well.

"I wanted to show you some more of my pictures," Auntie Eunice said when she was done, drying her hands on the dishcloth, then sniffing them as if afraid they still smelled of sponge. "I left that album here."

"Of course," Ella said. She followed her great-aunt into the dining room, where she had left the album sitting out on the table, still open to the page with her great-great-grandmother.

Auntie Eunice turned the page to the next and pointed to a baby in a flowing white gown. "That's my mother there in her christening gown. Did you know that my parents were cousins?"

Ella blinked. "Cousins?"

"It was much more common back then, boy," Eunice barked. "Look at the Roosevelts."

Ella shrugged, though she felt slightly disconcerted. "First cousins?"

"No, I believe they were second cousins. But my mother was a Keyes and she married another Keyes, which is why your last name Keyes."

Trying to follow that, Ella looked at the baby. Pudgy cheeks and dimples in the elbows. Ella had had those same elbow-dimples. She grinned. "Your mother was adorable."

"How they ever got babies to hold still for these things is beyond me," Auntie Eunice muttered. "Have you ever asked a baby to sit still? They don't listen."

"No, babies are known for being particularly poor listeners," Ella agreed.

Auntie Eunice flipped to the next page. "Mom met Dad up in Ontario one summer when the families got together. Did you know we had family up there?"

"Do we still?" Ella didn't remember ever hearing about it. Both of her parents were only children, and she didn't have any cousins.

"No, they're all dead now. My father was an only child. Seems to go like that in our family, Ella. Twins or onlies, and that's the end of it." Auntie Eunice frowned at the page. "Try to have a couple more kids."

Ella wasn't sure how to answer that. She listened as Auntie Eunice flipped through the rest of the album, which showed her great-grandmother growing up, dressed as a flapper in the twenties. That made Auntie Eunice giggle like a schoolgirl until tears eked from her eyes.

"My grandmother almost had apoplexy when Mom cut her hair. Mom used to tell us stories about how she'd try to wear the most shocking dress she could find when she'd go meet Daddy, just to see Grandma's face change color." Auntie Eunice wiped away a tear and hiccuped. "Ornery runs in this family, and don't you forget it."

When they reached the end of the album, Auntie Eunice shut it and pushed it across the table.

"I want you to have that," she said. "Now you know everything I can tell you about it, and someday your kids won't be lost and end up throwing it away because they think it's junk."

Ella didn't think any children of hers would grow up thinking a family album was junk, but she thanked Auntie Eunice and promised she'd make sure to pass on the knowledge.

"Are you going to show me your dress for the symphony or what?" Auntie Eunice pushed her chair back from the table.

"Upstairs," said Ella. She helped the old woman up the stairs to the second floor and settled her in on the bed in her room.

The dress was in a cheap garment bag in the closet, and Ella pulled it out to show her great-aunt.

"Well, put it on, boy. I can't tell what it looks like from here."

Ella smiled and nodded, taking the dress into the closet. She closed the door halfway to cover the opening and started to undress.

"You know, Helen and I used to play such pranks on each other. Did you and Stuart ever do that?"

Ella stopped with her fingers on the button of her shorts, thinking of the rocks. "Yeah, we did. He was my best friend."

"Helen was mine. Once when I was in college — she went to a different college across town — she came over and sneaked into my dorm pretending to be me. Then she let loose about a thousand crickets in the halls of my dorm. Bought out one of the local pet stores." Auntie Eunice burst out laughing. "You should have heard the racket they made. And I got blamed for it, because someone had seen Helen do it. I tried to tell them I had a twin sister, but they wouldn't listen."

Clad in only her underwear, Ella chuckled, pulling the garment bag from the dress. "That sounds like something Stuart would do, but he couldn't pass for me if he tried."

"You got lucky there." Auntie Eunice laughed too. "If we'd been fraternal, it would have saved me a lot of trouble. I got her back though."

There was a long pause while Ella shimmied into the dress, struggling with the straps.

"We used to do everything together, you know. We had our first alcohol together, got our first bras together, and we even lost our virginity on the same night." Auntie Helen's voice grew choked. "We should have died on the same day, but here I am anyway."

Ella straightened the straps of her dress. "I'm glad you're still here, Auntie Eunice."

"Well, thank you dear." The old woman's voice snapped back to it's normal no-nonsense tone. "Are you sewing that dress from scratch, or are you coming out while I still exist?"

"I'm coming out." Ella gave another little shimmy before opening the door and adjusted the key on its chain. It usually fell beneath her shirt, and she kept it tucked out of sight, but the low cut dress exposed the tiny key. She picked it up and gave it a kiss, then dropped it between her breasts again, where it hung an inch above the low neckline of the dress.

She pushed open the door and walked back out into her room. She spun in a slow circle. "What do you think?"

"I think my grandmother would have apoplexy," Auntie Eunice chuckled, then her laugh fell off in a choked gasp. "Where did you get that?"

"get what?" ella looked around, but couldn't see what Auntie Eunice was looking at.

"Where did you get that! All of this searching for the reset, for the keys!" Auntie Eunice had spittle forming at the corners of her mouth. "The reset, you had it all along! How could she do this to me?"

Alarmed, Ella took a step back. "Auntie Eunice, I don't know what you're talking about."

"The key, boy, the goddamned key!"

Ella's hand flew to the key at her chest. "This is what you've been looking for?" She'd worn the thing for years. Surely Auntie Eunice had seen it before. But it usually fell beneath her shirt.

Eunice jumped from the bed. "That's not for you!"

"Grammy gave it to me, Auntie Eunice," Ella said, taking another step back.

Auntie Eunice took a swipe at the key, and Ella trod on the back of her dress and slipped. She crashed onto the floor, scrambling backward. Her heart beat faster, faster. What was happening?

"You think you know, don't you?" Auntie Eunice asked. "But you don't. That's the problem with you boys, you never know what you think you know, and then it's just gone."

"What's gone?"

"Everything!" The old woman spat. "And you don't even understand, do you? You don't get it. Why they left. Why they won't talk to you. At least Jace gets it, at least she knows the truth."

A cold pit formed in Ella's stomach, and she backed up against the wall. Auntie Eunice stood over her, staring down with wild eyes that darted back and forth, but always returned to the key that hung between Ella's breasts.

"What are you talking about?" Ella pushed the words from her mouth, and they tumbled out like a dribble of whispers.

"It's you. You're why they left. Because they blame you."

Her parents. She had to be talking about Ella's parents. And the only possible thing they could blame her for...

Ella couldn't make herself think the words. Auntie Eunice did it for her.

"You think they just happened to go off to the one place they knew Stuart loved most? That they don't return your calls because they're off in the bush watching gorillas or because of the time difference? Don't be a fool. They left because they knew you should have been there. You should have answered his calls. You should have picked up your phone, then gotten in your car to go get him instead of leaving him there to die. And they know that. They left because they BLAME YOU FOR STUART'S DEATH." Auntie Eunice had crouched down more and more with her speech, and she roared the last bit into Ella's face.

Tears streamed down Eunice's cheeks, and Ella froze, her head pushed up against the wall. She had to be wrong. Auntie Eunice had to be wrong.

Eunice reached out and grabbed the key. Ella felt a sharp sting as the chain jerked against her neck, and Auntie Eunice fled.

Ella collapsed to the floor in her symphony dress, unable to follow, clutching at her bare chest where the key had been.

part four
doors and futures

chapter
twenty-eight

Ella wasn't sure how she made it to Jace's house or how she managed to climb out of her symphony dress and put on a t-shirt and a peasant skirt that didn't match. She arrived on Jace's doorstep with her mind still in a blur from Auntie Eunice's words.

For the first time in her recent memory, she tried to piece together the last time she'd spoken to her parents.

It had been over a year.

Even that conversation had been short and curt, and Ella had written it off as her parents being stressed with work. Could it really be that they blamed her for Stuart's death? Ella shook her head at Jace's door as if it could see her. She knocked on the door, her knuckles rapping quietly, then louder until the knock crescendoed into pounding.

Jace flung open the door a moment later, her bathrobe cinched around her waist and her hair dripping. "Ella?"

"Can I come in?"

Jace moved aside, and waved her in, her forehead creased in the center. "What's wrong?"

Ella tried to relate what had happened as best she could, but it didn't even make sense to her. Her neck felt naked; she couldn't remember the last time she'd gone anywhere without the necklace Auntie Eunice had ripped off of her, and even the lack of its almost nonexistent weight seemed like a part of her had been cut away.

Jace's frown grew deeper as Ella talked, and the shadow behind her dark eyes said she knew too well what it was like to doubt the affection of parents.

"I've known your parents for almost a decade. I can't believe that of them."

Ella met Jace's eyes. "Until this summer, I would have said the same about yours."

"But you know my parents. You know how judgmental they are."

"Judgmental is one thing. Disowning your kid is something else entirely."

"I guess," Jace said. "You don't know that what Auntie Eunice said was true for sure. She clearly wanted your necklace for whatever reason. Maybe she was just trying to shock you enough so she could take it from you."

"Well, it worked," Ella said.

"What do you think she wanted with it? I mean, do you really think that's what she's been looking for and tearing the house apart to find for the last seven months?"

"She acted like it was. She was saying something about a reset and that the key wasn't mine. I don't know exactly what she was talking about. She was kind of babbling."

"See? Something must have snapped in her brain," Jace said, taking a deep breath and shifting her shoulders. "I mean, if she wasn't making a lot of sense then, it only follows that she was just trying to bait you."

"Maybe." Ella sat back into the cushy couch, wishing she could believe it.

"I'm going to go make you some tea. You stay put."

Ella didn't feel like moving anyway. Move. She was supposed to go to the symphony with Callum in less than eight hours. She didn't feel particularly symphonic. If anything, the emotions that roiled through her felt discordant, like clashing notes when they ought to be in harmony.

What if Eunice was right?

The night Stuart died existed in Ella's mind like a scene from a painstakingly-drawn pen and ink. Every line clear, every line deliberate. She couldn't move them if she wanted, couldn't squint and wait for a three-dimensional shark to appear in the blur, couldn't stand back and watch dabs of color turn to a beautiful landscape. There was stark black and white that night, and it almost overcame her when she thought of it.

Jace had been just getting really serious with Alexa after one year of casual dating and a second of a deepening connection, and she'd wanted a night just with Ella. Just the two of them.

Growing up, Stuart had always tried to crash Ella's nights with the girls. To be fair, she did the same for him with his guy friends, but that night with Jace when he called the first time, she ignored him because she'd thought he was just going to be a pain again and show up with a couple of his buddies and leave Doritos crumbs in her couch cushions.

Her freshly-painted pink fingernails were still wet, and Ella'd handled her phone with the balls of her hands.

"It's just Stuart," she'd laughed and hit the ignore button.

Then he'd called again, and she'd gotten exasperated and turned her phone on silent.

And after that, he'd called again.

Ella hadn't listened to the voice mails until after the call from the police. She still remembered the officer's voice on the other line. "Ma'am, are you related to Stuart Keyes?"

"He's my twin brother," she'd said.

"I'm afraid there's been an accident. Please come to Kaleida immediately."

No more information. Nothing to assuage the deep, muddy thub-thub of her heart. Just that.

And Ella had listened to the voice mails.

Since ignoring them that night, Ella had probably listened to them a thousand times. She played them on repeat for the weeks after Stuart's funeral. She'd always blamed herself for what happened, but if her parents thought it was her fault, maybe it really was true. Maybe her negligence really had killed her brother.

"What did Eunice say about a reset?" Jace returned at that moment with two steaming mugs of tea, passing one to Ella over the back of the couch.

Ella jerked herself back to the present, blinking back the tears that threatened just at the edges of her eyelids. "Um, not much. I think she called the key the reset."

"The key she took from you," Jace said.

"The key she took from me."

"Didn't Grammy Helen's journal say something about the reset too?"

Ella took a sip of her tea and burned her tongue. It had. And Auntie Eunice had both the journal and the key.

They had to find out what it meant.

it was jace's idea to break into Auntie Eunice's house.

Ella hated it. But she also hated that Auntie Eunice had stolen two things from her; both Grammy Helen's journal and the key Grammy had given her years before were two of the most personal things her grandmother could have left to her. Ella didn't really think that she'd be righting those wrongs by sneaking into her great-aunt's house to hunt for two small objects that could be anywhere, but it gave her a vague sense of justice. Auntie Eunice had been going through Ella's things without shame for months.

Jace and Ella walked up to the front door as soon as they saw that there was no white Volvo in the driveway.

"You're sure you're okay with doing this?" Jace asked.

"Are you? I'm at least family."

Jace straightened her shoulders and flashed Ella her best real estate agent smile. "I'm just showing the house. It's privately listed as the elderly owner is in need of professional care."

"Got that part right," Ella muttered, then immediately felt a pang of guilt for the words and what they were about to do. "Okay. Let's break and enter."

The breaking part turned out to be a bit of an anticlimax when the knob turned easily under Ella's grip, and the door opened wide.

"She leaves her door unlocked?" Jace stepped over the threshold, peering into the house. She stopped a few feet inside the door. "I guess I can see why."

Ella turned, one hand still closing the door. The air in the house smelled like a used bookstore, musty and dusty and full of paper. "What?"

"Look."

At first Ella thought she was looking at a very strange castle. Then she realized it was towers of magazines, stacked several feet high and piled together like the battlements of a castle's outer bailey. They lined up along the back of Auntie Eunice's couch, stretching from arm to arm and from floor to above the headrests.

The walls of the house looked like Auntie Eunice was planning a move. Boxes, stacked three to five high, formed a perimeter of the entire living room. Ella tried to walk around the couch and met with more boxes.

"Are we on Hoarders? Where's the television crew?" Jace ventured into the living room, finding a path around the couch at the end opposite Ella. "Oh, god. The dining room."

Ella followed her into the dining room and stopped in the doorway. No table. At least at first glance, it looked like there was no table. Ella stared wide-eyed into the piles of papers and manila folders and books and boxes until a line of polished wood appeared below it like something out of a magic eye picture.

"Is she trying to see how much weight that thing can hold?"

"I don't think it could collapse if it wanted to." Jace pointed under the table, where even more boxes made their homes.

"Where does she live?" The question Ella really wanted to ask was how the hell they were supposed to find a hippopotamus in a house like this, let alone a single, handwritten journal and a gold key the size of a penny.

"Button, button, who's got the button?" Jace shook her head, her silky strands of black hair waving in front of her face.

"Where do you think she would have put the journal?" Picking her way through the dining room, Ella squeezed past a threshold of boxes into the kitchen. "I can't see that anything's been moved in ages."

Jace ran her finger along the top of a box, then examined it. "Dusty. I'd say you're right."

"So not in here."

"Look at us detectiving."

"Is that a word?"

"It is when you're me and grew up reading Sherlock Holmes." Jace wiped her dusty finger on her jean shorts and followed Ella toward the kitchen.

"I don't think Sherlock ever used the word detectiving."

"More detectiving now, less talking."

"See, talking's a word."

"Shut up."

"So's that." Ella fought the impulse to shake herself all over like a dog. She felt like Luke and Leia in the trash compactor with Han and Chewy. Even if the walls around her weren't moving, Ella worried they might start at any moment. The kitchen was only slightly better, with empty countertops and a single stool at the end of the breakfast bar where a coffee cup still sat, holding the still-wet dregs of what must have been Auntie Eunice's breakfast cup.

"Does she have a basement?"

"Not that I remember," Ella said. She had never spent a lot of time here, and she certainly didn't remember it looking like a fortress of backlists.

"Attic?"

"Crawl space, maybe. But it's only one level, and she has trouble getting up stairs." Though not, Ella recalled, much trouble running down them after stealing necklaces from nieces.

"Lucky us."

"We should probably try her bedroom first." Ella led the way back through the living room and into the short hallway. One look in the guest bedroom made a shudder run through her. She knew there was a bed by the way there were boxes stacked in the center of it, but she wasn't sure how she would even get to it through the clutter.

Auntie Eunice's room was the only place in the house that didn't wear a layer of boxes three deep across every exposed surface. Ella felt her chest loosen almost imperceptibly as she stepped through the door and into her great-aunt's room. Normal. Like a person lived there. How had it gotten that bad? The house was a red alert level fire hazard.

Ella and Jace combed through the room, opening jewelry boxes and drawers and flipping through the closet — which smelled of moth balls and Icy-Hot — but there was no sign of the journal or Ella's key.

"I don't think we're going to find anything here," said Ella, plunking down on the side of the bed.

"I found sneezes." Jace punctuated the sentence with a loud one, and she rubbed her nose. "My allergies aren't that bad, but this is enough to make someone without them get hay-fever."

"Let's just go." Ella stood and walked toward the door, wondering if Auntie Eunice would be paranoid enough to hide the journal under one of the ten thousand stacks of books that populated the guest room.

Her feet halted in front of the guest room door. Grammy Helen had hidden the journal under the bed in her guest room. Ella took a breath, scrunched her eyes shut for a moment, and stepped into the guest bedroom. Her first movement brought her toe into sharp contact with an obscured corner of the wall, and she cursed, biting down on her lip.

A couple feet into the room, she saw that she'd been wrong. There was a path to the bed; it just didn't look like it because of the way the boxes in the entry were arranged. She only hoped that Auntie Eunice's hiding place unconsciously mirrored that of her deceased twin. Stuart had never been able to hide things from Ella, and vice versa. Except the rocks. It made Ella wonder how Auntie Eunice never thought to look under the guest bed when she was looking for the key. Except, she decided, the old bat hadn't been looking for the journal at all, and that's what had been under the bed.

The moment Ella bent down, she saw it. Wedged between a pair of crumbling shoe boxes was Grammy Helen's journal. She pulled it out, straining her head to look over the boxes at Jace. She held up the journal.

"How did you know where to look?"

"Let's just say that twins think alike."

chapter
twenty-nine

"Do you think she's at your house?" Jace asked when they were back in her apartment. She washed her hands in the sink, then on second thought seemed to decide that the rest of her arms were dirty as well and stuck them under the faucet to the elbows.

"She could be at the salon, for all I know," said Ella. She opened the journal and paged through it, trying to find where she'd left off.

There it was, the entry from the day before Stuart's accident.

The next entry was written with sloppy handwriting, spikes and squiggles that Ella could hardly make out.

> *Stuart is gone.*
> *Whatever key I took yesterday...*

The entry trailed off there in a shaky scribble. The page bowed in small places, like it had gotten wet with raindrops.

Or tears, Ella realized. Her fingers traced over the wrinkled paper, feeling out Grammy Helen's grief at losing her grandson. And her guilt? She'd thought it was her fault for taking the key.

a hall of keys and no doors

> *I knew I shouldn't pick that one, but it was years since I'd picked a shiny key from the wall. I knew it when I touched it that it was wrong, wrong. Oh, forgive me. Please forgive me.*

The entry ended there.

Ella flipped through the remaining pages, but the entire last fifth of the journal was empty. She moved back to where the teardrops made the pages wrinkled. Only a sparse smattering of entries remained in the journal.

> *I don't know what it would do if I used it. Would it rewrite my entire life? Change every choice that was made? Slam every door those keys took me through?*
>
> *I never thought about it before now, but as I watch the grief on my son's face, my daughter-in-law, and my beloved Ella — I can't help but wonder. Is it worth the risk if it brings Stuart back?*

Ella felt dizzy.

The words swam together on the page.

Bring Stuart back.

Two sides of Ella's brain warred with each other. The logical, professor side said any talk of bringing a dead person back to the world of the living was as impossible as a three headed beast that could regenerate new heads the moment one was cut off.

But the sister side, the brokenhearted twin side that still had a gaping hole where a brother was supposed to be — that side clung to each word as if just clapping her hands enough would get people to believe.

> *I've come so close so many times to using it.*
>
> *Each time as I hold the box in my shaking fingers, I can't bring myself to do it. How selfish does that make me, to possibly hold the remedy to my family's pain at the tips of my fingers and yet be unable to do the one thing*

that would heal them? Perhaps the most selfish being in the world. I can't know if I caused it, if my decision is the root of this tragedy.

Oh, Stuart. My smart, handsome grandson. You would do something silly and tell me I'm being a crazy old bat for thinking any of this.

But then again, you don't live in this house. You don't know what those keys can do.

The next entry was the final one, and Ella read each word as carefully as she would excavate a fossil of a tiny bird from bedrock, as if reading her grandmother's words slowly were the equivalent of dainty brushes, chasing away the obscuring sand.

What I can't figure out is what would happen if I used it. What would happen if I put the key in the lock and gave it a turn?

So much of my life has been wrought of these bits of twisted metal. So many choices, so many memories. What I don't know is if turning that key would place me back at the age of seventeen where I first took a key down from the wall. If it would erase all my choices and give me a fresh start. Even if that were the case, how would my decisions possibly be any better the second time around? If not that, then what? Would it keep me here, a ninety-year-old woman in failing health, and simply change things to the way they ought to have been without my meddling?

There are too many questions and no answers at all.

That's why I can't do it.

If I knew it would bring Stuart back...

No. I can't even promise that. I've tampered far too much.

Knowing this makes me glad I gave the key to Ella all those years ago, removing the temptation. It didn't

> *remove it, and I know the dear girl would give it to me the moment I asked her, but I know now I won't go that far. I'll put the box away where no one will find it. Not even Ella.*
>
> *I'm sorry, Robert.*

A dip in the couch cushion behind Ella's head made her start. How long Jace had been there, leaning over her shoulder, she couldn't have guessed.

Ella closed the journal and set in her lap, shutting her eyes. A reset. Was any of this even possible? Ella thought of the elephant's rough trunk taking her hand and wondered if she'd ever know the real boundaries of possible again.

"What are you going to do?"

Ella looked at the clock on her phone. Already six o'clock. She was supposed to be ready to go by seven thirty, and she wasn't even home. She hoped the dress she'd flung onto the bed wasn't now covered in cat hair and wrinkled as an elephant's hide.

"For now, I need to get ready to go to the symphony."

if auntie eunice had been at Ella's house earlier, she wasn't there when Ella and Jace arrived at ten till seven.

Jace almost shoved Ella into the shower and set about removing Puff and Poof hairs from the dress, which had escaped with only half the damage Ella had expected. The hot water felt good against her skin, and Ella almost felt as though she were covered in visible grit from Auntie Eunice's house. The dust had settled onto her body, enough that the water streaming from her arms and legs turned slightly gray as it swirled into the drain.

She was just getting out when she heard the doorbell.

"Is that Callum?" she hollered out of the bathroom.

"Yep!"

"He's early!"

"Yep!" Jace stuck her head in the door, ignoring Ella's nudity. "You get dressed. I'll tell him we got held up today."

"Good. That makes me look only slightly less flaky."

Ella wrapped her hair in a towel and dried off as quickly as she could. She heard Jace talking to Callum downstairs and bolted into her room. The dress hung from the closet door, ninety-nine percent hair free. Ella pulled one long cream colored hair from the armpit of the dress and slipped it on over her head, thankful that the scooping necklines got past the towel without any trouble.

She felt an immediate surge of gratitude that the dress was black and didn't show water spots from her dripping hair. Ella towel-dried it as fast as she could until Jace reappeared.

"He said it's fine. He's going to read Nancy Drew while you finish."

"I feel like I'm in a rom-com."

"You'll live." Jace propelled Ella toward the bathroom. "You do makeup, I'll do hair."

Ella wasn't sure how good her makeup would be if someone were yanking on her hair, but she started anyway. Fifteen minutes later, she emerged from the bathroom only five minutes later than the original time Callum was supposed to arrive.

"Thank you," she said to Jace, tromping down the stairs in a pair of strappy blue sandals. Her chest felt even more naked for all the low neckline without her key hanging on its long chain. She'd replaced the star ruby with the sapphire necklace from downstairs, but its weight did nothing to soothe the sense of loss.

Jace patted her on the shoulder. "Bye, Callum!"

He put down Nancy Drew and the Secret of the Old Clock and stood.

Ella didn't notice Jace leave.

Callum wore an immaculate tuxedo, the lines of the cut emphasizing those of his body. His gray eyes stood out like a meld of the black and white he wore, and he smiled at the sight of Ella, his Adam's apple bobbing.

"You look amazing," he said.

"You too." Ella stepped into the circle of his arms and looked up, feeling more like her great-grandmother as a twenties debutante than an out-of-work college professor in the twenty-first century.

"Shall we?" Callum offered his hand, and Ella took it.

He took her to dine at a posh sushi bar. They laughed and had chopstick wars; the plum wine was sweet on Ella's tongue. Callum didn't bring up the events of the other night in Stratford, and neither did Ella. Instead, she watched him, listened to him, allowing herself to be cognizant of the warmth she felt when he was near. How the brush of his hand set off tingles in hers. How he sat quietly when she spoke and always let her finish a thought before asking a question.

By the time they left dinner, Ella felt more sure than she ever had that she was falling.

In spite of the nervousness, the uncertainty, and the length of time it had been from Brett to Callum, Ella was sure of one thing. That one thing was that she knew she couldn't just let Callum vanish.

He led her up the stairs into the amphitheater, an I-have-a-secret smile lighting his face.

"What's funny?" Ella asked him, his smile drawing hers across her face to mirror.

"Nothing," he said with a wink. "We're right up there."

He indicated the sixth row, centered in front of the stage.

The lights dimmed to a soft golden glow, and Callum leaned over to whisper in Ella's ear. "Keep an open mind?"

She started to ask about what, but the sounds stopped her short.

Boom. Boom. Boom. Boom.

The rhythm began like a heartbeat, deep and resonant. It hushed the dim chatter of the theater-goers like someone was turning a dimmer switch on their voices along with the lights. The sound continued with the curtains drawn. The lights in the amphitheater dimmed until only the emergency lighting could be seen around the edges of the stage and audience.

Boom. Boom. Boom. Boom. Boom-ch. Boom-ch. Boom-ch.

Ella closed her eyes in the darkness, listening to the gradual mutation of the drumbeat. The deep pulse continued, growing layers on top of it until the swish of smooth cymbals began to crescendo. A glow began, and Ella sensed the change in light even through her closed eyelids. There was a new scent in the room, like coal or brimstone. She opened her eyes. A line of torches filled the stage as the booms of the drums grew louder, faster.

The golden fire of the torches lit her face, the heat caressed her cheeks. For the second time in a week, Ella forgot she was part of an audience.

The beat halted, and silence reigned.

Callum squeezed her hand.

The curtain flew back.

A hundred drums burst into frenzied beat.

Ella sat with Callum on her porch swing, the stars bright in the sky above. Slightly veiled by Buffalo's lights, Ella could make out Pegasus galloping across the night's cloak of dark blue.

"What did you think?"

Callum hadn't asked her what she thought yet. She shifted on the hard wood, leaning into his side. What had she thought? Symphonies had movements; they flowed from part to part, fluidly telling a story with notes. This one had done the same. She'd never thought to hear such a story told with only drums — ninety-nine, the program said.

"It was chaotic, but kind of right," she said after a long beat. "Where did you hear about them?"

"They've been gaining some momentum in the past few years. A buddy of mine — who played Lysander in Midsummer — told me about them and that they were going to be playing in Toronto and Buffalo this summer. I missed the Toronto show, but I wanted to bring you to this one."

"What is it that drew you to it?" Ella was curious. She'd never asked what kind of music Callum listened to.

"I like the feeling of the drums. I love that you can really feel the pounding. It changes the tune of your heart when you hear it."

"I like that too."

"I also..." Callum paused. "This might sound dumb. But I like that for all the chaos, for all the loud cacophony of ninety-nine drums beating and beating and beating, there's an order to it. A rhythm that elevates it above noise. There's a carefully orchestrated rise and fall. It reminds me of life."

Ella pulled back a bit to look at him. "You think life is orchestrated?"

Even before what had happened to Stuart, Ella hadn't believed in some original prime mover in the sky. She didn't believe that someone was up there pulling marionette strings, ensuring that some people got a wonderful ride on the rock of Earth and others spent it covered in flies and feces, both alternately mourning the loss of hope and reaching for love. She watched Callum's face, carefully. Religion was such a personal thing, such a deep and intimate thing — and Ella thought it had to be shared with someone you loved.

She moved that last thought into a faraway corner of her mind to think about more later.

"No, I think life's chaos."

Ella took a deep breath and let it out slowly, the soft release of relief suffusing her chest. She agreed much more with that. "What did you mean about the orchestrated part?"

"Only that sometimes through the chaos, you see that rise and fall. Life gives way to death, which spins out life again. War. Peace. Other giant books. It reminds me of life because it's seeking out that order within the chaos that makes it bearable. We can't control it, so we might as well go with it and find what beauty we can." Callum turned his face toward hers, just inches away.

Ella couldn't see his eyes in the darkness, but the way he reached out a hand and softly brushed her cheek said enough.

She leaned her face into his palm. Ella knew she couldn't control everything. Maybe the last time she'd been with Callum had been her way of trying to remain in control.

Maybe sometimes she ought to allow herself to be out of control.

Her lips touched his, searching, moving softly. The swing swayed under them, its chains creaking like the crickets in the fields. When she pulled back, she could see a glint of his smile.

Then it faded, and he took her hand. "I want you to feel comfortable with me," he said. "I also know how much of a jackass that makes me sound saying that, like just voicing it will make it so. I just want you to know that I'll stick around as long as you want me to. All of this — you're in the driver's seat."

"Why?" Ella asked, the question emerging unbidden from her throat.

"I don't know. You're intelligent. A little weird. I like the way you look at the world. I've never known someone before who'd just go jaunt off to the other side of the planet alone for six weeks, and as maddening as it was to not be able to see you or ask you about your adventures, and as much as I hoped I'd be able to move on, I couldn't get my mind from returning to you." Callum swallowed. "You've taken tragedy and moved forward."

Ella wanted to protest that she hadn't, really, that the hole left by Stuart's death was still just as ragged around the edges as it was when she'd first seen his body in the morgue and had to nod through the crushing tears and identify him as her twin brother. Still just as ragged as collapsing into a heap on that cold tiled floor as soon as her chin had bobbed and the words, "That's my brother" came boiling out of her mouth like they existed in individual bubbles. How had she moved forward from that?

She looked at Callum's face, saw the self-deprecating smile that said he didn't expect her to feel the same way about him. "I'm still kind of broken."

Callum met her eyes. "You're not broken," he said. "Hurt and broken are two different things."

For a long moment, Ella listened to the creak of the swing and the singing of the crickets beyond. He was right.

"I wish I could give you more."

"I don't," Callum said. "It's like we were talking about a minute ago. Life is chaos. I'm not about to let a bit of the beauty slip away because it doesn't want to sprint. I don't need to sprint. Not anymore."

There was a brief ghost of a sadder emotion that moved across his face in the shadows, but it was gone in an instant, and he smiled.

Ella smiled at him. "How about a slow jog?"

For the second time, their lips met, and this time he slid his arms around her, pulling her close. His mouth against hers was searching, almost trembling, and Ella shivered at the shocks of pleasure she felt with each renewed kiss.

They stayed that way for a long time, until Pegasus had moved in the sky and the increasing tightness in Ella's hips on the hard swing suggested she move as well. She took Callum's hands and pulled him to his feet, pressing her body against his and kissing him once more.

She wanted to invite him in. She wanted to keep his hand in hers and lead him up the stairs to her bedroom. But he'd said he was okay to wait, and Ella wanted to be sure. She laid her cheek against his shoulder. "I'll see you soon?" On inspiration, she tugged on his lapel. "How about tomorrow night? Jace and Alexa can join us, and I'll cook dinner."

"Of course. I'd love to." He kissed her forehead, then took her hand and pressed something small and cold into it.

It was a tiny silver elephant.

She smiled as he walked away.

chapter
thirty

Ella laid in bed, thinking about Callum's words and the difference between hurt and broken.

She'd been broken at first, that was sure. Ella had taken two weeks off work right after Stuart had died, and she hadn't left the house. Jace had brought her food, brushed her hair, made her shower every few days. The weeks and months passed, and Ella had started finding the rocks left by Stuart around her house.

There was no getting over that kind of loss. She'd just learned to cover the hole with a tarp and some hasty stakes.

She pulled Grammy Helen's letter from the frame again, looking at the intense expression of concentration that covered her brother's face in the picture. Smashing rocks had been serious business.

The letter was serious too, but Ella still couldn't fully make sense of it.

Dear Ella,

I hope you'll forgive me for triggering old memories. You shouldn't fear them anyway. It'll drive you mad.

Lots of things will drive you mad. But I've always been a mad old bat. You know that. Look, I rhymed. Eunice would be proud, the old goat.

Here I am talking of goats and bats and madness when you're probably seething at me for giving you a house you don't want. I'm here to tell you that's just too bad. I only hope your sentimental side allows you to find this letter before you convince someone to buy the place off your hands and out of your life. You won't get anybody to sell it in the near future anyway, so don't even try. You're stuck with it for a while. I want it to be yours for a time, even though I know it's far from the refuge you want but won't admit you do. These last few years have been hard, and as much as it's been a pleasure to see you each week, to get to know the wonderful woman you've become, to become your friend as well as your grandmother, you need to find your strength now.

If, after a while, you decide that selling the house is what you want, you can.

I won't judge you for doing that. Some days I wish I'd done the same.

But this place holds a lot of keys, to a lot of different doors. Some of those doors you don't need or want to open. I know you've got your shiny, new loft, but Ella, sugar, that's not all that's important. Shiny and new aren't always the best options, you know. Sometimes even less than you think.

Sometimes you need a little old and cluttered. Like Eunice. Watch out for her. I know it sounds nutty telling an almost thirty-year-old to look out for someone three times her age, but you've been through what she's going through now. You can help her. Please do that, for your mad old bat of a Grammy.

Love,
Grammy Helen

Watch out for her, Grammy had said. What had she meant by that? When Ella first read the letter after Grammy's funeral, she'd assumed her grandmother had simply meant to help Auntie Eunice. Keep an eye on her, make sure she got care if she needed it.

Now Ella wasn't so sure. After Eunice barging in and rifling through Ella's personal belongings, stealing Grammy's journal, snatching Ella's key right from her neck — she couldn't help but wonder if perhaps Grammy Helen had been warning her, not admonishing her to care for a woman three times her age.

Help her how? Ella wondered what Grammy meant by that. Help her find the reset, or help her not to use it?

The same thoughts that surfaced in Grammy's journal now hummed through Ella's mind. Could she do it? If a reset for the keys really existed, could she put the key in whatever lock Grammy meant and give it a twist? What would that movement do to the rest of her life? Ella thought of the drums, of the beats that intertwined from booming bass to the rat-a-tat-tat of a bodhran. Change one and the whole feeling shifted. How much more would that be if she changed five things? Ten? Fifteen?

Would she give up everything in her life to bring Stuart back?

Ella punted that thought back into the recesses of her mind. She couldn't think like that. Not now. Not after three years of grief. If she entertained the idea of bringing Stuart back, if she admitted to herself that she believed in its possibility — she'd go madder than Auntie Eunice, if the old woman were even mad at all.

Ella curled up with her pillow and pulled Poof closer to her, waking him enough to make his purr rumble into being. Puff scooted closer, kneading the air above Poof's tail. Even in the warmth of her bed with her two kitties curled up with her and the feeling of Callum's lips on her forehead still whispering to her in the dark, it was a long time before Ella could sleep.

Of course, cooking dinner for four meant that Ella would have to go shopping. She spent the morning looking up recipes, including one for tiramisu that looked heavenly. After twenty minutes of double and triple checking her grocery list, Ella got into her car and headed to the store.

Shrimp scampi. Spinach salad with feta and sun dried tomatoes. Green beans with pine nuts.

Ella wheeled her cart into the aisle of Wegman's, a litany of food items flipping through her head like spinning a rolodex. She'd forgotten it was Saturday, and the produce section was crowded with people.

She filled the basket of the cart with baby spinach, fresh and sun dried tomatoes, garlic, ticking off the items down her list with satisfaction. She hesitated in the cookie aisle with her hand poised over a box of lady fingers, trying to decide whether she wanted to attempt making them from scratch. The recipe she pulled up on her phone looked simple enough. She left the box of cookies where it was.

As the meat counter attendant weighed her shrimp, Ella realized she was happy. Excited. She wanted to see how Callum fit in with her relationship with Jace and Alexa, and she liked the idea of this dinner party celebrating their soon-to-be new home together.

With every item on her list checked off, Ella headed toward the cashier, pushing her cart into the line behind a family of four with two full carts of their own. She looked to her right, searching for a shorter line and found nothing.

To the left was only the express lanes and the produce section again.

And there, sniffing the end of a cantaloupe, was her mother.

Ella's hand fell from the push bar of her cart.

This time she was sure. This was no glimpse through a tiny window over the heads of a crowd. This was certain.

Her mother wasn't in South Africa. She was calmly sniffing cantaloupes in a Buffalo Wegman's.

Ella felt as though someone had reached out, wrapped their fingers around her heart, and squeezed.

It wasn't possible.

How could her parents come back from South Africa without telling her? Did Auntie Eunice know?

She must. Ella replaced her hands on the push bar, tightening her grip on the cart's handle until the backs of hands corded and turned white mottled with pink. Auntie Eunice had asked if Ella had heard from her parents lately. She knew. She had to know.

Could she have been right?

Ella pulled her cart from the line and moved toward the cantaloupes, careful to stay out of sight. Her mother disappeared around the corner, carrying a cantaloupe in one hand and a honeydew in the other, and as Ella peeked one eye around an end display of half price Cinnamon Toast Crunch, her stomach dropped to her feet as her mother placed both melons in a cart and turned to her father to laugh just out of earshot.

They moved toward the cheeses, and Ella followed, staring at the backs of their heads.

Her parents, who she hadn't seen in years. Less than fifteen feet away and as oblivious to her presence as they would be were she a ghost.

It was them. Her father had regrown his mustache, which was now sprinkled liberally with gray, as was Mom's dark hair.

Any normal child would hurry toward them, embrace them. But Auntie Eunice's words resonated back and forth, ricocheting off the insides of Ella's skull.

Instead she followed.

"We're out of cheddar," her mother said. Ella knew that voice. Her mother had a singing voice that was a beautiful mezzo-soprano, but when she spoke, her tone was rich like honey.

Out of cheddar. Which meant they'd been back in Buffalo long enough to go through it. How long had they been home? How long had Auntie Eunice been keeping their presence a secret from Ella?

She couldn't keep thinking of it. Her whole body felt shaky, and Ella used the cart to support herself as she followed her parents on their shopping excursion, always just out of sight, lingering behind bags of tortilla chips and displays of the bakery's muffins.

There they were, fulfilling the most mundane of tasks, but doing it thousands of miles from where Ella had thought they were. Nausea rolled through her stomach.

She followed them until they finished, hovering in the health food section until she was sure they had paid, bagged their groceries, and left the store. Only then did she resume her place in line, her heart sloshy in her chest and her stomach churning like storm-swept waves on Lake Erie.

Ella watched them in the parking lot as she paid for her groceries. They took their time, smiling and laughing to themselves. Still in love after over thirty years of marriage. But without her. She was the missing piece in that family.

An urgency overtook her as she paid. She stuffed her change in her purse without taking the time to face her bills and tuck the coins into her coin purse. She gathered up her six grocery bags and hurried for her car.

They'd bought a new Honda. They hadn't had that when they left for Johannesburg two and a half years ago. She kept her eyes focused on the olive green SUV, throwing her bags in the back seat of her car. She pulled out carefully, watching the direction they turned and following.

Ella pushed the accelerator, seven miles an hour over the speed limit until she was only one car behind them.

Her parents weren't headed toward their old house. Ella didn't know where they were going, but she followed as they turned from the main roads onto side streets until they pulled up in front of a one level ranch, painted green with red-brown trim.

She parked down the block and watched them unload their groceries.

It was the normalcy of the scene that sent unease trickling down her spine. They'd gone about their lives. They'd come home from the opposite side of the planet, gotten groceries, and now they were heading inside to put them away.

It was as if they'd not only lost a son but forgotten a daughter.

chapter
thirty-one

She was about to pull her car away from the curb and go home when a familiar white Volvo cruised past her.

The sight brought the waves of nausea back to crest in Ella's stomach, confirming every thought she'd had at the grocery store about Auntie Eunice keeping her parents' presence a secret.

Ella watched as the Volvo pulled into the driveway behind the SUV, and Auntie Eunice clambered out, pulling her straw hat from the back seat and plunking it on her head. No sunglasses today. The old woman mounted the stairs to the house and knocked on the door.

A moment later, Ella's mother opened it, a smile lighting her face. She wrapped Eunice in a hug, then pulled back and fingered the brim of the hat, chuckling.

Ella wanted to cry, but no tears would come. Instead she sat and waited.

The groceries in the back seat would be fine for now. Ella cranked up the Converge album in her CD player as loud as she dared and tilted her seat back to watch the house.

There wasn't anything she could do. As much as she wanted to run up the stairs to that unfamiliar house and bang on the door, she had no illusions that she'd be greeted with the same warmth shown to Eunice.

No matter how Ella tried to reconcile the thoughts that swirled through her head, she couldn't change them.

Her parents had always been there for her.

As teens, she and Stuart had always had a sort of get-out-of-jail-free card. Her parents made sure they knew that if Ella or Stuart drank at a party, they'd come to get them. No questions asked.

Her mother had listened when Ella talked about her first time, fidgety and clearly nervous, but supportive and kind and relieved when Ella answered the question about using protection in the affirmative.

They had been her bedrock, laughing at her antics with Stuart. Never complaining when Stuart started brightening the blue in his hair. Never telling either of them they ought to be doctors or lawyers or businesspeople. They supported Stuart in his art, supported Ella in her studies. Because of them, she had no loans from college, because even a full ride didn't cover everything.

Ella watched the closed door of the house as if she could will it open, and with it, answers.

But none came as the minutes ticked by with the screaming of Converge's frontman and the frenetic pace of the drums. It reminded her of the drum symphony. Had that really just been yesterday? Less than twenty-four hours before, Ella had broken into her great-aunt's house and stolen something.

Auntie Eunice had to be there about the reset. She had Ella's key, and Grammy had said something about a box, though it was clear by Eunice's presence that however well Grammy Helen had thought the box hidden, someone had found it.

Two hours went by before the front door of the house opened again. Eunice came out, turning over her shoulder to smile at Ella's father this time.

In her hand was what looked like a small enameled box.

Ella waited until he door closed again and Auntie Eunice came down the steps toward her car. Then she opened her door, leaving the hard metal screaming behind her. She hurried across the street and met Eunice at the driver's side door of her car.

"Is that it?" She asked. Of all the questions in her mind, that was the first to spill out. "The reset Grammy wrote about? The reason you kept my parents' presence from me?"

Auntie Eunice turned, her mouth agape. "What are you doing here, Ella? You shouldn't be here."

"Oh, shouldn't I? My parents are supposed to be in South Africa!" Ella forced herself to straighten her spine, looking down at the old woman in front of her.

The brass box in Auntie Eunice's hands bore blue and green enamel in wave patterns across the lid. It looked ancient. In the front was a tiny key hole, just the right size for the key that normally hung around Ella's neck.

"They made me promise not to tell you they were here. I promised," Auntie Eunice repeated.

Ella sat back on her heels, feeling as disjointed as a Picasso painting. She hadn't had any promises of honesty from Auntie Eunice, but betrayal scraped its fingers down the inside of her ribcage. "You're my family, Auntie Eunice. You should have told me. You should have told me everything."

The old woman's fingers tightened on the box as if she were afraid Ella would tear it from her grasp.

"I'm not going to take it from you," Ella said, wanting to spit the words out. "Not like you took Grammy's journal and the key she gave me."

"I know you took the journal back," Eunice said. "How did you find it?"

"I looked where Grammy would have hidden it."

Auntie Eunice blanched at that.

"How could you, Auntie Eunice?"

"I had to." Auntie Eunice swallowed, holding the box tightly to her chest. "I can fix this family, Ella. I can glue these pieces back together. You'll see. I can make us whole again."

"It will never be whole again! Stuart's *dead*! He's dead, and he's not coming back!"

"And so is my sister!" The words bellowed from Auntie Eunice's small frame, and she took a step back to lean against the Volvo. "So is my sister."

So that's what it was about. It wasn't really about Stuart, or about healing their family. Ella closed her eyes and felt the sun warming her hair. It kindled the anger in her core, and she tried to smother it.

With her eyes closed, she didn't see the door open.

Her mother's voice cut through everything. "Ella."

Ella froze, opening her eyes. Auntie Eunice shot one look at the figure on the porch, then slid into her car and sped away.

Ella walked across the driveway on unsteady feet. Up the stairs. Until she stood at eye-level with her mother.

"Is it true?" she asked.

"Is what true?" Her mother looked at her, then past her at Ella's Subaru across the street with its door still cracked open.

"That you think it's my fault he died."

For a moment, the impassive facade of her mother's face slid away, but it snapped back into place as she opened her mouth to speak.

"It is your fault, Ella."

"No." Ella stepped back and ran into the railing of the porch. "You can't think that. How could you think that?"

The moment the question left her, Ella wished she could reel it back in. Because what came out of her mother's mouth next took her feet out from under her.

"Because it's true. He called you three times. He asked for your help. You should have been there for him, and you weren't. You were too busy painting your nails to pay attention to the brother who loved you more than anything else on this planet. Your selfishness is what did this to our family. You broke it. You killed him."

Ella's hand went to her chest, where her key was supposed to be. It wasn't there. Her other hand grabbed the blue lock in her hair, and she gasped, sinking to the porch floor. "I didn't kill him. I didn't kill him. I didn't kill him."

"You did."

Her father's voice, flat and hot like the surface of a lava floe.

"He begged you to come and get him. You couldn't tear yourself away from your friend for the thirty seconds it would have taken to hear what he had to say." Ella's father stepped onto the porch and took her mother's arm. "You broke our family."

"I didn't." Ella gasped a breath, but her parents' words repeated in her head like the skip in Grammy's Eric Clapton vinyl. *I shot the sheriff, I shot the sheriff, I shot the sheriff, I shot the sheriff.*

Ella tugged at the blue lock of hair. Blue for Stuart. Blue. Always blue. Always blue.

"You're not welcome here anymore," her mother said.

Her father pulled Ella's mother back into the house and shut the door. The sound of the latch clicking opened the floodgates, and Ella fell to the porch. Her tears beat her there.

somewhere, somehow, ella felt her phone buzzing.

It vibrated like the agony in her heart, made a sound like a thousand bumblebees against the wood of the porch as the phone buzzed, buzzed, buzzed in her pocket.

Ella pulled it out. Jace.

She answered it, but no words came out through the sobs.

"Ella? What's wrong? Where are you?"

Ella babbled something about parents, but her words dissolved into the thoughts in her head. *It's my fault. It's my fault. It's my fault.*

"What's your fault?"

Had she said that out loud? Ella breathed into the phone, trying to clear her head.

"Ella, sweetie, where are you? I'm coming to get you."

She got the address out and fell back to the porch. The shades were drawn. How was it possible that her parents could leave her out here? Jace's parents had done the same thing. The same thing. How?

Jace arrived what felt like immediately, Alexa at her side, and bundled Ella into Jace's car. Ella caught the murderous look Jace shot at the windows of the house, and she buckled her seatbelt, pulling the strap close to her chest.

"Alexa's going to drive your car to your house."

Ella nodded, not caring.

"You know you can cancel dinner tonight."

Ella nodded again.

"Do you want me to call Callum and cancel?"

Ella shook her head. She didn't want that. She didn't want any of this.

Jace was silent for several minutes as they drove. "Auntie Eunice was telling the truth, wasn't she?"

That time, Ella couldn't make herself move. Confirming it to Jace meant confirming it to herself. It meant admitting that her parents were right and that she'd killed her twin brother three years ago.

Her silence seemed to be confirmation enough. "God, Ella. I am so sorry you're going through this."

"Something else we have in common." Ella's voice sounded like it was underwater. Nebulous. Not real.

"No. This is different. My parents are crappy because they can't accept something about me. Yours are dumping something on you that's not yours to bear."

"It is mine to bear."

Jace slammed on the brakes and pulled the car over to the shoulder. "No. Don't you dare. You are not responsible for Stuart's death, Ella. Do you hear me?"

"He called me and I didn't listen. I didn't answer when he needed me. And he *died*, Jace. He died."

"I know exactly what happened that night. I was there, remember? I'm the one who told you I wanted a girls only night. You knew that. That's why you ignored the calls. If you have to blame anyone for his accident, blame me."

The engine of the car revved without any movement, as if accentuating Jace's words. Ella turned to her friend. "It's not your fault."

"Well, it's not yours either. Sometimes really horrible things happen to really wonderful people."

"They shouldn't." Ella knew she sounded like a child, that somewhere deep inside she had to blame herself because blaming life accomplished nothing at all.

"They do anyway." Jace took Ella's face between her hands. "They do anyway. All the time. Good people suffer and die, and they leave behind gaping holes of pain and confusion, and there's nothing we can do about it but move forward."

"I have no idea how to move forward from this, Jace. I don't know how to do this."

"No one does. I don't either. But the point is, your parents are wrong. Do you remember just a couple weeks ago when you told me the same thing? I never wanted the chance to say it back to you, but now that it's here, I'm going to. Your parents are wrong. They're so wrong, and they shouldn't have done that to you. No parent should do that. Family shouldn't do that." Jace let her hands drop away and scowled. "I think our parents need to join a support group for people who can't deal with their own issues."

"And you think I can deal better than they can?"

"You are dealing better. You are." Jace pulled the car back onto the road, knocking her sun visor down to diffuse the glare of the afternoon brightness.

They were silent for the rest of the drive. As they pulled into Ella's driveway, Jace turned to look at her.

"You're sure you want to still have Callum over tonight?"

"He's a part of my life now," Ella said.

She wanted that. Without her parents, without being able to trust Auntie Eunice, Ella would have to build a new family. But how?

chapter
thirty-two

Ella stood in the kitchen, mechanically putting groceries away. She pulled her crumpled list from her pocket and arranged the tiramisu ingredients in perfect rows on the counter. Mascarpone. Heavy whipping cream. Sugar. Flour. Eggs. Amaretto. Baking powder.

Her recipes for the night were in a tidy stack on the table, and she lifted the lady fingers recipe from the top of the pile. She didn't know where Jace and Alexa had gone to, but she needed to do something. Anything. So she began to separate eggs.

The four egg whites looked slimy and bulbous in the bowl. Ella stared at them for a long moment before digging in the cupboard to find the electric mixer. She fitted the beaters onto it and plugged it in.

The whirring blades and the sweet warmth that filled her nose as they churned the egg whites into froth reminded her of every moment she'd spent baking with her parents. Around Christmas, they'd always had three solid days of cookie making, from flat sugar cookies dipped in colored sugar to chewy molasses cookies and Russian tea cakes.

The frothy egg whites smoothed, growing fluffier and shinier until the beaters left their textured tracks behind. Ella turned off the mixer and pulled up. The forming meringue left a soft peak where the beater had been. She sifted in a couple tablespoons of sugar and turned it back on, watching as the whites stiffened, turning glossy in the beam of sunlight that slanted through the kitchen window. She flicked the mixer off again.

And heard raised voices.

"We've been planning this for years, and you're just going to postpone it?"

"She needs me."

"So do I —"

"Shh."

Ella sat the mixing bowl aside and slid the bowl of egg yolks over in front of her, rinsing off the beaters. Her breath came shallow. She dumped the remaining sugar into the yolks and turned the mixer on high. They had to be talking about Jace moving in with Alexa. Why would Jace want to postpone that? Ella had no doubt that the "she" Jace referred to as needing her was herself. They clearly hadn't wanted to be overheard. Ella concentrated on the paling egg yolks.

"Need some help?" Jace came into the kitchen, Alexa on her heels with a tight-lipped expression on her face.

"That'd be great," Ella said. "I need some really strong coffee brewed for this. I don't have an espresso maker."

Jace and Alexa exchanged a glance, and Alexa frowned.

Ella turned her gaze back to the mixing bowl.

The clicks and burbles of the coffee maker joined the whirr of the mixer, unpunctuated by speech. When Ella turned off the mixer again, Alexa and Jace had their eyes locked on one another. She thought she saw an almost imperceptible nod from Alexa, but she wasn't sure because a second later, Alexa spun around and left the room.

"Everything okay?" Ella asked. Wax paper. She needed wax paper. She found it under a bundle of plastic grocery bags in the pantry and spread a sheet out over a clear bit of counter.

"I have something I want to talk to you about."

Ella pulled Grammy's sifter from its hook over the stove and dumped the flour into it with the baking powder. Who came up with a recipe that required measurements like seven eighths of a cup anyway? "Shoot," she said, unsure of what to expect.

"You probably overheard Alexa and I a minute ago."

Ella gave a noncommittal nod, squeezing the trigger of the sifter over and over to dust the wax paper with the mixture. She dumped half the egg whites into the yolks, and started folding the fluffy clouds of meringue into the yellow goo.

"I know it's been three years since Stuart died. But there's been a lot of upheaval this year for you, and I hate seeing you go through it alone."

Ella's head jerked up mid-fold to look at Jace. "I'm not alone."

"Maybe, but things keep getting dumped on you, and I hate thinking of you in this big house all by yourself with the cats and a frog. So when my lease is up next week, I'm not moving in with Alexa. I'm moving in with you."

The mixture in the bowl started to look oozy, so Ella resumed her folding. "But Alexa needs this. You need this."

"We've waited five years. Another six months isn't going to kill either of us. I'm still getting used to being well and truly out, and this happened really fast. I know I didn't exactly ask your opinion, but I'm doing it anyway. I'm moving in here for six months."

"What about Callum?"

"What about him?"

"I'm not alone, Jace."

"That's fine, but anything can happen. I'll be out of your hair in six months, and he can move in if he wants then."

"That's not what I meant."

"I'm moving in, okay?"

Ella had her attention focused on slowly folding the flour mixture into the egg combo, but in her peripheral vision she saw Jace look toward the front of the house. Jace's words from the weeks before resurfaced in her mind. How moving in with Alexa was the one thing she'd been missing for five years. How it was what she wanted more than anything else. And now Jace was just going to give that up? Ella started to open her mouth.

"I know what you're thinking, and just leave it. Alexa will be okay."

As if to prove the point, Alexa returned to the kitchen a few minutes later with a big smile that didn't quite reach her eyes. Ella tried to smile back. When Alexa looked away, Ella stared into the batter she'd created.

"Damn," she said.

"What?" Jace moved to stand by Alexa and planted a kiss on her shoulder.

"I don't have a pastry bag."

Alexa bit her bottom lip for a moment as if considering something. She turned to the pantry, where she rummaged around until she emerged with a gallon-sized ziplock bag. Ella watched as she transferred the mixture into the plastic bag, then sliced off a half-inch chunk of the corner.

"There you go." She held it out to Ella.

As far as olive branches went, Ella thought it a rather strange one. But she nodded and took the bag.

pushing her parents from her thoughts proved harder than Ella expected.

Even as Alexa and Jace joked, whipping cream and mascarpone together with sugar and drizzling Jace's coffee reduction over the golden brown lady fingers, she couldn't help but think that she should have dragged herself off her parents' porch and pounded the door down until they answered. Until they explained. Until they sat down and gave her some sort of reasonable explanation for shunning her from their family.

But that was the problem, Ella thought, watching Alexa take a sip of amaretto and shove her glass under Jace's nose. Emotions didn't have much to do with reason or logic.

She'd thought her parents would have enough awareness to recognize that. Maybe they really did see a reason for blaming her. After all, hadn't Ella blamed herself? It wasn't until someone else strapped that yoke across her shoulders that Ella had truly felt it, and she had crumpled under its weight.

As always, it was Jace who was there to pick her back up again. And Alexa, in spite of whatever tension remained between her and Ella. She came through for Ella out of her love for Jace, and Ella couldn't turn her nose up at that.

Ella thought about her broken family. Looking back over the past three years, it seemed that Stuart had been the bridge between Ella and her parents, and his death had washed it out until nothing but ragged banks and an unfordable expanse of rapids remained between them. With him gone and the poisoning blame that had eroded her parents' love for her, Ella didn't think she would ever get it back. She'd lived without them for two and a half years already in blissful ignorance that packed her eyes and ears with wool.

Everything was different now.

Alexa flexed her arms, setting down a whisk, which Jace scooped up and licked. Jace met Ella's gaze.

Maybe the truest family was the one you built, through trust and kindness and loyalty.

She spooned the cheese and whipped cream mixture over the lady fingers until they were covered. Different components, layered together. Sometimes that made something beautiful.

Ella thought she'd been cried out, but she felt her eyes mist again and looked up at Jace, who was staring out the window.

"Thank you, guys," she said.

"What?" Jace shook herself, and Alexa shook her head.

"I said thank you. For helping out. And…everything."

"Of course," said Jace, her eyes lifting to the window again.

Ella insisted that the others relax until Callum arrived, bustling them into the living room with two bottles of chardonnay in spite of their protests. She was so focused on the finishing touches for dinner that she didn't hear Callum's arrival until he rapped his knuckles on the door jamb to the kitchen.

He strode toward her and kissed her. Ella sat down the wooden spoon she'd been using to stir the scampi and melted into his arms. The scent of garlic and butter surrounded them, the steam of the kitchen turning the air heady and warm and chasing away the chill of the air conditioning.

"Hi," said Callum after he pulled his face back. "Everything smells delicious. Can I help with anything?"

Ella smiled up at him and shook her head. "I've got it. You can grab a wine glass and join Alexa and Jace in the living room if you want."

"Now, that I don't feel like doing." He moved to stand behind her, wrapping his arms around her waist. "I think I'll just stay here and get in the way."

His lips touched the side of her neck, and Ella sighed, leaning back against him and giving the scampi a half-hearted stir. "I almost wish the food wasn't done."

Callum's arms tightened around her, and he murmured into her ear. "Me too."

Ella twisted herself around to face him. "Thanks for coming."

"And miss the promise of world-famous tiramisu? Never."

How could gray eyes look so warm? Ella looked up at him, and his eyes held a light, a glow when he met her gaze. He gave a small, whimsical smile that brought out the single dimple in his left cheek. It was then that Ella realized her parents hadn't left her today. They'd left her two and a half years before, when they jetted off to South Africa and blew off her calls, returning only short emails for a time, and then nothing. Ella had left for six weeks, and when she'd returned, Callum had still been here, waiting for her. She reached up and touched his cheek, words swirling just at the the edges of her tongue.

"Need help setting the table?" Jace clomped into the kitchen with an empty wine bottle, dropping it with a crash into the recycling bin. She winked at Callum, who gave her a wry smile in return.

"Sure," Ella said, turning off the stove and pausing to let out a slow breath. She turned back to face Jace and Callum. "I'm going to run and freshen up, then I'll be out to serve up the plates."

She put a hand on the small of Callum's back as she passed him and made her way to the restroom.

When she looked in the mirror with her hands under the water, she saw her own jaw drop. Her face was still puffy from her earlier tears, and her normal loose waves had almost matted together. The blue lock on her left side wasn't so much a lock as a blur, mixed together with the dark brown of the strands around it. Ella grabbed a brush and pulled it through her hair until it looked almost presentable. Her face she splashed with cold water and patted dry. It wasn't a great effort, but she looked like less of a mess.

Ella emerged from the bathroom to find that the others had already served themselves and were seated at the table. She took her place next to Callum and raised her wine glass to the others.

"To lessons learned," she said, thinking about family and the people she'd surrounded herself with.

Their answering murmur rippled across the table.

It wasn't until halfway through the tiramisu that Ella noticed Jace staring out the window for the fourth time since she'd sat down.

"What on earth are you looking at? You keep looking out the window."

Jace jerked her head back to face the table. "It's nothing."

"Nothing must be interesting to stare at," Callum joked.

Alexa's eyes were focused on her girlfriend too, and Ella raised her eyebrows, questioning.

Jace looked out once more, then took a breath. "I keep seeing Aunt Eunice's car drive by."

Ella turned to look out the window, but no one was on the road. "How many times?"

"At least six. Since we were putting dessert together."

Ella wasn't sure how much Alexa knew about what had been going on, but Callum certainly didn't know anything. "Why do you think she hasn't stopped and tried to come in?"

"I think it's because we're all here."

Jace had to be right. With two extra cars in the driveway, whatever Auntie Eunice's goal, she didn't think she could accomplish it with company.

Callum's face crinkled with confusion.

She could make up some story about a batty great-aunt that wouldn't be too far from the truth, but looking around at the table, Ella didn't want to lie.

"I'll try my best to explain," she said instead.

chapter thirty-three

Ella was certain that any explanation at all had to sound insane to Callum. He might be a creative spirit, but just because he got to play a fairy king of mischief on stage didn't mean he'd accept the idea of real magic and a great-aunt with the power to change possible centuries of lives.

His silence after she finished made Ella push a half-eaten chunk of tiramisu around her plate, hating the scrape of the fork on the porcelain but unable to stop herself. To her surprise, Alexa spoke up.

"I know it sounds nuts," she said. "But if you knew this family, you'd get it."

"I think I do know this family," Callum said quietly, looking at Ella. "So what do you think your Aunt Eunice is up to?"

The surprise Ella felt at his easy question made her drop her fork onto the plate. She picked it back up after a beat and shoveled the last bite into her mouth. "I think she thinks she can hit some magical reset button with the keys. Undo Stuart's death. And her sister's."

"You mean bring your brother back."

"I mean bring my brother back." After all, that's what Auntie Eunice thought had started all of this, right? Broken Ella's family. Begun Helen's spiral into obsession.

"Do you believe it will work?"

"I don't know."

Callum paused before asking a follow-up question. "Do you want it to work?"

Jace's mouth opened and then shut, and she looked at Ella.

Ella wasn't sure. Did she want Stuart back? More than anything in this world. She wanted to talk to him, to tell him how much she missed him. She wanted him to absolve her, somehow, of her guilt in his death. She wanted her parents to look at her, to love her, to comfort her. But if the reset really was what Auntie Eunice thought it would be, what would that mean for everything else? Every other key to touch every other finger. Grammy Helen's life — and Auntie Eunice's.

Would resetting all of it even mean that Stuart had been born at all?

She waited a long moment before speaking. "I can't let her do it. It could change everything. Every choice is too complicated; erasing all of them could erase all of us. Well," she said with a wry attempt at a laugh, "me, anyway. Who knows how long those damn keys have been in the family? It might even erase Auntie Eunice."

"I'm no physicist, but I'm not sure it's worth the risk either." Jace drummed her fingers on the table. "If there's anything I've learned from a lifetime of fantasy novels, it's that magic's more likely to bite you in the ass than not."

Alexa nodded, but Callum's eyes focused on Ella.

"If Auntie Eunice succeeding means you might vanish, I'm all for stopping her. Like yesterday."

"Gag," said Jace.

There was a light thud as Alexa kicked Jace under the table.

Ella looked right back at Callum. "You mean you believe all of this?"

"I believe you do. And that your great-aunt does. I'm willing to be open-minded. Just don't try and make me sacrifice any goats."

"No goats to be harmed, I promise," Ella said.

Jace was looking out the window again. "She just went by again. I think heading back toward town."

Ella stood and went to the window. Sure enough, she could make out the glow of Auntie Eunice's station wagon, pink in the light from the taillights. She didn't think Auntie Eunice would be back tonight. Not when she had company.

Instead, she turned to cleaning up, Callum at her side to dry the dishes. By the time her hands had wrinkled from the dishwater, Alexa and Jace had vanished.

Halfway through the washing up, Ella heard raised voices from her grandpa's office. She paused, one wet hand grasping a damp towel, and Callum met her concerned gaze.

Maybe it hadn't been as much of an olive branch as she'd thought earlier. Or maybe Alexa just liked her too much to be blame her for Jace's decision.

Ella set the towel down and wiped her hands on her jeans. "I'll be right back," she said.

Callum caught her arm, setting butterflies free to flap around her stomach. He stroked the side of her arm lightly with his thumb before letting go and continuing to scrub the tiramisu dish.

The heated voices grew louder as Ella stepped down the hall. She stopped in front of the closed door, unsure whether butting in was really a good idea.

"I love *you*," Jace said, and Ella winced at the emphasis. "You know that.

"I know. But we've been waiting for this for so long, and now the time's come to commit, you're putting Ella first again."

Again, Ella thought, hesitating with one hand on the door.

Alexa's volume dropped, and her voice took on a tortured tone. "What am I supposed to think?"

Jace was silent for a moment, and Ella's heart climbed into her throat. *Say something, Jace.*

The silence went on too long.

"Ella has Callum," Jace insisted finally, and Ella wanted to kick her.

"That says nothing about me or you," said Alexa so softly, Ella could barely hear her. "All this time, you kept setting her up with women, how am I not supposed to think you're secretly hoping she'll come out as a full-fledged lesbian and go for you?"

Jace barked a laugh. "That's what you think? I got over my crush on Ella years ago. All the set ups were just a distraction."

"For her or for you?"

"For her, goddamn it. I had to do something. You know how she was after Stuart's death. Or maybe you don't, because you didn't spend much time with her back then." Wistfulness seeped through the cracks in Jace's words. "You didn't know her before. How she was then. What she's like now in comparison. She's a shell, Alexa."

Jace's words shriveled Ella's insides. She couldn't disagree. The old pit threatened to resurface, the heavy grief. Ella bit it back.

Alexa countered again. "But Callum — I mean, a man in theater who's that well-groomed —"

"—Now you're reaching."

"Am I?"

That was it. Ella pushed open the door. "Knock it off, you two. You both love each other too much for your own good. Jace, you are not moving in here. Period. Alexa's waited long enough."

She stepped down harshly on a piece of curling-up rug. "If you're not ready for that, then you two talk about it, but don't put me in the middle."

Alexa turned her glare on Ella. The hot anger in her eyes made Ella feel about half an inch tall. "And Callum?" Alexa said. "You really think he's straight and Jace isn't behind this?"

It was Ella's turn to choke out a laugh. Here she'd barged in on their conversation and Alexa hadn't missed a beat.

"Gay or straight or somewhere in the middle, I'm falling in love with him," Ella said, the words tumbling out of her mouth.

She expected the jaw drops, but she didn't expect the two pairs of eyes to glue their gaze to the hall behind her. Until a footfall explained it.

Heat flooded Ella's cheeks. She turned slowly, hoping Callum wasn't actually standing there and that it'd just been Poof or Puff.

Nope.

Callum's face held a strange mixture of emotion that Ella couldn't sort out. He didn't speak.

He instead closed the distance between them and kissed her soundly.

The paired embarrassment and anxiety soldered her to him with the forging heat of his kiss.

Ella thought she might tremble, but then her hands snaked around Callum's neck, pulling him down closer to her. When the kiss ended and his lips parted from hers, Callum pulled back and leaned around Ella to look at Alexa and Jace.

"Definitely mutual," he said.

Ella wasn't sure if Alexa and Jace were okay or just putting on a good face, but when they closed the door to Grammy Helen's old bedroom and bid Ella and Callum goodnight, Ella thought she saw triumph in Alexa's eyes.

chapter
thirty-four

and then Callum and Ella were alone in the corridor altogether too close to Ella's bedroom door. Puff twined about her ankles, then Callum's, drawing figure eights between them.

Not trusting her words, Ella motioned to her door, her hand clumsily beckoning Callum to follow. His scent filled the hallway, clean and warm with the tiniest hint of the dragon fruit dish soap from the kitchen. She stepped into her room, avoiding the creaky floorboard, and perched on the bed. Callum followed her lead and sat next to her. His warmth was disconcertingly distracting, and Ella looked over at him. He made no move to touch her, only waited.

"I meant it," she said finally, knowing he'd understand exactly what it was she meant.

A slight give behind her followed by a smaller one told her Puff and Poof had arrived on the bed, but Ella ignored them.

"I know," Callum said. He met her gaze.

"How long had you been standing there?"

"Just a minute. Long enough to hear what Jace said about you."

Ella flushed, head falling forward. She stared at her knees, thinking. She didn't like that people thought of her as broken, as a shell. Was she, really? Had Stuart's death hollowed her out so much that everyone heard the echoes when she walked by? For once the passing thought of his name didn't tighten the knot in her gut, only whispered through her and was gone like a breath in winter. Was this the difference between hurt and broken?

"I wanted you to know that I don't think of you like that."

Alarmed, Ella jerked her head back up to look at Callum, a different knot tightening. Didn't think of her like what? Like a lover?

His next move both smoothed that knot and started threads swirling within her. His hand grazed her face, the other on her shoulder, guiding her body to face his.

"You're not a broken shell. You're a survivor, Ella. Most people think that means emerging from something with their face painted and a homemade spear dangling from their hands and a necklace of ears or something. It doesn't, not always. Sometimes being a survivor means being able to take those final steps to safety even when your legs want to give out and your stomach has shrunk to the size of a walnut. Sometimes it means doing what's best for you, and I've seen you do that. You're stronger than Jace gives you credit for. I know she means well, but I don't think a distraction is necessarily what you needed."

Callum's words were so earnest, so soft. Ella watched his eyes, the grey of his irises with flecks of silver like the cut beauty of a flawless gemstone. Pain lurked there, clearer now. What had he survived?

"What is it you think I needed?" Her own voice came out heavy and swollen and pendulous. Her words hung for a moment between them.

Callum looked at her, his hand falling from her cheek onto the bed beside them. "Time," he said.

Ella's heart felt as though he'd reached into it and squeezed gently. It ached like muscles after a workout or the remnants of a long-yellowed bruise. His closeness drew her like a magnet, but she didn't move, only sat inches from him, feeling the pull.

He looked down, but it only slightly weakened the spell. He spoke quietly, still with his gaze trained on the wood floor.

"I don't know what I would have done if you'd gone into the right coffee shop that day. I didn't think…" Callum trailed off like he'd been going to say something but decided better of it. He looked back up at her and turned to face her on the bed.

This time when his hand touched her skin, electricity sparked to life. It sent tendrils sizzling up her wrist, her arm. Ella's fingers sought his out, and it was as if his touch ignited something in her. She waited to hear what he would say, her breath catching in her chest with each inhale.

"It was all over for me that day," he said, his voice so soft it was almost a whisper. "And tonight when I heard you say those words, I thought I would crumble to the ground."

Callum's eyes captured hers, and Ella couldn't look away. She couldn't breathe.

"I love you, Ella Keyes."

Her heart soared in her chest. All knots melted away. Ella reached forward with her free hand and brought it to his cheek. He held it there with his own. His jaw felt strong and solid. Ella's fingers felt the beginnings of stubble, and she smoothed her hand back over his ear, into his hair. The touch of him felt like a drug. Slowly, slowly, she knelt on the bed, edging him backward until she could place one leg on the other side of him, straddling him. Callum still sat up, facing her, face calmer than she thought he should feel.

The first touch of her lips on his chased away any veneer of calmness from his body. His hands snaked around Ella's waist, and hers wrapped tightly around his neck. He still tasted of tiramisu and wine, and his lips against hers were full and soft and hot. She felt him beneath her where their bodies met through their jeans, the hardness she felt pressing between her legs.

Every point of contact opened up a vast chamber of hunger. Ella's mouth devoured Callum's. Parting her lips, she lightly moved her tongue against his, then deeper until their every touch demanded deeper closeness. Her hands left his neck, skimming down the flat planes of his chest and around his ribcage to his back, searching lower until she found the hem of his shirt and pulled it up. She didn't want to stop the kiss to pull it over his head. Her cool hands hungrily sought out the heat of his skin. She pulled her face back, lips tingling as the shirt came off and fell to the floor.

For a moment they looked at each other. There it was again, that face of calm. He was waiting on her, probably remembering the last time, when she'd fled his apartment without explanation. Ella felt no embarrassment now. Instead she pried herself from his lap, her body aching for the lack of his touch. On unsteady feet she walked to the door, shooing both cats into the corridor. She closed the door.

The walk back to the bed seemed to take ten years.

Ella stopped in front of Callum and reached to her waist. She pulled her shirt over her head and dropped it on top of Callum's. The air in her bedroom was warm, but still her skin pebbled into gooseflesh. She slipped her hands behind her and unhooked her bra, eyes on Callum's the whole time. He watched her, the calm look evaporating from her face and a new expression rising to replace it. His mouth fell open, lips still wet from their kiss.

The straps of her bra slid over her shoulders. The cups fell from her breasts and hit the floor. Ella closed the distance to the bed. Callum's hands met her waist where she stood in front of him, and there he waited, looking up at her.

His eyes held such longing that she wanted to dive into those grey pools and swim there forever.

"Yes," she said.

the touch of his hands sent tendrils blazing across the surface of Ella's skin. Instead of pulling her down to him, Callum stood, his arms wrapping around Ella's waist. The sensation of his skin against hers felt like an ice cold drink on a sweltering day. For every hint of satisfaction it brought came the burning need of unslaked thirst. Her skin drank his in. His hands kneaded her waist, changing to light touches that almost tickled their way up her ribcage to the sides of her breasts. Ella reached out mirror him, reveling in the taut smoothness of his skin. She remembered him on stage as Puck, gleaming in the lights. Here he was even more resplendent to her.

His hands cupped her breasts, and a small gasp escaped her lips. Her hands went to the button of his jeans and undid it with trembling fingers.

She wasn't sure how his jeans ended up pooled on the floor or how the legs of her own tangled in the denim. Ella fell back on her bed. Callum knelt over her, one leg on either side of her thigh. He didn't ask if she was sure; her simple yes was all she needed to say. He lowered his body down to her, his lips going straight to the crook of her neck, sending shivers and heat in webs outward from the spots they touched. His tongue skirted her collarbone as he kissed the line of her throat upward, tracing the edge of her jaw to the other side and back down.

Heat built low in her core, pulling at her, demanding for more, clamoring for the touch of his skin everywhere on her body. Ella pulled him down to her, edging her leg to the side, using both of her legs to wrap around his waist and pull him down.

The first touch of him through the thin layers of his boxer briefs and her panties made her buck up against him. Callum responded by pressing himself down, shifting his hips so that his length moved against her. He made a small sound into her neck, and Ella turned her face against his hair, hands running through its satin softness and down the back of his neck to the firm muscles of his back. Her skin seemed to yearn for his, and he seemed to feel it too.

He raised his face to hers. All Ella saw in the dim golden lamplight was the flicker of silver in his eyes. When he kissed her next, she didn't close her eyes, only held contact with his. It stirred something within her, stoked the heat between her legs where their bodies touched almost, almost. His hand journeyed down her body to her stomach until at the last moment, he propped himself up, still kissing her. His fingers met the edge of her panties and skimmed over the thin cloth. The murmuring moan that came from Ella's throat brought a glint to his eyes. Callum deepened the kiss, still with eyes open. His hand danced across her, and Ella raised her hips to meet his touch, feeling the coolness of the air where their bodies had been so hot, the teasingly cold shiver of moving air over her damp underwear.

All she could think was that she needed more.

Ella pulled him down to her.

Callum met her gaze again as he lowered himself on top of her. His hand traced her jaw, and she smelled herself on his fingers. That look in his eyes was pure hunger that said he knew exactly what he wanted to do, exactly where he would be in moments. Ella knew it was only a reflection of what she felt in her own.

Ella's body hummed like a struck dulcimer string, and Callum's tense torso above her thrummed in harmony. He lowered himself to her, their bodies half an inch apart. Electric heat sparked back and forth between them. He looked at her, and Ella looked back.

"I want you," he said, his voice full of the dark and velvet things that went with his words. "I love you."

"I love you." Ella drew a shuddering breath, moving beneath him, feeling him leap inside her. "I want you."

Then he was with her, and she with him, and she lost all sense of everything except the fire of their love.

chapter
thirty-five

hours later, her cheek nestled against Callum's shoulder, Ella started awake to the sound of a crash above her.

Heart leaping to a staccato beat, she sat straight up in bed. Callum followed a moment later. They hadn't even managed to turn off the single lamp, and the room was still bathed in golden light.

"What was that?" Callum asked.

"I have no idea." Ella waited for a moment of silence only the predawn hours can produce. She started to lower herself back down when a second crash came, followed by a thud and a cry.

Ella leaped from her bed and threw a robe over her shoulders, belting it even as she hurried to the door.

"Should I call the police?"

"No." Ella knew that voice. She flung the door open and ran to the staircase, flicking on light switches as she went. Dimly, she was aware of footsteps following her, but Ella paid no attention. Her bare feet took her up the stairs, and she skidded to a halt at the end of the hallway of keys, already knowing who was at the other end.

Auntie Eunice hadn't turned on a light, and she stood at the far end of the hall, the long chain of Ella's necklace dangling from one hand and the box Ella's father had given her in the other.

"Ella?" Jace's voice, still heavy with sleep.

Ella didn't answer, only advanced on the old woman. How had she gotten up the stairs? For months she'd struggled and made Ella help her up from the basement when she was done rummaging around in all of Grammy Helen's belongings.

"You can't be here, Auntie Eunice," said Ella.

Her great-aunt didn't turn or answer, but her hands shook on the box.

The hallway felt warm, uncomfortably so, far hotter than the remaining summer heat could make it. Something buzzed on the air, like a swarm of bees hidden in the paneled walls. Ella flicked the light switch, bathing the hallway in a halo of muted gold. It wasn't bright, but Ella found herself squinting. Her skin broke into gooseflesh under her thin robe, her skin tight with the perspiration dried and leftover from her lovemaking. She could sense Callum behind her like an otherworldly presence, but she didn't turn to him. A murmur began, quickly hushed. Alexa and Jace.

Ella tried to look at the keys on the walls to see if any were missing, but they seemed to blur beneath her gaze as if they existed in another plane and had somehow veiled themselves. She shook off the foreign thought, taking a bemused step toward Auntie Eunice.

"Auntie Eunice, what are you doing?"

"I have to fix it."

It was the first thing she'd said since everyone arrived, and now she turned to face Ella. Her skin looked like tissue paper, almost translucent in the golden light of the fixtures, somehow almost as blurred as the keys. Ella looked closer and realized that everything farther than a few feet away took on that elusive quality, as though she were watching the other end of the corridor through a mirror.

"You can't fix it," Ella said quietly. Then louder. "You can't fix death, Auntie Eunice!"

Eunice wrapped the dangling gold chain around her hand and fumbled with the enamel box. A bright light glinted from the old woman's closed fist, and when she turned, Ella saw where it was coming from.

Her necklace. The tiny gold key Grammy Helen had given her so long ago. It shone like a beacon, like a torch condensed into glittering metal. When Auntie Eunice opened her hand, the necklace's light spilled out like glowing honey, lighting the entire corridor with its brightness.

"What...is that?" Jace asked. "Is that your necklace?"

Ella half-nodded, taking another step toward her great-aunt. "Auntie, you can't do this." Something tugged deep in Ella's chest. The blur of the keys surrounding her made her blink and reach out a hand to steady herself on the paneled wall. She struggled to take another step, but her feet were snowshoes in mud. Why couldn't she walk straight?

The room tilted around her, and Ella's stomach lurched as if the planet had reversed the direction of its rotation.

"I have to save —" Auntie Eunice's voice blurred like the keys, and Ella missed the last words, seeing only the old woman's lips move soundlessly.

"You can't save him," Ella muttered. She fell to her knees and started to crawl.

Auntie Eunice opened the box.

Every key on the walls began to rattle.

Out of the corner of her eyes, Ella saw Jace and Alexa throw their hands over their ears, falling to their knees. Callum stumbled into one wall, barely managing to stay upright. A hum filled the air, deeper than the rattling of the vibrating keys, resonant like the Tibetan prayer bowl in grandpa's study.

"Don't," Ella said. She didn't mean it, though. She felt hope kindle in her chest, a wild hope, a desperate hope that brought every skinned knee, every teasing grin from Stuart, every hidden stone rushing back. She fell back onto her heels, hand going involuntarily to the blue lock in her hair. It wrapped easily around her fingers.

Eunice removed something small from the box that glinted in the light of the tiny gold key. She pressed the tiny object to the wall at the end of the corridor.

The hum changed pitch, higher and higher until Ella's ears rang and she fell prostrate to the floor.

It started with a tinkle, then a clatter, then a roar as every one of the hundreds of keys on the walls leaped from its nail and crashed to the wooden floor. They puddled around Ella's hunched form, a jagged-edged nest of twisted metal. All those keys. All those moments.

Silence drained all thought. Ella's ears buzzed from the sudden quiet, the lack of the resonant hum of the keys.

The keys.

Ella thought back to how her life had changed with each key she'd removed from the wall. Losing her job, her apartment. Finding Callum. Puff. Burst pipes and elephants. Panic rose in her stomach, crawling the rungs of her ribcage and up to her throat like a rising tide.

She cold see the end of the corridor now. Whatever Auntie Eunice had stuck to the wall glowed like the tiny key on the chain, bright like bottled sunlight.

As Ella watched, the glow faded. Purple, bruise-like afterimages floated in front of her face. She made another shuffling crawling motion toward Auntie Eunice. The reset. It was real. It looked so innocuous, a simple keyhole. But it hadn't been there before. It sat in the middle of the wall itself. No buttons or knobs, only a sea of fallen keys surrounded Ella on the floor. She pushed herself to her feet and took a step toward Auntie Eunice.

The inner part of Ella's mind tried to tell her that keyholes don't just appear out of nowhere, but she ignored that part. She had to do something. Stop Auntie Eunice or help her. She wasn't sure which.

The keys around her feet taunted her like chaos unleashed. She tried not to look at the bits of metal, tried not to think of what could happen tomorrow. A lottery win or a meteor crashing into the house. A hidden treasure in the field behind the house or the engine in her car spontaneously exploding. Anything. Anything could happen. The dizziness tried to take her again, and this time Ella didn't think it was because of the keys. It was the sheer spontaneity the keys pooled around her feet implied. Callum. She'd found him because of a key. What if he fled after this and she never saw him again?

Auntie Eunice stood only five feet away now. Her hand shook on the chain, the small gold key dangling and swaying in jerks and spurts.

What would happen? What would happen when the key hit that hole? Ella's eyes stung, and she blinked. Tears? Stuart.

Her heart pulled her forward.

Auntie Eunice fumbled with the key, her knobby fingers struggling to find purchase on the tiny curvature of the metal.

She raised the key, held in a white-knuckled hand, and pushed it into the keyhole.

"No," Ella whispered. She couldn't let this happen. Eunice could erase her, erase herself. Erase everything.

But what if it instead brought back Stuart? Tears danced at the lids of her eyes, flirting with the edges, ready to spill over.

"Auntie Eunice, please."

Ella didn't know if she was asking her great-aunt to stop or to turn the key.

Was that what she wanted? An end? Was she really a shell of a woman like Jace thought? Ella turned back to face her friend, her well-meaning friend. Jace who had risked her dearest relationship and love to make sure Ella would be okay. Alexa who fought like a tiger for her woman. And Callum.

Callum, who loved her and did not find her wanting.

Ella didn't want to cease to exist.

It was past time for her to fight for life.

Auntie Eunice turned toward the keyhole, her body obscuring it. There was a click.

"No!" Ella lunged forward, closing the distance between herself and the old woman. Her body connected with Auntie Eunice, and they tumbled to the ground. "You can't do this, Auntie Eunice!"

Eunice let out a wail, a high and keening sound that grated through Ella's psyche like the ghosts of everyone who had ever walked this hall. The old woman flailed her arms, and Ella tried to pin them down.

But Auntie Eunice wasn't trying to get away. Her arthritic hands grasped at Ella's bathrobe, taking handfuls of the fabric and pulling herself close to Ella's chest. Her body shook with sobs.

Ella looked up.

The key still sat unmoved in the hole. Ella reached up and wrenched it out, crumpling the fine chain and the key into the palm of her hand and making a tight fist around it.

"I couldn't," Auntie Eunice cried. "I couldn't do it." She yanked Ella close and sobbed into her hair. "Helen, I'm sorry!"

Ella didn't know what to do. How was she supposed to comfort someone who held the potential for wiping her from existence? She folded her arms around Eunice's thin shoulders. "It's okay, Auntie Eunice. It's okay."

"How do you do it, boy?" Eunice asked. Then her scream rent the air. "How do you do it?"

Startled, Ella flinched. "Do what?"

"Live. Without him. I can't. I don't know how to do it."

"Live without Stuart?" Ella felt his name leave her mouth like an accusation.

"Without Helen."

Of course.

For the first time, Ella looked down and truly saw her great-aunt. Not a batty woman who farted at odd moments and called her *boy*. Not an obsessive old lady trying to bring back a great-nephew who'd died too young.

A woman.

A person. A person who desperately missed her sister.

Her twin. The tears spilled over, hot on Ella's face. "I don't know, Auntie Eunice. I miss my brother every day."

Every day. How had she missed this before? She'd shared a womb with Stuart. Shared everything with him. Every day of her life revolved around him when she was little. As she got older, he was always still there. Not a day went by without speaking to him, laughing with him.

And the one day he'd needed her, asked for her, she'd failed him.

Ella would never forget that moment. She suddenly thought back to that bewildering telegram. *Grandmother expelled.*

Who had told Auntie Eunice? Had she gone to visit Grammy Helen and found her stolen away? Had Auntie Eunice cried out the way Ella had at the morgue?

Ella, who had had her brother only a quarter of a century.

And Aunt Eunice had had her Helen for ninety-three years.

Ella finally found her voice. "I don't know, Aunt Eunice."

Stuart. Her brother. Ella wrapped her arms around the old woman, feeling the shake of her shoulders echo Ella's own.

The key pressed into her palm, the metal denting into her skin. She could still use it. She looked up at the keyhole, then down at the weeping woman in her arms.

No, she couldn't.

She couldn't fix death. No one and nothing could.

The moment the words flitted through her mind, the keyhole stopped glowing, and a tiny chunk of gold dropped onto the floor. It glinted through the pile of keys, and Ella snapped it up before anyone else could touch it and shoved it inside the enamel box. Tomorrow. Tomorrow she'd bury that thing where no one would ever find it again.

Buried forever, like her brother.

Jace was the one who suggested tea.

Ella and Callum bundled a still-whimpering Auntie Eunice down the stairs and into the kitchen, where she sat on a chair, hugging the seat cushion to her chest.

Ella rummaged through the pantry until she found Auntie Eunice's favorite tea, a Moroccan mint blend in a tin. She opened the tin as she turned to hunt for a tea ball and stopped. There was a folded piece of paper in the tin.

The paper was creased and smelled sharply of mint as if the very essence of the tea had infused itself into the note. Grammy Helen's handwriting.

> *Dear Ella and Eunice,*
>
> *I know you'll be together when you get this, because Ella won't drink this, and it's all Eunice will touch. Unless, of course, Eunice is digging through my house when its owner isn't there. But you wouldn't do that, would you, sister?*

Ella stopped and felt tears moisten her eyes again. She could hear Grammy Helen's voice in her mind, the chuckle that came along with the last sentence, because Grammy would know damn well that her sister would hunt through the house with Ella gone.

> *I've hesitated so many times writing this. There must be an entire tree bemoaning the amount of paper I've scratched through, crumpled, and tossed across the room.*
>
> *Forgive me. I am a coward.*
>
> *I didn't tell either of you any of this because I was afraid. I feared what Eunice would do. I feared seeing her attempt at fixing this, fixing me. Because I know many things that the two of you do not, and for that I ask your forgiveness once more.*
>
> *As I write this, a bag of hideous yellow fluid is dripping into my arm. It burns like poison or like battery acid in my veins. This will be my last treatment. It won't save me, and I know it now. I'm ready to go. I'm ready to be done.*
>
> *This cancer is no fault of a key. It's the fault of failing genes that got confused and replicated until I felt them growing beneath my skin. I knew even at the beginning that it would not be enough — the chemo, the radiation. I told them only chemo, and even this has been halfhearted and not worth spending the remaining, dwindling days of my life in pain and sickness.*
>
> *It's the end. It's coming soon, and I can feel it in my bones.*
>
> *What a stupid thing to say. Forget I said that.*
>
> *Now, Eunice, I know what you're thinking. You're wanting to smack me upside the head and tell me to keep*

fighting. I have. I've done what I can, but I'm not so intent on living longer than my ninety-three years that I'll go to all ends.

Though I did, for me. I risked everything. I tried the reset. The key that she wears around her neck — I have its twin.

May all the gods have mercy on me, but I risked everything to save myself. For one glorious moment, I thought I might be taken away in a flash of gold light. But that didn't happen. The light faded into dimness and all that was left was quite a mess to clean up. I put the keys back, called my lawyer, and put Ella into my will. Eunice, you'll understand why I didn't leave this house to you. Ella is young. She, unlike us, has her whole life ahead of her.

That's a stupid thing to say, too.

Ella, I'm sorry. I'm sorry for the burden I've placed upon you. I'm sorry that you're probably only reading this after the worst has happened. If you ever even find it at all. Your parents might never get over what happened to Stuart; I know they've never forgiven me for standing by you through this. I thought better of my son than that. I hope my time with you in the last few years gave you back some of the family you needed.

Eunice, you old bat. The reset does nothing. Or perhaps it does something unknown, because I noticed the keys a little more clearly, like something had made their edges more distinct. This house has many secrets. Maybe someday Ella will discover them. Maybe you'll help her.

There is another key. You'll find it at the bottom of this tea tin. Twins run in our family. You know that, right?

I love you both.

Love,
Helen

There was a smaller piece of paper folded and taped to the bottom of the letter with Eunice's name on it. Ella handed the whole package soundlessly to her great-aunt.

The teapot whistled.

chapter
thirty-six

Callum, Jace, and Alexa helped Ella replace the keys on the walls upstairs.

There was no magical light this time, no hum or resonance. Just the odd warmth of the third floor corridor.

Together they hung each of the keys on the walls. At Ella's direction, they put all the shiny ones at the top where they'd be harder to reach. Touching each of the shiny keys made Ella want to throw them, but she made herself do it. It took an hour to put them all back, and when they were finished, the hallway was once again full. On the way back downstairs, Ella could hear Auntie Eunice snoring lightly in her bed. Ella had led her up the stairs and to her room, where Auntie Eunice had promptly announced, "It smells like sex in here," before flopping down on the bed and going directly to sleep, her twin sister's letter clasped to her chest.

Alexa and Jace went back to bed, both a bit wide-eyed. Ella wasn't sure if they'd sleep or not, but either way, she wouldn't be falling asleep any time soon.

She and Callum went downstairs together. The sky was beginning to lighten with the coming dawn. Without asking, Ella led Callum outside to the porch swing and sat, the swing creaking with their weight. It faced east, and together they swayed back and forth as the sky turned yellow and then rosy pink and the sun set the smattering of clouds on fire.

Ella looked over at Callum, then down at her feet, swinging them under the bench seat.

"What?"

"I think I'm surprised you're still here. You didn't turn tail and run when you found out that this stuff is real."

"Really real."

"Really real."

"I wouldn't have run." He took Ella's hand and kissed it, reaching over with his free hand to examine the key that now hung around Ella's neck again.

The other was in Eunice's pocket. Twins run in the family, Grammy Helen had said. Well, Ella and Eunice were the only twins left in this family.

A sliver of molten gold appeared over the horizon. It reminded Ella of the glow of the key, and when Callum dropped it, for an instant Ella thought she could see it again, contained somehow where it hung between her breasts.

"I was a little afraid," she said.

"Of what?"

"That if Eunice turned that key, you'd vanish from my life. Or that I'd vanish altogether."

"You're not going to get rid of me that easily."

Ella grinned over at him. "I think I'm starting to realize that." She sobered when she thought of their hands all over the keys upstairs. What would it mean for their future? That kind of chaotic uncertainty?

"Whatever you're thinking, it's not going to happen."

"I was thinking that anything could happen."

"Anything could."

Startled, Ella met his gaze. "What?"

"Anything could happen. Keys or not, Ella. People have freak accidents — or survive things that ought to kill them. Things work out or don't. Some people win the lottery and then lose their foot or a finger or something else they can't buy back. No one can ever predict life."

"So what is it?"

"What's what?" Callum looked at her sideways, and that moss darkness reappeared in his eyes. He knew what she was asking.

"You said before that you knew all I needed was time. Why?"

The first ray of sun filtered through the hedge on the far side of the porch, dappling the whitewashed wood floor with buttery yellow light.

When Callum spoke, it was with a softness like a summer zephyr. "Because of my mom. She died when I was thirteen. I'm the one who found her."

Horrified, Ella squeezed his hand, unsure of what else to do. "I'm so sorry, Callum. I shouldn't have asked."

"It's okay, really." He gave her that smile that made her insides turn to Jell-O. "I wasn't okay for a long time. Years, really. Theater saved me. The ability to step outside myself and deal with their problems, to overcome them in three acts. I needed that, needed time. That's what I saw in you, Ella. There's nothing that makes that hole go away, but sometimes you can plant flowers around it. Grow new things. Let the light shine in. All those things just take time."

Ella vowed then, looking into Callum's eyes, that if death could not be fixed, then she would be thankful every breath for each moment spent with love.

epilogue

The late summer sun beat down, drawing more sweat from Ella's already-perspiring brow. Jace shook the plastic jug at her. The remaining stones made a loud clatter that Ella thought Poof and Puff would probably run from even though they were still inside the house.

"This is the last of them."

"It better be," said Auntie Eunice. "I'm tired as one of Catherine the Great's horses."

Ella chose not to pursue that.

"It is the last bit." Ella stood back for a moment to survey the wall. They'd started with large river rocks at the bottom and inlaid the top with wide flagstones. Between the flagstones in a crack of mortar were Stuart's stones. Ella reached into the jug — the top of which Jace had sawn off with a hacksaw — and pulled out another handful. Only a small length of wall remained for the stones.

"Glad you decided not to sell the place?" Jace asked, wiping sweat from her upper lip with the back of her hand.

"I won't be doing that. Ever." Ella meant it. Grammy had said the house held secrets — she'd find them. In the wall behind her bed, she and Callum had already discovered a small cache of a child's treasures, hidden away years before Grammy Helen or Auntie Eunice had been born. A toy train and a tiny rag doll, three marbles and — what else? — A key, old and worn and caked with years of grime. After finding that key, Ella and Callum had added a new nail to the corridor on the third floor and placed the key on it.

The lawn beyond the wall was lush and green, tended by the community service group. Ella had taken to making them mint tea when they came each week, always using Grammy Helen's recipe. She told Rob Stevens, Junior that she knew about the checks he'd cashed and gotten her evicted, and for a long moment, she'd thought the boy would cry. But then he pointed to the weed-eater wielded by one of his friends and said, "That's what I spent it on. I wanted to help the church, and I was mad at my dad. I...didn't realize it would hurt anyone but him." Ella had raised an eyebrow at that, but she promised she wouldn't tell on him, then spent the rest of the afternoon mulling over the weed-eater she'd inadvertently paid for and how many people were getting free lawn care out of it and decided she was okay with how everything worked out.

The university had offered to reinstate her — at Easton's request (along with several other faculty members) — but Ella declined. Her new travel business had been an immediate hit; Ella had four tours booked up for the next year already, covering Scotland, Romania, Ukraine, and Norway.

Jace rattled the jug again, and the sun glinted off a shiny ruby on her left hand. Even though Ella had told her she ought to take the engagement ring off to work outside, Jace had refused. She somehow managed to keep it pristine. Every so often, Ella would catch her looking at it as she worked, admiring the way the sun turned the ruby to magenta and sent cascading red glimmers over the wet mortar. To everyone's surprise but Eunice's, Jace's mother had reached out to Jace and Alexa. She'd sent a bouquet of flowers after reading the engagement announcement in the newspaper, and she had asked to help with wedding planning. Jace's dad hadn't been as warm, but Mrs. Wong seemed to be holding the fire to his feet to thaw him.

Jace pulled a handful of stones out, the last handful.

"When's Callum coming?" Auntie Eunice asked. "That boy said he'd recite Hamlet for me."

"He'll be here any minute, Auntie," said Ella. "And I don't think he knows all of Hamlet."

"He does," Auntie Eunice said, planting one foot and crossing her arms. "He knows all of it."

Auntie Eunice had fallen almost as much in love with Callum as Ella had. Almost.

Jace placed a stone, then turned back to Ella. "Last one, hon. Want to do the honors?"

Ella looked at their handiwork. It had taken over a month to complete. Green grass, blooming roses — it was all ready. She saw the U-Haul come around the bend, kicking up a cloud of dust. As Callum pulled it into the driveway, he waved at them. Ella looked down at the stone in her hand. It was white, almost pearlescent. Perfect.

The wall stretched all the way around the entirety of the house to the side gates. All those stones from Stuart over the years. Enough to encircle her home like an embrace.

Ella pressed the final stone into the mortar and smiled.

about the author

Photo by Sara McQueen

Emmie Mears writes the books they always needed to read about characters they wish they could be. Emmie is multilingual, autistic, agender, and a bad pescetarian.

Emmie makes their home on planet Earth, and more specifically in Glasgow, Scotland. They live with two rescued kitties who call Emmie a forever home.

Lightning Source UK Ltd.
Milton Keynes UK
UKHW042356300120
357906UK00002B/28/J